STAR TREK™
PROMETHEUS

THE ROOT OF ALL RAGE

Also available from Titan Books

Star Trek Prometheus:
Fire With Fire
In the Heart of Chaos (November 2018)

STAR TREK™
PROMETHEUS

THE ROOT OF ALL RAGE

BERND PERPLIES   CHRISTIAN HUMBERG

Translated by Helga Parmiter
This edition published by arrangement with Cross Cult in 2018
Based on *Star Trek* and *Star Trek: The Next Generation* created
by Gene Roddenberry, *Star Trek: Deep Space Nine* created by
Rick Berman & Michael Piller, *Star Trek: Voyager* created by
Rick Berman & Michael Piller & Jeri Taylor

TITAN BOOKS

Star Trek Prometheus: The Root of All Rage
Print edition ISBN: 9781785656514
E-book edition ISBN: 9781785656521

Published by Titan Books
A division of Titan Publishing Group Ltd
144 Southwark Street, London SE1 0UP

First Titan edition: May 2018
1 3 5 7 9 10 8 6 4 2

A CIP catalogue record for this title is available from the British Library.

Printed and bound in the United States.

Did you enjoy this book?
We love to hear from our readers. Please email us at readerfeedback@
titanemail.com or write to us at Reader Feedback at the above address.

To receive advance information, news, competitions, and exclusive offers
online, please sign up for the Titan newsletter on our website
www.titanbooks.com

STAR TREK™
PROMETHEUS

THE ROOT OF ALL RAGE

PROLOGUE
NOVEMBER 18, 2385

Somewhere in the Lembatta Cluster

The universe knew how to keep secrets.

In the vast, hostile blackness of asteroids, meteorites, stars, and planets, every mouth remained silent. No one heard when Khan Noonien Singh's *U.S.S. Reliant* went up in flames in the Mutara Nebula, and when the genetically engineered warmonger drew his last breath within them. No one heard the tiniest noise when General Chang's Klingon Bird-of-Prey in orbit above Khitomer embarked on its final journey. And no ear witnessed the death of the Romulan usurper Shinzon in the vastness of the Bassen Rift on board his massive warship *Scimitar.*

And so the caverns where the machines did their work did not announce their presence to the rest of the universe. While the sounds they made echoed off the interior walls of the caverns, they did not extend to the all-consuming vacuum reigning outside their boundaries. The deafening noises of hull plates being connected and ship parts being hauled into position before being welded together pervaded the production facilities that were hidden deep within the rocks. Artificial lighting reflected from gleaming surfaces, half-completed hulls, engine housings, control panels, bulky computer consoles, and narrow disruptor gun barrels. Men and women standing at the work terminals carried the latter strapped to their backs. Complicated calculations scrolled across displays, schematic animations and holographic models of what they had been tasked to build: death in sharp and slender design, destruction with jet-black hulls.

Other monitors displayed detailed star charts highlighting the targets of their intended destruction: densely populated colonies as well as heavily frequented space stations were marked. Fleet movements, interstellar transport routes, and important military shipyards were also listed.

These targets all flew different flags. Some belonged to the Klingon Empire, others to the Romulan Star Empire, the Ferengi Alliance, the Cardassian Union, and the United Federation of Planets. But the hands working deep in the stony caves on the destruction of all these nations belonged to a single species.

"Don't slack off!" the foreman shouted over the din of the machines, looking down from his slightly elevated position onto the production lines that were his responsibility. Their sight filled the Renao with pride, and the artificial light inside the caves made the golden jewelry in his red-skinned face glitter. His eyes shone with pride like little suns. "We're working for the good of the Home Spheres, don't forget that. Our efforts serve the Harmony of Spheres!"

They were assembling tools of destruction, and they would carry death out to the large power blocs of the quadrant. The Renao knew with every fiber of his being that their work—which was almost completed—was a blessing. A salvation.

By bringing death to the Klingons, Romulans, Cardassians, Ferengi, and the worlds of the Federation, as well as all the other beings too blind to realize their massive mistake, they were healing the universe. They were healing the future.

And that was worth every sacrifice.

1
NOVEMBER 18, 2385

Xhehenem, Lembatta Cluster

Xhehenem was the agricultural paradise of the Renao realm, located deep in the heart of the red-glowing nebulae of the Lembatta Cluster. Almost seventy years ago, colonists set forth on the two-light-year journey to Xhehenem from the Renao homeworld of Onferin. The *yalach*-perennials didn't thrive better anywhere else in the cluster, and growing *basuudh*-tubers didn't require much of an effort. Xhehenem offered an abundance of water, warmth, and incredibly fertile soil. The spacious settlements that dotted the planet's surface each had dozens of silos filled with all the yields that the planet provided to those who farmed it.

Xitaal was one such settlement. The tiny community consisted of two relatively small arcologies—standard Renao multistory buildings reminiscent of the ancient *Griklak*-hives on Onferin, where the early Renao sought refuge from their hostile environment. Xitaal's arcologies stood on the vast plains of the northern continent of Xhehenem surrounded by farmland that reached toward the horizon. Sunlight reflected from the glass façades whenever the warming beams penetrated the agricultural planet's cloudy atmosphere, giving the two small arcologies the appearance of golden eggs looming on the plains.

Only the top two levels were inhabited. The lower levels

were reserved for agricultural purposes: water reservoirs, workshops for agricultural machines, hangars, and general storage rooms for both equipment and crops.

Every day was a busy day because every city on Xhehenem was mostly self-sufficient out of necessity—the distance to the next settlement was at least half a day's travel. Agriculture didn't know rest periods, because the land didn't know them either.

Nonetheless, that was exactly what Bosdhaar ak Mamuh had in mind when he left his hive on a bright violet morning, walking toward the landing pads for the *Kranaals*, the Renao's small, maneuverable flying transports. His companion was already waiting for him there.

"And you really think this is a good idea, Bos?" Kumseeh ak Yafor asked without preamble. Kumseeh was Bosdhaar's age, and he lived in a neighboring arcology. Both were passionate farmers, and—as was often the case in the Home Spheres—they had known each other since childhood. They had been through quite a lot together. "The southern fields won't last much longer. If we don't get there soon, we might as well leave the *basuudhs* in the soil. In a couple of days they'll be overripe."

Kumseeh was dressed formally in dark, ceremonial attire: a black, ankle-length robe with sewn-on adornments in bright red. Additionally, he had donned his best facial jewelry. His jet-black hair was combed back, and his glowing eyes showed skepticism.

Bosdhaar, who wore equally formal garb, raised his right hand, performing the Renao's traditional circular movement in front of his chest. "I also bid you a good day, Kum. Can't you leave the tubers be for just one day? We've got more important things to do today."

"More important?" Kumseeh snorted indignantly, though when Bosdhaar opened the hatch to his *Kranaal*, he readily climbed in. "Nothing is more important than harvest, Bos, you know that as well as I do. Least of all some obscure preacher."

Taking his place at the controls, Bosdhaar activated the on-board systems. "Custodian ak Daneel disagrees. He encouraged all of us to attend the ceremony. For the good of the spheres, were his words."

"Bah!" Kumseeh dropped into the passenger seat, looking out of the window toward their arcologies. "If good old ak Daneel really cared about our sphere, we would be in the fields, and not at … at … what was that event called again?"

"Iad's Awakening." Patiently, Bosdhaar repeated the words that the announcement on the news channels had drilled into his head. With his left hand he started the engines; with his right he programmed the course. *"The Harmony of Spheres and the Power of Space."*

"Power of space." Kumseeh scowled and folded his arms over his chest. "What a lot of nonsense. Why do I need space, hmh? Does space help me to fertilize the perennials? Do the stars know more about irrigation than you do? The thought itself is unnatural, Bos!" He shook his head vehemently. "And anyway … Iad? I'm past that age when you could excite me with fairy tales about Iad."

Bosdhaar knew where his friend was coming from, at least to some extent. There were more pressing issues this time of year than listening to a roaming, self-proclaimed missionary who traveled all over the cluster worlds. And Iad was a story for children and old fools. Still, the Harmony of Spheres was also important. And according to Custodian ak Daneel it was in danger; so much so that a traveling preacher was tolerated. Like most Renao, Bosdhaar neither knew nor cared about politics or questions of interstellar security. His life was the land and the fields, not space. There was hardly room in his thoughts for anything he couldn't cultivate, and that included the stars. But he knew that his custodian was worried, and so it behooved him and Kumseeh to leave their tubers be for one day.

The *Kranaal* took off into the skies above the plains. "We're going to do as the preacher asked because that's our duty to him. Afterward, we'll see what happens."

"We'll basically watch our tubers rot," Kumseeh grumbled.

The two inhabitants of Xitaal flew southwest toward the coast in their transport. Their destination was a tent that had been erected at a spot halfway to the famous algae-cultivating arcologies of Kharanto, which was the next settlement over. It was also halfway between the vastness of the plains and the open waters of the western ocean.

After three hours of tedious flight, Kumseeh marveled at the sight of the giant tent, supported by wooden struts tied together with thick wood poles and algae rope. "That thing is huge. And look at the landing area."

His surprise was understandable. The preacher's circular tent was surrounded by *Kranaals* and the occasional ground vehicle from Kharanto or one of the few farmsteads that had been founded outside of the arcologies. A constant stream of transports was approaching from the other direction, bringing more spectators for the mysterious preacher. It seemed as if visiting *Iad's Awakening* was compulsory in Kharanto as well.

Bosdhaar managed to put down on the edge of the makeshift landing area. Once the engines had died down and the rotors had stopped moving, both friends exited the aircraft, joining the stream of Renao walking toward the tent's entrance. Here and there Bosdhaar noticed some familiar faces in the crowd but it still felt wrong to be spending time several hours' flight away from home while work was waiting for them. He would never admit that to Kumseeh, of course.

Seeing all the people from Kharanto also irritated him. What did these people have to do with him? They didn't belong to his home, just like he didn't belong to theirs. Home … that was the place where you had grown up, that you belonged to. Home was immediate.

The things we do just to see this preacher. For the first time that day he asked himself whether Custodian ak Daneel knew what he was doing, or whether he'd grown too old to give useful recommendations.

The tent of the mysterious visitor from beyond the world's boundaries was ocher; the tarpaulin fluttered in the western wind. Its diameter had almost the same measurements as Kumseeh's small arcology. Bosdhaar had never seen a bigger tent in his life. But the inside didn't remind him of Xitaal's moderate luxury, being simply an elevated small stage with a dark red curtain, and lots of trampled-down grass.

"I guess our missionary doesn't believe in seats." Bosdhaar sighed as he joined the crowd of spectators gathering around the central stage. "If I had wanted to stand on my feet all day I would have stayed at home in the fields."

"Told you," Kumseeh whispered. He didn't dare raise his voice as Bosdhaar's disapproving comment had prompted quite a few of their neighbors to scowl at them. "This is going to be a complete waste of time."

Minutes passed. Silently, the two friends glanced

around. Wherever they looked, they saw Renao faces. Some were expectant, some were curious, some were doubtful. It seemed as if everyone who lived in either Xitaal or Kharanto was in attendance, and most of them apparently looked forward to this unusual event as a welcome change to their daily routine. On a market near the space port Bosdhaar had heard the first rumors that an increasing number of preachers had been travelling across the cluster's inhabited planets. Supposedly, they came from the heart of the cluster—from the inner worlds Bharatrum and Acina. He had never expected to see any of them on Xhehenem. Usually, the other Renao only paid attention to Xhehenem's food products and agriculture, not the people who farmed the land to provide that food.

These preachers seemed to mean business, even visiting those whom others didn't think worth the time of day. Again, Bosdhaar thought about Custodian ak Daneel and the concern he believed he had seen in the old man's eyes … concern about the harmony of the universe.

As the Renao faith stated, all things in existence had their place. Every single thing and every being in space had their very own position within the great game of life—its sphere. Bosdhaar and Kumseeh had been born in Xitaal, thus Xitaal was their sphere. They would never have dreamed of leaving it in order to settle elsewhere. That would be against nature, as there was no reason to do so. The Harmony of Spheres— the respect and dedication for the individual home—was the greatest good. As long as everything had its place, and that place was respected, everything was balanced and the way it should be.

But now, there were these preachers. Now, there was concern in the eyes of the old custodians. Now, there were rumors. And hadn't Bosdhaar wondered just a few weeks ago why some of his colleagues in the fields were very short-tempered all of a sudden? Hadn't he asked himself where their anger had come from, what had upset their inner peace?

For the good of the spheres, ak Daneel had said. *Go and visit that preacher. Do it for the good of the spheres.*

Bosdhaar felt uneasiness well up inside of him. Tense, he crossed his arms in front of his chest, waiting for *Iad's Awakening* to begin.

Eventually his wait ended, as the curtain rose to reveal a very old man. The preacher was even older than ak Daneel, though he had a lot more fire within him than Xitaal's patient custodian. The preacher didn't have a single hair left on his head and wore jet-black robes with golden applications. Glittering gold jewelry adorned his wrinkled, dark red face and his knotty hands. He walked with a stoop, using a cane for support.

"Brothers of Xhehenem," the preacher began. That salutation wasn't uncommon, as the men had gathered close to the stage and the women stood at the back of the tent, as was traditional. "I thank you for coming and for your hospitality, but I'm afraid I bring bad tidings." He straightened up, and the glow in his yellow eyes increased. With every word the burden of his age seemed to lessen a little. "We live in times of change, and yesterday's facts don't hold true today. The old values lose respect. The Harmony of Spheres is in grave danger!"

A murmur went through the crowd. Many faces expressed the same confusion and cluelessness that Bosdhaar felt. But he also noticed approval and fury in some of those around him.

"What is he talking about, Bos?" Kumseeh whispered.

Bosdhaar shook his head. "I have no idea." He did recall

other rumors he had heard at the market that two alien spaceships from beyond the cluster had arrived at Onferin, the Renao homeworld. The thought made him feel uneasy, although he didn't know why. "Just listen."

The preacher quickly had the attention of the entire audience. He spoke about unrest in space, about war and death, about incredible destruction and seemingly endless suffering. When he mentioned terms such as "Dominion" and "Typhon Pact," "Qo'noS" and "Romulus," his yellow eyes beamed ... maybe a little too brightly.

Those terms meant nothing to Bosdhaar. Still, the young farmer understood the preacher's general point. In fact, he understood it far too well.

"If you ask how it could come to all these atrocities," the preacher shouted, "and to years and decades of suffering, my brothers, all you have to do is look beyond our borders. Look toward the great powers in this part of the galaxy. Look at all those who don't want to understand that *their relentless hunger for expansion is disrupting the Harmony of Spheres!*"

Everyone broke into applause. They clenched their fists and punched the air.

The curtain had fallen behind the preacher, and now images were being projected on them: bright images that had to have originated from alien sources. Bosdhaar saw ruins of strange and exotic cities he didn't recognize. He saw shipwrecks tumbling through the blackness of space and armed beings in extremely martial uniforms. And he saw dead people. Beings died in their very own spheres because strangers had come and overwhelmed them. Harmony didn't exist for them any longer.

Not just for them, thought the young farmer. *There were no differing harmonies. There's just one entirety. Everything is interrelated. If you disrupt the balance of spheres, you disrupt life itself.*

That was the truth that every Renao learned as a child.

The preacher was filled with an energy that belied his age and his fragile physique. "Look at those who travel with their ships to locations where they have never been before. Look at those, who don't have a sense of home, and who don't respect the space of others. Brothers, you're looking at me and you want to know from me how to stop the destruction and the suffering that have turned space into a stronghold of misery and chaos. But you know the answer already: We stop it by stopping *them*! By restoring the harmony—if necessary by force!"

Again, his words were met with approval. Bosdhaar saw the fire in the eyes of many men near him. It reminded him of the workers on Xitaal's fields who had been much more short-tempered than before. It reminded him of the worried glint in ak Daneel's old eyes.

"Brothers, today we are at a crossroads." The preacher had by this point discarded his cane. Standing upright, he pointed at the crowd of farmers with open arms. "It's up to us whether we strive to stop this violation of the spheres' nature. It is our calling to end the chaos that our galactic neighbors have wrought, and to pave the way for a new beginning of life. Fate has tasked us with putting an end to the suffering. Thus, I am asking you: Will you be by my side when the calling reaches you?"

Everywhere Bosdhaar looked, he saw approvingly nodding heads and belligerently clenched fists. The crowd had been spurred on, and the preacher had them eating out of the palm of his hand. The few people who didn't seem convinced yet were hardly noticeable among the large number of those cheering loudly for the man on the stage.

"But how?" one of them shouted somewhere behind Bosdhaar's back. "How can we help, preacher? These alien beings you showed us may be sacrilegious sinners … but they're far away from our spheres."

The Renao on stage lowered his arms first, and then his eyes. "Oh, I wish it was like that," he said and his voice was calm and sad. "I really wish it was."

Bosdhaar turned to face Kumseeh. "Let's go," he whispered.

"What?" Kumseeh looked at his friend incredulously. "Now? Are you out of your mind? This is just getting interesting."

"That's exactly what I'm worried about. Come on."

He grabbed Kumseeh's arm, dragging him through the crowd toward the tent's exit. His thoughts were racing. What the preacher was effectively propagating was no less than a call to arms. This man hadn't come to inform people. He wanted to mobilize them, and he was advocating an attack on the big powers of the galaxy. He wanted to facilitate destruction, and he intended to fight fire with fire. And his fellow campaigners traveling across the other worlds outside of Xhehenem probably shared the same objectives.

But the Renao were a peaceful people! They lived secluded lives, yes, and cultivating contacts with their interstellar neighbors was of little interest to them, but that certainly didn't mean that they wouldn't take up arms.

Bosdhaar looked around. Disapproving looks followed him and Kumseeh as they pushed their way through the crowd. He noticed fury on several faces—fury against the intruders from alien spheres, but also fury directed at him and Kumseeh since they had obviously no intention of following the preacher.

Don't I want to do it? Bosdhaar asked himself when he and his friend finally stepped outside. *Or can't I do it?* Did it make any difference? If that preacher spoke the truth, these outworlders committed an outrageous sacrilege. In that case they deserved Bosdhaar's anger. But did they deserve to die? What's more, did they deserve to die at the hands of the Renao? The mob inside that tent seemed to be convinced of it, and the preacher quite obviously held that view anyway. But what about Bosdhaar?

"What's the matter with you?" Kumseeh snapped at him when they approached the landing area and the *Kranaals*. "First you want to come here no matter what, and then you can't get away fast enough!"

"Didn't you see it?" Bosdhaar asked. "The glint in their eyes? Didn't you hear the tone in their voices? Their disapproving looks?"

"What?" Kumseeh shook his head, clearly not understanding a word his friend was saying. "What are you talking about? Fair enough, some of them seemed to be pretty aggressive, I give you that. But …"

"No 'but.'" Turning around, Bosdhaar stopped and grabbed his friend by the shoulders. "Don't ask me how I know, Kum, because I don't know it as such. I just *sense* it. That in there …" He pointed toward the tent. "Renao taking up arms? Renao judging outworlders? That's not us, Kum! That's not normal. Something is happening to us, or at least to some of us. It makes them forget themselves, at least that's what it looks like to me, and this preacher …"

He sighed. Try as he might, he couldn't find the right words to express what he felt. How should he explain to Kumseeh what he found hard to describe? This strange fear that came over him every time he thought about the looks in the eyes

STAR TREK PROMETHEUS

of the others. This weird feeling out in the fields among the others—but also inside the tent. All those rumors about alien ships among the stars of the cluster above their heads …

"We're getting out of here," Bosdhaar said. "Right now." The young farmer turned right, looking over to the parked aircraft. He flinched when he noticed four large men appearing between them.

The men were built like seasoned farmers and looked like they weren't much smarter than their farming equipment. They grinned menacingly, and the plowing sticks—thick metal sticks with clawlike attachments—in their hands were even more menacing. Danger glowed in their eyes.

"And where are we going?" the first man asked Kumseeh, who had stopped dead in his tracks in surprise. The man's tone was mocking and overtly aggressive. "The preacher hasn't quite finished yet."

Behind his back, one of his companions swung the plowing stick.

"W… we need to get back," Kumseeh stammered. Raising his hand for the traditional greeting gesture, he made an attempt at an apologetic smile and failed miserably. "The *basuudhs* need to be harvested and they don't allow us …"

"Ah, *basuudh*." The man at the front nodded approvingly. "So, you're from Xitaal, eh?"

"Figures," growled one of his companions. He had rolled up the sleeves of his black cowl, displaying his massive upper arms. "Xitaal has always bred cowards. Apple-shiners who'd rather hide behind their seeds than face reality. Fools without foresight."

"Cowards?" Kumseeh clenched his fists. It was obvious that pride was warring with fear. "How dare you?"

"It's alright, Kum," said Bosdhaar, putting one hand on

his friend's shoulder. The gesture was meant to be soothing, but he also wanted to keep his friend under control. "We don't want any trouble."

"Oh, really?" The muscle-head looked at Bosdhaar. His grin broadened. "You could have fooled me."

"Anyone who doesn't want trouble," said the first of the four men, "makes sure that it doesn't get that far."

"Too right," said the one who kept swinging his plowing stick. "They fight back. *Before* it's too late."

"But you're not doing anything," said the first man, his gaze wandering from Bosdhaar to Kumseeh and back. "You don't care what the preacher says. You just have your stupid tubers in mind, and not the good of the spheres."

"That's not true!" Kumseeh cried.

"Wouldn't you be in the tent otherwise?"

Bosdhaar raised his hand defensively. "We don't want any trouble," he repeated, fully aware that it was too late. It had been too late right from the moment the men had approached them. Again he remembered the strange glint in the eyes of those people listening to the preacher. "No trouble."

The first man snorted derisively. "Oh, you already got that." He suddenly struck the first blow with his plowing stick. The ensuing fight could barely be called that. It was short and unequal. The agricultural tool with its sharp edges slashed wounds into the flesh of the two men from Xitaal, whose resistance faltered quickly.

The last thing Bosdhaar ak Mamuh heard before unconsciousness mercifully erased his pain were words full of hatred that the first aggressor screamed at him: "If you're not with us, you're against us, Xitaal! Don't ever forget that. The sphere is *everything*!"

2
NOVEMBER 21, 2385

U.S.S. Prometheus, in orbit above Xhehenem

"I really thought this would be easier." Captain Richard Adams let out a sigh, settling into his chair at the head of the long table. He looked around. "Didn't you?"

Everyone else present nodded or looked glumly toward the windows of the rectangular conference room aboard the *U.S.S. Prometheus*. Outside, they could see the Lembatta Cluster in all its exotic glory: giant red-glowing suns in swirling nebulae. The cluster bordered on both the United Federation of Planets and the Klingon Empire. But one look out of the windows here made everyone in this environment instantly feel like they were a very long way from home— alone and fending for themselves. The precarious mission that had brought Adams and his crew here seemed to intensify that feeling.

"Nothing is easy," replied Commander Roaas, Adams's first officer. He sat to the right of the captain. The Caitian officer wasn't known for long speeches; just now, though, his furry golden-brown ears twitched during this first internal briefing since their arrival at Xhehenem. "Not these days. It seems like the entire galaxy has lost its balance. The Dominion War, the Borg invasion, the Typhon Pact— and now this mess. We're not living in peaceful times, and 'simple' is just wishful thinking."

"I agree," said Lieutenant Commander Lenissa zh'Thiin. The young female Andorian security chief sat next to the first officer. Resting her arms on the conference table, she looked at her captain. Her short antennae, protruding from her white hair, were twitching. They betrayed her tension and her growing impatience far more than her tone of voice did. "It's been twenty days since the attack on Starbase 91, and here we are twenty days and several more attacks later, and we're still completely mystified."

"Not quite, Lieutenant," said science officer Lieutenant Mendon firmly. He sat across the table from zh'Thiin to the left of Adams. The respirator that he as a Benzite depended on for breathing soundlessly emitted vapor. "During our stay on Onferin, we have learned a lot; not least because of the Klingons from the *Bortas*. After all, we were able to trace the terrorists from Onferin to Lhoeel and now here to Xhehenem, and follow them."

The *I.K.S. Bortas* was a *Vor'cha*-class ship accompanying the *Prometheus* on its mission to the Lembatta Cluster, and currently also in orbit round the green and ocher globe of Xhehenem. Since one of their mining colonies had been attacked, seemingly by the same invisible enemies who had destroyed Starbase 91, the Klingons also had a strong interest in hunting down the perpetrators. Unfortunately, the ill-tempered commander of the *Bortas*, Captain Kromm, suffered from a severe lack of both patience and diplomatic skills.

"But we haven't made any progress." Zh'Thiin seemed particularly frustrated by this mission's status. "The trail went cold on Lhoeel after we barely managed to wheedle a permit for investigation out of them—and we're starting from scratch here. And the permanent saber-rattling from the Klingons doesn't make it any easier to deal with the stubborn Renao."

Adams leaned back in his seat, folding his hands in front of his stomach. "It's true, the Klingons are not so much helpful as …" Seeking help, he faced Roaas. "How can I put this diplomatically?"

"You can't," the Caitian answered dryly—and with audible frustration in his voice.

Adams nodded. So Roaas had also noticed it. He and the commander had just returned from yet another fruitless discussion with Kromm and his command staff—the first officer L'emka and the security chief Rooth. Rooth was a little too laid-back for Adams's taste. The *Bortas'* crew had proven only to be interested in fast results, and Kromm was uninterested in making a long-term difference in the Renao realm. The cluster's secrets didn't matter to him at all; neither did the recently substantiated theory that the Renao who lived within the cluster were being manipulated by an unknown power. This manipulation would explain their no-longer-deniable aggression toward strangers. Adams wanted answers, and he wanted to help the Renao. Kromm, on the other hand, just wanted to avenge the Klingon victims of the terrorist attacks in order to curry favor with his empire's government. He was only interested in answers if they were written in his enemies' blood.

But that wasn't the worst of it.

"The *Bortas* is keeping secrets from us." Roaas voiced Adams's concerns. "They know more than they let on. I can't put my finger on it, let alone prove it, but I can sense it. I think Kromm is seeking an edge over us. That might lead to problems when push comes to shove out here."

"What kind of secrets?" zh'Thiin asked.

Before Roaas had a chance to admit his lack of knowledge, the fifth and final person attending this internal briefing spoke up. So far, he had been listening quietly to the conversation with his eyes closed, his fingers steepled, and his fingertips resting against his nose. Now, leaning forward, Ambassador Spock of Vulcan looked at Adams. "I'm afraid I must agree with the commander, Captain. Kromm would appear to be filled with a keen ambition since the events on Onferin. It might complicate our task even further if we were to face internal problems in addition to the external difficulties. I was also under the impression that our Klingon counterpart believes to have some kind of concealed trump up his sleeve, if you'll pardon the Terran expression."

"And Kromm has no intention of sharing this trump with us," zh'Thiin said. She wasn't too impressed with the uncooperative behavior of the Klingon crew. The Andorian had a tendency to voice her displeasure much sooner than most other species would. Aside from that, she had been abducted and almost killed by radical Renao during their investigations on Onferin. Her kidnappers had been followers of a terrorist group called the Purifying Flame. In all likelihood this group was behind the terror acts, and following their trail had led the *Prometheus* and the *Bortas* into orbit around Xhehenem.

"So basically, we know that we don't know anything." Adams's gaze wandered to the windows and the strange new world that was waiting for them like so many others before.

Zh'Thiin added, "And they don't want us down here. Yet again."

This had become an irksome theme throughout their mission: Wherever the *Prometheus* and the *Bortas* stopped, the local Renao regarded them skeptically at best; usually, they were met with open rejection. The central government on Onferin had given both crews permission to move freely within the cluster and visit every world that might be relevant to their investigations, but that didn't mean they were welcome on these worlds, as zh'Thiin had pointed out.

Quite the contrary—when Adams had contacted Barrah ak Samooh, Xhehenem's custodian, the slim-faced man had made it clear in no uncertain terms how he felt about visits from outworlders. Ak Samooh had strongly condemned the terrorist acts, for which the Purifying Flame had claimed responsibility, but he saw no reason to allow total strangers to search his Home Sphere and consequently disrupt its harmony.

Adams sympathized with the custodian. That was part of the problem. The captain was sixty years old, and during his travels, he had experienced and seen enough in the vastness of space to make him respect ak Samooh's views. Every world had its morals and traditions, and he respected the outlook on life held by the citizens of those worlds. That was the foundation of the Federation: strength through diversity and mutual respect.

All things being equal, Adams would gladly have heeded the wishes of ak Samooh and pretty much every other Renao he had met on this mission. Yet he had no choice but to go against those wishes for the sake of all Renao.

"If the Purifying Flame is indeed present on Xhehenem," Spock said, "we have no other choice but to visit the planet. The needs of the many outweigh the needs of the few." He briefly hesitated, and when he continued, his voice was as quiet as a whisper of a distant memory. "At least that is mostly the case."

Roaas nodded. "I agree. Some of the Renao are definitely suffering from mental manipulation by a strange power. The deeper we advance into the cluster—"

"The more intense this strange influence becomes," Mendon finished the sentence a little overeagerly. He touched a padd in front of him on the table and the large monitor embedded in the wall behind Adams sprang to life. "Look at this. I have combined our current stellar cartographic information with a star chart of the cluster. My staff update this map continuously. When I press here—" he touched another button on the padd, "—you will see the evaluation of our encounters with the locals …" Mendon fell silent. He cocked his head in confusion. Nothing had changed on the star chart he had brought up. "One moment, please," he mumbled, confused, staring at the padd. "I'm sure I did … Ah, now it should work." Again, he touched the square flat data device, and again, nothing happened. "What?" the Benzite whispered, aghast in light of his failure.

Adams left him to it. While waiting for the lieutenant to get his presentation going again, he regarded Commander Roaas. "Have we learned anything new about the strange drive in the Flame ships we encountered above Onferin?"

"Not much, sir," the Caitian replied. "Commander Kirk has spoken to Yilaah ak Brekuul about it. He's the Minister for Industry and Research, and part of Councilor Shamar ak Mousal's staff on Onferin. According to the minister, Renao industry has indeed been working on a new propulsion system for quite some time now. It allows so-called 'solar jumps' across distances of up to thirty light years—in absolutely no time at all."

Zh'Thiin's antennae bent forward, alarmed. "Thirty light years?"

Adams also frowned. The memory of the ship's strange and sudden disappearance above Onferin had been preying on his mind for days. However, knowing the reason for it had done nothing to make him feel any better.

"Ak Brekuul insisted that the technology is still in development," Roaas continued. "They just have one prototype, which is currently in testing. Ak Mousal himself verified that."

"That doesn't change the fact that this drive exists," said the Andorian woman. "We saw it with our own eyes. The Flame has got it!"

"The minister presumes a case of industrial espionage," Roaas said. Judging by his expression, he didn't like that fact any more than any of the others in the room. "But, yes, the Flame does have this drive. It has been under construction on Onferin for four years, or so we were told. If the Federation had been able to maintain closer contact with the Renao, we probably wouldn't be so surprised now."

Adams nodded. The Renao's reluctance to communicate with outsiders was indeed a serious problem, and it increased with every passing day.

"What do we know about its specifications?" he asked. He had fought hard to keeping the ice-cold feeling in his stomach at bay. Roaas touched his combadge.

"Roaas to Kirk."

"Kirk here, sir," the chief engineer's voice answered straight away.

"Commander, could you please brief us on the Renao's solar-jump drive?"

Kirk sighed. Apparently, she also didn't like this technology much—at least not in the hands of their enemies.

"Sir, so far I've only been able to scratch the surface of the technological progress of the Renao. That said, I believe that their research has made impressive progress during recent decades—including in the field of propulsion technology. In theory, the solar-jump allows ships to jump from one sun to another within a

certain radius without notable time loss."

"From one sun to the next?" Adams repeated.

"Yes, Captain. That's what Minister ak Brekuul's documents state. Apparently, the drives are capable of folding space and creating a rift, which the ship can use to jump to its destination. The gravitational fields of both the starting and the destination sun are being used as anchors to contract normal space between them. The underlying technological and quantum physical calculations are extremely complex. I must admit that I have difficulty grasping all the details."

"Perhaps I may be of assistance," Spock offered. "My time as science officer might be several decades in the past, but I do attempt to keep abreast of the latest developments."

"Very well," Adams said. "You and Lieutenant Mendon should work more closely with Commander Kirk. Everything we can find out about this drive before we encounter the terrorist's solar-jumping ship again could be important." He looked up. "Commander, is there anything else you can tell us about it? Does it have a weakness?"

"Oh yes," Kirk replied emphatically. *"These jumps require an enormous amount of energy. The distance the Renao can cover depends largely on the ship's individual level of performance. Also, after a jump, they require a twenty-four-hour regeneration period before they can use the drive again."*

"They can cover a maximum of thirty light years with this technology, correct?" Roaas asked.

"Yes, sir. The energy requirements would be too high for longer distances, and the space rift's hyper geometry would become unstable. As our target ship was fairly small, I assume that the drive's capacity will allow jumps of no more than twenty light years."

"That's bad enough. Even at maximum warp, that would be a close run."

"*That's true, sir. The minister was suitably horrified by the thought that this experimental technology might have fallen into the hands of terrorists.*"

"The Romulans were also horrified," zh'Thiin said. "But the Flame still stole their *Scorpion* attack fighters."

"Thank you, Commander Kirk," Roaas said, cutting the link.

"That's not good news," Adams mumbled. He gazed at Mendon. The Benzite had listened intently to the conversation. Now he returned to attending to his own technical difficulties.

Spock had risen and walked around the table. He stood next to Adams, regarding Mendon's star chart on the monitor. His gaze wandered to the windows and the red nebulae beyond Xhehenem.

"We know where we are, Captain," said the old Vulcan quietly. "But do we know against whom we are fighting?"

Adams sighed once again. "I hope so, Ambassador. I really hope so."

3

NOVEMBER 21, 2385

The Starboard 8 was probably the most popular recreational facility aboard the *Prometheus*. Moba, a very jovial and talkative Bolian, ran the small club on deck eight. Both the club and its proprietor enjoyed a good reputation among the crew. Many officers relaxed there after duty, informally chatting to fellow officers, perusing the latest reports from Starfleet Headquarters while enjoying a steaming cup of Klingon coffee, or reading the odd novel. So the club was fairly crowded when Chief Engineer Jenna Winona Kirk walked in that afternoon.

Moba waved at her from behind the elongated bar where several crew members sat, with various others at the tables near the window front, raising their synthehol-filled glasses and generally enjoying their after-work hours.

Still, something was putting a damper on everyone's mood; Kirk could sense it immediately. Initially she assumed that their current mission was the reason for the subdued atmosphere. But then she realized that the reason was much more specific, sitting by one of the small tables right next to the windows.

"Jass," she greeted her friend and colleague from the bridge crew when she arrived at his table. Beyond the thick window panes, she saw Xhehenem in front of a red and black backdrop. Near its north pole, thick clouds drifted across the atmosphere. "Have you been waiting long?"

"Not very," Jassat ak Namur replied quietly. His yellow eyes glowed faintly. "Mind you, I probably couldn't stand being alone in this place for long."

Kirk took the seat across the table from him. The uneasy feeling that had welled up when she entered the Starboard 8 turned to consternation. "Because of the others?" she asked, glancing quickly at the other guests. "Have they been treating you poorly?"

The young conn officer shook his red head. "No, of *course* not. Starfleet members always display exemplary behavior, didn't you know that?"

Kirk snorted derisively.

"Precisely." Regret and remorse resonated in Jassat's voice. "Jenna, I can't even take exception to their hostile demeanor. My people have, after all, admitted responsibility for the terrorist attacks."

"A radical group among your people," Kirk said. "Don't subject yourself to kin liability, Jass. It's bad enough when others do it."

He smiled faintly. "But I really can't understand my own people. Neither can the others. The Renao have never been full of anger like this. That's not us. Still ... you saw the vids claiming responsibility, Jenna. You know about all the casualties. Dammit, Captain Adams's niece died on Starbase 91! *Captain Adams's niece!*"

"You're not a terrorist!" Kirk stated emphatically. "And you're certainly not the enemy—you're a Starfleet officer."

"The only one of my kind," he said. "That speaks volumes."

"That doesn't matter at all." She waved a hand

dismissively. "You're my colleague and friend. The casualties are not your fault, just like they're not the fault of most of the Renao we've dealt with so far." Once again she remembered the kidnapping on Onferin, and she thought about the Klingon crew member from the *Bortas* who had died while they had been held hostage. She pushed that memory aside. Exceptions must never confirm the rule, and prejudices didn't help anyone. "Anyone who blames you or any of the other peace-loving Renao for the atrocities of the Purifying Flame has lost a few marbles somewhere along the way, if you ask me."

"And yet, the events on Onferin have left their mark on the crew," ak Namur said. "Don't you notice the looks?"

Kirk wanted to object again but she couldn't. Although she sat with her back toward the lounge, she felt herself and ak Namur being watched. The chill toward the young Renao was almost palpable. Kirk knew that ak Namur had had to deal with several racially tinged confrontations since the first video claiming responsibility had surfaced, and the knowledge horrified her. That kind of behavior was inconsistent with everything that Starfleet and the Federation stood for.

But the proud and honorable nation had been pushed to its limits during recent years by the numerous conflicts. Several government decisions of late seemed to convey that morals and ethics were a luxury that they could not afford under these bitter circumstances. Kirk absolutely detested this kind of reasoning, and she didn't know anyone among the command staff of the *Prometheus* who would feel otherwise.

"Just ignore them," she said. "These guys should know better than to tar all Renao with the same brush. That's not worthy of them as Starfleet officers or as *people*, much less citizens of the Federation. Why are we out here, hm? Why did you join us? For the same reason I did. Because you want to learn. Explore. Help. Because you're convinced that progress arises from solidarity, rather than fear."

Ak Namur's smile remained faint, but it became a little warmer. The glow in his eyes also increased. "You should sign up as the speechwriter for the new Federation president, Jenna. You really have a knack for pathos. Probably runs in the family." At Starfleet Academy, he had obviously heard the legends surrounding Jenna's great-great uncle, the famous Captain James Tiberius Kirk.

"Don't even mention that," the chief engineer replied, pretending to be crabby. She didn't like being reminded of the other Kirk whose boots were far too big for anyone else to fill. But then she snickered, leaning back in her comfortable seat and crossing her legs. "I leave politics to other people. I'm much more comfortable between dilithium crystals and EPS relays than with diplomats. A computer might be frustrating at times when it doesn't want to function properly but at least it's completely honest at all times."

"Totally unlike him," a new voice suddenly sneered to her right.

Kirk looked up. She hadn't noticed the man who had approached her and ak Namur. She knew him by face; his uniform and insignia showed him to be a lieutenant from security on the *Prometheus*. He had ginger hair with a side parting, and his beard was neatly cropped.

"Excuse me?" Kirk faced the human officer. "What is that supposed to mean, Lieutenant …?"

"Jansen." His gaze was fixed on ak Namur. "Bjorn Jansen, security. The others by the bar reckoned I shouldn't come here, let alone disclose my name. I, on the other hand, figure that everyone may know my name. Because I *am* completely honest."

"What do you want, Lieutenant?" Kirk snapped at the security officer.

"Leave it, Jenna," ak Namur said quietly. "We should go."

"I'd say that's an excellent idea!" Jansen's voice grew louder, giving the impression that he was drunk. But Kirk knew very well that Moba never served alcohol to the lower ranks, and never served it to anyone who was on duty. "You're not wanted here, red-skin! Someone needs to say it!" He glanced around. "You're all thinking the same thing! But no one else wants to say it!"

"Because you're wrong, Jansen," one of the medical staff spoke up. The slender Tellarite, whose name Kirk didn't know, stood up, looking at the security officer. "And anyone with a modicum of common sense realizes that. I certainly *don't* think like you do!"

Several people nodded, and some voiced their approval: "Shut up, Bjorn!" "You're a xenophobic idiot!" Many seemed to be either embarrassed by or angry with Jansen's behavior.

But Jansen shook his head. Sneering, he glared at the medic. "In that case, you're a fool."

"And you're a disgrace to the uniform!"

"Stop it!" Kirk shouted angrily. "That's an order!"

Jansen ignored her and ran toward the Tellarite, raising his fist for a blow. But other patrons of Starboard 8 intercepted him and held him back. Furiously he tried to shake them off.

"I've had enough!" The security officer raised a hand that trembled with fury, pointing at the combadge on his chest. "At least this still means something to me! This is something I must defend, just like I've always done! I can't just sit idly by and watch while we're losing ourselves!"

The medical officer and his companions dismissively waved their hands. All of them seemed to be ashamed of Jansen's undignified behavior, and Kirk noticed from the corner of her eye that they weren't the only ones. Several patrons shook their heads, while many others pointedly looked the other way. Interrupting their 3-D chess game, two ensigns from Mendon's staff stood up by the window, expressions that mirrored disgust and fury at Jansen's performance on their faces.

But Kirk also noticed isolated approval among some of those present: by the bar and at some of the tables, people were nodding and whispering to each other. The sight frightened and confused her. That was definitely not appropriate conduct for a Starfleet officer.

Something is going on here, she thought, and a chill ran down her spine. *Something more than meets the eye.*

Jansen was still the most immediate problem, though— and it needed solving urgently.

"Is there anything else you want to say, Lieutenant?" The engineer spoke menacingly slowly to Jansen. "What's so important that you're risking an official complaint to Commander zh'Thiin? Because I can assure you of one thing—I've had more than enough! If you have taken it upon yourself to come all the way from your bar stool to our table to say what I'm worried you're going to say, I *will* inform your superior officer. And once I've done that, I'll also speak to Commander Roaas." She raised her right hand, placing her index finger over her combadge. "So?"

Jansen blinked. He had clenched his trembling fists again. Maybe he wasn't sober, after all? Had he smuggled alcohol aboard the ship and given himself liquid courage to cause this scene? Kirk almost hoped that was the case, because the alternative—unadulterated xenophobic hatred—was even more horrifying.

And yet … it wouldn't explain the way the other cowards had reacted.

"You're murderers!" Jansen screamed at ak Namur. "Fanatics without morals! You disgust me, *Lieutenant*! You and your entire species."

Kirk stood up, planting herself threateningly in front of the security officer.

Ak Namur had also gotten up, putting a hand on her shoulder, pleading. "Jenna, he … It's not worth it. Really."

"Bridge to Lieutenant ak Namur," Commander Roaas's sonorous voice came from ak Namur's combadge.

He hesitated briefly before tapping his combadge and saying, "Ak Namur, here. Go ahead, sir."

"Lieutenant, we need you in the captain's ready room. Custodian ak Samooh has just informed us that he will allow an away team on Xhehenem, and we need your expertise in order to plan the mission."

Kirk was relieved to hear that. Onferin had guaranteed the *Prometheus* and the *Bortas* free passage in the entire cluster. However, Adams didn't want to be regarded as an intruder. He had felt it necessary also to get the cooperation of the local governments, even if it was just reluctant acquiescence.

"Understood, Commander," ak Namur replied. "I'm on my way." Nodding, he glanced at Kirk.

"Good luck, Jass."

He smiled gratefully, stepping past Jansen. The stares of the other officers followed his departure but he ignored them ostentatiously.

"Yeah, off you go," the security officer growled angrily.

"Go back home where you belong!"

Kirk grabbed the man's left upper arm. Her grip was firm, and her voice even firmer. "The only one who should be sent home is you, Lieutenant. We are now heading to your cabin, where I will inspect your closet very thoroughly. And if I find what I think I will find in there, you will spend the night in the brig, mister, where you can read the Starfleet manual to refresh your memory as to what it means to be a Starfleet officer!"

And before Jansen knew what was happening, Kirk ushered him through the door of the Starboard 8.

No one watched their exit.

4

NOVEMBER 21, 2385

I.K.S. Bortas, in orbit above Xhehenem

Nuk liked his engines. They were more reliable than any living creature could ever be. To those who were able to interpret their performance, their vibrations and their sounds, they were like an open book. And old Nuk's favorite book was right here, surrounding him. This was his little realm, where he knew every nook and cranny better than even the ridges on his own forehead.

The *I.K.S. Bortas* was the Klingon Empire's aging former flagship. Her chief engineer stood deep within her engine room, breathing in. The air in the rather confined compartment of the *Vor'cha*-class cruiser was warm and calm. The ship's red illumination had been dimmed down to a minimum. It was barely bright enough for him to make out the computer consoles and the metal grids on the deck.

Faint clattering sounded from smaller chambers nearby. The engineers of the night shift went about their routine. Nuk gladly ignored them. The majority of his staff were asleep in their quarters on different decks, and Nuk enjoyed the thought of having the engines to himself during the ship's night. He liked being alone—just him, the night, and the soothing humming of his engines.

The past few days had been hectic, and although the sixty-year-old Klingon with the long, dark gray hair and bushy eyebrows had conquered all challenges successfully, he was no longer used to that kind of effort. The *Bortas*'s record of battle hadn't contained anything worth mentioning for many years; she had only been deployed for patrol flights and escort missions. The current assignment to the Lembatta Cluster along with that Federation ship, tracking down professed enemies of the Empire, was a most unusual task for the *Bortas* these days, which made it a very welcome change for the younger crew members.

Nuk himself was far beyond such considerations at this point in his life. He had grown up as a solitary offspring of the house of Kruge, which was famous for its dockyards. Even as a child, Nuk had preferred the company of schematics and tools, rather than concerning himself with other Klingons. While his contemporaries sought their first experiences with games and fights, he had roamed around half-built ship hulls or climbed steel gantries. During his childhood days, he regarded the shipyard as most adventurous and full of tales. He watched the workers going about their craft, built his technological expertise, and imagined how he would serve in the belly of such a proud warship some day in the distant future.

Somehow, Nuk had achieved his goal. The *Bortas* used to have an excellent reputation. She had been the flagship of no less than Chancellor Gowron; proud warriors had walked her corridors. But times changed. Gowron had been dead for more than a decade, and new commanders had diminished the reputation of the formerly proud ship, rather than enhance it.

Especially the current one.

"Still awake?"

Nuk turned around. Usually he sensed changes in the

ambient noises instantly. But the footsteps of his old friend, security chief Lieutenant Rooth, had eluded him.

Too much thinking, he concluded with a sigh. The night was Nuk's trusted friend, but it was also a time when flights of fancy and superstition were allowed to rule his mind. He quickly recovered from Rooth's startling approach, and nodded.

"Thought as much." Rooth smiled. "That's why I brought this."

The security chief stood in the doorway to the corridor with his hands hidden behind his back. Bringing them forward, he presented a bulbous bottle of firewine. The red translucent liquid shimmered in the light that the quietly humming warp core emitted.

"A good choice." Nuk grinned as he stepped to one of his computer consoles. Bending down, he opened the casing at the bottom with one purposeful blow with the side of his hand, which revealed a small secret compartment. He removed two tankards.

"The captain doesn't need to know about this," he said, his grin widening.

Rooth was three years older than Nuk, and hailed from the penal colony Rura Penthe. His parents were prison guards there. Rooth was a born strategist and was also totally at ease with himself. His gray locks cascaded down his shoulders, and he had very prominent brows.

Straightening his shoulders, he spoke with a complete lack of sincerity: "You've got a warrior's word of honor."

Nuk chuckled.

Across the engine room, on the other side of the warp core, stood an oval table for briefings. The piece of furniture featured a variety of holoemitters, plugs, and displays, and up to six people could be seated around it. Nuk and his nocturnal visitor sat down on two of the stools surrounding the table. The old engineer pushed the tankards to the center of the table, and the security chief poured the wine.

"To old and new times," Rooth said as they raised their tankards.

"To old times," Nuk limited the toast, grumbling, and drank. Firewine was considerably rarer than the more popular bloodwine and posed a problem for the digestive systems of many species, but it was exquisite. It warmed Nuk's intestines and put a happy smile on his lips.

"Don't be so skeptical, Engineer," Rooth chided, but Nuk knew that his rebuke wasn't serious. Rooth shared Nuk's views on their commander. "Captain Kromm is taking our vintage barge to new heights. Back to fame and glory, didn't you know that?"

Nuk snorted. He had never been a man of many words— they usually didn't come to him soon enough—but as far as Kromm was concerned, Nuk considered every word an utter waste of time.

Kromm was a descendant of one of the highest houses in the First City back on Qo'noS. He had been born an honorable man, but the young warrior had done nothing to add to that in the years since. The glorious feats with which he had been credited had truly been achieved by others. His House's place in imperial society had opened every door for him, while his commanders had fought his battles for him. Kromm was considered the "Hero of the *Ning'tao*", a warship that had been destroyed during a heroic battle ten years ago. But Nuk knew that while Kromm had indeed been part of the crew of that honorable ship, he had left it well before its heroic self-sacrifice.

Even the Klingon High Council seemed to have been aware of Kromm's useless nature very early on. Why else make him commander of the *Bortas*—Nuk's and Rooth's beloved home in space—and then limit the ship to nothing but minor missions? This smart move by the fleet leaders had given Kromm a position that was adequate to his social status, as the high-born could benefit from the former flagship's glory; however, at the same time the Empire ceased to have any expectations regarding this ship. They had promoted Kromm while stashing him in a quiet corner so he couldn't do any damage. And the *Bortas*'s crew had been discarded right along with him.

But then the Klingon mining colony on Tika IV had been destroyed. Much to everyone's surprise, the reclusive Renao had claimed responsibility for this atrocity, while announcing further attacks. Since the battle cruiser happened to be close to the border of the Lembatta Cluster, Qo'noS suddenly remembered the *Bortas*. Since then, Kromm had been dreaming about a glorious future for himself and the ship. He was hoping that this Renao mission would breathe new life into his career. That, thought Nuk, was yet more proof of both Kromm's blatant ignorance and his exaggerated opinion of himself.

"Have you heard the latest from the bridge?"

Nuk's rambling thoughts were once again interrupted, and he shook his head. He had lost all interest in the things happening on other decks a long time ago. Colleagues and superior officers were no machines. They were subject to mood swings, they sometimes made mistakes, and they often acted only in their own best interest. Why should he bother with them more than absolutely necessary?

"The wait is over," his old companion told him.

"Xhehenem officially invited us down to the planet's surface. It took them a while, but it's still sort of voluntarily. Kromm and Adams are now putting together mixed away teams. As soon as the night shift is finished, we're finally moving out. Let the search for the Purifying Flame commence."

The engineer gulped down the contents of his tankard before waving it demandingly at Rooth. "Tomorrow, when even the last fanatics have had ample time to dig themselves a hole to hide in."

Rooth sighed. "Adams likes to be thorough. Especially where preparations are concerned. If it was up to Kromm, we'd already be down there, taking prisoners."

Nuk nodded. The Empire was changing, or so it seemed to him. Way back in his youth, a captain of the Imperial Fleet would not have been slowed down by a human. At least not in the past that existed in his memory. No one would have ordered a Klingon commander to find conclusive, individual evidence for any one person's guilt; the entire people would have felt the rightful wrath of the Empire.

The engineer grabbed the wine bottle, refilling his tankard. *The past is long gone,* he pondered, taking another swig. *Today, everything is different.*

But different didn't necessarily mean worse, did it? Different was just that ... different.

Rooth also took a refill from the bottle. But then he hesitated. "Is anyone else in here?"

Nuk tilted his head quizzically. It was obvious that Rooth wasn't referring to his colleagues in the adjacent rooms. But what was he talking about?

Suddenly, Nuk also heard it. A very faint grunt reached his ears, the source of which seemed to be close by. Another sound he had missed! He was either going deaf or all this thinking he'd been doing had impaired his other faculties.

That's a ghost, his nocturnal imagination whispered in his mind. *Your little empire is haunted.* For a brief moment, a chill went down Nuk's spine. That was complete nonsense. There were no ghosts on ships of the Klingon Empire.

Or were there?

Again, he noticed the faint grunt. It sounded hollow and pained—just like in the old horror stories his sister used to tell during their childhood. And it seemed to come from everywhere and nowhere at the same time. Nuk's eyes widened. His hand holding the tankard froze halfway in the air, as he looked at his old friend in confusion and—if he was completely honest—with a certain amount of fear.

"Do you have a visitor?" the security chief asked quietly. Placing his tankard on the table before him, he stood up.

Nuk shook his head. All the other technicians had left this area of the engine room quite a while ago. As long as the bridge didn't issue new orders, they wouldn't return any time soon.

"In that case, you probably have an *unwanted* guest," Rooth whispered in his ear. His hand reached for the disruptor that was dangling from his hip. He pulled the weapon and activated it with one smooth movement, before looking around.

Silence. The grunting didn't repeat, and all they heard was just the familiar humming of the engines.

But Rooth didn't seem to be satisfied with that. While Nuk watched him uneasily, the lieutenant went to the room's back wall, tilting his head, sniffing the air. He moved on, past the warp core to another wall where he repeated his actions. Shortly after, crouching in front of the bulkiest computer console, he put his free hand against the casing.

He seemed to be looking for irregularities of the surface texture, or maybe disturbances to the soft, barely noticeable vibrations that the drive sent throughout the ship's decks. Again, he seemed to be breathing in deeply, sniffing.

Nuk slowly got up. He grabbed the bottle, intending to use it as a club if push came to shove. Stepping behind his friend, his eyes asked silently, *"What?"*

And the grunting returned … hollow, deep, echoing, and full of pain!

Rooth stood up, his eyes fixed on the ceiling of the engine room. Without explanation, he climbed onto the console that had been deactivated for the night. He reached for the ceiling and hit it twice with his fist. Immediately, one of the access hatches opened. These hatches were scattered all over the ship, leading to service crawlways. They were only used if something needed to be repaired, replaced, or serviced. It was completely dark inside.

Standing on the balls of his feet, the security chief lifted his disruptor up to the hatch, peering into the darkness inside the crawlway.

Nuk tightened his grip around the neck of the firewine bottle, just in case. Countless stories from Klingon mythology and ancient superstition shot through his mind. Legends full of death and destruction, revenge, atonement, and lost honor.

But Rooth lowered his weapon, reaching into the opening with his other hand. "Come on," he said with a strange undertone, half request, half order. "Get out of there."

Sounds of movement came from the ceiling. Nuk heard hesitant rustling, and the scratching noises of a body crawling through the narrow, dark maintenance tunnel. Shortly after, a ghostly white face appeared in the open hatch. The head reminded him of a very old horror story, as it didn't feature even a single hair. Not only that, it was also devoid of any wrinkles, and there were no ridges on the brow. But the eyes seemed to be even more black than space itself.

The engineer gasped a moment later when he recognized the creature. The Rantal! What was this wretched *jeghpu'wI'* doing in his little realm?

Rooth tucked his disruptor away at the hip before helping the slender being down from the tube onto the deck. The creature originated from one of the conquered empire worlds and held the rank of *bekk* aboard the *Bortas*.

"Who did that?" the security chief asked tersely.

Only then did Nuk notice the multitude of wounds all over the snow-white body of the Rantal. Almost every inch of skin that wasn't covered by his dark blue coverall was scattered with bloody scratches, bruises, and cuts.

Someone had given this *jeghpu'wI'* a good thrashing, the engineer realized. And this someone had either thrown the creature into the crawlway from one deck above and locked him in there, or the Rantal had hidden from his tormentor in the depths of the ship.

"I asked you a question, *Bekk*!" Rooth barked.

The Rantal—Nuk finally remembered that his name was Raspin—winced when he heard the harsh tone of Rooth's voice, but he remained silent. His deep black eyes were fixed on the floor. He seemed to be ashamed of his appearance and his situation.

Nuk also felt ashamed. A *jeghpu'wI'*—one of the conquered people—here ... among his engines? Without him noticing and preventing it? *Jeghpu'wI'* were impure, dammit! The value of the planets they came from was measured by their strategic location or their resources, but not by the strength or character traits of their inhabitants. *Jeghpu'wI'* were beings without honor or pride. Their social status was equal to vermin, far below the honorable warriors of the Empire. And Nuk, who had always been prone to irrational superstition, was convinced that they brought bad luck!

"Very well, *Bekk*," Rooth said, impatiently. "If you do not wish to talk here, you will do so elsewhere—but you *will* talk!" He pointed toward the exit to the engine room. "Move!"

Reluctantly, the *bekk* with the snow-white skin complied. Rooth followed him silently. In the doorway, the security chief turned around. "Are you not coming?" he asked.

Nuk shook his head, resting his hand on one of his consoles.

A faint smile played in the corners of Rooth's mouth. "It's just a Rantal, old man," he said in a futile attempt to chase away Nuk's worries. "Your visitor was Raspin, not Fek'lhr." With these words, he left, taking the *jeghpu'wI'* with him.

The engineer was left behind alone, and suddenly, he didn't consider that state to be quite so accommodating any longer. He didn't need Fek'lhr, the mythological gatekeeper who brought dishonorable warriors to the Barge of the Dead, to ruin his enjoyment of his little realm. A simple *jeghpu'wI'* was sufficiently capable of doing that. He wondered whether spilling Renao blood would help restore the honor of the engine room. He sincerely hoped so. He also hoped that Kromm would finally follow up his bold words with the glorious deeds that he had been promising ever since they had embarked on this mission.

If he didn't, Nuk feared that Kahless himself might not be able to do anything for the heart of the *Bortas*. That thought left Nuk, taciturn at the best of times, completely speechless.

* * *

It didn't require an astute investigator to figure out the facts. Rooth realized that just as soon as he entered the Rantal's quarters. All that he needed were two healthy eyes.

Raspin lived in a glorified closet on the ship's lowest deck, well past the cargo area. Except for Nuk's engineers, no crew member had any reason to come here ... especially not since the *jeghpu'wI'* had come aboard. Raspin's abode measured only a couple of square meters. The door needed to be opened manually. The only light sources were a lone ceiling lamp and the small computer terminal, which was located right next to a tiny commode and sink.

Rooth was down here for the first time, but he wasn't surprised at all. The Rantal might hold the rank of *bekk* and serve on the ship's bridge but he wasn't respected or even welcome. He was merely tolerated, albeit grudgingly.

For reasons probably only known to the Klingons' long-dead gods—and perhaps the decision makers in Command—Raspin had an incredible talent for working at the ops console. Rooth had witnessed it first-hand: no one, absolutely no one was capable of handling the functions and technical intricacies of this workstation better than the slender, hairless *jeghpu'wI'*. Someone somewhere had realized the strategic advantage this creature might present on an Empire ship. So Command hauled Raspin from his shoddy world and put him aboard a cruiser; an experiment they obviously considered to be extremely beneficial. Of course, they put him on the *Bortas*, a ship of little consequence, so if the experiment failed, it would only affect a vessel whose honor was already quite well diminished in the eyes of the Empire. If it succeeded, they could try again on a ship that actually had a strong position in the Defense Force.

Raspin's cabin looked like a warzone. The narrow bed

and the table had been knocked over and damaged. The computer terminal lay flickering on the deck covered in dents and cracks. Dried blood and something that Rooth believed to be dried feces were on the walls.

Right in the center of this chaos stood the *bekk*, his gaze still fixed on the floor, not making a sound.

"What happened here?" Rooth asked, although the answer was fairly obvious.

Raspin remained silent.

Seconds passed. Finally, the Klingon decided that he had been patient enough. Rooth was among the few people on board who was indifferent to the Rantal's presence, but even his leniency had its limits.

"Go and report to the medical bay, Raspin," he said sternly. "I will take care of the rest."

And he knew exactly where to begin.

Commander L'emka was many things: first officer of the *Bortas*, the scion of a family of farmers, seasoned veteran of the glorious Dominion War. Despite her young age she had left an impression with the right people during that war.

Right now, though, she was simply furious.

"Klarn," she growled just as soon as Rooth had finished his brief report.

The security chief nodded. "It would appear so." He sat across from L'emka in her quarters. Rooth had come here just a few minutes ago ... his second visit since she had moved in here, and for the same reason as before. "Lieutenant Klarn has never bothered to hide his irritation about the Rantal's presence."

"*Everyone* is irritated about that," L'emka said, crossing

her long legs. As her shift of duty had finished she was clad in civilian clothing. "But that doesn't mean that everyone resorts to physical violence. We're a warship, not a pirate sloop where everyone does as they please."

Candlelight reflected off the edged weapons mounted on the wall behind her. The air in her cabin smelled of wax and sweat. The smell was pleasant to Rooth ... inspiring, exhilarating. It reminded him of his youth.

"Apparently, Klarn doesn't remember that. I'm afraid I should have seen it coming. After all, Klarn stood in my office a few weeks ago, spouting absurd conspiracy theories about Raspin."

L'emka cursed under her breath. Her dark hair almost touched her breasts, which were covered by a dark brown top with a very low neckline. Her facial features were both hard and gracious. "And the *jeghpu'wI'*?"

"I sent him to the doctor," he said. "But I'll wager he won't be able to make him talk either. Raspin is not a Klingon, Commander. Klarn's attack didn't infuriate him or galvanize him, it traumatized him. He doesn't stand up for himself—he escapes, withdrawing into his pain, leaving it to us to do justice."

"Justice." L'emka snorted. "For a Rantal?" She shook her head as if she, like Rooth, couldn't believe that such a thing was being considered—what's more, that it would be necessary. "This is all because of what happened on Onferin. Klarn wanted to kill that radical preacher that we had apprehended, but Captain Kromm forbade it. And Klarn doesn't like it when someone puts him in his place."

Rooth nodded again. He thought about Joruul ak Bhedal, the preacher in question, who sat in the *Bortas*'s brig. It was thanks to him that they had a trace to Lhoeel and from there to Xhehenem. Ak Bhedal was a member of the Purifying Flame, and he had established a small network of agitators on Onferin. These agitators spread the xenophobic and aggressive sermons of their terrorist organization among the people. As middle man between Onferin and the fanatics who allegedly were located on Xhehenem, the hatemonger was an invaluable informant for the mission of the *Bortas* and the *U.S.S. Prometheus*. Rooth had been present on more than one occasion when Kromm had questioned the man; and it had been Rooth who usually called the ship's medic as a precaution to ensure that enough was left of ak Bhedal to allow for another interrogation. This lasted until Captain Adams had learned about Kromm's methods and had insisted on a "more humane" treatment. Since then, the preacher had probably only been suffering from boredom.

"So it seems Klarn has found another outlet for his urge to kill someone," he said. "If he's not allowed to brutalize ak Bhedal, he turns instead to the Rantal." Rooth himself wasn't too keen to have a non-Klingon aboard ship, and to a certain degree he could understand those who regarded that fact as a downgrading of their vessel—a collective loss of honor, so to speak. But in his mind, that fact didn't justify Klarn's behavior. Raspin might be a *jeghpu'wI'*, but he was also a member of the crew and as such, he deserved a minimum of respect.

L'emka hesitated. "I agree that Klarn was likely looking for easy prey to let off some steam. But I'm surprised that he chose the Rantal rather than the Renao couple on deck twenty-four."

Surprised, the old security chief raised his eyebrows. "What Renao on deck twenty-four?"

"Evvyk ak Busal and her partner Moadas ak Lavoor used

to work for our preacher. They were captured on Onferin and officially they are dead. The captain wants it kept that way. Most of all, he doesn't want the *Prometheus* to learn of them. For Kromm, those two serve as a clandestine source of information that will allow us to stay ahead of Adams and his crew."

Rooth almost lost his temper. "That is outrageous! Nobody informed me about those two still being alive! And what are they doing on deck twenty-four? We have cells for such purposes!"

"We also have a very headstrong commander," the first officer said angrily.

Rooth knew that there wasn't much love lost between them. Before Kromm had been made her commanding officer, L'emka's career had been moving up swiftly. Since being assigned under Kromm, it had stalled.

"The captain feels as if he's been put on a leash by both Adams and the Federation. He has other ideas with regard to this mission."

The security chief snorted. "Don't we all." Then he remembered Nuk. "Well, most of us, anyway. That doesn't justify leaving security in the dark, however." It wasn't the betrayal of confidence concerning their mission partner Adams that made Rooth's blood boil—it was the realization that his own captain obviously didn't think enough of him to confide in him concerning matters that clearly came under his purview. How was Rooth supposed to serve under a commander who, in essence, took his job away from him?

The first officer was just about to say something, when Rooth jumped to his feet. "Deck twenty-four, yes?"

L'emka nodded. "What are you going to do?"

"My job," he answered harshly. "This ship ... this *mission* can only succeed if all of us perform at maximum capacity. I can understand Kromm's desire to keep those two prisoners from Adams. But, by Kahless, I'm going to pay them a visit right now!"

Sighing, the younger woman also got to her feet.

Rooth had almost reached the door to her quarters. Facing her, he stopped, squinting. "What exactly do you think you're doing?"

L'emka smiled. "I'm going to take you there."

5
NOVEMBER 21, 2385

Paris, Earth

Warm sunlight reflected from both the smooth river surface and the façades to the right and left of the Seine. In the distance, beyond charming old buildings made of stone and brick and much younger palaces made from transparent aluminum and plastisteel, the Eiffel Tower reached to a cloudless crystal blue sky. Outside small, picturesque street cafés, locals of all ages sat next to visitors from other countries and other worlds, reading their padds or watching passers-by. On many of the *ponts*—the bridges spanning the river that were as typical for Paris as the bells of the Notre Dame cathedral and the governmental seat of the United Federation of Planets—tourists walked past the small traditional stalls of portrait painters and holoartists who were offering their works. The city of light, as humans had called it for many centuries, smelled of fresh coffee, bread and cheese, and vitality.

Lwaxana Troi almost hated it for that.

"I swear," the ambassador from Betazed, who was quite clearly in a very bad mood, snorted, "if I have to make one more step in these streets, I will call my office, have them beam down the Sacred Chalice of Rixx, and then I will stuff it down President zh'Tarash's assistant's throat!"

Mr. Ru also stopped. Patiently, the large humanoid, who

never left Troi's side in public, waited out his mistress's tantrum. Ru had been accompanying Troi for several years on many of her travels. Ru was the latest of many valets Troi had gone through in her time and, much like Mr. Homn— who had served Troi for many years until he died during the Dominion attack on Betazed—he had the accommodating tendency to remain silent.

Emmeline Mokhtari, third and final member of the small walking party, stopped. Unlike Ru, she didn't seem to be patient at all. "My sincerest apologies, Madame Ambassador, I was under the impression that you were enjoying this little guided tour around Paris."

Mokhtari was a dainty, purposeful person with dark, carefully styled hair. She was always polite and courteous, and she probably stored more business appointments and diplomatic details in her head than there were bottles of red wine in Paris ... but she always seemed as if she had swallowed a Klingon painstik that prevented her from ever being relaxed or casual.

"I assure you, I *am not* enjoying it," the ambassador answered pointedly and abrasively. "I *would* enjoy making my appointment, which is the reason for my long journey from Betazed to Earth. But the gatekeepers of your new president apparently prefer to leave me waiting while trying to distract me with all sorts of sights."

Nervously, Mokhtari licked her lips. Tantrums had obviously not been scheduled as part of today's agenda. "President zh'Tarash is delighted that you came, Madame Ambassador ..."

Troi waved her hand dismissively.

"But since she's been in office, her schedule is even more crammed than before. Countless dignitaries from every corner of the Federation aspire to pay her a courtesy visit—much like yourself. And some of them even appear after making an appointment and not on a whim."

"Bah!" Troi said, loudly.

"As you were told in her anteroom, you will be contacted the minute the president's schedule has an opening."

"An opening," the ambassador repeated incredulously, facing her male escort. "Did you hear that, Ru, what I am in this city? A stopgap! That really needs to be added to my long list of dignities. Daughter of the Fifth House, holder of the Sacred Chalice of Rixx, heir to the Holy Rings of Betazed … and stopgap on Earth." She sighed deeply. "I must say, I really didn't envision my best years like this."

Ru remained dutifully and wisely silent. He only changed the way he clasped his hands in front of his stomach.

Mokhtari, however, looked at her, obviously embarrassed.

There you go, little girl, Troi thought with a hint of pride. *There's a spark of life inside of you yet.*

"I truly didn't mean it that way, Madame Ambassador," the human woman with the dark skin apologized for her faux pas. "I hope you can forgive my bad choice of words and …"

Again, Troi waved her hand dismissively. For a brief moment she was tempted to read Mokhtari's thoughts and amuse herself with the younger woman's unnecessary embarrassment, but she didn't. As a powerful telepath, she was capable of perceiving the thoughts of the people surrounding her. But in recent years she had found herself refraining from using her ability for decency's sake—it would be an intrusion into the personal freedom of others to delve into their emotional life. This was yet another insight that came with age and experience.

"Nonsense," she said, sounding slightly more forgiving.

"None of that, now. After all, it won't bring us closer to the president. But one thing is certain: I'm not taking another step. Just look at the way I'm dressed." She pointed at herself, specifically at the heavy, layered dress, at the jewelry she had donned, and at her high-heeled shoes, which had been polished until they were gleaming. "If I had anticipated a slog through Paris, I would have worn more casual clothing. Or my wedding dress, which would have been even more comfortable."

Mokhtari's chocolate-colored brow furrowed in confusion, until she recalled what kind of attire was customary for Betazoid weddings: none at all.

"Madame Ambassador…" she began, horrified.

But her visitor from Betazed wasn't listening any longer. "What do you say we leave the sights and spend the afternoon drinking a nice cup of coffee? Wherever I look, that seems to be the most common pastime here. Although I'm not entirely sure if the soup bowls they use in these small cafés to serve coffee in still deserve the term 'cup'." She looked at Mokhtari. "Zh'Tarash's minions will still find you if we're *not* moving, won't they?"

"But … but of course, Madame Ambassador," the French woman stammered, somewhat taken by surprise.

"Superb." Without waiting for any objections, Troi stepped from the cobblestone street onto the sidewalk, heading toward the first available restaurant. It was a small brasserie with a large outside area, and according to the menu displayed in several languages on waist-high stands near the street, it specialized in a mixture of traditional French and terrible Klingon dishes. The thought of *gagh monsieur*, which was at the top of the list, almost made Troi's stomach turn. Warm and faintly sweet Brioche bread with cheese, salt, and pepper … and living worms from Qo'noS? What would these modern cooks come up with next to horrify the palates—or the mucous membranes used for the intake of food—of their customers? Bajoran *jumja* sticks with a sauce from fermented Regova eggs from Cardassia Prime? And for dessert boiling hot fish juice with cherries?

"May I order you a dish, Madame?" Mokhtari asked after the three had settled at one of the restaurant's few vacant tables. "I noticed how intently you studied the menu, and …"

"Coffee," Troi interrupted her quickly. "Black. And definitely not a *mix* of beans, do you hear me? Just supplies from this planet."

Mokhtari blinked, and nodded respectfully, before beckoning the *garçon* to their table.

In the meantime, Mr. Ru opened a small suitcase that he had been carrying since they disembarked from the transport that had brought them from Betazed. He took out a golden fan and tried to cool his mistress down with it. It was late fall and the day was bordering on chilly, but a daughter of the Fifth House wouldn't tolerate servants who didn't know how to make themselves useful. Ru knew that; it was how he had kept his job.

The soup bowls full of coffee had been served, and the black brew was exquisite. Finally, Troi felt inclined to act a little friendlier towards the tour guide that zh'Tarash's office had assigned to her.

"Tell me, dear, are you married?"

Mokhtari was in the midst of a sip of coffee, and so she responded by simply shaking her head.

"Good girl," Troi said. "And if you want my advice— don't. I can understand that the atmosphere here can fill the mind of a young woman such as you with all sorts of romantic nonsense. All these little alleys, the street musicians, the history that's oozing from every house wall. But listen to me—I've been married countless times ... to a human man, a Tavnian, almost to a Kostolainian, and even to a changeling from the Gamma Quadrant, believe it or not. And did it make my life any richer?" She took another sip from her soup bowl. "It became more hectic, that was all. Louder, full of debates. Do you want debates when you come home from a long day at work? Or do you want to do as you please? There you have it."

Helplessly, Mokhtari looked at Ru, who continued to fan his mistress dutifully.

Satisfied, Troi continued her monologue. She hadn't really wanted any answers, anyway. "Men!" she said derisively. "You prefer men? Forget it. Too much maintenance, not enough profit. Of course, there are exceptions, but I'm telling you ... for each Ian Andrew there's at least one Q—for each Odo an avoidable Jeyal. It's not efficient, at least not for me." She paused. Pensively, she frowned, raising her coffee bowl again. "On the other hand, this is France, right?"

The young French woman nodded eagerly. She seemed pleased to make some manner of contribution to this conversation.

"Ah, France." Troi sighed. "In that case, it's possible that the exceptions outweigh the disadvantages. After all, Jean-Luc is French, *n'est-ce pas*? Well, *he* certainly is a man. Strong, educated, well-traveled, at peace with himself—and he's been head over heels in love with me for decades."

Finally, it seemed as if Ru wanted to say something. Troi shot him a sidewise glance that silenced him.

"No, really," she insisted, losing herself in her infatuation. "The captain of the *Enterprise* is unique."

Mokhtari blinked, even more confused than ever. "Forgive me. You … and the captain of the *Enterprise*? I thought he was married!"

Once again, the ambassador waved her hand dismissively, speaking in a patronizing tone. "Oh, child, leave that subject to the experts, won't you?"

Troi was both amused and surprised that the young woman was about to protest, but she didn't get a chance to do so, because the white-haired man at the table behind them raised his voice considerably.

"I've had enough of this," he announced with a booming voice, hitting the table with the palm of his hand. His glass full of anisette took a leap sideways. "I say: make short work of all of them!"

"Well," said the other person at the table. He was considerably thinner than the white-haired man, and definitely not as loud. He sat with his back toward Troi. "You can't quite put it like that."

"I can't?" The man with the white hair looked at him incredulously. "These red-skins have *admitted* to being behind those atrocities!" Again, he hit the table with his flat hand. "What's more, they've been announcing even more of them for days. Don't give me that 'too vague' or 'far too general' bullshit! As if that mattered anymore. It's bad enough that the new president doesn't have the guts to do something about it. Why did we elect her again? So she can twiddle her thumbs while we're heading full speed ahead towards the next crisis?"

"You're right," the other man said. "But you shouldn't shout it out into the world. You know how peeved some people can be when …"

"Do I look as if I care?" the man with the white hair

ranted. "I'm just speaking the truth, Mathieu, and that must be allowed! The Renao don't just look like the biblical devil, they *are* devils. And our politicians are do-gooders or far too tolerant to do something about it. How long has the *Prometheus* been in the Ciabatta Cluster now? Two weeks? Three?"

"*Lembatta* Cluster," Mathieu corrected quietly.

The white-haired man just snorted. "Three weeks, isn't it? I think that's what they just said on FNS. And what, I ask you, has happened since then? Nothing! These red-skins are busy planning the next attack but the Federation and Starfleet are sitting idly by." He laughed humorlessly, expressing fury as well as mockery. "We should be glad that the Borg are no longer a threat. The state we're in, those machines would assimilate us within minutes." He picked up his cup. "Seriously, Mathieu, if I had any say here, all these red devils would be locked up. For security reasons."

Troi, who was listening to the outburst at the next table with a mixture of repulsion and horror, looked at Mokhtari. "What in the world ...?" she whispered.

The young woman from the president's staff seemed saddened and ashamed in equal measure. She leaned toward Troi. "I'm afraid these types of xenophobic attitudes have become commonplace during the past few days," she confessed quietly to the ambassador. "Since the destruction of Starbase 91 and the appearance of the first vids claiming responsibility, an aggressive mood toward the Renao has spread among the people—it is directed against the entire species and not just the Purifying Flame."

"That's disgusting," Troi said, horrified.

"Without a doubt," the French woman agreed. "And completely intolerable."

The white-haired man's companion also seemed to

have his doubts. "Punish an entire species for the deeds of individuals? Some people might consider that to be radical also, Jerome. It brings back memories of the darker chapters in human history."

"Pfff." Jerome snorted, sounding unimpressed. "I don't care what it reminds others of. I know what's necessary, and what isn't. I know what I would do. We're all targets, aren't we? This spawn of the devil can strike again at any time. And we're supposed to keep still until that happens? It's about time we fought back. That we recognized our opponents and stopped them."

"That sounds like war," Mathieu warned him.

"Are you not listening, you old fool?" Again, Jerome hit his fist on the table. "This *is* war! And if we don't take up arms soon, we're going to lose it. We've had ships on location for weeks but they don't achieve anything. Is Starfleet incapable of putting the terrorists in their place?"

"Even Starfleet's options are limited."

"Bullshit! Limited … The *Prometheus* should bomb the Renao back into the Stone Age! That would solve the problem once and for all."

Troi stood up. "Right, that's enough!" This time, it was her turn to bang on the table. She smashed her fist down so hard that even Mathieu and Jerome winced. Furious, she got up, facing the two men with her fists on her hips. "What the hell is this? Is this Paris, the city where the heart of the United Federation of Planets beats? Or am I in some kind of dive full of Orions and Nausicaans?"

Both men stared incredulously at her.

"You should be ashamed of yourself!" Troi cried. "All Renao are terrorists? Starfleet is supposed to crush them? What you're spouting here, gentlemen, is nonsense! Since when can problems be solved that way? The universe is far more complex than that. You can't just flick a switch, or fire a phaser, and expect everything to be alright again!"

Jerome wanted to say something, but the ambassador silenced him with a wave of her hand. "Be quiet, it's my turn. I can understand your fear. We have been through terrible times; you don't have to tell me that. Betazed was conquered by the Dominion—I barely survived my house being destroyed around me. And then we suffered again from the Borg. None of us needed the fanatics of the Purifying Flame, I agree with you there. But that does not justify racism! It takes some extremely stupid individuals to let fear cloud their minds. Are you extremely stupid individuals?"

"No, Madame," Mathieu said quietly.

"Prove it! Remember what the Federation stands for. Remember our basic values. And act accordingly. If you can't do that, at least keep your stupid mouth shut in public, because what I heard coming from you will spoil anyone's day who has an educated mind." She gave Ru and Mokhtari a nod. "Come on, I've suddenly lost all interest in coffee. This is an enchanting little restaurant, but the clientele leaves a *lot* to be desired."

Mokhtari sounded apprehensive as she rose to her feet. "Madame Ambassador, if you could tell me where you want to go... I'm afraid President zh'Tarash is still busy."

Troi waved her hand dismissively. "Forget zh'Tarash," she said resolutely, leaving the outdoor area of the small brasserie. "I know now that I came to the wrong place to ask for an audience."

Mokhtari ran after her, frowning. "The wrong place?"

"Without a doubt, because this is not one of the usual courtesy visits. My help is not required in the presidential office, but instead in California."

Once again, her companion could only blink in confusion. "Pardon me?"

Troi stopped dead in her tracks on the sidewalk. Mr. Ru almost walked into her. She was tempted to dismiss him for his clumsiness, but she decided she was going to be forgiving today. Instead, she looked at the young French woman. "Take me to Starfleet Headquarters. Take me to Admiral Akaar."

Mokhtari hesitated briefly, before nodding.

What had become of the Federation? Troi wondered as they headed toward a transporter station. Sometimes she hardly recognized it, and she sensed that she wasn't the only one to feel that way.

6
NOVEMBER 21, 2385

First City, Qo'noS

Night had fallen, covering the First City, the wild and beating heart of the Klingon Empire, in darkness. It made the grand old buildings look like black mountain ranges and the streets between them like dark ravines. The darkness dominated the skies above Qo'noS as if intended to defy the gods of old that the Klingons had discarded eons ago.

Most of all, though, it dominated behind the forehead of Chancellor Martok. Tired, the old warrior rubbed his wrinkled and scarred face, but when he lowered his hand, the malcontents still stood in front of his throne.

"Our patience is wearing thin, Martok," Grotek shouted. Those around him nodded, mumbling approvingly. Fury showed in their eyes, and the glow from the braziers in the council chambers reflected off the buckles and clasps of their robes, and from the ceremonial sashes full of medals and emblems that some of them wore. "We not only expect answers, we *demand* them!"

Grotek was a narrow-minded fool who had never managed to think further than his next meal. His impressive gray beard, his broad shoulders, and the merits he had earned as a considerably younger warrior made the representative of one of the planet's most important Houses behave as if he was extremely dignified and even more important. Neither his brain, nor his loose tongue could live up to these delusions of grandeur.

"You will get your answers," Martok replied immediately, asking himself how often he had said the exact same words since the beginning of this session. Five times? Seven? "The mission is going according to plan, and ..."

"Bah!" Grotek interrupted him.

Other chancellors would have answered that lack of respect with brutal punishment, and just for a brief moment Martok felt tempted to emulate them. But he pushed that notion aside. Violence against Grotek would not solve the problem.

"We've heard these tiresome reassurances for days now," Grotek continued. "But what answers do we need? The Renao have been clearly identified. Captain Kromm stated it in his latest report: The red-skins in the Lembatta Cluster are without the shadow of a doubt responsible for the terrorist acts. They have so-called 'solar-jump technology' at their disposal, which enables them to appear out of nowhere in order to wreak death and destruction! And what does the High Council do? How does our oh-so-honorable community react?"

"By staying silent," Britok answered the rhetorical question. The muscular son of Graak wore his old Defense Force armor. As a member of the House of Konjah, he was among the Empire's most influential warriors, and he had become a prime opposition voice during the past few weeks. He had challenged Martok during almost every council meeting. "Our enemies point their weapons at us, and we do nothing, as if we had all the time in the world." He glanced at the larger-than-life statues of ancient empire leaders and warriors lining the walls of the great hall. "We besmirch the memory of our ancestors! This empire has grown through actions, not through hesitation."

Approving, appreciative, and furious noises echoed throughout the vast hall. It seemed as if the entire High Council stood behind Britok and Grotek. Martok couldn't really blame them, but he knew that their short-sightedness was a mistake with regards to the Renao crisis. In the beginning, he had been able to appease the council members by sending the *Bortas* into the cluster with Federation Ambassador Alexander Rozhenko aboard as a scout. Later, he had amassed a small force of battleships near the border. They had been waiting for his orders to attack ever since. All these measures had helped him to take the edge out of the debates and to keep the critics in check.

But that was no longer the case. Since Onferin—since the allegedly unmistakable evidence of the Renao's guilt—the opposition had been out of control. And it grew stronger with each passing day.

"The size of the Empire is not your concern, son of Graak," Martok snapped. "Last time I looked in the mirror, I was still ruler, and not you!"

Britok seemed to have waited for that reprimand. As soon as the words had left Martok's mouth, the younger council member took two steps toward the chancellor's throne. "Still," he snarled, his iron gaze fixed on Martok. "But as I already stated, Chancellor, the time demands new actions."

A murmur went through the hall, echoing from bare stone walls and rising to the ceiling. Satisfied, Martok noted it, as it proved to him that even the most short-sighted among Britok's followers weren't inclined to stage a coup. Even these fools weren't misguided enough to rob the Empire of its leadership during this critical hour of need.

Still, he had no intention of leaving Britok's outrageous

motion unanswered. "The House of Konjah would be well advised," he said loud enough to silence the murmur, "to have someone attend the next council meeting who is able to keep their tongue in check." Martok rose and drew himself up to full height. "Otherwise, I won't guarantee that their representative returns home *with* their tongue." The man in uniform wanted to protest but Martok simply continued. His thundering bass choked off any protest. "Invading the Lembatta Cluster would be foolish. It would cost the lives of innocent civilians, which does not bring honor to our dead. Captain Kromm and Captain Adams are seeking the true culprits, the members of the Purifying Flame. As soon as they have been found…"

"As if not all of the Renao deserve to feel our wrath!" Grotek shouted, clearly inspired by the courage of his fellow campaigner.

"… we will react accordingly," Martok continued, ignoring the objection. "Until such time, the council would be well advised to listen to its supreme commander, and to remember the decisions he reached along with our allies in the Federation!" He threw his cassock of office from his shoulders, dropping it on the now empty throne for effect. He stepped off the small dais and left the council chambers without a word or another glance at any of the gathered councilors, deliberately turning his back on them, a calculated insult.

Korrt, one of his many assistants, was waiting for him in the corridor.

"Chancellor," the ever pale, ever frantic man from Munjeb III greeted him. The upper lip on Korrt's narrow face was blemished by an absurdly tiny mustache. Since Martok didn't stop, Korrt scampered next to him toward the exit of the Great Hall. "You have defended yourself firmly and clearly, if I may say so."

Martok grunted. Suddenly he had the taste of bile in his mouth, and a mixture of fury, concern, and impatience tied his stomach into a firm, ice-cold knot.

"Only for the moment, Korrt. There is trouble brewing in the council, and words alone are not going to change that. Britok, Grotek, and their foolish minions are taking advantage of the current situation to undermine my position. If Kromm and Adams don't come up with a decisive breakthrough before the next session, I will be forced to accede to their wishes."

Silent, and without looking at his aide again, the mightiest man of the Klingon Empire stepped out into the night. He was a victorious veteran of countless battles, but today felt far more like a defeat.

7
NOVEMBER 21, 2385

I.K.S. Bortas in orbit above Xhehenem

A long time ago—the Klingons had been telling this story for generations—a great storm approached the proud city of Quin'lat. Fearful, the citizens left the streets and squares, hurried home from the fields, and sought shelter within the great walls of the city. Concerned, they locked themselves in their houses. They nailed broad boards before their windows, and locked their heavy doors behind themselves. They hoped to weather out the approaching force of nature. Only one man refused to acknowledge the danger. Instead of hiding from the might of the storm like his comrades, he stood with his legs apart outside the city gates, his hands resting on his hips, scowling at the approaching dark clouds.

In those days, according to legend, Kahless the Unforgettable, the divine progenitor of Klingon honor and culture, spent some time among the citizens of the city. Just before the storm's arrival, Kahless learned about the audacity of this man. Immediately, he left his secure shelter, and walked outside Quin'lat's city walls to ask the warrior what he was doing.

"I am not afraid," the man declared. "I will not hide my face behind stone and mortar. I will stand before the wind and make it respect me!"

The wise Kahless nodded, as he accepted the man's

choice, before returning to his secure shelter, where he would wait for nature's force to run its course. When the storm finally arrived, it shook the walls and roofs in the proud city as they had never been shaken before. And they also swept the proud citizen off his feet—and he consequently died.

The next morning, the skies cleared, and the danger was finally over. The remaining citizens of Quin'lat asked Kahless why the wind hadn't bent to the dead man's will. He had been a man of honor and strength, after all, and—as Kahless confirmed—he had deserved respect.

Again, the unforgettable one nodded. Silently, he let his gaze wander from one Klingon to the next. Finally, he said: "The storm does respect a warrior. But did you truly expect it to respect a fool?"

Lieutenant Rooth, security chief of the *I.K.S. Bortas*, had liked this legend about the wise Kahless ever since his childhood days. Although he had heard and read various versions of it, he had never found an account divulging the name of the stupid inhabitant of Quin'lat. Now that Rooth stood inside the makeshift cell on deck twenty-four of his ship, looking at two Renao who were more dead than alive, he wondered if that stupid man from Quin'lat might have been called Kromm. He thought that would explain a lot.

"Are you satisfied, Rooth?" Captain Kromm pointed impatiently with his outstretched arm at the unconscious prisoners slumped in their chains. "Now you know about them. They're still alive. Can we return to more important matters?"

Ignoring the question, Rooth stepped closer to the two prisoners. Evvyk ak Busal and Moadas ak Lavoor were a pitiful sight. Their clothes were in tatters, their hair was greasy and sweaty. Their nose bridges were no longer adorned by gold jewelry, and the dim light of the ceiling lamp revealed numerous wounds all over their bodies— deep, untreated cuts on their thighs, broken fingers, lips that had been split by blows, and dark bruises on their shoulders, cheeks, and backs. Their wrists were also bloody, and the dirt and rust of the chains mingled with their blood.

"These people have been tortured," Rooth said quietly. He felt a fury approach him like the storm had approached Quin'lat, but he kept it at bay. For now.

"What else?" Kromm laughed abruptly. "Do you think these two will give up their secrets willingly?"

Undeterred, Rooth continued to survey the prisoners. Ak Busal seemed to suffer from a fever. She kept wincing slightly, and her red forehead was gleaming in the light of the dim lamp. "They require medical assistance." Again, the captain laughed. "Perhaps a roast *targ* or a large helping of skull stew and a tankard of warnog?" Kromm snorted. "They're our enemies, Lieutenant, not passengers! Whatever happened to them, they brought upon themselves by rising up against the Klingon Empire. Their existence aboard this ship gives us a crucial advantage over the *Prometheus*. For us—and for the entire Klingon Empire."

"That's if they had anything more to disclose," Rooth commented dryly.

"Oh, they do, surely." Kromm stroked his dark mustache with his left hand. "I just have to … persuade them a bit more."

Rooth was not sure there was anything left to persuade them with. Both Renao were at the end of their tether, both physically and mentally. What little mission-relevant knowledge they might have, they would have divulged to Kromm on Onferin. Their information had led the crew to the fanatic ak Bhedal and put them on the track of the

Purifying Flame. But they were minor players in the terrorist organization, distributing flyers for ak Bhedal, nothing more. Their only crime was following the wrong preacher and not thinking for themselves. They were no longer a source of information. Instead, they were a valve to let off some steam, and they served to keep up illusions.

Captain, you are so keen on impressing Qo'noS that you can't distinguish between valuable and useless sources. Half furious, half regretful, Rooth looked at his commander. *Your ambition gets in the way of your reason. So far, only these two poor creatures had to suffer because of that. But this mission is perilous. And perhaps all of us will suffer because of your blind ambition.*

The old security chief knew that he couldn't let that happen. He had been able to ignore Kromm as long as he was only involved in pub brawls, made loud noises, and emptied bloodwine barrels. Since Onferin, Kromm had been doing things just for the sake of it, and that could have dangerous consequences. It was one thing, keeping information from Captain Adams and the *Prometheus*. It didn't matter much to Rooth whether the Federation was on a level with the Empire, or whether it trailed behind. But mindlessly tormenting two prisoners didn't bear witness to honor and strength, but instead to undignified hatred. And, what was more, to hubris.

I will stand before the wind and make it respect me. Rooth was almost tempted to laugh out loud while slamming his fist into his captain's face. Almost.

"We will call a doctor right away," he said with a quiet but firm voice. The glare he bestowed upon Kromm spoke volumes. "And then we will relocate them to a cell where they belong, and where I can watch over them personally. *Sir.*"

Kromm's eyes widened with both incredulity and

amusement. "We will do … what? Lieutenant, you're overestimating your importance aboard this ship! If you don't wish to end up in a cell yourself …"

Rooth had expected nothing less. Even before Kromm had finished, he took his communicator from the belt of his uniform, opening a channel. "Bridge, this is Lieutenant Rooth. Requesting previously discussed link with the *U.S.S. Prometheus*."

"Very well, Lieutenant," Commander L'emka's equally harsh and sweet voice answered from the small device on the palm of his hand. *"Unfortunately, the nebulae are causing interferences. We will need approximately one minute to establish a stable connection."* She paused briefly, as they had rehearsed. *"Will you still require it then?"*

"Good question, Commander." Rooth glanced at Kromm. "What do you think, Captain?"

The commander of the *Bortas* gaped, which made him look even more stupid than usual. "You wouldn't dare."

"I already *have* dared," Rooth replied, unfazed. "The only question is, whether I will succeed or not."

"Dammit, Rooth, that's mutiny! I will have you thrown out of the fleet in disgrace, you old fool!" Kromm's hand reached for his hip also, but not for the communicator. "Or perhaps I will simply ram my *d'k tahg* into your wrinkled body right here and now!"

The security chief remained calm. "Be my guest, Captain. That won't change anything. Captain Adams *will* learn about these prisoners. Unless …"

Rooth could see that Kromm was struggling with what to do. The young commander's inexperience was surpassed only by his hubris, and his mind was racing.

Finally, the captain snarled. "What do you suggest?"

"The doctor, treating them in a proper cell."

"And in return, you will honor the promise you made to keep the existence of these two Renao to yourself?"

Rooth nodded. "I'm already keeping my oath, sir. Can't you see that? It will be much easier for me to keep it when the prisoners are in my custody where they belong. That's where I can guarantee the utmost secrecy regarding their existence because *I'm* watching them."

The captain snorted again. Kromm was visibly struggling. Rooth knew that the captain wanted to kill him on the spot. But even a fool like Kromm who had been drowning his wits in alcohol for most of his life knew that the result of such an emotional act would be less than desirable. Rooth had no intention of betraying the ship. He just wanted a more honorable treatment for the two Renao.

"Lieutenant?" L'emka's voice sounded from the comm device in Rooth's hand. *"We're ready. Do you want me to patch you through to the bridge of the* Prometheus?"

The security chief looked at Kromm.

"Negative, Commander L'emka," the captain replied. "The matter has been resolved. Inform sickbay that we require Doctor Drax to report to the prisoner cells."

"Understood, Captain. Bridge out."

The connection was terminated. Rooth nodded appreciatively. He was just about to open his mouth, when Kromm beat him to it.

"Take custody of your prisoners, Lieutenant—and rest assured that this is *not* over." The captain pointed at Rooth's face. "You may think that you're an intelligent man, but I can assure you, you're nothing but a potential risk. And I keep an eye on trouble spots, Rooth. Remember that." With these words he turned on his heel, leaving the room.

Rooth watched him leave until the heavy door closed behind him. Then he permitted a grim smile to play on his lips. "My sentiments exactly, sir."

"Bridge to Lieutenant Rooth. Doctor Drax is on his way."

He took the device from his belt, speaking into it. "Understood, bridge. And L'emka? I believe we should talk. Don't you agree?"

A storm had been raging inside of him, just like the one at Quin'lat all those years ago. But now, the old security chief mused, the skies were clearing. And nature didn't respect fools.

U.S.S. Prometheus

Lenissa zh'Thiin saw red—and she fully enjoyed it. Grunting, the Andorian security chief twisted herself, throwing the man, whose large hand had grabbed her unprotected throat, over her side and onto the mattress next to her.

"Is that the best you can do?" she asked when his fingers brushed against her neck … and they did so far too gently for her liking. She was sweating profusely from all pores, and her chest lifted and lowered with the rhythm of her panting breath. Her white hair stuck to her forehead, and her blue antennae seemed to vibrate with every beat of her hammering heart. "You should make a better effort if you want to keep up with me!"

The man simply laughed. Again, he leaned toward her, searching for an unprotected part of her body to attack. She felt his warm breath on her skin, and his teeth came dangerously close once again.

Zh'Thiin avoided them with ease. She wrapped her long legs around her opponent, interlaced her feet behind his back, squeezing him hard. She buried the fingers of her right hand in his short, curly hair and began to pull.

"Ouch," Geron Barai exclaimed. The ship's chief medical officer winced, and his hand, which had advanced toward her chin, retreated. "Pulling hair is not fair."

"Just like stopping right in the thick of things," zh'Thiin said. Impatiently, she pressed her body against the Betazoid man. Her thighs squeezed his hips. "You're far too timid today, anyway. Come on, put up a fight, you son of a ..."

"Careful, Commander!" The mischievous glint in his eyes stood in contrast to his Hippocratic Oath. "One wrong word and I'll have you locked up in the brig."

"You would need the new access codes, first, Doctor." She removed her hand from his hair, spreading her arms on the mattress, challenging him to a new attack. What was the matter with him? He never handled her with kid gloves when they enjoyed each other. "And those are only known to the captain, the first officer and me. So, come and get them."

A smile flickered across Barai's sweaty face, when he attempted to free himself from the clasp of her legs. "Thanks for the advice," he whispered. "I guess I'd better return to the bridge, then."

"Don't you dare!" Laughing, she grabbed his bare shoulders, throwing him and herself around again.

The game they were playing wasn't new, and they weren't the first ones to play it either. But both of them had mastered it. Every touch, caress and quiet word was an important milestone on their journey to breathlessness. Hands, lips, legs, and antennae—their bodies reacted instinctively to the movements of the other party; their skin yearning for the warmth of another being. Like most Andorians, zh'Thiin was hot-blooded and easily excitable by nature. Usually, she suppressed these traits in order to stay level-headed during her service in Starfleet. But right here and right now she succumbed to them fully. She *wanted* the stimulus, she *wanted* to feel her blood rushing through her veins, and the sweat on her naked breasts. She wanted to live!

The whatever-this-was between her and Barai had been going on for quite a while, and although they didn't go to great lengths anymore to hide their evenings together from the rest of the crew, no one seemed to have become suspicious in any way. Although zh'Thiin didn't think it would matter to Barai if anyone had.

But then, he wanted more than just an occasional sex partner. He didn't say as much, but she figured it out from his gazes and from the touch of his hands. If she was honest, she knew the truth.

And therein lay the problem.

But this was hardly the moment to ponder truths. Not with her blood boiling, her lust reaching warp nine. She was beyond considerations of the past, or of the future. There was just a most joyous *now*.

"More," she hissed, her eyes closed, and it sounded almost like an order. "More!"

And Barai screamed.

This time it was her turn to wince. When she opened her eyes, he just rolled away from her. His face was distorted with pain, and his hands touched his sides.

"What's wrong?" she asked, and felt guilty—especially since her question had sounded more reproachful than concerned, and she hadn't meant it that way.

"A bilateral fissure of my pelvis. The colossi of Delta Teka are weaklings compared to your thighs, Commander!"

Zh'Thiin immediately became overwhelmed by a guilty

conscience. "Geron, dammit. I ... I'm sorry, I ... damn, where is my uniform top? I will call sickbay and ..."

His hand grabbed her forearm. "Forget it, Niss. I'd really like to spare Trik that sight—and myself the embarrassment. Besides, it could be worse, honest." Propping himself up, the telepath swung his legs over the bed's edge, and promptly winced in pain. He barely managed to stifle another scream by pressing his lips together.

"So much for 'it could be worse'. You can hardly move, Doc," zh'Thiin said as she got up, quickly getting dressed. Once her tunic was in place, she tapped the combadge on her chest. "Zh'Thiin to Emergency Medical Holographic program. Trik, we need you right away on deck..."

"Disregard, Trik," Barai's voice said behind her. He was audibly in pain, but his voice was firm. "Don't trouble yourself. I'm on my way."

The holographic physician sounded confused. *"Erm. Understood. I think. Doctor, what's going on?"*

Zh'Thiin looked at her bedmate. Barai stood on both legs, albeit unsteadily. Slowly and gingerly the attractive Betazoid bent down to pick up his clothes, strewn all around her bed. The Andorian woman quickly helped him.

"It's fine, Trik. Thanks. Barai out."

She looked at Barai quizzically. "Are you sure?"

"Positive," he gasped and even managed a smile. It looked rather strained. "If you could help me ... with this?"

She helped him get dressed, before putting his arm around her shoulders, supporting him on his way to the door of her quarters. "I'll take you, alright?"

He laughed briefly. "And what are we going to tell Trik when the two of us turn up arm in arm and covered in sweat?" His hand brushed against her forearm. "Don't worry, Niss. I

THE ROOT OF ALL RAGE

know the way. And I know my hip. A few minutes with Trik and our regenerators, and I'll be as good as new." He groaned quietly. "I need to be as good as new, anyway. Tomorrow morning we're leaving for Xhehenem, and anything can happen down there. Sickbay needs to be prepared."

Xhehenem. That word proved to her more than anything that the time for games was over.

"Agreed," zh'Thiin said, nodding. "I ... I'm sorry."

"Save your remorse for the JAG office, Commander," he replied, joking. Again, he winced when she removed her supporting shoulder. "It won't get you anywhere with me." Another smile—warm but strained—and then he was gone.

Zh'Thiin remained behind in her quarters. Silently, she looked around, saw the rumpled sheets, the half-empty glasses, and her uniform boots in front of her bed. She took a deep breath.

What exactly was she playing at? It was beyond reasonable, or was it? She had already decided that she shouldn't continue with this. He was getting too close for comfort. She needed emotional distance and the certainty that she was just playing and having fun with him. And what about him? He didn't want any distance whatsoever. That was why he never mentioned it. He knew that she would end it if he decided to be honest with her.

But he is honest, she thought, recalling his far too gentle hands on her eager skin. *Not with words but with ... just about everything else.*

Damn. Why didn't she follow through then? It was better to make a painful break than draw out the agony—wasn't that what humans always said?

Why? She answered her own question. *Because of Onferin. Because of the Flame. Since this kidnapping ...*

Her blood yearned for life, for pleasure without consequences. That was the problem. Onferin had left marks on her. That was why she didn't turn Barai away when he looked in on her.

That's one of the reasons. Be honest with yourself, Niss, she chided herself. *You of all people. He has been treating you gingerly since you reported back aboard, and you know how much you resent that. But you're not doing yourself any favors when you refuse to face the truth. If you do that you're just as naïve and overcautious as he is. Can't you see that?*

Everything had consequences. Absolutely everything. If you tried to avoid them, you didn't understand life.

Lenissa zh'Thiin lay down on her bed, closed her eyes and waited for reason to kick in.

8
NOVEMBER 22, 2385

Kharanto, Xhehenem

Xhehenem's cities were small, its plains vast. Facing away from the ocean and the rising sun, Lieutenant Jassat ak Namur let his eyes wander over the arcologies of the city of Kharanto near the shore. The small settlement primarily subsisted on the treasures the water offered it. Sunlight reflected from the glass and various other sea-green surfaces, casting the oval structures with a breathtaking glow. It was majestic, touching Jassat deep within his heart.

"That's quite decadent," Alvar Bhansali commented. The lieutenant from zh'Thiin's security team hailed from the colony world of Deneva. Jassat hadn't noticed that Bhansali had joined him on the pier. Bhansali pointed his tricorder at the water but his gaze was fixed on the shimmering golden façades of the city. "Condemning other people for their lifestyle, while living in palaces."

The words weren't directed at anyone in particular. Bhansali's habit of thinking out loud was well known by everyone on board. Under normal circumstances he would have ignored the mumblings of the bearded man. But these circumstances were far from normal, and Jassat was not aboard the *Prometheus*, but back home. And although his eyes and his heart assured him with every step that this was home, he felt like a stranger.

"Would you like me to report you to your superior officer right away," he turned to the other lieutenant, "or would you like to finish voicing your prejudices first?"

The Denevan had been deep in thought and the harsh tone of voice startled him.

"Hm?" Bhansali mumbled, blinking. "What's wrong?"

Your big mouth, Jassat thought. *And you don't even realize it.*

"It's beautiful here, isn't it?" he asked with an aggressive friendliness. Inside, he fought to maintain his patience. "A view that makes it difficult to avert your eyes."

The other lieutenant nodded half-heartedly. "If you so say," he grumbled, pointedly attending to his tricorder.

Jassat sighed quietly, and left Bhansali to the ocean and his appalling prejudices. One more person to think like that, what difference did it make? Why get agitated?

Silently, the young Renao left the pier and walked toward the arcologies, leaving Bhansali to his work at the harbor. The streets and the airspace in between the sky-high buildings slowly came to life. The first pedestrians appeared on the sidewalks, in the open storage buildings and in the green spaces near the shore. Some *Kranaals* flew through the air.

Connecting the arcologies at approximately two-thirds of their height were bridges filled with lush green plants. At this hour, many inhabitants probably gathered there in order to watch the sunrise and to greet the new day. They would at best regard their visitors from space with considerable reluctance, Jassat was sure of it.

Renao loved keeping to themselves. Jassat and his interest in all things foreign was a rare exception to that rule. The majority of his people preferred turning their backs on inhabitants from other worlds, or foreign areas in space. This behavior had nothing do with xenophobia; it was based on the conviction that every living being had a fixed sphere within the universe and didn't need other places, and leaving that sphere would severely harm the galactic harmony. Therefore most Renao spent their days at the place where they had been born. That was what they deemed the right thing to do. Jassat had been taught that ever since he could think.

Renao taking up arms and violently punishing other species for changing their locations, however, was new and, in his opinion, unnatural. Based on what they'd learned on Onferin he believed that his people were being mentally manipulated. *Spock also said that. Ev, Moa ... These fanatics don't know what they're doing anymore*, he thought. *Or do they?*

The scientific evidence for this assumption still wasn't very solid, but Jassad found himself relying on it, as it was the only way to reconcile his people's behavior. The alternative was that his people were truly like this, and that would have hurt him even more than Bhansali's inconsiderate words or Jansen's abusive behavior in Starboard 8. As Jenna Kirk had so rightly pointed out, he should do his best to ignore them.

But how do you ignore being met with rejection everywhere you go? Or when home didn't feel like home any longer?

By doing your work, he chided himself. He hadn't been put on the away team to mull over his private problems. He was here because Captain Adams had assigned him a particular task, and Jassat would rather turn up in Chancellor Martok's living room with a target painted on his chest than disappoint Richard Adams.

"Go, lie low and sing small, Lieutenant," his captain and mentor had said to him just before Jassat had beamed down. "You are the least conspicuous of us. Go where Xhehenem's inhabitants would never allow us. Find the Purifying Flame."

So the young Renao didn't roam around with the other

officers but kept to himself. He wore civilian clothes in order to blend in. Only his combadge and his phaser would identify him as Starfleet, and he kept them both hidden in the folds of his black-and-gold casual top.

Minutes turned to hours. Jassat roamed through the harbor town's parks, scoured the first floors of several arcologies, listened to the conversations of other visitors in public *ley*-taverns, and he even briefly visited a temple of sphere harmony. The small sanctuary was situated at the top of one of the arcologies but because of the early hour it was completely empty. At the algae stores near the water he enjoyed a locally cooked meal which was tastier than any replicator could ever have prepared. In a *Kuruul*—a public information center with modern computers and a plethora of instructions for working with, above and below the surface of the ocean—he found Purifying Flame flyers, as if it was completely normal. But when he asked an employee, pretending to be interested, the man just shook his head.

This was not his only encounter with the mysterious organization. The longer Jassat stayed in Kharanto that morning, the more traces of the Flame caught his eye. There wasn't anything blatantly obvious, but rather, subtle indications. Sometimes, the flame symbol had been painted on a park wall or the back of one of the uglier algae stalls as a colorful reminder; sometimes a local with stacks of "eye-opening specialized literature"—his words, not Jassat's—stood by the entrance to one of the *Kuruuls*, attempting to engage passers-by in conversation. That man reminded Jassat painfully of Ev and Moa, the childhood friends he had been reunited with on Onferin, whom he had lost to this madness.

This Flame advocate from Kharanto was barely intelligent

enough to distribute the propaganda materials. He knew as much about the people behind all this or their attack plans as Bhansali did about quiet contemplation. Following him wouldn't achieve anything. Downhearted, Jassat left the man to his misguided beliefs and continued on his way.

Around lunchtime, Jassat sat in a public transport *Kranaal*, traveling to one of the two algae growth stations offshore, when he overheard a racist exchange between two elderly passengers who ranted about the "visitors from the outworlds" with their prejudices and their irrational fears concerning the sphere harmony.

Seeing an opening, he looked at them curiously, raising his hand in greeting. "We have visitors from outworlds?" His two fellow travelers stared at him incredulously. The man on the right had deep wrinkles in his face, and his opaque eyes indicated that he was almost blind. His seatmate was small but very stocky, and his scarred hands proved that he had been working around the ocean and its violent fauna for much of his life.

"Have you only just now gotten out of bed?" the smaller man replied. "The whole of Kharanto is talking about nothing else. My neighbor says that he saw two Klingons outside the power plant, when he went for his morning stroll!"

His wrinkled companion shook his head vigorously. "That's against nature! I don't even want to think about it."

Jassat nodded, trying to express concern and incredulity on his face. "That's peculiar. The strangers would need permission from Custodian ak Samooh for their visit here. Anything else would be considered an attack."

"Ak Samooh." The smaller Renao almost spat the name of the planet's administrator. "Forget ak Samooh. He's just masticating what Onferin is feeding him."

"But his duty is to the welfare of Xhehenem's inhabitants ..."

The man with the wrinkled face snorted derisively. "According to the news feeds, yeah. That's what they say during their speeches, especially when an election is imminent. Talking about the ordinary Renao citizen, about the will of the people, being seen with algae growers and field workers and mechanics. But once the elections are over?" Again, he shook his head. "Forget it. Even custodians of the planet are just puppets of other, bigger institutions. If today can prove one thing, it's that. Ak Samooh can claim to be standing for Xhehenem—and to defend Xhehenem—but as soon as Onferin gives him a different order, he will float with their tide ... and not with Xhehenem's."

"It's plain disgusting," the little guy agreed. He frowned with utter revulsion. "Our home's highest authority actively working against harmony."

"And no one is doing anything about it?" Jassat mimicked the consternation of both men as best he could. Again, he remembered Moa during his visit to his and Ev's little dwelling in Auroun on Onferin. He tried to emulate how Moa—the Moa of today, not the one of their childhood— would react in light of these latest developments. "We need to fight back!"

There was a glint in the eyes of the old man when he looked at him. "Oh, but we *are* fighting back."

"Khey," his companion said in a cautious tone.

Jassat leaned forward. "You're telling me that there's true sacrilege happening? What can I do about it? Whom do I have to speak to?"

Khey reached between the creases of his black and golden clothes but his companion touched his arm to caution him. "Don't, Khey. You know what they said."

Snorting derisively, Khey said, "They also said that we need all the support we can get, didn't they? And this young man *does* want to offer support."

Jassat nodded, trying not to look *too* eager.

Khey's friend eyed him suspiciously. "Be that as it may, but ... Forgive me, sir, but where did you say you came from? I don't seem to recall your face."

"I'm not from Kharanto," he said quickly, having been ready for this. "I come from further inland. I'm here to help with harvesting algae." He followed this statement with several details about harvest season that he had picked up this morning in the *Kuruul* he had visited. Would it be enough? Did it sound plausible? He didn't know but he sensed that he had found the trace that Captain Adams wanted.

When he finished, Khey nodded approvingly. "There you go, Oba. No reason for any secrecy. Every Renao is needed—and every Renao is a friend."

He produced a small, rectangular card and handed it to the lieutenant. The card was made of dried algae, and it showed the symbol of the Purifying Flame on one side, with a single cryptic line of text on the other:

N 23 / A 15 / 3

Confused, Jassat looked at Khey. "I'm afraid I don't follow."

"Well, then it's maybe not for you," Oba said quickly, snatching the card from Jassat. "Don't lose any sleep over it. You will surely find other ways to convey your disfavor toward our visitors."

The *Kranaal* began its final approach. Through the windows the passengers saw the algae growth station atop three broad support columns that towered above the shimmering waters. Inside were laboratories, production lines, and elevators. Vast algae fields expanded in all directions.

"But I'd like to know ..." Jassat started.

Oba, however, considered the conversation over. "And we need to go." He quickly raised his hand for the traditional greeting, before shoving Khey toward the exit hatch. "Have a nice day."

Khey gave Jassat a glance that was half amused, half apologetic. The *Kranaal* touched down on the landing platform of the algae growth station, and the rotors fell silent. A few moments later the hatch opened.

The lieutenant followed the other passengers outside, surreptitiously watching the two old men walk across the platform. They made their way toward the station office, which was a multistory circular building made of metal and glass. It was on the right side of the complex above the ocean's surface. Neither of them turned back.

The other passengers also disappeared quickly—into different entrances, some into hatches that led into the support columns and deep under water toward the algae.

Quickly, he found himself alone on the landing platform with the pilot. "You don't want to go back already, do you?" the latter asked, laughing at his own joke.

But Jassat turned back to him, nodding. "Oh yes, I do."

N 23 / A 15 / 3

The more he thought about it, the more hopeful he became.

Kharanto's northernmost arcology was also the largest. Just like most other main complexes, it was surrounded by annexes with three or four floors. They were primarily used for business purposes. It was also the city's only arcology to feature exactly twenty-three floors. Jassat stood on one of the green bridges leading to that building, looking up at its sun-flooded façade, and took a deep breath.

This just has to be right. Otherwise, I'm back to square one.

Silently, he crossed the bridge and disappeared into the belly of the arcology. A solar-powered elevator swiftly took him up to the top floor. Once there, Jassat strolled in a leisurely manner along the circular corridor until all the other passengers from the lift had entered their flats and other destinations. When he was finally alone in the corridor, he hurried along to his right until he reached the door with the number 15.

The door seemed as inconspicuous as all the others. No signs indicated that anything but a small working-class flat waited behind that door. But then Jassat noticed a flame symbol that had been clumsily carved into the silver metal casing of a small rectangular pad to the left of the door. A good sign.

He touched the pad with his hand. An acoustic signal sounded on the other side of the doorway.

One, Jassat thought, touching the pad for a second, and then for a third and last time. N 23 / A 15 / 3

Seconds passed. Nothing happened. Had he been wrong, after all?

Of course, I'm wrong, he chided himself. *It was so foolish of me to believe it could be that simple.*

Then the door opened.

"We don't know you," the Renao on the other side of the door stated, as if he'd been watching Jassat for a while. "And we know *all* of our friends."

The man was at least ten years older than Jassat, and he seemed to be even more mistrusting than Oba. His hair was jet-black, and he wore ceremonial robes. His facial jewelry was among the most glamorous Jassat had ever set eyes on.

The young lieutenant swallowed. A heavy scent of candles, incense, *ley*, and sweat wafted into the corridor from the doorway. And yet, there was complete silence.

"My name is …"

"Unimportant." The older man raised his hand for the traditional farewell, took a step backward, and started to close the door slowly.

"Oba sent me!" Jassat shouted quickly.

The man stretched his raised arm, and the door remained half open.

"Oba?" he asked, doubtful.

Jassat nodded. "My name is Moadas ak Lavoor." He quickly recited his false identity, before the chance would be irretrievably gone. Again, it came easy to him to imitate the local accent, and to sound like one of them. His nervousness was only half pretended.

"I'm a laborer on one of the growth stations. Oba and Khey thought I would be in the right place here. You know, because of the strangers."

"Oba and Khey," his counterpart mumbled. He seemed to ponder for a moment. Finally, he looked at Jassat skeptically. "They say there's a Renao among the strangers. So we're wary of people we don't know."

Jassat shook his head, desperately. "All I know about is Klingons in the power plant."

That seemed to be enough. The man laughed, stepping forward to open the door again. "Come in then, friend of Oba."

Grateful and relieved, Jassat entered the premises. A narrow, short corridor painted in warm earth tones led to a large room of approximately thirty square meters. It looked more like a temple of sphere harmony than the dwelling of a worker. The right wall consisted of a panoramic window front. The view of the ocean would have been breathtaking if the other arcologies hadn't blocked it. The wall was adorned with an impressive painting of the cluster's seven spheres. In the center was the legendary planet Iad, where all Renao came from, according to their mythology. This legend had fascinated Jassat as a child, but at the same time he had always considered it implausible. "Iad's Awakening" had been handwritten on the front wall beneath the symbol of the Purifying Flame.

So far, so good, thought Jassat, hoping more than ever that he wouldn't make any mistakes now.

Approximately twenty people, all male, were present. They seemed agitated and restless. They acknowledged Jassat's arrival with suspicious and even hostile glares.

"Oba sent him," the host explained. "The old algae-caresser probably wanted to put our call for missionaries into action right away."

"Moadas ak Lavoor," Jassat introduced himself, raising his hand respectfully. "I'm here to …"

"What does Starfleet promise these days if you betray your own people?" An older man who stood by the window with his back toward the others interrupted him. Now, he turned around. "How much does the United Federation of Planets pay a spy?"

A murmur went through the group. Even the host, who stood in front of the wall with the painted flame as if that was his usual place, looked at Jassat expectantly.

The lieutenant didn't hesitate for one second. "Hopefully not very much," he answered, and his voice was just as firm as the one of the stranger by the window. "Because that would mean that the traitor had forfeited his life for nothing, and that would serve him right." His gaze wandered across the small group, from one face to the next. "So, what's going on here? Oba said this is where we fight back. And this is where the work is being done that ak Samooh neglects to do. Have I come in vain or was the old fool right for a change?"

For a moment, no one said anything. Finally, the man by the window began to laugh. The others joined him several seconds later. Jassat sensed that he had been accepted and sat down without further ado.

Xhehenem, somewhere in the Southern Plains

"If this is supposed to be food, I'd rather starve." Disgusted, Jenna Kirk dropped the *basuudh*-tuber back into the oval harvest silo. She and her companion stood on the roof platform. "Just the thought of taking a bite off that makes me sick."

Lieutenant Rooth laughed out loud, showing her the small Klingon scanner he held in his right hand. Angular shaped characters scrolled quickly across the small display. Even if they hadn't moved as fast, Kirk would have had difficulty reading them. In the top left corner of the display flashed a green circle.

"They should really whet your appetite, Commander Kirk," the *Bortas* security chief stated, shaking his white-haired head in obvious amusement. "These tubers may not appeal to you visibly, but they contain a vast number of nutrients that are essential for humans."

Kirk snorted. If she wanted to listen to a lecture about local agricultural products, she would have joined Mendon's away team, instead of traveling around the southern areas of Xhehenem with Rooth, Ensign Gupta from xenobiology, and another Klingon called K'aybrok. "How would you know what's essential for humans?"

Rooth flashed his teeth in a predatory smile. "It's my duty to know the physiology of the space-traveling species that matter. You never know when this knowledge will be useful for killing an enemy."

"Charming." The chief engineer grinned at him, humorless. "You can spare me the advertising campaign, Rooth. You will not make me like this slimy, reeking stuff, I can promise you."

"And that is the core problem of your Federation, Kirk," Rooth said, saving his scanner readings. "They don't know how to adapt to new conditions."

"Says the man who'd rather shoot first, and ask questions never," she retorted dryly.

Rooth looked at her with a mischievous glint in his eyes. "Careful, Kirk. Don't mistake me for Kromm."

Ignoring him, she turned away from the open hatch of the silo and the disgusting stench emanating from it. She glanced at the open range in front of her—a blue and green plain reaching as far as the horizon. Water seemed to be a rare commodity here. If it hadn't been for the annual intensive wet season and the subterranean wells, Kirk would never have guessed that this world of all worlds was the most valuable and productive harvesting area of the entire Lembatta Cluster. She didn't see any rivers or lakes anywhere.

Instead, the afternoon sun presented vast fields where the slimy tubers and various other foodstuffs were being cultivated. She saw sandy pastures, where worm-like livestock burrowed through the ground, oozing some kind of viscous secretion that was supposedly extremely healthy. Apparently, there was a forest near the range of hills in the distance but that was another team's area. Kirk and her companions were supposed to search the farms and fields of this region.

"*Gupta to Kirk,*" a female voice jolted the chief engineer from her thoughts.

Quickly, she touched the combadge on her chest. "Go ahead, Aahi."

"*Commander, we're wasting our time here. K'aybrok and I have scanned each and every field in a diameter of several dozen kilometers. The data might be interesting for the science department on the* Prometheus, *but they don't tell us anything about the terrorists.*"

How could they? Kirk thought, sighing inwardly. *Those slimy tubers are just good for an attack on our taste buds, nothing more.*

She shielded her eyes and looked up to the sky. Up there, just a stone's throw from the tuber storage, hovered the shuttle *Jacob Marinsky* in Xhehenem's blue sky. Inside sat Gupta and K'aybrok, leaning over their computer readings and analyzing the lands from up above.

Unlike Onferin's atmosphere, Xhehenem's wasn't riddled with interferences, so Adams and Kromm had been able to launch smaller ships for surveys from a bird's-eye perspective. Two additional Starfleet shuttles as well as two small transports from the *Bortas* had also been dispatched. Like curious satellites they hovered above selected regions of the foreign planet. The captains had agreed to deploy the ships solely above scarcely populated or uninhabited areas. They had no intention of provoking the population any more than necessary, and a visible presence in the skies above their cities probably wouldn't have done anything to improve relations.

"Understood, Aahi. You can land right here in the yard. We'll come aboard soon. Kirk out."

"We will?" Rooth asked, amused, as soon as she had terminated the connection.

Shrugging, Kirk faced him. "Unless you want a sunburn. Because that's all you'll be getting here, Lieutenant."

The old Klingon made a tiny noise that was probably supposed to sound reproachful. At least that's what his tone of voice indicated when he continued. "And there was me thinking you were like your famous ancestor."

"Don't even mention him." What did it have to do with her that he was a legend? And why did everyone she met feel the urge to mention him to her? Sighing, she went to the edge of the narrow roof platform, stepping onto the hoverlift that was waiting for her.

Rooth closed the harvest silo's hatch and followed her. "Many songs are being sung among my people about him, even today," he said while the lift moved downward. It was no more than a square grid without any protective walls or a safety rail.

"And I bet he's the punchline in all of them," she said brusquely. "Seriously, Lieutenant, you would do me a favor if we could change the subject. Let's consider where we're going to continue our search. Damn, it would be a lot easier if we had more than just vague information from that uncommunicative preacher to find our way around."

"Hero," Rooth said.

Kirk didn't believe her ears. "What?" She had heard many terms for Joruul ak Bhedal, such as demagogue, fanatic, and—if Spock's assumption was correct—most of all victim … but she would never have used this one.

"Hero," Rooth repeated. "Not punchline."

Finally, she understood what—or more to the point, who—he was talking about. "Jim Kirk is a Klingon hero?"

Rooth nodded. "For decades, he bravely thwarted us. He lost his son at our hands. Yet he closed ranks with us when we needed him most. That, Commander, is the conduct of a hero."

She glanced at the Klingon with a mixture of perplexity and surprise. The mischievous glint she'd expected to see had vanished from his eyes. He was being serious. "You're right, Rooth. It's definitely impossible to mistake you for Kromm." *Or for most other specimens of your species I have met so far,* she added silently. The old security expert's inherent calmness was almost unnatural. Rooth was always in control of himself and his temper.

The harvest lift reached the ground. It jerked to a halt, and the two passengers got off. Kirk glanced at the circular two-story hive, which was the accommodation for the local farmhands. It was approximately a dozen meters away, and there didn't seem to be any movement.

"Our hosts were serious when they said that they didn't want to see or hear us," the engineer mumbled to herself, remembering the two Renao who had been occupying Doctor Barai's sickbay ever since they had left Onferin. Were Xhehenem's inhabitants just as deluded as they were? Did the strange radiation that Captain Adams allegedly found within the depths of the cluster affect them as well? A lot of their gathered evidence suggested that.

Deep in thought, she touched her combadge again. "Kirk to *Prometheus*."

At first, nothing happened. Finally, a voice came from

the device on her chest, along with the inevitable weak crackling that accompanied every communication within the cluster.

"Prometheus *here*," said Paul Winter. "*We hear you, Commander. Come in.*"

"We're almost done here, *Prometheus*. Next, we'll fly to this *yalach* plant in the west near the mountains. Unless you have other orders for us."

"*Negative, Commander.*" She heard Captain Adams himself now. "*Continue as agreed. But proceed with caution. There have been sporadic altercations in Kharanto. Chief Schnieder was in need of medical attention.*"

Kirk blinked in shock. Gordon Schnieder, the ship's quartermaster, was a jovial man in his early forties, and was the last person Kirk would expect to be part of an altercation. She looked over to Rooth, who was listening intently. "The madness is even more present here than it was on Onferin."

"Indeed," the *Bortas* security chief said. Again, he looked at the display of his small scanner.

A swooshing noise indicated that the *Marinsky* flew overhead. The shuttle headed for the tenement, descending behind it as ordered.

"Understood, *Prometheus*," Kirk said, closing the connection. She faced Rooth. "Shall we?"

Nodding, Rooth started walking, holding his scanner under Kirk's nose again. "Are you able to read Klingon characters, Commander?"

She shook her head. "Not very well." Soil crunched under their soles, and the light of the strange sun shone straight into their faces. "My Renao is much more fluent than my Klingon."

The old security chief regarded her pensively. "I thought as much," he said.

Then he pulled out his disruptor so fast that Kirk didn't stand a chance to react.

9
NOVEMBER 22, 2385

Kharanto, Xhehenem

They spoke of death and destruction, of outrages against the spheres, about the doom of galactic harmony.

And they spoke of Iad.

With every passing minute that Lieutenant Jassat ak Namur spent in the company of these so-called concerned citizens of Xhehenem, his horror grew. Were these really his people? Did these approximately forty men—the group had increased considerably since his arrival—with the mad glint in their eyes and the belligerently clenched fists really belong to the same species as he did? The phrases they spouted didn't have anything in common with the reserved demeanor that Jassat had known all his life. Whoever called for the demise of entire realms couldn't be a typical Renao. Or could they?

The mind of this poor woman is unhinged, Jassat remembered Spock's words back in sickbay, when they had been standing next to the manipulated Renao of Onferin. *She no longer has control over her life. She believes she is doing the right thing—but she is no longer able to ascertain the difference between right and wrong.*

This also seemed to apply to the men who had gathered in secret here in the northern arcology to voice their xenophobia, to listen to the preacher, and to indulge in fantasies about violence and what they would do to the strangers from space. With each new sentence, they psyched each other up; with each clenched fist they gave each other strength for the attack that they obviously longed for.

"The strangers must leave," Golaah ak Banuk said emphatically. The host of this little gathering still stood by the wall with the symbol of the flame. He glanced at the congregation. "What's more, they need to understand that their coming here is a crime against nature. A slap to the face of sphere harmony."

"Them and all others," a man to the right of Jassat shouted. He wore dark clothes with silver lapels. When he moved his head, his nasal jewelry gleamed in the light of the afternoon sun that shone through the windows. "We should make an example of the strangers to let everyone and anyone outside of the cluster know what it means coming to Xhehenem without invitation."

"Make them listen to us," another one shouted.

Ak Banuk smiled. "Oh, they're already listening," he said with a serene, distant expression. "They're hearing us loud and clear. But … they will hear us even clearer soon, I promise."

"What do you mean?" Jassat asked. He knew that he was pushing his luck, but he had been silent so far, simply listening to the others. If he wanted to remain believable, he needed to participate. "Clearer … how?"

"Just wait and see," was ak Banuk's evasive answer. His smile froze to a mask. "Bharatrum leads, we follow."

"Bharatrum leads," some of those gathered repeated approvingly. Jassat saw nodding heads and heard appreciative murmurs. Wherever he looked, he saw the same strange expression on their faces: a mixture of joy and fury, of awe, and the will to act.

They believe they're doing the right thing.

"What's on Bharatrum?" Quizzically he looked at ak Banuk. How far could he push his luck? "A ... source?"

That was too far, and he realized it immediately, if a bit late. "You're pretty nosy for a simple laborer," Hachtoo ak Laban said. He was the man who had been standing by the window when he had arrived. Now he was sitting on the edge of the group, eyeing the lieutenant skeptically. "You're asking an awful lot of questions."

Jassat made himself sound defensive. "I want to help. I need to know how, don't I?"

"I know someone else who would like to know as much as possible," ak Laban said. His tone of voice indicated quite clearly what he thought about Jassat.

Golaah ak Banuk also regarded Jassat suspiciously. "Someone else you say, Hach?"

Ak Laban nodded slowly. "Someone who wears the enemy's uniform. That person would ask a lot of questions here as well, don't you think?"

That was enough. Jassat sensed that he was losing the group. They all stared at him with incredible fury. All the madness they felt toward strangers, and the anger they had incited within each other, was directed at him now.

Jassat stood up. "You're wrong," he said with a firm voice, although his knees began to weaken considerably. Slowly and without taking his eyes off the others, he moved backward in the direction of the front door. "All of you. I hope you will realize that before it's too late for you. I hope you can find help."

"You will find death, you traitor!" ak Laban snarled. He leaped to his feet, pursuing Jassat. His face was a mask of hatred.

* * *

Somewhere in the Southern Plains

Jenna Kirk caught her breath when Rooth pointed the weapon at her. She imagined she could hear the humming of the energy reservoir inside the lethal device.

"Dammit, Rooth, what …" she began quietly. She was just about to raise her hands when the barrel of the disruptor moved away from her, pointing toward the entrance of the two-story farmer hive that was just behind them.

"Someone is watching us," Rooth whispered, nodding toward the small building. "And he's got a weapon."

Finally, Kirk understood. Quickly she drew her weapon as well, before whirling around. She didn't get a chance to take a closer look at the building because someone fired a shot. Luckily for her it was not very well aimed. The small projectile whistled about three handbreadths past her head.

"Take cover!" Rooth shouted, firing back.

Kirk dove behind one of the vehicles that was parked on the yard between the harvest sheds and the hive, Rooth following suit a moment later. The square vehicle was made of some kind of metal, was one and a half meters high, and brown like the soil on the fields. Volleys hit the harvester's side facing the hive.

"Rooth to *Marinsky*," the Klingon barked into his communicator. "K'aybrok, here we go!"

Kirk also fired. Cautiously, she peered from her cover and saw the two farmers who had initially greeted them out here in the open entrance of the building, along with two others who looked like farmhands.

Why now? she thought while firing a warning burst at the

building's façade just above the group's heads. *If they intended to kill us, why wait until now instead of when we first got here?*

There was only one explanation: the Renao had lost their nerve, which meant that their farm was anything but clean. Apparently, Kirk and Rooth were on to something. They had come too close for comfort, and they were obviously just about to discover a secret that the farmers, a husband-and-wife team, were desperately trying to keep under wraps.

Well, in that case you should have kept quiet, Kirk thought. Because two farmers had nothing on the combined forces of the Klingon Empire and the Federation.

Five minutes later it was all over. A well-aimed burst from Rooth's disruptor and one from Kirk's phaser had stunned two of the three male Renao. The third man withdrew hastily into the building. The woman didn't follow him, though. Instead, she dropped her weapon and walked clear of the entrance, holding her hands in front of her in a submissive gesture. Kirk covered Rooth, who quickly searched the woman before handing her over to Gupta and K'aybrok, who had landed the shuttle nearby.

"Take care of the unconscious men," Rooth said.

"What about the other one?" Kirk asked.

"We'll get him." The Klingon walked ahead while the woman began gesticulating and shouting at her captors.

The security chief and the chief engineer advanced into the building. Even there, Rooth could hear the curses and insults that the agitated woman screamed at the unwelcome armed guests.

The bottom floor of the farmhouse consisted of one large room. Rooth saw walls with earthen colors, various pieces of furniture, some kind of oven, and the painted symbol of the Purifying Flame on the back wall. Apparently, it hadn't been there long. The red and gold color looked fresh and bright compared to the dull, worn tones of its backdrop ... and his scanner verified what his eyes told him.

So you've only recently converted to fanaticism, have you? the Klingon thought. It was an interesting detail, provided it was true. But it didn't change anything about the guilt of the two Renao, nor did it make any difference to their value as informants. Which left the question, what had happened to the fourth individual? "Where *is* he?"

"Not here, that's for sure," Kirk said. "There's hardly ..." She trailed off and pointed. "Look, there!"

He also saw it. In one of the corners at the back of the room, barely covered by pieces of furniture, was a hatch, leading underground.

Rooth didn't know why they hadn't noticed the basement during their approach in the shuttle. The Federation pilot Gupta was probably incompetent. Or maybe the hive's walls somewhat shielded it against sensor detection. If that was true their hosts had been very foolish to attack, as it had led to them giving their secret away.

The security chief wasn't sure if these fanatics had truly lost their mental faculties, like the old Vulcan had been saying repeatedly for days. After all, you didn't necessarily need to be insane in order to have secrets.

Quickly he approached the hatch. As soon as he reached it, someone fired at him from below, but Rooth was able to dodge.

"Apparently, there are some more left," Kirk said dryly.

Rooth nodded. *And whoever it is, he's probably cleaning up ...*

They couldn't let that happen. Scanners overlooking

important details due to geological features was one thing, but he had no intention of wasting a chance to get answers.

"You go left, I'll go right," he said, raising his disruptor.

Kirk nodded. Cautiously but swiftly, they approached the open hatch.

"This is Starfleet," Kirk shouted. "It's over. Surrender, and nothing will happen to you."

Again, the Renao fired a shot. Apparently, he was not inclined to listen to the woman from Earth. That didn't surprise Rooth in the slightest.

"Right, let's do this my way." The Klingon took a leap forward, firing a volley of random disruptor shots into the opening in the floor. Not a sound was audible from the hatch anymore.

"Shoot first, and ask questions never," Kirk said, looking at him in disappointment. "That's your way, is it?"

"It's efficient, wouldn't you say?" Rooth replied, unfazed, pointing at the hatch.

He ventured forward again, peering into the secret basement. The Renao down there no longer posed a threat. He lay unconscious on the floor, his projectile weapon only a few steps away, probably dropped when one of Rooth's stun beams had found its target. The hideout was crammed with all sorts of devices and crates, and a small lamp at the rear end illuminated the scene. Kirk and Rooth climbed down a small ladder from the hatch into the basement. While Kirk attended to the unconscious man, Rooth took a closer look around.

The basement was extremely small, a glorified hole in the ground. Various private items belonging to the Renao had been piled into small niches that looked as if they had been dug manually into the ground some decades ago. Rooth saw crates full of preserved food and tools, but nothing that would have been worth fighting for. Or did the looks deceive him?

"K'aybrok to Rooth," his subordinate said over his communicator.

"What is it?"

"Sir, the Renao woman out here is behaving oddly. She's talking about something called Bharatrum. She says we can torture her all we want but she will not tell us about Bharatrum. And that we can't stop Bharatrum."

"I really don't like the sound of that," Kirk said. She had picked up the small lamp. Slowly, she let the light cone wander over the niches.

"Nor I," Rooth said. "Understood, K'aybrok. If she reveals anything else, let us know. Out."

Suddenly he remembered something that L'emka had told him. Back in the council hall on Onferin, there was a painting of the spheres on the ceiling: seven planets in seven overlapping circles. Bharatrum had been the innermost circle.

He looked at Kirk. "Do you see a circle somewhere around here?"

The engineer from the *Prometheus* raised her eyebrows, apparently recalling the same thing. "Good question. It's worth a try."

Together, they searched the niches, peered into crates made of algae-based cellulose, and turned over every single item. Finally, the wooden ladder caught Kirk's eye; or rather the corner *behind* that ladder. "Lieutenant!"

Going round the ladder, she grabbed some dark cloth in the corner.

"Somebody tried to cover something," Kirk said. Her cone of light moved across the material. It seemed to be some kind of blanket, as long as the basement was high and approximately one meter wide. Kirk handed Rooth the lamp and grabbed the ladder with both hands, pulling it from the hatch and out of the way.

Rooth stepped past Kirk. With his free hand he pulled the blanket aside—and his eyes widened!

There was indeed another niche, and within it another crate, bearing the symbols of the spheres. It was open, and inside they found several isolinear data rods. All of them had been destroyed.

Kharanto

Jassat ak Namur ran. His steps echoed loudly off the corridor walls. He expected attackers to be hiding everywhere, ready to lunge out from their cover to intercept his escape. Behind him he sensed Hachtoo ak Laban and the others chasing him.

Just as soon as he reached the first floor, the young lieutenant faced four furious Renao hurrying toward him. Obviously, ak Laban had informed these men, and now they waited for the fugitive at the arcology's exit. Their faces were distorted with fury.

Jassat whirled around. The situation was becoming increasingly precarious. Quickly, he ran back the way he had come. He needed to find another exit. Or some kind of hideout where he could wait until …

"There you are!" Hachtoo ak Laban appeared at the other end of the corridor with Golaah ak Banuk by his side and three more men from the gathering. "Did you really think we would let a traitor escape?"

All of them held beam weapons in their hands, and they stared at Jassat. Their eyes glowed ominously with the fire of madness.

The lieutenant stopped. In front of him were ak Laban and his companions, behind him he heard the four other men approach.

Relying on the instincts that had been honed over four years at the Academy, Jassat pulled the phaser from the depths of his robes, whirling to his right and firing at the front door. The energy beam disintegrated the door within a fraction of a second, and before its glowing had completely subsided, Jassat lunged into the quarters behind it.

"Ak Namur to *Prometheus*," he yelled, his free hand tapping his combadge. "Beam me up *now*!"

He knew that he was taking a risk, which was one of the reasons why he had waited so long to play this card. The atmospheric interference meant that beaming simply wasn't a safe means of transport … Chief Wilorin had made that abundantly clear during the mission briefing. However, while a transporter malfunction *might* kill him, staying here definitely *would* kill him, since it was obvious that ak Laban and his lunatics had no intention of taking him prisoner.

From the corner of his eye the lieutenant noticed movement. The flat's owner stormed out of one of the rooms, alarmed by the racket. He was also armed, and he aimed at Jassat.

At that moment, the transporter beam finally took hold. A familiar white-blue glow engulfed the lieutenant just as the Renao pulled the trigger.

U.S.S. Prometheus

"Are you alright, Lieutenant?" asked Wilorin.

Jassat blinked. The glowing had subsided, the arcology

had changed into the transporter room on the *Prometheus*. But the Renao had to pat himself down before he would finally believe that he was still alive.

"Y … yes," he finally stammered. "Thank you, Chief. That was in the nick of time. I was about to be shot to death."

"Well, apparently, the stars are smiling down on you, sir," the Tiburonian replied. "You were neither shot, nor were your molecules scattered during transport, which might well have happened. Fortunately, I was at the control panel myself."

"Yes, that was lucky indeed." Jassat nodded slightly. "If you would excuse me, Chief." His knees still trembling, he left the transporter room. He had to report to Commander Roaas.

10
NOVEMBER 22, 2385

U.S.S. Prometheus, in orbit above Xhehenem

Geron Barai was panting heavily as he and the Vulcan nurse struggled to hold Kumaah ak Partam in place on the biobed.

"Another dose, Trik, right now!" Barai shouted over the Renao's screams.

"Doctor," the Emergency Medical Hologram said, "the applied dosage is already above normal parameters. Do you really think it's wise to increase it even further?"

"Dammit, Trik, don't you see what's happening here?" Without waiting for the EMH to answer, Barai nodded toward Nurse T'Sai.

The young Vulcan woman acted instantly. She released one hand from its grip on Kumaah. This made Barai's struggles more difficult, as T'Sai's greater strength was a boon when trying to keep the crazed Renao under control. She grabbed the hypospray from the small table by the bed, double-checking the contents before pressing it against Kumaah's carotid artery. The quiet hiss indicating that the sedative was being released into the man's bloodstream was drowned out by his screams. But even before T'Sai removed the hypo from Kumaah's neck, the man finally calmed down. His arms loosened and fell to the bed, his legs stopped twitching, and he closed his eyes.

Barai looked at the monitor that showed the patient's

vital functions. "He's asleep. It worked."

At the next bed over, the EMH followed T'Sai's example with Kumaah's female partner, aided by Nurse Chu. The Renao woman had already hit him in the face twice, but she also responded immediately to the sedative.

"Cerebral parameters returning to normal, Doctor," Trik said. He and Chu released their grip on the sleeping woman.

"What in the world was all that about?" Chu asked. She was one of the most experienced and capable members of Barai's team, but even she seemed to be at the end of her rope. Cautiously, she took a step back from the biobed. Her black hair was disheveled, as if she had been involved in a fight.

"That's a very good question, Mikyung," said Barai. "And I will be damned if I don't get an answer soon." The Betazoid stepped away from Kumaah's bed. Both of his patients were guarded by security details. He tapped his combadge. "Barai to bridge."

"Roaas here," said the Caitian first officer.

"Commander, during the past few minutes our Renao patients have behaved as if a joint armada of the Jem'Hadar and the Borg had amassed outside the doors of my sickbay. They were flailing and screaming in a fit of spontaneous hysteria, which almost led to them losing their voices. And their brainwaves … sir, I have never seen anything like it! The parameters changed within seconds, with no obvious stimulus or change in treatment on our end. We're completely mystified, Commander. I thought you should know about this."

The Caitian remained silent for a moment. Barai frowned, looking quizzically at Trik, T'Sai, and Chu, who were attentive to the unconscious patients.

"Understood, Doctor," Roaas finally said. He sounded

pensive. *"Could you come to the bridge? Mr. Mendon thinks there's something here you should perhaps see."*

Trik faced Barai. "Do you want me …?"

Barai waved his hand dismissively. "Save yourself the trouble." Trik was part of the ship's computer, and it would have been easy for him to access Mendon's "something," so Barai could have looked at it right there. But Roaas obviously wanted him on the bridge.

"I'm on my way, Commander," the Betazoid said. "Barai out."

Trik nodded.

"I'm intrigued," Chu said quietly, while T'Sai began cleaning up the small tables at the top end of the biobeds.

"You and me both." Barai shouted toward the adjacent room, "Doctor Calloway, I'm on the bridge. You're in charge."

His deputy looked through the open door. "Understood, Doctor Barai." The blonde human woman from Meezan IV looked at the Renao. "Anything I should know?"

"No, Trik will continue to look after our guests." He faced the EMH. "Trik, if there are any problems …"

"I will apply further sedatives," the hologram finished the sentence.

"That's one way of dealing with it," Barai said helplessly. With one last nod at Calloway he turned and left the room.

Several minutes and one short turbolift journey later he entered the bridge of the *Prometheus*. The ship's control center displayed its usual focused and busy atmosphere. Lieutenant Commander Mendon stood next to Carson at ops, his hands folded in front of his stomach. Captain Adams joined them when Barai walked in.

Commander Roaas rose from his chair at tactical, facing the turbolift. "Thank you for coming so quickly, Doctor. You said the Renao have been hysterical? A few minutes ago?"

"Something like that," Barai answered. Suddenly, he felt insecure while climbing down the few steps to the lower area of the bridge.

"Exactly how many minutes ago, Mr. Mendon?" Adams asked without looking at Barai.

The Benzite didn't need a second prompt. "If my theory is correct, it should have been exactly five point three nine minutes, sir."

Now Adams looked at Barai. "Doctor?"

The Betazoid blinked, confused. What were they hinting at? "That sounds about right. I would need to check the logs to be more precise ..."

"That won't be necessary, Doctor," Adams said. "There will be enough time for that later."

"I'm sorry," Barai shook his head helplessly. "Would someone please care to explain to me what we are talking about?"

"We are speaking of madness, Doctor," a deep, coarse voice answered behind Barai's back, "and attempting to determine its cause."

Barai looked over his shoulder in astonishment. Spock stood at the science console that Mendon had abandoned at the back of the bridge. Barai hadn't even noticed him when he had entered the bridge. The Federation ambassador had staffed a similar workstation back in the days of the great James T. Kirk on the *U.S.S. Enterprise*. He looked up from the displays of his console, turning toward Barai and the others. He wore an ash-gray robe, and the wrinkles in his face seemed deeper than the Lembatta Cluster.

"What do you mean, Ambassador?" Barai asked.

"Our sensors registered an unusual activity out there

six minutes ago now," Adams answered in Spock's stead. "Some kind of radiation that—so Mr. Mendon assured me—contradicts any normal or even probable physical parameters within this region."

The medical officer frowned. "An artificial radiation?"

"Possibly." Spock stepped into the center of the bridge and stood next to Commander Roaas. His eyes were fixed on the main screen where the red nebulae and distant giant stars beyond Xhehenem were visible. "Or its source is natural—and our knowledge of the Lembatta Cluster is even more insufficient than previously believed."

Mendon said, "We registered this radiation exactly when the two Renao in your sickbay became agitated. And if you ask me, that is such a remarkable coincidence that I can't even call it that."

"I tend to agree," said Captain Adams. He glanced at Sarita Carson's ops console. Barai noticed that the readout showed not only sensor readings but also cerebral scans of the two Renao in sickbay. The captain continued: "I'm wondering why we haven't noticed this radiation sooner. If this has been a frequent occurrence, shouldn't we have detected it earlier? We've been in the cluster for weeks. Was it simply not there before?"

"It is possible that it increases the deeper we advance into the cluster," Mendon said. "It was too weak to detect sooner, but now that we're theoretically closer to the source, we're finally detecting it."

Spock nodded. "A fascinating hypothesis, Mr. Mendon."

Barai remembered Spock's notion that the Renao's fanaticism and their aggression were the result of a foreign influence that manipulated them unnoticed. This new observation might support Spock's assumption.

"Alright," said Adams, clapping his hands. "Mendon, you investigate this as thoroughly as you possibly can. I want to know what just happened, whether it will happen again, and where it originates."

"Right away, Captain." The Benzite beamed with pleasure, obviously thrilled at the chance to do this level of research.

"If you have no objection, Commander," said Spock, "I would be honored to assist you in your research."

"The honor would be mine, Ambassador."

Adams turned to his chief medical officer. "Doctor, you and Commander Carson will provide them with all the data they require."

"Of course," Barai replied.

"Aye, sir," the ops officer said. She had been sitting quietly, content simply to listen to the exchange without participating; now, her fingers danced across her station.

Adams glanced at the Betazoid. "And let me know if the situation in sickbay deteriorates."

"Understood, sir," Barai nodded, turning to leave. He was already halfway to the turbolift when Paul Winter spoke up.

"Captain," the communications officer shouted from his console. "We're receiving a message for you from Xhehenem."

"Custodian ak Samooh?" asked Adams.

Winter nodded slightly. "It would appear so, sir. The message is coming from his office."

"Thank you, Ensign. I'll take it in my ready room." Adams looked at Roaas and Spock. "I'd appreciate your company, gentlemen. Something tells me that our host doesn't bring good tidings."

"No shocks there then," Commander Roaas growled quietly.

The doors closed behind Barai, and the turbolift started moving down.

Captain Richard Adams stood by the window in his ready room, looking down on Xhehenem. Reddish nebulae filled the space beyond the agricultural world, and the distant sun shone on the planet's southernmost continent. Adams had listened to the initial reports of the away teams hours ago. Some of them were still investigating down there, and slowly but surely he pieced together an image in his mind. He didn't like that picture one bit.

"*Did you read me*, Prometheus?" the voice of the planetary custodian sounded from the comm system. "*Was that clear enough?*"

Barrah ak Samooh wasn't a nice person; Adams had realized as much during their previous conversation the night before. The narrow-shouldered Renao always came across to Adams as shady. He also seemed aggressive every time he dealt with him and Kromm. His hollow cheeks and the thin, pointed nose that was almost too small for the traditional Renao gold jewelry didn't hide the fact that the custodian from Xhehenem was a strong-willed man. Ak Samooh had little patience, but he also stood by his convictions. It had taken several long conversations and a direct, clear order from Onferin—issued by Councilor Shamar ak Mousal, the president of Renao's Home Spheres himself—for him to allow the visitors from the *Bortas* and the *Prometheus* access to his world.

"We abided by all agreements," Adams said. He still hadn't turned around to face his desk and the computer monitor that showed the faces of the custodian and of

Captain Kromm. "We have limited the number of away teams, we have tried not to disturb everyday life and work routines, and we are in permanent contact with your office, Custodian. We are observers, not conquerors. There is no reason to ban us from the planet now."

"*There isn't?*" Ak Samooh raised his voice. "*Captain Adams, against our better judgment, my people have opened their doors and extended hospitality to you. But what did I just hear from my outposts and their law enforcement officers? What do my agitated people tell me?*"

"*Oh, please,*" Adams heard Captain Kromm's voice from the* Bortas, *dripping with sarcasm. "*Don't keep us on tenterhooks. Nothing is more interesting to me than your agitated people!*"

Adams turned around, intending to soothe ruffled feathers, but then he realized that ak Samooh was just ignoring the Klingon. "*They are telling me about shots being fired and arrests. They speak about spies in our Temples of Sphere Harmony, and inside the workers' settlements. They report suspicious figures near our power plants, our breeding stations, and our water production plants. My people are nervous, Captain Adams, and when my people are nervous, I get nervous. I can't tolerate you being here any longer, and I never wanted you to come here anyway.*"

"Custodian, please." Adams had delivered quite a few pleas for reason since they had arrived in orbit here—indeed, since arriving in the Lembatta Cluster.

But ak Samooh had no intention of letting Adams finish. "*No, and once again, no, Captain. President ak Mousal may force us to tolerate you and your kind within the cluster, but I'd rather face ak Mousal's wrath than allow you to remain one second longer on our world. This is our sphere, Adams! It's far too important for compromises, too sacred! Withdraw your people or I will make them withdraw! Am I clear?"*

"You will make *them withdraw?"* Kromm laughed witheringly. *"Don't overestimate your powers, you filthy—"*

"Captain!" Adams interrupted sharply. "Please, leave it to me. I'm leading this mission, and I'm making the decisions." He was just as angry as Kromm at the custodian's impudence, but Adams had no other choice than to obey the Renao. He and the *Bortas* might have ak Mousal's permission to move freely within the cluster and to carry out their investigation, but the captain was dead set against ignoring the will of the people's representatives. It would be akin to an invasion, which would be against Starfleet's fundamental principles, which Adams would sooner die than violate.

Adams continued. "We will withdraw our people, according to your wishes. Thank you, Custodian ak Samooh, for your coop…"

But he didn't get a chance to finish his sentence, because ak Samooh terminated the connection. Apparently, the Renao had heard all he wanted to hear.

Which wasn't the case as far as Kromm was concerned. *"Have you completely lost your mind, Adams?"* He sat on his chair in the center of the bridge. Once again, Adams couldn't help regarding this piece of furniture as some kind of medieval throne, and Kromm as an ill-tempered despot. *"I do not recognize your authority to tell me what to do with my own ship, whether or not the Federation is 'leading' this mission or not. I'd rather sleep in a freight hangar full of tribbles than listen to the wishes of this pompous red-skin. Furthermore…"*

"Furthermore, Captain Adams acted perfectly reasonably and correctly," a second voice spoke from the comm system. At the same time, the camera angle widened, and the person next to Kromm's chair came into view. It was Ambassador Alexander Rozhenko. Like Spock, he was a Federation ambassador. The son of the *Enterprise*'s first officer, Commander Worf, he had been accompanying this mission from the beginning. Also like Spock, he shared very few of Kromm's views. *"We can't deal successfully with the Renao if we work against them."*

"These creatures are the enemy!" Kromm screamed.

"They are victims," Rozhenko said firmly. *"They are under some kind of strange influence."*

Kromm snorted. *"The only one who's under a strange influence is me!"* There was a grim determination in the Klingon's eyes, which chilled Adams to the marrow, as did the snarl in the Klingon's voice. *"And I'm fed up with playing games, Adams."*

Adams recalled the reports from the away teams, their stories about the overt aggression the locals had displayed toward the visiting aliens. He still hadn't heard back from all the teams, but he knew that there had been altercations, small gunfights, even. This was possibly only the tip of the iceberg. Violence usually spiraled out of control if it wasn't met with consideration and a clear head—and sometimes it did even if this was the case.

Then he thought about Barai's patients, about mysterious radiation emissions and their possible consequences.

"Your objection has been noted," he decided brusquely. *"Prometheus* out."

He pressed one button and the connection was terminated. But as he shifted his gaze from the terminal on the desk to Spock, Adams knew that the dispute had only just begun.

* * *

"I'm afraid my report won't do anything to improve the situation at all." Clasping her hands behind her back, Jenna Kirk gazed at her captain across his desk. She was the only visitor in his ready room, and she wished she had better news—especially in light of recent developments. "It's … complicated."

"It usually is, Commander," Adams replied, interlacing his fingers and leaning back in his chair. "We will have to live with that. So? What did you discover?"

"Not a lot, sir," Kirk admitted. "Lieutenant Tabor is still working on the data along with Captain Kromm's technicians, but I'm afraid their efforts will be in vain. The Renao down there on Xhehenem knew that we were in their yard. And even if they initially believed that they could escape discovery, the Renao man in the basement had enough time to render the data useless, once the shooting had begun."

"A secret hideout in the basement of a farmhouse," Adams muttered. "Not exactly the place where I would suspect important information about the Purifying Flame."

"Maybe that's why it was the ideal hiding place. Even more so, because our sensors missed it. It was Lieutenant Rooth who discovered it. And I haven't been able to reconstruct enough of the data to figure out if it's of any value or not."

Kirk groaned inwardly when she remembered how they had found the half-melted crate with the isolinear rods; the hopes that this find had raised within her, hopes that were dashed upon realizing that they'd been all but destroyed. It would take a technical miracle from an army of Federation computer experts to recover the data. Frustrated, the chief engineer ran her fingers through her hair. She was tired and wired, and it would be quite a while before she could rest.

"Important enough to shoot at Klingon and Federation officers," said Adams.

Kirk nodded. "One thing is certain. The farmers caused quite a ruckus. Rooth and I had to stun two people before we could even gain access to the house. And the third person opened fire on us in there. But we couldn't control the woman at all. She ranted at us, sir, saying over and over again that we couldn't stop Bharatrum and that we were too late."

Adams frowned. "Too late for what?"

"I have no idea, and the farmers refused to answer. Rooth and I handed them over to the planetary security forces, and they promised to continue the interrogation, and to inform us if the prisoners started talking. Somehow I doubt they'll remember that second part, if they even remember the first. Lieutenant Rooth agrees with me."

"The plot is certainly thickening," said the captain. "*Something* is happening on Bharatrum. Lieutenant ak Namur has returned from his undercover mission with that name as a clue, and now you have as well. The Purifying Flame seems to be very active there." Adams brought up a map of the cluster on the monitor on his desk. "Bharatrum is the most central inhabited world in this region. If the Flame has its seat there, we should take a closer look."

Kirk's combadge beeped, followed by the voice of her Bajoran deputy. *"Tabor to Kirk."*

She tapped her combadge. "Kirk here."

Lieutenant Tabor said, *"Commander, I can report an initial success, albeit a small one."*

Adams looked at Kirk and said, "Let's have it, Lieutenant. We can do with some good news for a change, no matter how insignificant it seems to be."

"*Sir, I was able to retrieve a small fraction of the data on those isolinear rods. It would appear that we are looking at technical drawings … three-dimensional animations of one-pilot battleships. They remind me of the fragments we found at Starbase 91.*"

"The modified *Scorpion* attack fighters," Kirk said. "Black market goods from Romulan war supplies."

"*That's what it looks like to me,*" said Tabor. "*But there's something else. The text files, which are attached to the animations, repeatedly mention one particular location. We haven't been able to retrieve much from these files but this one term keeps coming up.*"

"Let me guess, Lieutenant," said Adams. "Bharatrum?"

The Bajoran was audibly perplexed. "*Um, correct, sir.*"

Again, Adams exchanged a knowing glance with his chief engineer.

"Thanks for the update, Tabor," said Kirk. "Keep at it, and report anything else you find."

"*Understood, Commander. Tabor out.*"

"I don't like this," Adams said once the connection was closed. He got up, walking over to the small window of his ready room, staring at the view of Xhehenem. "What do these *Scorpion* replicas have to do with Bharatrum?"

Kirk nodded. "Maybe they have a secret shipyard there. It could be the source of all the attacks."

"Perhaps," said Adams. "In any case, we have to follow up on that lead." He faced Kirk. "This is a region full of mysteries, Commander. It's about time we unraveled some of them."

11
NOVEMBER 22, 2385

San Francisco, Earth

The mighty Pacific smelled of salt, and the blue of the cloudless sky framed the ocean's vastness. Lwaxana Troi stood on the rooftop terrace of Starfleet Headquarters—one of the many bright and friendly-looking buildings near the Californian bay—staring down onto the Golden Gate Bridge and the extensive campus of Starfleet Academy. Cadets from many different member worlds walked in uniform along narrow pathways between well-kept green areas.

Small shuttles flew across the ocean before landing on designated platforms behind Academy buildings. Just an ordinary day in the City by the Bay.

Ten years had passed since the attack of the Breen that had left this campus in ruins. But no matter how long Troi let her gaze wander across these grounds, she couldn't find a single trace of the atrocities that the people here had endured back then. It really looked as if the Federation—and Starfleet—had left the past behind and found their peace again.

But looks were deceiving. The Betazoid woman knew this, not just because her home of Betazed was also attacked during the Dominion War and had rebuilt over the past decade, but also because of the reason for her visit here today.

The man she had come to see said, "As I have already

told Ms. Mokhtari, Madame Ambassador, my time is limited. As much as I'm honored by your unexpected visit, I can't devote any time to you today."

Troi's gaze remained fixed on the campus and the bay. The warm wind played with her dress while she listened to her host in silence.

Fleet Admiral Leonard James Akaar, commander-in-chief of Starfleet, was truly a giant. The humanoid from the planet Capella IV was almost one hundred and twenty years old, had broad shoulders, silver-gray hair, and a face that Troi had never known to smile. The admiral, with whom she shared a decades-long professional acquaintance, was one of the most influential people within the Federation. He had taken it upon himself only a few weeks ago, together with Jean-Luc and her delightful son-in-law Will, to chase the treacherous interim president Ishan Anjar from office, before he could be elected as long-term leader of the Federation. Ishan had been the murdered Nanietta Bacco's successor. The actions of Akaar, Will, and Jean-Luc could have cost each of them more than just their career, but they had exposed Ishan's treachery and cleared the way for both Kellessar zh'Tarash and a new and better future.

And now Akaar didn't have time for her.

"I understand," Troi said quietly. Again, she let her gaze wander across the bay, the sky, and the blue vastness.

"The events in the Lembatta Cluster demand most of my attention," the Capellan continued. His tone was polite and apologetic, but determined at the same time. "Not to mention the Typhon Pact and various other hot spots of various importance and size."

Troi simply nodded.

"We're still in the process of re-arming, Madame

Ambassador," he continued. "The Borg, the Dominion … Recent events are weighing heavily on the fleet, and despite our best efforts we simply haven't achieved sufficient strength to deal with new crises."

"I understand," she repeated placidly. A snow-white ferry floated on the waters beneath the bridge. The observation deck was full of tourists, or so it seemed from this distance. Troi imagined how these San Francisco visitors would be enjoying the view of the famous Golden Gate Bridge.

"So I would welcome it very much," Akaar finally came to the point of his little monologue, "if you could return to Paris and your appointment with the president. Or at least direct your query to your son-in-law instead of me— although he, too, is very busy right now, I'm afraid—as are we all." He sighed and his tone became softer again. "I'm sorry, Madame Ambassador, truly. President zh'Tarash will surely be glad to accommodate you in Paris, once …"

That was the end of the feigned peace. Troi turned around, facing Akaar. "I understand, Admiral, but I'm afraid, *you* don't. I appreciate your intention to 'take a few minutes out for a breath of fresh air' with me, as you stated to Ms. Mokhtari, despite all the stress that your busy schedule undoubtedly burdens you with."

Akaar nodded. He seemed trapped between his sense of duty—Lwaxana Troi wasn't just anyone—and the call of duty from his office within Headquarters.

"But you couldn't be more wrong," the Betazoid woman continued, "if you mistake my coming for a courtesy visit or some kind of diplomatic exhibition. Make no mistake, I don't expect a red carpet or some kind of promotionally effective press conference with you by my side. And I am very aware of my dear William's workload, as well as yours. Yet some things can't wait. Some things need to be addressed immediately—and with the appropriate people, right at the top. With you."

"In that case, I'm afraid I don't follow you, Madame Ambassador."

Troi looked around. They were alone on the small rooftop terrace, which had two white benches, exotic plants in large pots, and a small fountain. Mokhtari and Ru, who had accompanied Troi to San Francisco, had remained indoors, cooling their heels on the top floor.

"Then I shall come straight to the point." She turned back to the admiral. "Perhaps I don't know all too much about the situation in the Lembatta Cluster, but I know what's going on here on Earth. I hear people talk, Admiral, and—believe you me—I recognize a ticking time bomb when I see one."

The tall commander-in-chief frowned. "What are people saying?"

"Too much!" She waved her arms emphatically. "Stupid phrases, Admiral! Rumors and prejudices, combined into a conglomerate of dangerous foolishness. The people are getting agitated. They are full of fear; and fear that isn't met with therapy usually results in rash actions, injustice, and hatred."

Akaar seemed to understand, but he drew the wrong conclusions. Instead of nodding, he smiled. "All credit to you for your concern, Madame Ambassador, but I assure you that we're doing our best to defuse the situation. The U.S.S. Prometheus and the I.K.S. Bortas are looking for the roots of the Purifying Flame as we speak, and ..."

"I know hatred, Admiral," she interrupted him, shaking her head. She recalled the two men from the street café in Paris, whose shameful behavior had been so absolutely out of character for humans. Yet in her mind they transformed into Jem'Hadar warriors, the likes of which had been everywhere on Betazed during the Dominion War. "With all due respect for your efforts, the damage has already been done, right here on your doorstep. Don't forget Earth, Admiral Akaar, and all the other Federation worlds where frightened citizens are spouting slogans. If you really want peace, you mustn't just de-escalate matters within the Lembatta Cluster."

The Fleet Admiral fell silent for a while, gazing thoughtfully at his unexpected visitor. A warm and fresh ocean breeze blew through his shoulder-length hair and made his Starfleet uniform sleeves flutter.

"I have a confession to make, Madame Ambassador," he finally said. "I'm afraid that I have underestimated you."

She chuckled quietly. "You would hardly be the first, dear. Besides, I've found that being infamous has its merits."

"I don't doubt it." Akaar actually smiled. "Your visit honors me, Madame Ambassador, and I do not merely say that out of courtesy. You wish to help?"

Gratefully, she clapped her hands. "At last, we're on the same page." Troi was just about to begin listing the measures that she had come up with when the door to the rooftop terrace flew open, and a Vulcan stepped out.

Akaar turned around to face him. "What's wrong, Sendak?"

"Please excuse the interruption, Admiral," said the aide, "but I thought it would be best if I relayed this message personally. You must return to your office immediately, sir. President zh'Tarash will contact you in five minutes."

The admiral was already on his way, and the Betazoid woman followed him, uninvited.

"What's this about?" both of them asked simultaneously.

"Korinar, sir," Sendak said. "Apparently, the Purifying Flame has struck again."

12
ONE HOUR EARLIER

Korinar Prime, Korinar System

The Korinar system was located near the border to the Lembatta Cluster on the outer edge of the Klingon Empire. A little over one hundred years ago, the Tholians had attacked Korinar. They had brought bloodshed, death, and agonizing destruction over this remote region in space, claiming that their actions were taken out of vengeance for past evils done to the Tholian Assembly by the Klingon Empire, whether real or imagined. But those atrocities were in the past, and even though the people living there today still sung heroic songs about those days, they mainly did so because there were no songs from more recent times. Nobody came to Korinar anymore, and nothing ever happened there. Life in the Korinar system predominantly consisted of boredom, silence, and emptiness.

Some settlers liked it quiet; the workers, for example, who dug up liquid from the planet's core. Apparently, Qo'noS very much liked that liquid, even though it smelled horrible. Lurnga had overheard that this didn't bother the workers since the smelly liquid was very valuable indeed.

Lurnga wished it was not quite so boring. Ever since her birth on Korinar Prime ten moons ago, the Klingon girl had longed for more action in her homeworld … for more glory than mining dirt. Until a few days ago, Korinar had continuously disappointed her in that respect.

But now ... "Don't think much of the Federation's words, Commander," Lurnga heard the visitor's voice. He was a warrior in a dark uniform who had suddenly appeared a few days ago at her home, there to speak to Lurnga's father. According to him, an entire fleet of Klingon warships had taken position just this side of the cluster border. "The humans and their lackeys have once again proven their utter incompetence when it comes to recognizing a crisis before it turns dangerous."

Lurnga was hiding behind one of the unused computer consoles, as she often did when she wanted to eavesdrop on the adults. She pricked up her ears. Had the visitor really mentioned danger?

Danger ... that sounded like adventure, a welcome change from boring normality. Lurnga decided that danger had to be something good, and suddenly, she liked the visitor even more than before. She was also happy that she had managed to slip into the command center tonight. Otherwise, she would have missed out on this thrilling conversation. That made it the first thrilling thing she'd encountered in her entire life.

Smiling, she looked at Brolt, the small toy *klongat* that she carried everywhere, and who was her best friend.

"You see?" she whispered to the fairly well-worn puppet that consisted of cloth and leather. "And you said I shouldn't listen in. You said this was only for true warriors. Bah!"

Brolt did what it always did when she chided it: it remained silent and patient, baring its impressive *klongat* teeth.

Lurnga shook her head reproachfully. *For such an apparently dangerous beast, you're pretty cowardly, Brolt*, she thought, before concentrating on the conversation of the adults again. At least they weren't as childish as the *klongat*.

The listening post that Lurnga's father and mother operated was situated high within the mountains of Korinar Prime—the boring main world of the just as boring system—and it wasn't very big. Basically, it only consisted of one large, windowless room. It was crammed with consoles, sensors, monitors, and all sorts of other technological equipment. The girl didn't know anything about the devices and their functions. Her father had explained to her once that the sensors were listening into the cluster at the order of the High Council, but Lurnga didn't consider that to be terribly exciting. After all, the cluster had been even less eventful so far than Korinar Prime ... and that said something. The technology generally worked automatically, that much Lurnga knew, as long as her parents serviced it meticulously. They also had to send regular reports to the chancellor, although he gave—as her father had put it quite a while ago—"a *targ*'s wet fart" about those reports. The devices seemed to be as unimportant as the entire system, Lurnga thought. Why else had the majority of them stood idle and deactivated in the listening post until a few days ago?

All that had changed drastically after the visitor had appeared. Drastically. Now, just about every console hummed and flashed around the clock, and not an evening went by when Lurnga didn't hear her father, the great and honorable Commander Bak, complain about how outdated all this equipment was. Her mother, the even greater and much more honorable Commander Lapsok, would chide him for not bringing it up to date sooner. She would complain that he had been foolish to let his laziness tie him to Korinar. She would sigh deeply, calling herself foolish as well because she had gotten involved with a fool like him back then, when she had other options.

Lurnga's parents raised their voices considerably when they were talking with and about each other like that, and they used many bad words. Lurnga could hear them from her bed every evening, and she was annoyed with them because they didn't realize just how wrong they were. They were Bak and Lapsok, by Kahless, the most important people on Korinar!

Honorable warriors were no fools, and definitely not lazy. It was a disgrace that they didn't realize that, when even Lurnga understood it.

The sound of someone clearing their throat brought the young Klingon girl back to reality. It was her father; she recognized him instantly. The great and honorable Bak was a man of many wise words, but this clearing of his throat was the first noise he had made since the visitor had entered the remote listening post today. That was yet another confusing fact for Lurnga. She didn't get a chance to think about it much, though, because the fascinating visitor continued.

"President zh'Tarash may be new," said the warrior, "but she is proving as bloodless as her predecessor. Staring the Renao in the face and not spilling their blood right away …" Their visitor laughed derisively. "It's unbelievable. Don't you agree, Bak?"

Lurnga lifted her head slightly when her father's name was mentioned. But she didn't dare to crawl to the edge of the console to peer around it. If her father spotted her, he would use words far worse than those of his evening arguments, that much was certain.

"Bak?" the visitor asked. "Have you gone deaf? Do you think I'm talking to myself here? Answer me!"

"It's unbelievable," Lurnga heard the great and

honorable commander say. But Bak didn't sound great, or honorable. In all honesty, he almost sounded like Brolt: small and cowardly.

"But?" The visitor sounded challenging. Apparently, Bak was too quiet for his liking.

"No 'but,' sir. You're correct."

Lurnga heard a deep sigh, even deeper than those of her mother in the evening, before their visitor continued. He sounded somewhat dissatisfied.

"You must speak openly, you pitiful worm! Do you think that the Empire became what it is because of spineless weaklings? If I ask you a question, Bak, I want to hear your opinion!"

Weaklings? Had he just called her father a weakling? Lurnga wasn't quite sure. Still, the fascinating stranger had just lost quite a bit of fascination in her eyes.

It took a while for Bak to answer. "Aren't we doing the same thing?" Lurnga's father asked, and he did sound weak. Almost as if he was afraid of his own words.

The visitor laughed. "Bak, Bak, Bak, you don't even dare to look up when a superior officer is talking to you. And you really did allow the *targs* to gnaw away at your little mountain retreat when you didn't see the need to accept the upgrades that Qo'noS had been offering you for years. But behind your anxious little face beats the heart of a true Klingon! You're actually capable of *thinking*, Bak!"

Lurnga caught her breath because she was suddenly furious. How did this man dare? Who did he think he was? He suddenly appeared, talked about armed forces and some red-skinned enemies, grumbled about the allegedly bad condition of the listening post, and insulted the operators. Didn't he know how to treat honorable commanders? And hadn't anyone told him how little the chancellor cared for the reports from Korinar? The rest of the Empire just cared about the smelly liquid, and not about the data from the Lembatta Cluster. What was all this nonsense about?

"So, keep on thinking," the man now demanded from Lurnga's father. "Come on. Keep it coming."

Bak hesitated. When the words finally came, they seemed to trickle one by one. "I … I'm just saying, sir. You blame the Federation for not doing anything—and rightly so. But, we're not acting either …"

"Wrong, Bak," the man said. Lurnga asked herself why she had ever found him fascinating. He was nasty, with no honor. "It would seem you're not that intelligent after all. What a shame. I expected more from you." He clapped his hands. Apparently, he touched the consoles where he and Bak sat; at least, Lurnga heard the noises those devices always made when they were being touched. "You see? Here, here, and here, Bak. *That* is the difference between the glorious Klingon Empire and the pitiful Federation—we're doing something. That's why I'm here."

Silence. Lurnga still didn't understand what the two adults were talking about, but she sensed that her father had an objection, which he was reluctant to voice.

"Yes, Bak?" the visitor urged him as if he had also sensed it.

"Sir." The great and honorable commander cleared his throat nervously. "Sir, we …"

The visitor growled. "Out with it. Your cowardice is hardly bearable. Are you afraid I will cut your head off?"

Lurnga looked at Brolt, horrified. Cut his head off? By Kahless, would the *klongat* and she have to intervene and defend her father? *Klongats* were wild animals. If you encountered them unarmed, you usually didn't breathe for much longer.

"Sir, are we really doing something?" her father asked, hesitantly. "Your fleet ... it's just in position outside the cluster. They are also not spilling blood. They are not avenging the dead the Renao have left behind."

The man in the black uniform laughed again. But there was no more mockery in his laughter. "Oh, Bak, your heart is in the right place, if nothing else. And if you knew what's transpiring at the High Council right now ... Well, let me put it this way—Martok's days are numbered. There are powers within our honorable government that will no longer tolerate the chancellor's dependence on the Federation. Before too long, my fleet will not only wait outside the border, but it will become active. It will kill. Avenge. That's the sole reason why it's here. And, Bak? I can hardly wait."

He laughed again, and the great and honorable commander joined him this time. Lurnga relaxed a little as the edgy mood seemed to have subsided.

Until the alarm sounded.

"What?" The visitor seemed shocked. "That's impossible. Bak, your machines must be showing their age. Tell me that this is a malfunction!"

Bleeps and humming sounded along with the wailing sirens. The consoles were doing their job because Bak sat at their controls. Lurnga could hear him. The commander was at work.

"Bak!" the stranger shouted, imperious. "Explain!"

"I ... I can't, sir," Lurnga's father stammered. The little Klingon girl was petrified when she noticed the horror in his voice. "This is impossible. The long-range sensors should have picked it up ages ago."

"How many are there?" the man asked.

Bak didn't say anything.

"How *many*, you pathetic fool?"

The shout echoed from the walls in the small control center, drowning out all the other noises. That was enough. Lurnga gave in to her fury about the unsavory visitor, and did what she had never done before—she left her hiding place.

"One more word from you," she snarled at the stranger like a true warrior, holding out her wild Brolt, "and I will set my *klongat* on you, you wretched *petaQ!*"

Commander Bak turned pale. Bewilderment stood in his eyes when he stared at Lurnga. On the monitors behind him, the little Klingon girl saw a map of the Korinar system. Twenty unknown flying objects were entering orbit around her boring homeworld. According to the display next to the map, their weapons were enabled.

"Get that child out of here," the stranger said without giving her a second glance. He was a tall man with broad shoulders, and looked as important as the men from the High Council did. His face was twisted with fury, gaze fixed on the monitors as if he didn't believe his eyes.

Bak ignored his rage. The great and honorable commander went to Lurnga, crouching next to her. "They will sing songs about us," he whispered in her ear, closing his arms around her and hugging her tightly. It sounded terribly sad. "Songs in all eternity."

The sirens wailed even louder. The displays on the monitors blinked in warning. The twenty objects had almost reached them.

Breathing in her father's scent, Lurnga closed her eyes, and finally understood what all the other inhabitants of Korinar had been talking about all this time.

13
NOVEMBER 22, 2385

First City, Qo'noS

"... *and thus, it is more important than ever not to act rashly. The mission is taking longer than we had hoped, but it's still very much a success. I understand that you want vengeance against those who wronged both our nations, but the important thing is to make sure that the vengeance is directed properly. It would be dishonorable to commit acts of violence against an entire people when it is only a subset that is responsible. I assure you, honorable councilors, that the* Bortas *and the* Prometheus *are closing in on the* Purifying Flame *as we speak. They are the ones who have committed these acts, and they are the ones against whom you must take your vengeance, not the entire Renao species. We need to have patience if we ...*"

Ambassador Alexander Rozhenko continued but the rest of his recorded speech was drowned out by the protests of the council members. The outrage of the assembled members echoed from the stone walls of the chamber. Grotek took his eyes off the holographic display of the Federation ambassador that hovered below the ceiling, and looked around. Wherever he looked, he noticed the same fire that burned within him. Every face was distorted with fury. Fists were clenched and shaken at the image of the ambassador. Korinar was engulfed in flames, but it was Qo'noS where the fire raged!

And so it should be, Grotek thought. The fury that surrounded him was like a river, and he enjoyed floating along in its waters. *Finally, they understand.*

There wasn't a single member of the High Council who was opposed to an immediate military strike. Grotek sensed it clearly. Earlier, word of Korinar's fate had arrived: yet another Klingon colony world had been attacked out of the blue, and there had been thousands of casualties. That had been the last straw.

Not just in the council, either. The streets of the First City—and indeed in *every* city and every village—were in turmoil. The fury severed the restraints that had been holding back the Klingon people. Grotek knew it ... sensed it in the current of the river he floated in. And he enjoyed it even more than he cared to admit.

"Enough!" The recording had barely finished when the old warrior stepped out of the crowd of council members. He raised his hands, seeking attention with moderate gestures. His low bass could be heard over the furious screams. "Enough, I said!"

One by one the dignitaries fell silent. They looked at Grotek, agitated.

"We have heard this foolishness before," Grotek said. He stood amidst the assembly. Slowly, he pivoted to make sure that there wasn't a man in the house whom he hadn't looked in the eye. "We also know what has happened yet *again*, this time on Korinar. We hear the anguished cries for vengeance from the dishonored dead, not just on Korinar, but from all the other places that the Renao have viciously attacked." Accusingly, he pointed at the hologram above his head. "And we've heard the reaction the Federation expects from us once again today. Rozhenko may look like a Klingon but he simply regurgitates what Earth is telling him."

Councilor Britok jeered. "Of course, he does. What else do you expect from the son of two Federation sympathizers? K'Ehleyr and Worf never managed to put the Empire above the Federation. Why should their degenerate offspring act any different?" His hand rested on the disruptor's grip on his hip, as if he intended to make the first officer of the *U.S.S. Enterprise*-E pay here and now for the lack of honor of his offspring, although he wasn't present.

Grotek nodded. Drawing closer to Britok, he rested his hand on his shoulder, but he addressed all those present when he continued. "That's right, and everyone who still refuses to see that will have Korinar's blood on their hands. Everyone who refuses to acknowledge that is spitting on the graves of Tika IV just like the Renao did, and they are depriving our honorable dead from entering *Sto-Vo-Kor*. Do we really want to stand idly by while these red-skinned murderers aim at the next Klingon target? And the next one after that? And yet another one? Or shall we finally rise up like true Klingons, and take action?"

"Act!" those around him shouted furiously, a choir of anger and thirst for revenge. "Act! Act!"

Grotek took a deep breath. Satisfied, he allowed the choir to sing, inspired by their inner fire. He finally faced the man to whom he had been truly talking most of all.

Chancellor Martok sat on his throne, several steps above everyone else. His wrinkled, scarred face was inscrutable. The cassock that other chancellors had worn before him seemed to weigh heavier than usual on his shoulders. And the only fire that Grotek believed he saw in Martok's remaining eye was the reflection of the braziers that stood alongside the council chamber walls.

The old warrior took a step toward the chancellor and stopped just before the bottom step. "What say you, Martok?" he asked challengingly, and he deliberately made it sound like a threat. He had to raise his voice because the choir behind his back was loud. But he knew that Martok heard him. "The people are stating their will loud and clear, as they have done for weeks. It hasn't changed. What about yours?"

Silence. Martok completely ignored him. The chancellor stared into the distance, stroking his gray beard with his calloused fingers. Not even the choir seemed to faze him.

Grotek was impressed. What was more, he was incensed.

"*Chancellor!*" the old council member shouted furiously. One word like the crack of a whip. Dignitaries everywhere winced, but Martok hardly moved.

Grotek was losing the last bit of respect for the office. Martok had never impressed him much as a politician, but now he was wondering if the notion of a chancellor was outdated. The constant, agitating shouts of "Act! Act!" from his supporters rang in his ears, so Grotek lifted his foot in order to climb the steps to Martok's throne.

He didn't even notice Martok unsheathe his *d'k tahg* until it was millimeters from his nose, the fires from the braziers reflected in the metal blades.

"Not one step further, son of Braktal," snarled the chancellor, "or this disgraceful day will see the blood of yet another Klingon!"

Now everyone present had fallen silent. Grotek didn't dare to turn around—or make any other movement for that matter—but he sensed that the council stood behind him, gawking. It was far easier to demand action when there wasn't cold steel threatening you.

Martok rose to his feet; the blade remained where it was. "I can bear many things, Grotek. Protest, opposition, jealousy, stupidity … the head of the High Council encounters all these things every day that he reigns."

The silence was almost deafening. The entire council seemed to hold their breath as Martok descended the steps, his *d'k tahg* still in front of the motionless councilor.

"But remember that I *do* reign! Regardless of what you and the likes of you demand or at what volume you demand it. No matter what the people might supposedly want. Because the people want one thing first and foremost: that someone else does their thinking for them."

Grotek was aching to object, but not a whisper escaped his lips, as he was paralyzed with fear for his life. Worse, he was sweating and had difficulty swallowing, making his fear obvious to everyone present. But he couldn't keep it in check.

"I did not wish for my position, but someone must be chancellor, and fate has chosen me. As the father of the 'degenerate offspring' reminded me when he slew Gowron, supreme power is not something you seek, but something that is thrust upon you. It also requires strength and foresight—the very thing that Ambassador Rozhenko has just demanded from us."

"Chancellor Martok," Britok interjected in Grotek's stead. Grotek could hear him in the silence behind his back, and he saw the addressed man glowering menacingly at Britok.

"Be silent!" Martok screamed. "The House of Konjah would be well advised to accept that *I* rule the Empire! That will change only if you have the courage to change it. Do you, Britok? Do you, Grotek?"

Grotek stood still. No one spoke. No one drew a blade. Britok's disruptor remained holstered. Martok nodded. "But although I appreciate the son of Worf's words, they are no longer ones we can hear. Our efforts have only resulted in further deaths at the hands of this Purifying Flame. And that, we *cannot* accept! The Federation has had their chance to resolve the situation with their methods. They are our valued allies, and we would be well advised never to forget that—they were by our side after Praxis and against the Dominion. But they are not infallible, and in this case, their course is the wrong one."

"What are your intentions?" Grotek managed to ask weakly.

Martok grinned, but sadness stood in his eyes. He lowered the *d'k tahg*, holstering it. "A chancellor never has any *intentions*, son of Braktal, a chancellor takes action. As of now, we will triple our presence at the border to the Lembatta Cluster. Once our battleships have reached the border, we still strike! For the protection of our Empire, to honor our dead, and to warn everyone who thinks they can follow in the footsteps of those murderers!"

14
NOVEMBER 22, 2385

I.K.S. Bortas

The day had been long and unyielding, but to Captain Kromm's surprise, the evening promised glory, honor, and revenge. He knew that entire careers could be decided on evenings like this. That certainty left him almost drunk with excitement.

The eyes-only message from Qo'noS had arrived approximately twenty minutes ago. Kromm had taken the message in his cabin, and he was now playing the recording for the third time, because he was so pleased with its contents. This wasn't a message of greeting from home, nor was it Federation babble in disguise.

It was the answer to all his prayers—it was nothing less than a call to arms. Oh, not in so many words—Martok didn't specify that he should aim disruptors at Xhehenem in order to pulverize Custodian ak Samooh and his clumsy farmers as such. But Kromm was skilled at reading between the lines, and he knew the order *behind* the order, as it were.

"Kromm to Commander L'emka," the captain said into his comm device when the recording finished for the third time. An inner fire burned within Kromm, and he enjoyed its warmth with all his might.

"L'emka."

"Commander, do you happen to be on the bridge?"

As usual, L'emka couldn't resist the opportunity for a snide remark. *"No, sir, I don't happen to be here, I'm deliberately here."*

Kromm did not begrudge her this little joke. Why should L'emka's whims still bother him? "Await my arrival, and summon Rooth to the bridge as well."

"May I ask why, sir?" She sounded skeptical.

"Of course, you may ask, Commander," Kromm answered, grinning triumphantly … and closed the connection.

A few minutes later he arrived on the bridge. The heart of the *I.K.S. Bortas* was still busy, despite the late hour. Officers stood at their respective consoles. As far as Kromm was concerned, communications and ops didn't have enough to do since Captain Adams had given in to the planetary custodian, calling back the teams from the planet's surface.

Kromm was still annoyed when he recalled that decision. Though he commanded a warship, Adams was a pacifist fool. Martok had been wrong in agreeing to allow the man to command this mission. If the chancellor hadn't made this mistake, a lot would have been different throughout the past few weeks—more glorious and efficient.

It's the result that counts, Kromm thought, as he approached L'emka and Rooth. *Not how you get there.*

And he would play a deciding role in the result, just as he had always hoped he would.

"We are here," the second in command said without preamble. "Why?"

Kromm grinned. He savored the moment. This was the first of many triumphs to come. He was just about to answer, when Rooth beat him to it.

"Qo'noS has caved in," the old commander said calmly.

Rooth's gaze was fixed on the bridge's main screen just like it had been when Kromm had entered the bridge. It displayed the *U.S.S. Prometheus* in orbit of Xhehenem. "The opposition has finally won through in the High Council." Then Rooth turned to face his captain. "Isn't that right, sir?"

Kromm saw regret in the eyes of the seasoned security chief, and his tone of voice didn't express any joy or relief. Quite the contrary.

L'emka's eyes widened. "Are you saying we're going to attack?" She sounded incredulous and horrified in equal measures. "Us against … a world full of farmers?"

Kromm's smile vanished. The reaction of both his trusted officers was insulting. The Klingon Empire had been attacked! It had every right to defend itself, to avenge the dead, and to thwart a repeat of this attack. It was the Empire's duty to make an example of the dishonorable murderers so that their fate would serve as a cautionary tale. If there was collateral damage, so be it!

"The Renao are dishonorable animals," he growled. "They didn't feel sorry for the mine workers on Tika IV, nor for the settlers on Korinar Prime. I don't feel sorry for them."

L'emka put her hands on her hips. "This is not about pity, sir, this is about justice!"

"You're even more attractive when you're furious," he replied, unfazed. "Did you know that?"

"What did you just say?" The first officer narrowed her eyes to slits, and the muscles on her neck twitched rhythmically. Kromm knew that L'emka was proud of her career, which had led her from the agricultural fields of her homeworld to the bridge of the *Bortas*.

However, her fast track through the officer ranks did not give her leave to ignore the chain of command when it didn't reflect her own viewpoint, which Kromm was going to enjoy reminding her.

"I've paid attention to the complaints of others for far too long," Kromm said. "That ends now." The fire inside of him flared up again. Kromm felt its warmth and followed it.

"What are your orders, sir?" asked Rooth. The old warrior sounded strange, as if resignation was wrestling with the last of his courage behind his ridged forehead. Rooth had been an accomplished hero of the battlefield, but he had grown philosophical with age. Sadly, that reflected badly on his record of battle.

"My orders are Qo'noS's orders," the captain answered, and for the first time in years he felt as if he really deserved that rank. "We're going to attack. On this day, Xhehenem will finally feel the wrath of the Klingon Empire!" He looked at the screen, his gaze steady on the globe beneath them. This was his path to glory. "Commander, charge the disruptor banks and ready the torpedoes. Now!"

"But, sir, the *Prometheus*—"

Kromm raised his hand, silencing his subordinate. "Leave the *Prometheus* to me." He could already see the sculptors at work, carving his face into a stone statue that would be erected in the Hall of Warriors someday soon. That swept aside all remaining doubts.

U.S.S. Prometheus

Xhehenem wasn't a world capable of defending itself. There had never been the need to build armies or even battleships, because the solitary Renao didn't have enemies.

That, Captain Adams thought dolefully, *is something else that has changed drastically, thanks to the Purifying Flame, and not for the better.*

"You can't be serious," Roaas cried. The normally taciturn Caitian stood next to Adams on the bridge, and Adams couldn't blame him for shouting at the Klingon captain whose face took up the viewscreen. "The inhabitants of this world haven't done anything to you. The majority of the Renao have absolutely nothing to do with the Flame!"

We're going round in circles, Adams thought angrily. And he knew from many crises in the past that this usually signaled the end. Talking in circles meant nobody really had anything new to say. And if you didn't talk to one another, you made mistakes.

Kromm's face was twisted into an angry snarl. *"Commander Roaas, the species has wronged me and the Empire! When the Flame raised their hand against Qo'noS they brought our wrath over the entire Lembatta Cluster. And now they will feel it. Just like they should have felt it a long time ago."*

From the corner of his eye, Adams saw Lieutenant Jassat ak Namur at the conn looking horrified. Adams felt pretty horrified himself, but it was far worse for Jassat, whose people were the target of Kromm's wrath.

Paul Winter reported from behind Adams's back. "Captain, we're being hailed from the planet surface. Custodian ak Samooh requests to speak to you urgently. He sounds nervous, sir."

I can believe that. Adams clenched his teeth. *Xhehenem may not have sufficient defense mechanisms, but it realizes when someone is targeting it. Especially from its orbit.*

"Put him through, Ensign," he requested tersely. "Conference call."

The main screen separated into two halves. Kromm was

pushed to the right. He was shaking his head mockingly. On the left, the horrified face of the planetary custodian appeared.

"Captain Adams, I must protest strongly! Your escort ship has just pointed its weapons toward ..." ak Samooh fell silent, and his eyes widened even more. He seemed to have realized that he wasn't the only one speaking to Adams, and that the other person was the man pointing the weapons he had just mentioned. *"You! How dare you!? Haven't you insulted us enough? Do you need to threaten us as well now? We're not the aggressors here, Captain Kromm, you are!"*

The Klingon merely grinned, and his grin was as cold as space itself. *"You heard me, Adams."* He spoke to the human captain as if ak Samooh wasn't part of the conversation. *"I have fulfilled my duty as mission partner by informing you of our intentions. Bortas out ..."*

The turbolift door had hissed open during the custodian's diatribe against Kromm, and now Ambassador Spock walked across the bridge, standing near Winter at the communications console. The half-Vulcan diplomat seemed calm and collected as always, but Adams couldn't help but feel that his own grave concern was mirrored in Spock's dark eyes.

"One moment, if you please, Captain," Spock said. "I have just spoken to Ambassador Rozhenko, and he informed me that he has strongly advised the High Council *not* to resort to violence as a reaction to the attack on Korinar Prime."

The Klingon snorted. *"I can believe that. For someone whom the chancellor values so highly, the ambassador has precious few Klingon traits."*

Spock shook his head. "That is an incorrect assessment, Captain."

"Coming from a Vulcan, Ambassador, your opinion means nothing to me."

"It is coming from a Vulcan, as you say, who has faced the *Dahar* Masters Kor, Kang, and Koloth in battle. It is coming from a Vulcan who was present at Chancellor Gorkon's death and Chancellor Azetbur's inauguration. It is coming from a Vulcan who has travelled your empire extensively and whose dealings with Klingons date back to a century before you were born. On the basis of all of that, I believe I am qualified to say that you are wrong."

The words had hit home, Adams noticed immediately. Kromm's face showed shock mixed with admiration and the number of heroes of the Empire that Spock had crossed paths—and swords—with. Would mentioning them be enough to change the captain's mind?

Kromm leaned forward in his command chair. *"You may have met all these impressive personalities, Ambassador Spock. But you're not a Klingon. Still, don't let that fact trouble you. Once today has become history, and songs are being sung about this great day, you can tell people that you knew Kor and Kang and Koloth and Gorkon—and also Kromm."* He glanced sideways, nodding at someone who wasn't visible on screen.

It's happening, Adams realized, and a cold fist seemed to clutch his stomach. He had been dreading this moment since the beginning of the mission, and now it seemed to have arrived. *It's really happening.*

"I demand to speak to Ambassador Rozhenko," Spock said with a firm voice.

Kromm didn't even flinch. *"You can speak with whomever you want. Kromm out."*

The connection was closed. The monitor display changed again, and now only a very frantic Custodian ak Samooh was visible.

"Captain Adams!" The Renao spoke with horror and outrage. Adams recognized the custodian's office in the background, and he noticed a panorama window with a view to the mountains of the northern continent that hadn't been visible in the smaller split-screen. *"I demand that you cease all hostile actions against us. Furthermore, I feel impelled to report this incident to Onferin. I'm convinced that your permission to stay will be revoked instantly. You're no longer tolerated here; do you hear me? Leave this sector at once!"*

"The *Bortas* has readied all weapons, sir," Sarita Carson reported from ops.

"Confirmed," Lenissa zh'Thiin said from the back of the bridge. The Andorian woman who had taken over at tactical from Roaas sounded on edge. "Disruptor cannons and torpedoes are aiming at Xhehenem's larger settlements: Kharanto, Bunhao, Sebelleb …"

Suddenly, the image on the monitor became distorted by static interference before the transmission ended abruptly. The custodian's office was replaced by the *Bortas* in orbit above Xhehenem again.

"The Klingons are disrupting all Renao communications," Ensign Winter said.

Frustrated, Adams clenched a fist. *Kromm did say that he had heard enough.*

"These wretched …" The words had slipped out of Lieutenant ak Namur's mouth, before he pulled himself together again.

"Sir." Roaas turned around to face Adams. His face expressed both tension and fury. "The mission is clearly defined. Kromm and Qo'noS have just violated everything we are here for."

"Without a doubt, Commander," Adams said quietly. He

stood next to Carson, staring glumly at her displays. His mind was racing.

Akaar and zh'Tarash would strongly condemn Kromm's actions. The Federation Council would rebuke Qo'noS sternly, for sure. But the president, the admiral and all the other top brass weren't here. What's more, they were out of reach. They were too far away from Earth for subspace contact in real time, even without the interference from the nebulae in the cluster. Adams didn't have time to wait for an answer from Starfleet Command or the Palais de la Concorde. He had to act now. Kromm had forced his hand. If Adams didn't do anything, the fate of thousands of innocent Renao would be sealed.

Spock drew close to Adams. "You know what to do."

The captain of the *Prometheus* nodded, before looking up to the screen. "Red alert! Commander zh'Thiin, charge the phaser banks and raise the shields. Mr. ak Namur, position us between the *Bortas* and Xhehenem. Mr. Winter, get Kromm back."

Adams had to hand it to his bridge crew—they acted instantly and flawlessly. All the 'Aye, sirs' hadn't even faded yet when Jassat maneuvered the ship into its new position, and one view on Carson's console showed that the phasers had been charged immediately.

"Shields are up, sir," zh'Thiin said, while the red-alert siren echoed through the bridge and the rest of the ship.

"I've got Kromm for you, Captain."

"Very well, Ensign. On screen."

The Klingon commander once again appeared on the main screen but this time, his smug demeanor had given way to incredulous amazement. "*Adams, what are you doing?*"

"Whatever is necessary, Captain. This is Starfleet's

strongest battleship. Our armament dwarfs even that of the *Enterprise*. If necessary, I can separate us into three smaller segments, and—"

Kromm raised one hand irritably. *"I know your equipment. Why are you telling me all this?"*

Richard Adams straightened his shoulders. "So you know who you are dealing with, Kromm. If you want to attack Xhehenem, you have to go through me first!"

15
NOVEMBER 22, 2385

Paris, Earth

The Place de la Concorde was situated in the eighth arrondissement north of the Seine, and it was lined with many impressive buildings. None of them could compete with the fifteen-story-tall Palais, though, where the new Federation President had taken office just like her many predecessors. This wasn't Lwaxana Troi's first visit to these venerable premises, but she also knew from those many previous occasions that every visit was different from all the others.

Emmeline Mokhtari knew the Palais de la Concorde like the back of her hand. Without hesitation she led Troi, her valet Ru, and Fleet Admiral Akaar—the man to whom Troi owed this spontaneous audience—to one of the conference rooms on the top floor. "Right here, Madame Ambassador, Admiral. The President suggested the Wescott Room for your meeting. I hope that suits you as well."

Troi shrugged. One room was as good as any other, whether it carried the name of a presidential predecessor of zh'Tarash or not.

"It does," Akaar said. "Thank you."

They arrived at a wide door made of dark fine wood. To the right and left of it stood heavy pots with exotic plants. Troi was no botanist, but she recognized Cardassian *perek* blossoms and Ferengi *Zan Periculi*. Much to her surprise, the scents of these two disparate flowers matched perfectly.

Akaar knocked on the door. Mokhtari grabbed Ru's arm, withdrawing with him discreetly.

As Akaar opened the door, Troi saw the oblong, slightly curved conference table that dominated the Wescott Room. It was made of dark wood, white glass, and intricate ornaments. There was room for almost twenty people to sit around it, and every chair featured a small control panel for the technological devices in the room, such as the holoemitters in the center of the ceiling, the lighting, the in-house communications, and the computer system.

Beyond the table was a broad window with a breathtaking view out onto the lights and roofs of the metropolis. The view of Paris conveyed peace, life, and romance, a city that had not only shaken off the hardships of the past, but had found a peaceful present. It was often symbolic of the entire Federation, though it felt much less so lately.

Opposite the window was a white wall with an oil portrait of Kenneth Wescott. At his inauguration in the twenty-third century, he had been the youngest Federation president in office. Another painting showed Captain Jonathan Archer from the famous NX-01 *Enterprise* and one of the founders of the United Federation of Planets. In front of these two paintings stood Kellessar zh'Tarash. The Andorian *zhen* was tall and had dark blue skin. Her face expressed wisdom and an inner strength. Three undoubtedly stressful weeks in the highest political office of the Alpha Quadrant hadn't been able to alter that expression.

"Admiral," said the president, walking around the table towards her visitors. "Ms. Troi. I'm glad to see you both—especially you, Madame Ambassador. I'm sincerely sorry that it has taken so long, and I regret that it happens under these unfortunate circumstances."

The Betazoid woman nodded. "The regret is all mine, *Zha* President. Thank you for receiving us."

"How could I have not, after all what the admiral has reported to me?" zh'Tarash pointed invitingly at three chairs on her end of the table. "Shall we?"

"I thought there were to be four at this meeting." The admiral settled his considerable girth into a chair he barely fit in.

"I'm afraid Ambassador K'mtok will be a little late," zh'Tarash said, sitting down next to Akaar. She beckoned Troi to take the empty chair to her left.

"Typical Klingons," Troi muttered under her breath as she took her seat. "I really haven't met many representatives of their species who were able to think further than their *bat'leth* blade. And that explicitly includes the ominous Mr. Worf whom Jean-Luc sees fit to bestow my son-in-law's duties to. No really ... Klingons!"

"What about Klingons?" a raspy voice asked as the door to the room flew open to reveal a large Klingon. His hair flowed halfway down his back, and he wore a military uniform beneath his cassock. The ridges on his forehead looked like boulders on a moon landscape, and in his eyes burned the fire of unbridled self-confidence.

Mokhtari appeared behind the Klingon, looking pale and very flustered. "Ambassador K'mtok, you can't just burst into the room like that and ..."

"It's alright, Emmeline," said President zh'Tarash, waving her hand. "Thank you."

The dark-skinned French woman visibly struggled, coming to terms with K'mtok's uncouth behavior, but she did as the *zhen* told her to. Nodding quietly, she backed out of the room and closed the door behind her.

"Ambassador." Zh'Tarash rose from her chair and nodded respectfully. But her tone of voice had an unmistakable edge that even the universal translator couldn't conceal while translating her words in real time from Andorian. "How nice of you to join us."

Without invitation, K'mtok pulled up the chair to Akaar's right. "My time is limited. You know what's happening at the border of the Klingon Empire and the Lembatta Cluster."

"Which is exactly the reason why we are here," Troi spoke up. She had never met this K'mtok, and she wished she could have gone longer without having the dubious pleasure of doing so. "What's possessed Martok all of a sudden? Overnight he forgets everything that we have so meticulously built up during recent weeks? Just like that, he tears down the entire mission in Lembatta single-handedly?"

Akaar winced. She sensed a combination of outrage and admiration in his surface thoughts, and for a moment she was tempted to take a closer mental look. But that would have been rude.

"Don't worry, Admiral, I'll remain diplomatic." She sighed.

"That would be appreciated," the Capellan mumbled.

But K'mtok laughed, baring his filed teeth. "I like women who speak their mind. Especially in my bed."

"Ambassador!" zh'Tarash cried.

"And I like men with more brains than a tribble," Troi snapped. She hoped that her stern gaze spoke volumes. She would most certainly not be intimidated by such a brute. "The incident on Korinar is a disaster, Ambassador. Still, the High Council must be able to realize that simple retaliation will not accomplish anything but further disasters!"

K'mtok rested his hands on the table. The light of the small lamps that were embedded in the ceiling reflected from his high, ridged forehead. "You are wrong, Ambassador Troi. It will accomplish something else: avenging the dead and paving their way to an honorable afterlife in *Sto-Vo-Kor*."

Troi hit the table with the palm of her hand with such force that the small padd in front of her leaped. "By shedding innocent blood?"

Her counterpart straightened himself in his chair. "The Renao are *not* innocent! They attacked *us*, and now they will pay for it. Martok has waited long enough ... too long if you ask me."

"Those are honest words, Ambassador," zh'Tarash said quickly to prevent Troi from answering. "That is a rare commodity in our circles. I appreciate your honesty. But you know as well as I do that the High Council's reaction is intolerable. Unfortunately, our efforts to contact Chancellor Martok haven't been successful thus far, so we appeal to you to convey our displeasure to the High Council."

K'mtok merely laughed.

Akaar didn't seem to like what he was hearing. His gaze was reproachful, his demeanor expressing barely suppressed impatience.

Zh'Tarash went on, glowering at the Klingon. "The Federation Security Council will convene after this meeting for emergency talks, Ambassador. I would appreciate it—we all would—if you'd join us, and use your influence on Qo'noS, convincing them to be patient until our talks have finished."

"You can hold as many meetings as you like, it won't change anything," K'mtok said dismissively.

Once again Troi couldn't help but admire the Andorian woman's self-restraint. In the face of all the Klingon arrogance that had been on display all day, most other—

weaker—people would have exploded with frustration and anger by now … diplomacy or not.

But Troi knew just as well as zh'Tarash did what was at stake here. The well-being of an entire planet and its inhabitants was so much more important than a president's pride. Zh'Tarash fought for Xhehenem—and for the deceptive, idyllic scenery outside the Palais's windows.

She fought for peace.

"Speak to the Council," the president pleaded. "Do you really want to plunge us into another war? To shatter our alliance?"

"You're talking to the wrong man, *Zha* President," said K'mtok grimly. "Martok has made his decision, and just like the High Council and the majority of our people I stand by that decision. It was wrong to keep the *Bortas* on a leash. It was wrong not to send an entire fleet to Onferin. These red xenophobes are fanatical murderers, and they deserve all of the suffering that's coming to them now! We will begin with Xhehenem, but I can guarantee you that will just be the beginning of our revenge. There are seven inhabited systems in the Lembatta Cluster. Our safety will only be restored once we control each and every one of them."

That was the last straw. Rising abruptly, zh'Tarash rested her hands on the table and leaned toward K'mtok. Her self-restraint wasn't gone but it had made way for a very purposeful aggression and sharply formulated words, which surprised Troi.

"And you, Ambassador," the *zhen* said, "are first and foremost the representative of your people to the Federation! You are a diplomat. You would be well advised not to forget that. Do your work, K'mtok, or we will do it for you—and I can assure you … I can be very undiplomatic if I want to be."

The Klingon also got to his feet, menacingly raising his index finger. "You shouldn't threaten us, Madame President. We have been allies for years, but friendships are not indestructible."

Troi almost didn't believe her ears. She reached out with her mind to K'mtok in order to find out how serious he really was. Much to her dismay, she sensed his conviction that he was doing the right thing. K'mtok knew that he had the upper hand. Even if Martok's actions led to unpleasant diplomatic consequences, such as economic sanctions, military saber-rattling, or even an open fight that would abrogate the Khitomer Accords—in K'mtok's eyes the chancellor was acting well within his rights by not paying much attention to the Federation's priorities and wishes. Personally, K'mtok didn't have much to fear. Even if zh'Tarash banned him from Earth, he would be praised like a hero at home for being the man who had dared to stand up to the Andorian woman. And one way or another, the Renao would suffer. Troi sensed that this fact was all that mattered to the Klingon.

While her attention was focused on the ambassador's emotions, Akaar and zh'Tarash made another attempt to appeal to K'mtok. They argued, and threatened him more openly with consequences. The Klingon also raised his voice.

Finally, he threw his hands in the air. "I see no reason to listen to this any longer. I have more important things to do than hear political lectures from the pair of you. So, if you would excuse me." With these words, he left the conference room as abruptly as he had entered it twenty minutes earlier.

"That could have gone a lot worse." Akaar sighed, rubbing the bridge of his nose. He looked tired, the recent crises obviously preying hard on his mind, and here he was facing another one. And clearly, he could neither control nor influence it. Unlike all those who were discussing the matter here and on Qo'noS at that moment, Captain Kromm *was* at Xhehenem, and was ready to wreak destruction upon that world.

Troi hesitated. Kromm—there was something familiar about that name. Captain Kromm from the *I.K.S. Bortas*. The *Bortas*.

"Of course!" She hit the table again. This time, she was frustrated with her own forgetfulness. "The *Bortas* is the former flagship of the Imperial Fleet, isn't it?"

Akaar nodded. "That's right. Under Chancellor Gowron, Martok's predecessor. But since then, it has veered well off course in the fleet hierarchy, so to speak."

Troi glanced from him to the president and back. She had been looking for an outlet to put the energy within her to good use; and now, she hoped, she had finally found one. "*Zha* President, give me an hour, a communications terminal, and a private transporter, and then I can give you Qo'noS!"

La Barre was located in the northeast of France. The romantic sleepy village and its surrounding lands had survived on a combination of agriculture and tourism for centuries. Of all the things that grew in La Barre's soil, the most prominent were the grapes produced by the local vines.

Lwaxana Troi took a deep breath once the glittering transporter beam had subsided, and found herself on a vineyard. The fresh evening air filled her lungs, La Barre's tranquility proving a welcome change from the hustle and bustle of Paris. Her gaze fell on dark soil, wintry vine tendrils, and even on the moonlit Ognon River down in the valley.

Suddenly, she heard footsteps behind her. "It is quite beautiful, isn't it?"

That voice! A pleasant shiver ran down her spine, while a smile appeared on her lips. "Indeed." She sighed, contented. "I always knew how important this place was. But now, I think I finally understand it as well."

He didn't say anything for a moment, and this silence communicated more approval than words could ever have done. It told her that he understood why she had beamed here and not into his house.

"Welcome, Ambassador Troi," he finally said, "to Chateau Picard."

She turned around. Jean-Luc Picard, captain of the famous *U.S.S. Enterprise*-E, who would soon take off for yet another of his famous deep-space missions, didn't look a day older than he had done when they had last met … but considerably more relaxed. His almost completely bald head showed nothing but laughter lines, and his always thoroughly fit body was covered by civilian clothes that were more than suitable for this rural region. His shirt was tailored from coarse gray and white linen, he wore a dark, moist-looking apron to protect his chest and brown pants, and the boots on his feet were covered in soil and the juice of fresh grapes.

"I would like to shake your hand, Madame Ambassador, but I'm afraid my sister-in-law and I are in the middle of the production process." He held up his right hand. It was just as dirty and sticky as his boots and the apron were. But the smile that lit up his face was that of a dear, old friend. "Come."

Troi walked next to him across the vineyard. She knew that her grand dress wasn't in the least suitable for this environment, but time was of the essence, and so she had gone without getting changed. The Palais transporter station had beamed her directly to this location, and when her conversation here was over, she would return to Paris the same way. And then find somewhere to get the dress cleaned.

"You're fortunate to find me here," Picard said. "I'm only on Earth for a few more days before the *Enterprise* sets off again."

"I heard that Admiral Akaar had assigned an exploring mission to you," Troi said. "To the borders of the Federation and beyond. I hope you're not running away from me." She laughed.

Picard also smiled. "I assure you that is not the case, Madame Ambassador."

They drew closer to the small estate, which stood at the edge of the vineyard among several trees. One of the windows was lit, and the light shone warm and welcoming. Troi asked how Picard's wife, Dr. Beverly Crusher, and their son Rene were faring, and while Troi had a pang of jealousy for the doctor having with Picard what she had always wanted, she could not deny that the captain was actually happy, and his being so pleased her greatly.

"To what do I owe the pleasure of this visit?" Picard asked as they reached the house. "The communiqué from the president's office led me to believe that this is not a friendly visit."

Troi nodded. "Of course it's a friendly visit!" she said emphatically. "I have been dreaming for eternities about visiting the place where you grew up, Jean-Luc."

"And?"

"And … it's not a social visit." Sighing, she turned her attention back to reality and outlined recent events for him. She didn't have a lot to report that he didn't already know.

Picard might be officially on leave—his ship was undergoing a general overhaul in orbit because it hadn't escaped unscathed from the events leading up to the presidential elections—but he obviously stayed abreast of matters.

She finished with: "And now Martok has obviously lost his mind … or his last remaining supporters in the High Council. Or both."

Picard grimaced. The news weighed heavily on him, she could see it. Without a word he walked to the house, pointing at a small wooden bench beneath the illuminated window. It was the end of November but neither the daytime in Paris nor the evening here were cold. Troi sat down, and Picard settled down next to her. Both gazed at the vineyard, the valley and the silhouettes of the small village in the distance.

"Martok is no fool," Picard said finally.

"Be that as it may, but he's acting like one," Troi said. "Violence is not the answer, especially not to other violence, Jean-Luc. If Qo'noS avenges the atrocities of the Purifying Flame with death and destruction, they're not any better than those fanatics!"

"Who seem to be under the control of someone else. I heard that Captain Adams and Ambassadors Spock and Rozhenko support the notion that the Renao themselves are victims and no longer masters of their own fate."

She nodded again. "I hope they're right."

"I have every confidence that they are," Picard said with conviction. "I know Spock very well, and I can say with certainty that he is rarely wrong."

That was enough for Troi. "Your word is the only proof I need," she said, gratefully. For a brief, glorious moment her old infatuation with him returned, and she basked in it. Once again, she pondered all the times she had met the great

Jean-Luc Picard in the past. She recalled the family bonds they had tied when her daughter Deanna and his former right hand, the recently promoted Admiral William T. Riker, had gotten married. It was evenings like this one, and sitting side by side with Picard in La Barre's romantic idyll, when she was more or less convinced that all these events had to have been orchestrated by fate.

Contentedly she thought that maybe, there was a man in her life who was the right man, after all. Maybe, true love—*her* true love—was something that could only be defined individually, and on a case-by-case basis.

"Jean-Luc?"

"Mhm?"

"Say something in French."

"Merde!"

The quiet curse dragged her back from the moment into reality. Surprised, she looked at Picard. His right thumb was bleeding. With his left hand, he pulled a small knife from a pocket in his apron.

"What happened?"

Frustrated, he sighed. "I was looking for my handkerchief. And I had completely forgotten what I had just pocketed."

"You cut yourself. With that … thing."

He showed her the sickle-shaped knife. "A pruning knife, for use on the vines. The tool goes back to the Middle Ages, and my father and brother both preferred to utilize modern technology as little as possible. I used to find that attitude tiresome, but lately I've come to appreciate the value in getting your hands dirty."

"And I appreciate the value of getting them clean." From one of the many pleats of her dress she produced a small dermal regenerator that she always carried with her. Someone who traveled as much as she did liked to be prepared. "Let me have a look." Slowly, she moved the medical device across his wound, which closed immediately.

"As good as new," Picard decided, wiggling his thumb. "Thank you very much, Madame Ambassador."

"Don't mention it," she said, waving her hand dismissively. "How many times do I have to tell you, Jean-Luc? Call me Lwaxana."

Picard smiled wryly. "I'm afraid protocol demands a more formal tone. Madame Ambassador," he replied, and she thought she could sense a bit of embarrassment. "There's one thing I don't understand about this whole matter," he said, pocketing his knife again. "How can *I* be of assistance? I don't know Martok very well, and he will not even speak to anyone from Ambassador Rozhenko's staff. I doubt that I would be able to get through to him."

Troi shook her head. "Not you, Jean-Luc," she said, resting her hand on his. "Your new first officer. Doesn't Mr. Worf come from the House of Martok?"

Picard's face brightened. "Of course. Worf and the current chancellor have known each other since the days of the Dominion War. They fought side by side on Deep Space 9. Martok owes Worf a great deal. As I recall, Worf was instrumental in liberating Martok from a Dominion prison camp."

"And he should listen to him, shouldn't he? Even at short notice?"

"Perhaps," he said. "It's certainly worth the attempt. Worf is on board the *Enterprise*, overseeing repairs." Picard offered Troi his arm. "Would you accompany me into the house of my ancestors, Madame Ambassador?"

Troi smiled, and not just out of gratitude. "I thought you'd never ask," she said, rising to her feet and taking the arm.

16
NOVEMBER 22, 2385

I.K.S. Bortas

This was to be Kromm's moment of triumph. Nothing would spoil it, he was going to make certain of that.

The captain stood in the center of the bridge, staring at the main screen. Minutes ago, he had been content. His crew executed his orders efficiently, and the *Bortas* was ready to fulfill its duty and serve as the Klingon Empire's weapon to be wielded against its enemies.

Now, though, something stood between him and his glorious task: the *Prometheus*. On the bridge's main screen, he saw Captain Adams's ship hovering in space like a silent promise, bristling with weapons. He couldn't help but think about the Mark-XII phaser arrays, the quantum torpedo launchers, the ablative plating, and the ship's multi-vector assault mode.

"A confrontation with Adams would be suicide," Commander L'emka whispered into his ear. The first officer stood by Kromm's side, her face expressing unconcealed criticism, if not contempt. "The *Prometheus* is far superior to us. A true captain would know that … sir."

"And a true first officer would know how to create the deciding tactical advantage, instead of whining like a coward," he said. "And I will *not* retreat from Adams, Commander! Never again! Our orders are clear!"

"That's madness, Captain," L'emka said. "The *Prometheus*

stands between us and Xhehenem. We wouldn't be able to get past her, even if our attack on a world full of farmers *was* an appropriate reaction to Korinar!"

Kromm whirled around to face her. He had been tolerating L'emka's behavior for far too long, and that was going to change once he led the *Bortas* to new heights. "If *Prometheus* stands between us, then we will go around it."

"You really believe that Adams will let us pass?"

"Which choice does he have?"

The first officer jutted her chin forward. "Sir, that ship can split into three segments. Even if we managed to evade one of their sections, there would still remain two to open fire on us. Where should we escape to?"

He snorted. "And I thought you were a Klingon warrior. We have no need to 'escape.' Are you afraid of the phaser arrays of a Starfleet ship?"

"The only thing I fear, Captain, is the dangerous foolishness of my commanding officer!"

That was the final straw. Kromm's eyes widened incredulously and he clenched his fists. "How dare you! Commander, I have tolerated your misconduct as my right hand in the past, but rest assured that I will not repeat that mistake. If you stand in my way I will sweep you aside."

"You are welcome to try, sir," she said defiantly, her hand moving to her *d'k tahg*, her eyes blazing with righteous fury. "It wouldn't be the last mistake you'd want to commit today. But at least it would only cost your own life, and not that of the entire crew. I'm ready to let you make that mistake. Are you?"

That was it. The challenge.

Tense silence ensued on the bridge, the only sounds coming from the automated functions of the consoles. Everyone seemed to hold their breath, waiting for the result of this confrontation between captain and first officer.

Kromm thought of all the times he had been furious at L'emka. All those objections, all the criticism. She had never been on his side. Why should she be there today of all days? It wouldn't be her fault if she died now, it would be his, because he should have killed her for her insolence a long time ago.

"I've been ready for a very, very long time." He unsheathed his *d'k tahg*. The blade shimmered blood-red in the light of the bridge's illumination.

"Sir!" Lieutenant Klarn's voice cut through the silence like a blade through the flesh of an opponent. "A message for you is incoming. Priority level one."

Kromm did not take his eyes off of L'emka, who had also drawn her blade. He was dying to put her down, once and for all. "That can wait. There's something I have to finish here."

"Sir, the message is from Chancellor Martok."

L'emka and Kromm stared at each other ferociously. The captain raised his blade, pointing at her. "This isn't over yet."

"No, Captain," she said, unfazed, "it is not."

Both of them sheathed their weapons. "Put Martok through to my quarters, Lieutenant," Kromm ordered Klarn. "I wouldn't want to watch this message in the wrong company."

"Understood, Captain."

Silent, and without looking at L'emka again, Kromm left the bridge. It wasn't far to his quarters, and as soon as he had entered, he activated his comm console. But it wasn't the chancellor's face that looked at him. It was someone whom Kromm would never have expected to call.

"*Captain Kromm,*" the Klingon wearing Starfleet uniform said, "*my name is Worf, son of Mogh, of the House of Martok. The chancellor tasked me with speaking with you. I have news for you, Captain …*"

17
NOVEMBER 22, 2385

U.S.S. Prometheus

Captain Richard Adams knew from painful first-hand experience that violence didn't so much solve problems as create new ones. He stood to Roaas's right, staring at the tactical console alongside his Caitian first officer. The displays told him the current armament status of both his ship and the Klingon ship on the main screen.

Two hours had passed since their memorable conference call. Both ships had spent these hours in an awkward state of uncertainty. Adams had no doubt that he would emerge victorious if he had to fight Kromm's *Bortas*. The *Prometheus*'s weapon systems were second to none, and the Klingon commander could only dream of such weaponry. Many ships had surrendered when Adams attacked from three different directions, though he had his doubts that the stubborn Klingon captain would ever surrender.

However, even if the *Prometheus* won a conflict against the *Bortas*—and the odds were very much in their favor— just the act of getting into a fight would mean that Adams had lost. Because the fragile peace between the Federation and the Klingon Empire would be shattered.

"No change so far," Sarita Carson said from the ops console. Since the beginning of this awkward stalemate in Xhehenem's orbit, she had been reporting at regular intervals, regardless of whether anything had changed. Adams was grateful for that.

Sometimes, no news is good news. So far, Kromm hadn't married violent action to his provocative words. So far.

"Thank you, Commander. Keep me posted."

"No changes on the planet's surface, either," Ensign Paul Winter replied to Adams's quizzical glance. "Ambassador Spock is still in direct contact with Custodian ak Samooh and Ambassador Rozhenko."

Adams nodded, relieved. That was at least something. Spock had secluded himself in the observation lounge in order to speak to all parties involved without interruption. Winter had once again proven his mettle by finding a way to circumvent the jamming devices that Kromm had employed. Now they were at least able to reach the planetary administration.

Which was good, as the people on Xhehenem were in a full-blown panic in the face of the Klingon threat. Custodian ak Samooh had already informed Onferin and taken measures to evacuate the largest settlements on Xhehenem. But those efforts were for the most part in vain, as the Renao were philosophically opposed to the notion of abandoning their home spheres.

There would be casualties. Adams could sense it with every fiber of his being.

"Mr. Winter, try reaching the *Bortas* again. Get me Kromm."

"Aye, Captain." The young ensign's tone of voice betrayed his lack of confidence in being able to raise Kromm—considering the previous four attempts had failed.

We have no other choice, Adams thought grimly. *So far, nothing has happened except for saber-rattling. We might be able to avoid disaster—maybe. I need to try.*

Winter stared at his console, grimacing. "No answer, sir. The *Bortas* doesn't respond to our …" He hesitated.

"Ensign?" Adams made two steps towards Winter's station. An awkward chill went through him. "Talk to me."

"Sir, I … don't ask me why or how, but you're being hailed by the *Bortas*."

"On screen, Ensign," Adams said tersely, walking to the center of the bridge. Commander Roaas joined him.

The *Bortas* vanished and was replaced by Captain Kromm's face. Kromm appeared to have moved from the bridge to his quarters. Adams saw bare blades mounted on the walls and light shining through grids.

"Are you pleased, Adams?" the Klingon snapped at him. *"Have you gotten your will once again?"*

Adams glanced at Roaas quickly and quizzically, but the Caitian shook his head barely noticeably.

"I'm afraid I don't understand, Captain," Adams said. "What are you talking about?"

Kromm snorted. *"So like a human not to gloat when given the opportunity! You should bask in your triumph."* He leaned forward, and his face came so close that it almost filled the entire screen. *"Have you ever noticed how theoretical democracy is within your oh-so-very freedom-loving Federation? In theory, everyone gets their say. Everyone will get a seat at your table. But in the end, it's always Earth's bidding that's done."*

"With all due respect to your philosophical deliberations," said Adams, "I'm afraid that I have no idea what you're talking about, Kromm."

"I promise you, Adams, this is not *over. You and I will meet again on the battlefield. Maybe not today, but soon enough. Don't forget that, Captain."*

The cryptic transmission ended, Kromm's image

replaced with that of the *Bortas*.

Carson said, "Sir, the Klingons are standing down. Weapons are no longer armed, shields are lowering."

"Communications are no longer being jammed," Winter added. Adams looked at him, and saw that the ensign raised his eyebrows in confusion. "And there's another recorded message incoming for you, sir. From Admiral Akaar at Starfleet Command."

"On screen, Ensign," said Adams. "Let's shed some light on this. And stand down from red alert."

"About time, too," mumbled Roaas.

Once more, the *Bortas* disappeared from the screen, this time replaced by the face of Starfleet's commander-in-chief. Leonard James Akaar sat in an office that Adams didn't recognize, so it couldn't be his own. The admiral's face was serious.

"Greetings, Captain. I bear good news for a change—Qo'noS has reversed their position, at least temporarily. Captain Kromm is under strict orders not to open fire on innocent Renao."

Adams noticed that Lieutenant ak Namur at conn breathed a huge sigh of relief.

"But, as I said, this development is temporary. We were only able to partially dissuade Martok from his decision to avenge Korinar immediately."

"I really don't like the sound of that," zh'Thiin muttered under her breath.

"Prometheus, you have exactly one hundred standard hours from now to hunt down the Purifying Flame and to stop them. The High Council has given us an ultimatum. If you and the Bortas *are unable to detain the guilty parties in that time, Kromm has orders to initiate the attack on* all *cluster worlds. And there's a fleet of Klingon warships just over the border, the size of which is increasing*

daily, waiting to support him." Akaar hesitated, and then his tone softened. *"I'm sorry that I can't do any more for you, Dick. This is a respite, not a solution, but our hands are tied. Qo'noS is not open to discussion on this matter; it's nothing short of a miracle that we were able to get these one hundred hours as a compromise."*

"I can believe that," Adams said quietly. He felt for Akaar, and although the news that the admiral had sent them was bittersweet, Adams was grateful for it. Even temporary peace was peace, and every new moment opened new opportunities.

"Look after yourselves, Prometheus," the Capellan said. *"Akaar out."*

The message ended. Adams looked at his first officer. "Let's make the best of this." He needed to make good use of this valuable time that Akaar had granted them.

Nodding, the Caitian moved to his station. "Your orders, sir?"

"Inform ak Samooh and the authorities on Onferin that Kromm no longer poses a danger to them. Afterward, speak to Ambassador Rozhenko, and ask him for his opinion about Kromm and the situation on his homeworld. And ask Ambassador Spock to join me in my ready room."

"Aye, sir." Roaas turned around and began his work.

Adams glanced around the bridge one more time. They had forestalled the violence for a hundred hours, but only for that long.

It's down to us, he thought. *Let's do this.*

Spock leaned back in the visitor's chair, steepling his fingers in front of his face. The cup of tea that Adams had replicated for him sat on the desk in front of him, steaming hot and untouched.

"The *Bortas* will not simply return to business as usual," he said. "Kromm's pride has been hurt … what's more, his ambition has been roused. In his mind this mission is an opportunity to increase his standing within the Empire. He has no intention of wasting that opportunity, regardless of what orders he has received."

Adams sighed. The captain sat behind his desk, elbows resting on the table surface. He massaged his forehead with his right hand. "I know. Kromm may do as he's told for now, but he's just waiting to pounce. In fact, he said as much."

"Diplomacy has never been a strong suit of our Klingon companion," Spock said gently. "Neither has patience."

Adams buried his face in his hands and nodded, before sitting up, straightening his shoulders and facing Spock. "The clock is ticking, Ambassador. Martok's forces are marshalling at the gate, so to speak, and we can see them from our fortified walls."

Spock thought about Xhehenem. The agricultural world was merely the latest stop on their journey in search of a solution. They had neither found the instigators of the Purifying Flame, nor gained any more intelligence regarding their next targets. All they had to work with were Lieutenant ak Namur's information about fanatical preachers and a people who had become ever more aggressive, as well as the data that Kirk and Rooth had discovered in the farmhouse cellar, which the chief engineer was still attempting to access.

Sighing, Adams continued. "I'm open to any suggestions you might have."

Spock lowered his hands, raising an eyebrow. "It is my considered opinion that only one option is viable. We must proceed to Bharatrum." Spock recalled the Son of the Ancient Reds, and thought about the assumed drydock full of recreated *Scorpion* attack fighters.

Leaning forward, Adams regarded the ambassador. "That's a thin thread. All we've got are a few damaged rods found in a cellar, the words of a farmer, and the delirium of some agitated Renao."

"I understand your reservations, Captain. However, our time is limited, and we must make do with what few facts we have available to us. The evidence we have, such as it is, points us toward Bharatrum. And my instincts also tell me that it is the next logical stop on our journey."

"Instincts?" The captain of the *Prometheus* got up and wandered over to the window where he could look down at Xhehenem. "You of all people are giving me the advice to make decisions based on instinct, Spock? Where's the logic in that?"

The faintest hint of a smile played in the corners of Spock's mouth when friends from days long gone appeared before his inner eye. The memory warmed him. "Over my decades of life, Captain, I have learned that even logic might be subject to certain limitations and that instincts should sometimes be followed. I had the benefit of a particularly fine teacher."

Turning around, Adams smiled. "So Kirk would fly to Bharatrum, would he?"

"No, Captain Adams," Spock replied wryly. "James T. Kirk would already be there."

18
NOVEMBER 23, 2385

Paris, Earth

A new day was dawning over Paris but no one in the oblong, windowless chamber of the Federation Council noticed it. One hundred and fifty representatives of various Federation worlds had gathered in the early hours of the morning within the second-floor chamber of the Palais de la Concorde in order to talk about the galaxy's various hot spots in general and the situation in the Lembatta Cluster in particular. At the front of the room was a dais surrounded by marble columns. On the dais stood a lectern and three white shell-type seats in front of the Great Seal of the Federation, which was mounted on the wall. A holoscreen showed images of the death and destruction on Korinar. Klingon Defense Force warriors searched the ruins of shattered buildings for bodies and for evidence of the perpetrators. It was tragically obvious that they wouldn't find any survivors in this utter destruction.

President zh'Tarash and Admiral Markus Rohde from Starfleet Intelligence occupied two of the three seats. They listened to the man who had vacated the third seat in order to stand at the lectern and talk about the horrifying images everyone was watching.

Admiral Akaar didn't even look at his notes during his speech. His gaze wandered across the rows of his audience, to the dignitaries from Andor, Tellar, Vulcan, and the other members of the Federation. He looked at his fellow admirals and esteemed colleagues who had also gathered to listen to his words. And to Lwaxana Troi, sitting in one of the back rows and listening intently like everyone else.

The night had been short and full of concern. Once the imminent disaster in orbit around Xhehenem had been successfully delayed, Troi had withdrawn to her suite in the Parisian hotel that the president's office had booked for her and Ru. Unfortunately, sleep had been out of the question. All the concerns and apprehension of Federation and Fleet Command had weighed down on the Betazoid woman.

Over the course of a life of sufficient vintage that Troi avoided thinking about the exact duration, she had witnessed enough interstellar crises to know that it didn't take much for them to escalate. Cold shivers ran down her spine as she remembered the day when she had learned that her beloved Ian had died on a mission to Raknal V while serving on the *U.S.S. Carthage*. Burning fury added to that when she remembered the Jem'Hadar soldiers who had overrun Betazed several years ago in order to enslave it. Wars were terrible constants; if people weren't careful, they would rekindle time and again.

"And therefore," the tall Capellan reached the end of his short speech, "the *Prometheus* and the *Bortas* are making their way to Bharatrum, the centermost world of the Lembatta Cluster."

A map of the region appeared on the holoscreen. Troi saw the cluster's seven inhabited worlds, of which Onferin—the main world—was closest to the Federation. Xhehenem was two light years further inward, and Bharatrum even further. According to the legend next to the image, it was just under three light years.

She found herself recalling the files about the cluster that she had studied during the previous night, including details of an unusual number of red giants. Their radiation and matter emissions made navigating through the cluster and contacting it all the more difficult. "Demon Cloud" was the name that the Klingons had given to this region because of its dangerous, eerie nature. Troi wasn't inclined toward superstition, but after everything she had learned during the past twenty-four hours about the home of the Renao, she was almost tempted to agree with that description.

Akaar continued: "Unfortunately, our attempts to prepare Bharatrum for the arrival of the two ships have failed so far. The radiation and emissions in the cluster are part of what is making it very difficult to contact the planetary administration."

"Part of?" a man two rows in front of Troi asked loudly. He was the Tellarite representative, Kyll. "What does that mean, Admiral?"

Kyll's tone of voice might have been unduly belligerent—on the other hand that was to be expected from a Tellarite. Aside from that, many other dignitaries seemed to be tired of talking as well. Troi heard approving murmurs from the assembled crowd. The council wanted actions; they even demanded them.

"There have been initial talks with Bharatrum's administration," Akaar answered patiently. "But, Councilor Kyll, these have proven to be somewhat slow and unsuccessful. Just as with Onferin and Xhehenem, we're trying to prepare the officials on the planet cautiously for the visit of our ships. Please remember that contact with strangers is something that the Renao are not accustomed to. It is not only unusual but unwanted. We therefore consider it to be prudent and appropriate to announce our visit well in advance."

"Why is that?" Kyll replied indignantly. "Onferin has given both ships permission to travel unrestrictedly throughout the entire cluster."

"That's correct," the admiral said, "but the Federation is striving to be a partner to the Renao, not their oppressor. It would be wrong for us to force ourselves upon them."

"Wrong? Don't make me laugh!" The woman to the left of Troi snorted derisively. She was human, but her wonderfully exotic garments indicated that she came from Aldebaran III. Her almond-shaped eyes suggested Asian ancestry. "Do we have permission, or don't we? With all due respect, Admiral, you're sounding alarmingly indecisive."

Respectfully, Akaar tilted his head. "The situation is indecisive, Councilor Park. The deeper we advance into the cluster, the more resistance and reluctance we encounter."

"But Onferin is the homeworld," Kyll said uncomprehending. "Onferin has the final say, yes?"

"That is correct," Akaar said. "But Onferin is considerably closer to the border than all other Renao settlements. Compared to the planetary administration of Bharatrum, Custodian ak Mousal and his staff on Onferin come across as very cooperative. And that—you will have to agree with me if you have read Captain Adams's report about his stay in the local arcologies there—says a great deal." He sighed. "Contact with the Renao is much more difficult and cumbersome than you or I wish for, Councilor. But we must deal with that as best we can. Anything else is not acceptable."

"There are lives at stake!" a Deltan shouted, agitated. He rose to his feet. The light of the lamps embedded in the ceiling reflected on his hairless skull, and his silver robe with colorful lapels wasn't able to conceal his bony shoulders and lanky build.

"And are we to react to a threat by becoming a threat ourselves?" Akaar replied instantly, and with a certain edge in his voice. "The Renao are not our enemy, Councilor Zoona. They deserve our respect, just like any other interstellar neighbor. And as long as we are guests in their territory, they deserve for us to adapt to them. We mustn't expect anything else, let alone force it upon them. Yes, the contact to the deciding powers on Bharatrum is difficult. Yes, Bharatrum seeks to block our attempts to negotiate with them, rather than welcome them. But as much as it pains me to say this, they are well within their rights. And it is my duty to continue to seek talks with them, in order to prepare a path for the *Prometheus* and the *Bortas* that they so urgently need."

There was a moment of silence in the room. Troi leaned back in her chair, observing the councilors, politicians, and diplomats. Akaar's speech had been well presented, and he had found true and important words to dissipate the delegates' doubts ... or at least to counter them with valid points. Surely, most of those present shared his point of view. But there were still council members demanding a more hard-line approach. Democracy couldn't exist without difference of opinion. The art was to stand together, come what may; and the Federation was nothing if not the paradigm of this very special—and extremely important—art form.

"Still, I think we should be cruel to be kind where Bharatrum is concerned," the Deltan said, slightly offended, sitting down again. "It's in the Renao's best interest if we stop the Flame. We're doing what they are not capable of doing."

Akaar was just about to reply, when President zh'Tarash

spoke up. The Andorian woman didn't need an amplifier as her voice carried through the entire chamber effortlessly. "The sovereignty of foreign worlds is sacrosanct," she said, friendly, but stern. "The right of self-determination and individual freedom is the keystone to any coexistence. Whoever denies anyone else these rights, even with good intentions, commits a sin against life itself ... just like the terrorists of the Purifying Flame. The United Federation of Planets will adhere to its principles, if need be until its collapse. If it didn't, it would no longer be the organization that I vowed to uphold and lead. The end, Councilor Zoona, doesn't always justify the means—regrettable as that might be for us sometimes."

That hit home. Troi felt a lump in her throat when she recalled the past that zh'Tarash had just hinted at, subtle but nonetheless unmistakable. The Dominion War, the Borg, the Typhon Pact and the chaotic weeks in the wake of the murder of zh'Tarash's predecessor Nan Bacco—all these events had happened in quick succession, and they had pushed the Federation to its limits and sometimes beyond. Zh'Tarash's admonishing words had hit home because the Federation *had* recently forgotten what it was all about.

Everyone present had witnessed first-hand what became of the league of worlds when it abandoned its principles. The latest, horrifying example lay only a few weeks in the past.

And everyone in the council chamber knew that something like that must never happen again. *That* was the unity in this hour of need. That was the great art.

"We are an ideal," Akaar said, expressing what Troi was thinking. The Capellan spoke quietly, with a gentle tone of voice, and his usually stern face mirrored confidence and faith. Hope too. "Just as every noble goal is an ideal. But the past—the two hundred and twenty-four years since the Federation was founded—have proven just how important, how precious, and most of all how right our ideal is."

He touched a button on his lectern, and the map of the Lembatta Cluster disappeared from the holoscreen. It was replaced by a still image that couldn't have been more symbolic. The shot had been taken on Onferin when the visitors from space had been met by Councilor Shamar ak Mousal and his political entourage. Ambassador Spock, Ambassador Rozhenko, Commander L'emka, and Captain Adams stood side by side with both the Renao's highest-ranking politician and his defense minister ak Bradul in front of a valuable-looking polished stone table and beneath the ceiling with the exquisite painting of the cluster and its spheres. It was a typical press photo—a group picture like any other taken during diplomatic receptions. And yet, it featured something special, and this detail said more than words could ever do: Although the gesture was not customary to the Renao, Councilor ak Mousal shook Captain Adams's hand in this picture. Both smiled. They smiled like partners.

Maybe this smile had little meaning in the grand scheme of things. Maybe it had only been a brief moment, and the next moment had been completely different. Troi didn't know. But she knew—and so did the entire Federation Council—that there had been this particular moment out there in the Lembatta Cluster. And that was all that mattered, wasn't it? It conveyed what was possible, given half a chance. A gesture of cordial unity, good will and mutual understanding.

"Bharatrum is a long way away from here," Akaar said quietly, "and, yes, it's alien to us. It's so alien, in fact, that the *Bortas* and the *Prometheus* are virtually left to their own devices out there. But they're not lost. Neither is peace. Let us hope, esteemed council members. Let us dare to hope." He paused briefly. "Thank you for your attention."

19
NOVEMBER 24, 2385

I.K.S. Bortas, en route to Bharatrum

The engines' humming sounded like an opera to Captain Kromm's ears. Finally, something was happening. Finally, they were moving forward.

He stood in the wardroom, his gaze wandering across an illustrious assembly of hand-picked warriors surrounding Lieutenant Klarn. "Your task is simple: Turn over every stone on Bharatrum. Don't leave any of the red-skins undisturbed, and don't ever take no for an answer. The Empire has ordered us to find the Purifying Flame and to render it harmless, and, by Kahless, that's what we're going to do!"

Klarn, whose right hand rested suggestively on the disruptor attached to his uniform belt, grinned eagerly. "And what if the population puts up resistance?"

Kromm jutted his chin forward. "Then they will learn the hard way that there isn't anything in the universe that will stop a determined Klingon."

Thirty warriors surrounded the lieutenant, and they all enthusiastically threw their arms in the air, howling battle cries. Just as on Onferin and Xhehenem, Captain Adams had requested that Kromm contribute security and science officers for his half of the away team. But Kromm had no intention of honoring that request. The time for compromises was over, and consideration was merely another word for weakness. If you wanted results, you had to act instead of talking and hoping. Kromm's choice of warriors therefore consisted entirely of seasoned soldiers—Klingon men and women who yearned to shed Renao blood.

Satisfied, Kromm bade farewell to the members of the away team. He knew that, as soon as they materialized on Bharatrum, those warriors would do him proud.

Commander L'emka regarded him with a typically skeptical expression. She stood by the wardroom entrance. Kromm hadn't noticed her enter, not that he cared much. "What do you think you're going to achieve, sir? You instructed them to indiscriminately attack Renao regardless of whether or not they are part of the Purifying Flame. That is hardly conducive to completing our mission."

Kromm pushed past her and went through the doorway. Without a word he walked out into the corridor.

But the first officer had no intention of dropping the subject. "Sir!" she said sharply. She caught up with him. "We're looking for answers, not for more deaths. Enough people have died already!"

Stopping dead in his tracks, he whirled around to face her. When he made a step toward her, L'emka already stood with her back against the corridor wall.

"Don't remind me of the dead, Commander! I have not forgotten the many Klingons who have died dishonorably at the hands of these cowards!"

"Killing random Renao just as dishonorably won't avenge them, Captain."

He snorted. "Do you *really* consider your babble worthy of a true Klingon? I assumed those were ridges on your forehead, Commander. In truth, they're probably implants that make you *look* like a warrior. Deep inside you seem to be as weak as any human."

"Hegh neH chav qoH," she said with a nasty snarl.

Kromm threw his head back, laughing derisively. "It's possible that a fool's only achievement is death, Commander," he repeated her words. "But it won't be mine, I assure you. Today, the perpetrators will die, not the avengers."

"Innocent Renao?"

He shook his head. Her blindness was disgusting, and her pretty head clearly wasn't capable of producing anything else but obstinacy. "There's no such thing as innocent Renao, Commander L'emka. If you were worthy of your position, you'd know that."

"What are you trying to say, sir?"

For a brief moment Kromm was tempted to finish it here and now. He knew that he would do himself a favor, and that he would only bring to an end what had been long overdue. He was fighting for Qo'noS, after all, for those who had already died, and those who were being targeted by the enemy. His task was important, and whoever got in his way was against him and against Qo'noS.

He quickly pushed that thought aside. Martok counted on him fulfilling his duty, and contributing to the Empire's honor and glory. The truth was, there was no one else in his misbegotten crew who could fulfill L'emka's duties as well as her. He needed each and every warrior under his command, no matter how stubborn. Revenge was a dish best served cold—after longing for it for a while and looking forward to it. He would settle his score with L'emka when the mission was completed and he had achieved his deserved glory.

A sardonic smile crept onto his face. "Your words do not concern me anymore, Commander, if ever they did. Simply do your work, and leave the decisions to me."

"Aye, sir." She spoke those words as a declaration of war. "The ship is on schedule, Captain, and we will arrive at Bharatrum at supper. All systems are working as normally as can be expected, considering the disturbances within this region. And the agreement not to orbit the Renao world without permission of the planetary administration still hasn't changed—just in case you intend to go against the *Prometheus* again."

Her cynicism was like water on a *bat'leth* blade to him. "Precisely, Commander. The good of the Empire outweighs Captain Adams's need for a good night's sleep. Old agreements don't hold any value for me. We are the vanguard of our chancellor's forces. We don't need invitations. We take what we need—by force if necessary." With these words, he turned around and walked toward the bridge.

U.S.S. Prometheus

As far as Ensign Goran Tol was concerned, sickbay was one of the most boring areas of the entire ship. The unjoined Trill with freckles and jet-black hair was part of the security staff aboard the *Prometheus*. He liked being in the thick of it and seeing action, but his duties to date had been anything but exciting.

"Join Starfleet," Tol mumbled, "discover new worlds and new civilizations." Only the empty corridor was listening.

Yet another uneventful hour was behind him, and another one had just begun. He understood that the two Renao who had been taken aboard on Onferin—this Kumaah something and his female companion—needed to be guarded around the clock. Both of them were potential informants, alleged victims themselves and under the mental influence of someone else … they might even be dangerous, although Tol doubted the latter. But most of all, they were unexceptional. What danger did people pose who had been in some sort of coma for days now?

It wasn't the guard duty itself that annoyed Tol. It was the fact that he had been picked for the second shift in a row. Yesterday when less experienced colleagues had left for Xhehenem in order to see new things and face challenges, Tol had had to settle for standing outside the door to sickbay with his phaser, where nothing actually happened for hours on end. And today, just one hopeful night later, Security Chief zh'Thiin had given him this tedious duty again. Tol couldn't help but feeling that she was punishing him for some reason. Even a walk on the observation deck would have been more exciting than this boring task. At least there, Tol could have stared at the so-called "Demon Cloud" instead of the plain wall on the other side of the corridor.

He laughed quietly. What a bizarre name. Admittedly, the region did come across as a bit demonic if you really looked closely. And, yes, Tol had looked intently out into space like most of the others on board before starting his duty shift. And he had marveled at all the changes that their environment had undergone while the *Prometheus* had been advancing deeper into this alien region of space. There had been both red glowing nebulae and energy storms near the border and Onferin, but on the way to Xhehenem their intensity had increased on a surprising scale. Since they had left Xhehenem, however, they had increased almost by the hour—at least that's what it had looked like to him in the morning. The red seemed to be everywhere. Tol imagined that it must have been very difficult for Lieutenant ak Namur to navigate the ship safely through these regions.

Years ago, Tol had been in the Badlands, a region of space on the Cardassian–Federation border known for intense plasma storms and gravitational anomalies. Compared to a flight through the Badlands—when Tol's little runabout had shuddered continuously from energy turbulences, and all his cockpit consoles had been permanently acting up—their journey through the Lembatta Cluster had been relatively smooth. The deck only shuddered slightly on occasion, and sometimes the lights flickered nervously. But Tol assumed that they owed this smoothness to the skill of the bridge crew in general and their conn officer in particular. Still, he was worried that their situation might deteriorate.

A loud clatter coming from the room behind his back jerked the Trill back to reality. Tol winced, turning his head to look at the closed door.

Suddenly, the lights flickered at the same time as a spine-tingling shriek came from sickbay.

The Trill's training kicked in and he reacted instantly despite not knowing what was happening. Unholstering his phaser, he double-checked its setting—stun, like it should be—then pointed the weapon at the door.

Another shriek—no, two shrieks! It reminded Tol of ghost stories from his childhood. It was then joined by a hollow, wailing moan. Those sounds chilled him to the marrow, and they were scary beyond belief. The dead souls from Earth's mythology must sound like this when the ferryman crossed the Styx with them. Those were the sounds of Gre'thor, the Klingon hell of the dishonored.

"Tol to security," the Trill said, his free hand tapping the combadge on his chest. "Requesting backup in sickbay."

"Zh'Thiin here," came the prompt reply from his superior officer. *"Understood. What's happening, Goran?"*

"Stand by, Commander," he said. "I'm just about to find out."

He touched the control pad next to the door, entered the security code and checked his phaser one last time. The door hissed open.

The sight was bizarre and horrifying. The two Renao were still in their biobeds, but they were no longer comatose. Their glowing eyes were wide open, and they were writhing in their restraints. The woman had white foam in the corners of her mouth and Kumaah's head twitched in spasms. Tol didn't know anything about medicine, and even less about Renao, but the displays on the monitors above the biobeds seemed dramatic even to him. Red and golden lights were flickering everywhere, and alarms sounded.

"Don't shoot!" Trik shouted. The Emergency Medical Hologram stood between the beds. His face was frantic and he looked at Tol, appalled. "Will you put your phaser away, Ensign? What we need here is a second hypospray, not weapons fire. Get on with it!"

Tol blinked in confusion, even as the woman screamed again. Her torso reared up, and her arms tugged fiercely but in vain on the black leather straps.

Trik accusingly waved the hypo that he held in his right hand.

"I can assure you, Ensign, that I don't have more than two hands."

That finally got through to Tol. "Of course, Doctor," he said quickly, holstering his phaser and entering the room.

Tol knew that Barai had given orders to the hologram to activate himself as soon as the Renao required further medical attention. That case had obviously arisen—and the medical assistance seemed to be late.

The Trill hurried over to Kumaah's bed, while Trik attended to the woman. "What am I supposed to do, Doc?" he shouted over the wailing sounds of the red-skinned strangers.

"The hypo … on the small table over there," Trik said loudly. "Apply Melenex to our guest, ten …" He caught himself, as the woman seemed to become ever more agitated. "*Twelve* CCs, at least for now."

Tol looked around, noticed the small end table with the medical instruments, and did as he had been told. He pressed the hypospray against the man's neck, and squeezed. The small device emitted a hissing noise that was almost drowned out by the fits of the two Renao.

"Are you sure that's enough, Trik?"

The hologram in the black and blue Starfleet uniform sighed, looking at the displays above his female patient's bed. "I'm only sure about one thing, Ensign," he replied, applying a dose from his hypo to the woman. "It's never been that bad before. Today is the first time these two have behaved like this."

Kumaah threw himself into his bonds with full force again. Tol saw his muscles cramp, and the carotid on his neck pulsate—and suddenly, it was over. Unconscious, he fell back on his cushions. The woman also fell silent and closed her eyes.

The door leading to sickbay opened, and Doctor Barai stormed in along with a male nurse. "Report!"

At the same time, two shapes materialized next to the beds. Silver energy columns turned into zh'Thiin and Cenia from security. Both had their phasers drawn, but they relaxed as soon as they saw that Tol had holstered his own weapon.

"Everything back under control?" asked the Andorian woman tersely. She exchanged a look with Barai. "Doctor."

"Commander," he answered, nodding, before approaching the beds in order to check the Renao's vital parameters.

"Sir," Tol said, ashamed. He had completely forgotten to report back to zh'Thiin.

"It's all settled for the moment, Doctor," Trik said to Barai. "It was another fit." The hologram focused on zh'Thiin. "However, I obviously have to reiterate that this is an infirmary and not a shooting range! So I'd be obliged if you could all refrain from showing up with drawn weapons."

"Sure thing, Doc," said zh'Thiin, glaring at Tol. "We definitely have better things to do than go on wild goose chases. Thanks for the timely all-clear, Ensign."

The edge in her voice was unmistakable, just like the reproach. "Sir, in the heat of the moment I must have …" Tol began.

"Save your breath." Zh'Thiin ignored Tol and looked at Cenia. The man with the black hair studied the display above Kumaah's bed, and clearly didn't understand anything. "Come on, Dominik. Let's go."

"Sir, I *am* sorry!" Tol shouted after her, but the security chief was already through the door. Cenia just shrugged his shoulders before following her.

"I guess Commander zh'Thiin is slightly irritable today," Trik said as soon as the door hissed shut behind them. The hologram exchanged a questioning gaze with Tol and Barai.

"Who isn't, Doc?" Goran Tol replied, silently cursing himself and his superior officer.

Jenna Kirk had the mother of all hellish mornings. Not only did she have to reprimand two extremely ill-tempered subordinates in the engine room even before she'd had her first cup of coffee, the technology itself also seemed to be conspiring against the chief engineer. What other explanation was there for the dozens of minor malfunctions that had occurred since they had left for Bharatrum? Kirk's team didn't have enough hands to adjust all the displays that had acted up, or to change all the overloaded controllers of the EPS conduits.

"I'm telling you, Commander, it's the cluster." Mendon smiled, looking down at Kirk. The science officer stood to her right, next to his station on the bridge, while she was on her back underneath it. "These storms and that mysterious radiation ... They're affecting the ship somehow."

"Somehow," Kirk repeated dryly. Then she cursed quietly when fusing two cables didn't bring the anticipated solution to the problem, but instead another blue streak of lightning. "Well, thank you for that extremely insightful expert analysis."

The Benzite was still smiling when he crouched next to her. "No, seriously ... if you ask me, all of that has to do with the cluster. The technical problems, and even your mood."

Kirk didn't know what annoyed her more, his exhausting friendliness or his insinuations. Mendon was always excited when he could explore something new, no matter what it was, and today in particular it was unbearable.

"My mood," she growled, "is the result of years of extensive training, and as much as I hate to say it, Lieutenant, it doesn't improve when my work is being interrupted by small talk."

Once again, too much energy bolted through a cable that wasn't ready for it, and once again, Kirk winced as this energy ended up in her right thumb instead of the console. "Dammit!" Furiously she crawled out from under the console, pressing her hand against her chest. The pain subsided quickly but the anger remained.

Mendon studied her pensively. "You weren't like this yesterday." He produced a tricorder and pointed it at her. "And neither was my console."

"So?" snapped Kirk. She was tempted to wrench the stupid device that he waved in front of her face from his blue and gray hand, but she managed to rein herself in just in time. "I'm the chief engineer, Lieutenant. Am I not here to share the pain of my engines?"

"And most of all, you're not usually this snide." Mendon stared at his tricorder display. "Tell me, Commander, have you had unusually bad headaches during the past few hours? Do you frequently feel irritable?"

This time, she *did* snatch his tricorder from his hand. "I'm working," she said as a warning, and she hoped that her glare was even more expressive. "And yes, I'm irritable. I always am when I'm being disturbed."

Mendon nodded. He looked concerned. "Captain?" He looked toward the bridge center. "Could you spare a minute, please? I'm afraid it's important, sir."

Well, I'll be damned … Kirk pushed herself up from the floor, ready to give him a severe dressing-down, when Adams joined them.

"What's up, Lieutenant?"

Mendon took the tricorder back from Kirk, and held it under Adams's nose. "This, sir. I've been observing strange mood swings in certain crew members. Irritability, a harsh conversational tone—the Starboard 8 almost became the scene of a brawl, shortly after gamma shift ended. And the sensors don't have anything to say about it."

"What's your point, Mr. Mendon?" Adams asked in a

tone of voice suggesting he already had a suspicion.

"That's what I'd like to know," Kirk mumbled impatiently. "Captain, this nonsense is taking valuable time away from—"

"Just one moment, Commander," Adams said, his gaze fixed on Mendon.

"Sir," the Benzite said quickly, "in my opinion, the psychological influence that we have detected in the Renao has by now reached an intensity that also affects non-Renao. On the one hand, that would mean we're definitely getting closer to our destination. But at the same time, it apparently poses a considerable danger."

Kirk shook her head. "Nonsense. The shields are able to keep out almost any known radiation."

"Exactly, Commander." Mendon nodded gravely. "Any *known* radiation."

Kirk snorted again. She understood what her crewmate was trying to say but that didn't make it any more plausible for her. "Sir," she said to Adams, "with all due respect for Mr. Mendon's expertise, the lieutenant is imagining things. The absence of counter-evidence is not evidence."

"And yet I can't just dismiss that notion," Adams said. "Especially in light of the latest developments that Doctor Barai has just reported to me."

Kirk raised an eyebrow. "Sir?"

"Our guests, Commander. Kumaah ak Partam and the other, Alai ak Yldrou, are reacting to the progress of our journey. They are still hardly ever conscious or responsive. The closer we come to the center of the cluster, the doctor says, the more agitated and uncontrollable the two Renao are. So far, Barai and his team have been able to sedate them with medication. But apparently their condition—

and their madness—is deteriorating."

"That matches my theory," Mendon said. "The Renao's madness gets worse, and now the influence becomes noticeable in us as well." His hands were trembling with excitement.

"There's no proof of that," Kirk said. It was unbelievable, how much Mendon annoyed her! Why couldn't he see that his speculations were hair-raisingly counterproductive? "An allegation, nothing else."

"And yet I'm tempted to act on that." Adams nodded. "Well spotted, Lieutenant. Get together with Commanders Carson and Kirk, Doctor Barai, and all other departments you need, to put your theory to the test. Modify our shields. Try anything in your power. I want to know whether your assumption is correct—and if that's the case, I want to do something about it."

"Aye, sir," Mendon replied.

Kirk rolled her eyes.

20
NOVEMBER 24, 2385

U.S.S. Prometheus, in orbit above Bharatrum

Captain Adams looked out at Bharatrum through the conference-room window. It was a russet, cloud-covered globe, with heavy storms crossing its northern hemisphere, and high-energy discharges—the heaviest lightning the captain had ever seen—streaking through the black clouds. *This doesn't look at all welcoming*, he thought.

The planet was approximately the same size as Earth. Initial scans had revealed that around one and a half million Renao lived down there, predominantly in city-like settlements. Considering the difficulties that the on-board systems had been displaying these past few hours, Adams hesitated to trust those results. The reality of the planet might have been much different.

Almost two-thirds of the planet's surface consisted indisputably of landmasses. An enormous continent covered the southern hemisphere, while a small ocean with a large island shaped the image of the northern hemisphere. There were vast deserts, high mountain ranges, jagged and hostile coastlines, and several settlements consisting of various arcologies that looked like the insectoid hives they had already seen on Onferin, Lhoeel, and Xhehenem.

"A breathtaking view, wouldn't you say?" Captain

Kromm had joined Adams. His face showed an expression that might have been awe.

"It is indeed formidable," Adams said.

Kromm laughed briefly. "Respect is good, Adams. As long as it doesn't slow us down."

Adams nodded at his mission partner. "Shall we begin?"

"I thought you'd never ask."

Both turned around. Selected representatives from both ships sat in small groups divided according to their affiliation around the oblong conference table. Adams's gaze fell on Commander Roaas, Lenissa zh'Thiin, Jenna Kirk, Doctor Barai, Jassat ak Namur, and Mendon. Kromm had brought his first officer, L'emka, and his security chief, Rooth, as usual. Both ambassadors were also in attendance. Spock and Rozhenko sat at the foot of the table next to each other, as if they could form a bridge between the two estranged teams sitting at the long sides of the table.

The atmosphere was tense; Adams sensed that clearly. Kirk and zh'Thiin glared at the Klingons as if they wanted to jettison them from the next air lock. Kromm seemed to harbor similar aversions to Jassat. Rooth seemed to ignore everything and everyone. And a certain aggression was almost palpable between Kromm and L'emka. Adams wondered if this was the influence of the radiation, like Mendon believed it to be? Or was it due to the deadline for Klingon forces near the border to strike?

Adams was deeply concerned about the atmosphere, yet he couldn't do much about it. He could only keep going … and hope.

Kromm and Adams took their seats at the head of the table. Adams cleared his throat and commenced with the briefing.

"Thank you for coming. I know that the circumstances

are by no means easy, but we still have a common task. A lot depends on our success. As you already know, Bharatrum's planetary administration hasn't responded to our contact attempts. The latest communiqué from Earth suggests that Starfleet Command has similar problems in that department. Of course, we will continue our efforts to establish contact."

Kromm snorted derisively. Qo'noS, of course, hadn't made any attempts to contact any cluster worlds since the mission had begun, nor would they.

"In order to point out potential risks in this region," Adams continued, "I've asked my chief medical officer to join us. Doctor?"

Geron Barai nodded, touching a control in front of him. A holographic recording appeared hovering above the center of the table. It showed the two Renao who were in sickbay— ak Partam and ak Yldrou—during one of their fits. Although both patients were strapped to their biobeds, they were in a frenzy, twitching, throwing their heads from side to side, and uttering guttural noises. Those were followed by half-howled, half-shouted verbal abuse of the nursing staff that the ship's computer was unable to translate. Instead, Jassat ak Namur began providing the Federation Standard equivalents of their words: threats, promises of violence, and so on. The "invaders from space" and the "criminals against the Harmony of Spheres" would, they promised, be treated horrendously. And they heard prophecies that they would face every possible punishment in the universe for their sacrilege.

Adams waved his hand dismissively after a few minutes. What good did it do, listening to this?

"What you see here," Barai said quickly after a signal from his captain, switching the sound off, "is Bharatrum. At least, everything points to the fact that this reaction is directly linked to our location. We have been assuming for quite a while that there's a connection between the Renao's madness and the center of the cluster. These two patients seem to confirm our assumptions, as it's grown worse as we've approached the planet below."

"Are you saying that the people down there are just as insane as these two?" Kromm pointed at the world outside the window. "And that they are not in control of their actions?"

"I doubt that very much," Barai said. "We're assuming that the radiation doesn't affect everyone the same way." He looked at Mendon, who promptly got up, straightening his uniform top.

"Commander Kirk and I are currently in the process of analyzing this radiation," the Benzite said. "So far, with little success, unfortunately. The radiation is so extraordinary that we initially found it difficult to isolate it with our sensors. It was—and it pains me to say this—almost a coincidence that we discovered them. For the same reason, we're lacking reference data and can't come to any conclusive results. As Doctor Barai has just indicated, we have many reasons to believe that the Renao's madness is connected to this radiation—and apparently, it doesn't just affect the Renao."

Commander Roaas then spoke up. "Since we have entered the Lembatta Cluster, there's been an underlying aggressive mood among the crew," the Caitian reported. "At first, no one really noticed it, but the closer we came to the cluster center, the stronger the effects became." He looked at zh'Thiin.

"We're talking about verbal altercations," the Andorian woman said. "Arguments for ridiculous reasons. Brawls, nasty rumors, and even two cases of clear paranoia. Lieutenant Da Silva from astrophysics and Medtech Lersch complained to security that the crew members in their neighboring cabins were changelings and infiltrators from the Dominion, and that they had spied on them for weeks. Both are now in therapy."

"With Counselor Courmont?" Adams asked.

Barai replied, "No, we're treating them with medication, as this is probably a physical—possibly hormonal—and not a psychological problem. Counselor Courmont has been informed, and she's offering to settle disputes. But if speedy assistance is required, we need medication, just like we do for ak Partam and ak Yldrou."

"How are our guests right now?"

"Most of the time, they're sedated. But I can't continue this treatment indefinitely. I've had to increase the dose each time I've sedated them, and eventually, the sedative will pose a threat to their health. And there might come a point when we will face the same problems with our crew."

Adams looked at Kirk. "Can we block that radiation, Commander?"

"We're working on a solution in the shape of a modification to our shields," Kirk said, also touching a control. The Renao hologram vanished and was replaced by long columns of numbers, technical specifications, and calculations from the ship computer. Adams didn't understand them in the least. "However, it's early yet, I'm afraid, and it remains to be seen whether we're able to reach that goal at all. So far, we simply don't know enough about this radiation."

Mendon added, "We're experimenting with variations in the metaphase area, and with modifications of the deflector dish. I'm sure it's only a question of time before we find the correct settings to protect ourselves from the radiation."

"We hope," Kirk mumbled under her breath.

Looking more closely at the calculations, Adams at last

recognized schematics of the main deflector array and the shield grid among all the numbers and technical terms, but Kirk didn't seem to be inclined to explain them further. Did she doubt that their Klingon guests were trustworthy? Adams would have understood that notion but he doubted that Kirk's ill-tempered behavior was only due to Kromm and his two escorts.

The radiation is already affecting her as well, the captain thought, recalling her testiness on the bridge when Mendon had first reported to him. *There's nothing we can do about it. At least not yet.*

"What you're telling us is all well and good," Kromm said. His eyes were fixed on Kirk's holo, but his smile proved that he either didn't take those figures seriously, or that he didn't understand them. Or both. "But all these wonderful theories of yours are mere thought experiments. If this radiation was as strong as you're making out, more people should be affected."

"Not necessarily," the Benzite replied. "It has different effects on different species, and on different people within species. That's our working hypothesis, Captain Kromm."

"One with which I concur," Spock said. The old ambassador looked at the Klingon commander as if he intended to nip his doubts in the bud. "Since my mind-meld with Alai ak Yldrou, there can be no doubt that the minds of our guests are under some kind of outside influence. I was, however, not able to ascertain the source of this influence. This mysterious radiation would offer a feasible explanation for the source of the Renao's fanaticism. It greatly increases the basic xenophobic attitude of the Renao culture. It transformed a people who cared little for the galaxy outside of their spheres into one that actively and aggressively combats all things alien. And the further we advance into the cluster the stronger it becomes."

Jassat nodded with gratitude toward Spock, who met his gaze with a short nod back.

"In that case, we've finally arrived at its source," said L'emka. "Bharatrum is the most central of the inhabited cluster worlds. Acina and Catoumni, the two planets beyond Bharatrum, are clearly located closer to the border."

Adams looked at Kromm. "I suggest we assemble a joint science team to look into the radiation and a possible protection from it. Let's combine our resources. That way, we might find a solution for this mystery much more quickly, and we can cure the people affected by it."

Kromm shook his head. He turned to Rooth, who had been staring silently down into his lap. "Lieutenant, have you noticed any unusually aggressive behavior aboard the *Bortas*?"

Is that a trick question? Adams thought, barely stifling the comment. He was glad that he had managed to bring the Klingons to this table after the events in Xhehenem's orbit. Rhetorical jibes might satisfy his anger against Kromm in the short run but they would surely not help anyone else.

"Yes," the security chief answered casually and without raising his head.

Kromm laughed incredulously. "Oh, really. And would you be so kind as to elaborate on these observations?"

"No," Rooth said in the same indifferent tone of voice.

Adams frowned. He sensed that he was scratching the surface of something important here. But neither Rooth nor Kromm seemed willing to escalate the matter. Adams was just about to follow up when L'emka spoke up.

"I think that such a cooperation is an excellent idea,"

the first officer stated emphatically, without even looking at Kromm. "Our scientists and chief medical officer Drax will report to you."

Satisfied, Mendon tilted his bald head. White steam rose from his respirator. Barai also nodded affirmatively.

"Maybe another look at Renao mythology might be worth a try," Ambassador Rozhenko suggested. The Klingon had partially grown up among humans, and Adams thought that he had a special sensitivity toward each of the two disparate mission halves. His intuition might well bring them together after all. "Local phenomena often have an influence on the legends and myths of those living with them. Mr. ak Namur, do you recall stories from your childhood involving a radiation from space that would make you aggressive? Or about generally inexplicable aggressive behavior?"

The Renao shook his head. "Unfortunately not, sir. External influences are extremely unpopular among my people. Even in our legends there's hardly any mention of them, as far as I'm aware."

"Still, the suggestion isn't all that bad," Adams said. "Lieutenant, I want you to do some research, both on our computer and hopefully on Bharatrum itself."

Jassat nodded. "Aye, sir."

"If I can be of any assistance …?" L'emka took the initiative again without waiting for the approval of her commanding officer.

Even Jassat noticed the clear violation of the chain of command. Quizzically, he glanced at Adams and Kromm. But Kromm remained silent.

"Absolutely," Adams said quickly before Kromm changed his mind and decided to object. A cooperative mindset was what they needed, especially under these circumstances.

Then he turned to his own first officer. "Mr. Roaas, what's the status of our away teams?" They had intended to send mixed teams down to the surface again. But since the narrowly avoided disaster above Xhehenem, Adams didn't take anything for granted.

"Our halves of the teams are ready, and they're awaiting your command, sir," said the Caitian. "Captain Kromm?"

The Klingon noticeably took his time to answer. Almost defiantly, he finally looked away from the conference-room window, facing Roaas. "Our teams are ready," he said casually, as if that point had never been in doubt.

Roaas nodded. "Alright. As soon as Bharatrum deigns to notice us, we can begin."

"Oh, they *have* noticed us," said Kromm. "I'm sure of it."

"Me too," Adams said. "And if we don't receive a response to our efforts to contact them within the next half-hour, I will personally approach their administration. Time is of the essence."

"Indeed," Kromm said with a guttural grunt.

Ignoring the accusing tone of the Klingon, Adams looked at Kirk. "Commander, do we have any news about the data that you and Lieutenant Rooth discovered on Xhehenem?"

"Negative, sir," the chief engineer said with obvious dismay. "Tabor and everyone else are doing their best to recover data from the isolinear rods. But as I said just after we had discovered them, the material has been very badly damaged."

Abruptly, Kromm rose. "Are we finished? My bridge is waiting for me."

Yet again, Adams couldn't believe Kromm's audacity; and yet again he had the feeling that Kromm had no concern for the *Prometheus*. That he was simply humoring Adams by even attending this meeting, but that he would pursue his own agenda soon enough.

The thought was extremely disturbing.

Then Spock spoke up again. "If I might be so bold as to make another suggestion?"

Adams looked at Spock. "Of course, Ambassador."

"I feel we should give our cooperation a new foundation," Spock said. "We should draw a line under the past, and move forward with new determination."

"What do you suggest?"

"A change of personnel. Ambassador Rozhenko and I have already discussed the idea before this meeting, and he agrees."

The Klingon diplomat nodded. "In order to bind the *Prometheus* and the *Bortas* closer together, Ambassador Spock and I would like to change our positions. He will continue the journey aboard the *Bortas*, and I will move to the *Prometheus*. This is a sign of our cooperation, and our will to combine our efforts. It's a new beginning, and a symbol that conflicts like the one above Xhehenem won't happen again." He looked at Kromm and Adams. "Of course, we will only do so with your permission."

"Granted," Adams said promptly—and also gratefully, as both men were part of the Federation Diplomatic Corps, not Starfleet. They didn't need Adams's permission—and they certainly didn't need Kromm's—but Adams appreciated the fact that they showed the courtesy of asking. "That's an excellent suggestion. Don't you agree?"

Kromm snorted. It was obvious that he didn't care in the least. "If that's what you want."

"Alright." Straightening his uniform jacket, Adams got up. "We all know what we have to do. And we know what's at stake. Let's do this."

21
NOVEMBER 24, 2385

I.K.S. Bortas, in orbit above Bharatrum

There had been a time when the sight of two suffering enemies of the Empire would have deeply satisfied Commander L'emka. It would have brought forth a triumphant feeling equal to being victorious in battle. And she was convinced that she would feel the same today if she was faced with two Jem'Hadar, two Romulans, two Kinshaya, or two Breen.

But Evvyk ak Busal and Moadas ak Lavoor didn't evoke this inner jubilation in the Klingon woman; they didn't even generate a feeling of superiority.

Instead, she felt ashamed.

"You see what I mean, Ambassador?" She leaned over the unconscious ak Busal.

Spock stood in the doorway of the small room in the medical bay, and while his face was nominally inscrutable, L'emka could see that the sight before him had an impact on him.

And understandably so. The two Purifying Flame henchmen they'd captured on Onferin, ak Busal and ak Lavoor, appeared to be more dead than alive. Their bodies were covered in wounds, their will to live broken. In contrast to Doctor Barai and his staff, who applied sedatives and care to calm down the Renao afflicted by the radiation, Lieutenant Klarn and Captain Kromm had been applying brute force to silence their prisoners. Beatings instead of medication, malice instead of help.

Ak Busal lay on her bed like a piece of dead meat. Her eyes were closed, her breathing shallow and irregular. Ak Lavoor, on the other hand, suffered from a fever. He wasn't conscious but his lips were twitching, and he uttered strange noises that seemed to L'emka to match the eeriness of the blood-red space outside the ship.

"How long?"

Those were the first words from Spock since L'emka had brought him here. They were very quiet, almost a breathless whisper, but the soft voice carried a terrible fury. Spock had only been aboard the *Bortas* for just over an hour. He had been assigned to Rozhenko's vacated cabin. L'emka hadn't wasted any time, taking him here immediately … and also secretively.

She asked, "How long have they been here? Since Onferin."

"Officially, they have been declared dead," Spock said.

"Correct. Captain Kromm believed it to be for the best. He felt that having his own informants gave him a strategic advantage."

A dark shadow appeared on the old half-Vulcan's face. L'emka knew Vulcans to be calm and collected, but she was also knew that a hot flame of passion burned deep within them that they suppressed with their logic. The ambassador was also part-human. She had the feeling that she had just caught a glimpse of that buried fire.

But it vanished just as soon as it had appeared.

"They are not informants." Spock entered the room and went to ak Lavoor's bed, checking his pulse. "They are victims."

L'emka couldn't help but agree with him. Since she had been made aware of the presence of the two Renao, she had been seething. She wasn't too keen on the Federation, and she was generally prepared to overlook morals when it served the protection of the Empire, but she was also able to distinguish between wrong and right. And Captain Kromm proved with every passing hour that he lacked that capability.

"You're committing treason by showing me your prisoners," Spock said matter-of-factly. He placed his hand on ak Lavoor's hot forehead. "Kromm will not be best pleased when he finds out."

"Kromm is never pleased," she answered calmly, "and I don't care what he thinks. The way he's treating these two is wrong. His conduct towards the *Prometheus* is also wrong. Both show a complete lack of honor. Kromm was an arrogant drunkard when we began this mission, and the only difference now is that he hasn't been drinking as much. He's here to make a name for himself, and I wouldn't be surprised if he was prepared to sacrifice the mission in order to achieve that."

Spock studied her silently with his old, wise eyes. "You are a disloyal first officer."

"I'm doing what's necessary," she said sharply. "The mission is more important than the chain of command. Honor is more important than Kromm."

"Is the mission also more important than your reputation, Commander?" he asked. "I'm sure Qo'noS will be extremely displeased with you acting against Kromm's wishes."

"I'm acting *for* Qo'noS!" she snapped. "The goal is more important than the means to reach it, Ambassador. I thought you of all people would understand that."

The corners of his mouth twitched slightly. "Worry not, Commander, I understand very well."

The tense atmosphere subsided. L'emka understood that

she hadn't been wrong about Spock, and his reaction proved to her that she was doing the right thing. She had helped the oblivious Renao whose only faults had been naïvety and falling for a hatemonger's rhetorical tricks. She had helped the mission by building a bridge to the *Prometheus*. And she had helped herself by using the ammunition that Rooth had given her to weaken the dishonorable Kromm.

Spock turned away from the Renao to face L'emka. "Both of them require further treatment."

"And they will get it," growled a Klingon, pushing past them into the room. "Leave it to me."

"Are you Doctor Drax?" the Vulcan inquired.

"Yes, and you're in my way."

Much to L'emka's surprise, Spock didn't seem to be insulted at all. "My apologies," he said and stepped aside.

She and Spock observed Drax and another medic attending to the two prisoners, treating their wounds, and applying medication. Spock's presence wasn't entirely appreciated. It was obvious that Drax only tolerated the ambassador because L'emka was with him, but he answered the questions that Spock asked about the Renao's recovery prospects.

"I will inform Captain Adams." Spock turned to L'emka again. "I hope you are aware of that."

L'emka nodded. "I ... I have been down here frequently during the past two days—watching them, listening to them, talking to them, when their mental condition allowed for a conversation."

"And?" Spock raised an eyebrow. "What did these encounters bring forth, Commander?"

"These prisoners know even less about the Flame and their instigators than you and I do, Ambassador. These aren't criminal geniuses, bloodthirsty avengers, or clever terrorists.

They are naïve young Renao from a rural province who have fallen for the words and the madness of a false idol. And thanks to Kromm they are paying a terrible price for it." She shook her head. "If what you say is true … if this radiation is the cause of the Renao's behavior, and not deliberate actions … then Kromm has made a terrible mistake."

"One of several," Spock said.

Moadas ak Lavoor's head fell back. His mouth opened, emitting hissing, gurgling noises.

"Come, Commander," Spock said, leading L'emka out of the room so the doctor could do his work. "Let us inform the *Prometheus* and ensure that they receive even better help."

L'emka nodded in agreement and followed the ambassador.

Captain Adams should have expected that something would go wrong. Things had been going well for a bit. Goraal ak Behruun, the planetary custodian of Bharatrum and an extremely unlikeable character, had finally agreed—albeit grudgingly—to comply with Onferin's orders to tolerate away teams on his world. Commander Kirk and Lieutenant Mendon worked fervently on a shield modification that actually looked quite promising thanks to the help of the Klingon engineers. With the masterstroke of exchanging the ambassadors, Spock had worked wonders. The solidarity between the crews of the *Bortas* and the *Prometheus* had been rekindled.

And yet, Captain Adams felt like screaming, and the reason was once again Kromm.

"You're exaggerating, Captain," the Klingon said dismissively from the monitor on the desk in his ready room.

"And you're interfering with internal matters of the Bortas."

"Don't even think about using that excuse," Adams said with a snarl. He glared at his counterpart, while noticing from the corner of his eye that Roaas had folded his arms in front of his broad chest. "The two Renao should never have been imprisoned in the first place, Kromm. Not like that. There is such a thing as ethics!"

"Absolutely." Kromm nodded, unfazed. *"And there's an end that justifies the means. My end is the security of my Empire, and punishing those who act against it. Everything else is your problem."*

Adams could barely suppress the urge to slam his fist on the table. Since Spock had informed him about the two Renao aboard the *Bortas*, he was livid. Kromm had been a hindrance to the mission since day one … since Xhehenem his behavior had been absolutely unacceptable.

No, he corrected himself. *Since Onferin. Since he started to keep secrets from us that endanger lives.*

"I will inform Starfleet Command about this incident, Kromm," he said sternly. "And I'm sure that President zh'Tarash will put in an official complaint with the High Council. Until then …"

The Klingon just laughed.

"Until *then*," Adams repeated pointedly and with an unmistakable edge in his voice, "I expect that Evvyk ak Busal and Moadas ak Lavoor receive whatever medical treatment they require. Furthermore, I expect you to treat them like patients, and not like terrorists."

"They are terrorists!" Kromm slammed his hand down on his chair's armrest.

"They are victims," Roaas said. The Caitian stood to the right of Adams, leaning toward the monitor now. The expression on his face was as furious and stony as his tone of voice. "Just like the dead on Korinar. Like the dead on Tika IV Beta."

"Ambassador Spock will see to it that all concerned will be properly treated," Adams said. His index finger pointed at Kromm's face. "And I'm warning you, Captain! If I find out that you use prisoners as punching bags again, the High Council will receive a lot more from zh'Tarash than just a complaint."

"Was that a declaration of war, Captain Adams?" the Klingon asked snidely.

"You tell me," Adams answered brusquely, closing the connection.

22
NOVEMBER 24, 2385

Paris, Earth

Paris never slept. At least that was the impression Lwaxana Troi got from the city on the Seine. The night only seemed to be all the more reason to enjoy life and celebrate in the streets, and the clubs, and bars. Nothing seemed to be able to slow this city down—especially not the fear of terrorism.

Smiling, the Betazoid woman looked down from the window in her suite on the hustle and bustle—on countless lights and people milling about. She looked over at Ru and asked, "Don't you wish sometimes that you were a few years younger?"

Her tall factotum sat behind the desk in the middle room, looking at the monitor of the computer terminal there and did what he did best: work and be silent. He didn't seem to have heard Troi.

"I'm talking to you." She pointed at the Parisian night. "Aren't you itching to go out there and throw yourself in the fray of the nightlife?"

Blinking, Ru looked up before shaking his head.

"Never?" Troi frowned incredulously. "You're fibbing."

Another shake of the head. The thought of being part of something that was called "nightlife" seemed to horrify him.

Pensively, Troi tilted her head. "Oh well, you're a few years older than me, I guess. That probably explains it."

Her assistant knew better than to reply to that. With a quiet sigh that could have been born from frustration or contentedness—or both—he focused his attention back on his monitor and the data research that Troi had tasked him with several hours ago. Suddenly, his dark eyes widened.

"What's the matter?" Troi walked away from the window to join him. "You look as if you're reading a love letter from my Tavnian ex-husband—and you don't want to read one of those, I assure you."

Ru turned around to face her, pointing at the monitor. Numerous data windows were open but one was especially large and attracted Troi's attention.

"*U.S.S. Valiant*?" she read out loud. "What am I supposed to do with mission reports of a century-old starship?"

Ru pointed at a passage in the text.

"Yes, fine, the *Valiant* went to the Lembatta Cluster one hundred and twenty years ago," Troi said, skimming over the text that her factotum had dug up from the depths of the data banks. "But those are yesterday's tales, Ru. They won't help us much today." Nonetheless, she read over the ship's history, about her charismatic and determined young commander, Jeremy Haden, about the cartography mission in the cluster—and about the tragic technological disaster, which had obviously destroyed her in the cluster.

And then she realized why Ru had wanted her to read this. *They never found any conclusive evidence for that assumption. They never knew for certain why the* Valiant *had disappeared. They had assumed technical failure because the ship had been prone to technical difficulties, and so they never had reason to suspect another reason—for example the involvement of a third party.*

But now … did they have such a reason? Troi glanced at

Ru questioningly. The taciturn giant nodded emphatically.

"Fair enough," the Betazoid said. "It's worth a try. Put me through to Admiral Akaar, Ru, *tout de suite*."

Less than ten minutes later, the Capellan looked at her from the screen of her room terminal. Presumably, he was in San Francisco as the sun shone into his room. His hair and his uniform were immaculate, his face alert and focused. His eyes, though, were full of skepticism even as he stared at a padd containing the information Ru had sent to him.

"The Valiant? That ship had always had issues with its engines. Today, no one would allow it to leave drydock, let alone give permission to fly into uncharted territory."

"And yet, the fate of Captain Haden's ship has never been entirely unraveled." She held a padd with the relevant data in her hand, just as he did. "Explain that to me."

Akaar shrugged with his broad shoulders. *"I cannot, but we are speaking of a time before even I was born. But if Starfleet had entertained a notion that foul play might have been the reason for the* Valiant's *destruction, they would have investigated. The* Valiant *vanished in the Lembatta Cluster—no survivors, no witnesses. Sometimes accidents do happen, regrettable as that may be."*

"Maybe there wasn't foul play involved," she said, leaning back in her seat while defiantly crossing her legs. The fabric of her skirts rustled. "Maybe it was because of that radiation that Captain Adams reported."

Akaar frowned. *"You mean …?"*

"What if Haden didn't have technical problems? What if he and his crew weren't in full command of their mental faculties when their ship went down in the cluster? Admiral, back then, Starfleet might not have seen any reason to assume anything but technical failure. Today, knowing what we know of the cluster, the situation looks different, wouldn't you agree?"

The Capellan looked down at his padd. *"A moment, please, Madame Ambassador."*

The Betazoid woman gave him the time he asked for, motioning for Ru to bring her a glass of water. She closed her eyes. It *had* been a long day, and she wasn't young any more—although she was younger than Ru, of course.

Several minutes later, Akaar lowered the padd. *"Apparently, a chain of unfortunate events prevented a search for the* Valiant. *A lack of resources, a hasty decision from admiralty, perhaps a lack of technical capabilities. When first contact was made between the Federation and the Renao in 2332, Captain Rachel Garrett of the* Enterprise-C *suggested launching another search. However, the Renao were digging their heels in and closed their borders. Our philosophy of colonizing space didn't seem to match their own principles. When we finally came to an association agreement in 2377, the* Valiant *had been all but forgotten. The version that technical failure was the reason for the ship's disappearance remained in the records."*

Troi shook her head, placing her glass back on the table. "Call it Betazoid instincts, Admiral, but I have severe doubts about that version …"

U.S.S. Prometheus, in orbit above Bharatrum

"Superficial knowledge." Sighing, Captain Adams glanced into his synthehol-filled glass. Even the amber liquid reminded him of the cluster and all the problems it posed. "There's not much worse than superficial knowledge."

Commander Roaas smiled wryly. "The Borg were worse."

Adams looked up. Roaas sat in a chair across from him and grinned, which was an extremely rare sight, both in general and particularly recently. The Caitian had persuaded Adams to come here to the Starboard 8. Only a mind that occasionally relaxed could remain vigilant, he had told the captain. But Adams had a difficult time relaxing while the away teams searched for answers on the planet below. However, there was very little *to* do while waiting for those teams' reports, so Roaas's notion was a good one.

"You know what I mean," the captain said with a friendly glower at the Caitian.

"And you know that Starfleet will not accept any half-baked facts," his first officer replied quietly. "Sir, I've looked into the files regarding the *Valiant*. Ambassador Troi must be wrong."

"She was pretty clear." Adams thought about the bizarre message that he had received from Earth less than an hour ago. "I was on a call with both her and Akaar. The admiral couldn't get a word in edgewise. She thinks that the *Valiant* fell victim to the same thing that we're investigating here—whatever it is that turns Renao into insane fanatics."

Roaas looked toward the window. Silently he watched Bharatrum, lost in thought. "It's possible," he finally said. "At least in theory. I mean, it is one possible interpretation of what happened to the *Valiant*. But that's all it is, an interpretation."

Adams sighed again. "Do you know Ambassador Troi? I sat at her table many years ago during a diplomatic reception. She has an extremely … obstinate personality, Commander. If Lwaxana Troi is convinced of something, there's no way to dissuade her, and it doesn't matter whether you're discussing the advantageous effects of Bajoran cocktails on official gatherings, or the fate of spaceships that have mysteriously disappeared without a trace."

"That have allegedly mysteriously disappeared," Roaas

said. "Starfleet never had any reason to believe that Captain Haden's ship suffered anything other than an accident."

"But they also never had any conclusive evidence for the accident notion."

"True," the Caitian said.

Adams placed his glass on the small table. "It definitely warrants further investigation. For now, let's consider the notion that Ambassador Troi is correct—especially since she usually is." Adams allowed himself a small smile. "The reception *did* become much more bearable once the bar offered Bajoran cocktails. Inform Mendon and Winter and all the away teams to keep an eye out for signs of the wreckage of the *Valiant*."

The Caitian nodded. "What about the *Bortas*?" Adams's face turned stony. "Don't even mention the *Bortas*. I'd just as soon send her home." He looked at Roaas questioningly. "I assume you've already heard?"

"Of course," his second-in-command replied. "I believe the entire ship knows about it by now—except maybe one or two crew members who haven't emerged from their labs since the beginning of the shift."

Adams shook his head, recalling their initial contact with Goraal ak Behruun. Bharatrum's planetary custodian wasn't an approachable man by any stretch of the imagination. These first talks had made that clear, especially when ak Behruun abruptly ended their conversation after less than half a minute. It took three attempts and Jassat ak Namur's cautious but nonetheless persistent advocacy to persuade Bharatrum's highest-ranking Renao to negotiate. These negotiations were also kept very brief, as ak Behruun refused point blank to give the visitors any more freedom of movement than he absolutely had to. Onferin's order was clear and concise, the custodian claimed, and he would follow it to the letter: The away teams of the *Bortas* and the *Prometheus* were allowed to search for traces of the Purifying Flame, nothing more. They would not be given access to buildings, regions, or data storage that didn't have any verifiable connection to the terrorist organization.

"You're not welcome here, Captains," ak Behruun had said, and in his glowing eyes they had seen the fire of a passionate representative of his people. *"Don't forget that. We tolerate you because President Shamar ak Mousal orders us to. But we do not welcome your presence by any means. You are sinners against the Harmony of Spheres. You don't belong here."*

After this conversation, Sarita Carson had reported to Adams that Kromm had not heeded the custodian's wishes. The Klingon had deployed additional away teams made up of *Bortas* crew members who went to areas that ak Behruun had explicitly declared to be out of bounds.

Adams understood Kromm's impatience. A lot was at stake. But his recklessness would cause more problems than it would solve. What little peace they had achieved with ak Behruun was in danger again. Adams was sure that as soon as the custodian heard about Kromm's additional forces, he would ban *all* away teams from his world. And Adams wouldn't blame him if he did.

"Kromm's course of action is unacceptable," Roaas said. The Caitian's ears twitched—a clear sign of his anger.

"And he's been ignoring all our attempts to contact him," Adams said. They sat on a diplomatic powderkeg. The clock that Qo'noS had wound up was still ticking, and the end of the ultimatum was approaching rapidly. *We need answers,* the captain thought, *but not at all costs. Never at all costs. And yet, with every passing hour, that sentiment becomes more difficult to justify.*

He remembered his niece, Karen, who had died in the Purifying Flame's attack on Starbase 91. Would she want Starfleet to ignore their principles because of her? Did it help the dead if Adams threw his ethics into the waste extractor?

No, he thought with grim determination. *We either respect our counterpart, even if they go against us and make our lives difficult, or we don't.* The Federation had been born out of respect towards others. The diversity of cultures and opinions was the Federation's strength and blessing ... in all things great and small.

"You've observed ak Behruun, Commander. Did you feel that he was under someone else's influence?"

The Caitian looked out into space. "Difficult to say. My first impression? A definite no. He's unapproachable and hostile towards us, but that doesn't constitute madness."

"No, he's entitled to that attitude," Adams agreed. "Whether we like it or not."

"Dammit, I'm done with this!"

The loud shout made Adams wince. Looking up from the table, he swung around. The Starboard 8 was fairly empty at this hour. Alpha shift had finished about thirty minutes ago, but most of the officers apparently preferred spending their spare time elsewhere today. And suddenly, Adams thought he knew the reason.

A Triexian stood at Moba's small counter. He had a bald, orange head, a haggard face, and three slender legs. Adams had met the man briefly. He was an ensign working in the engine room, Ricat Na Bukh. He wore civilian clothing, a comfortable jumpsuit and a light black vest.

"Are you listening to me?" the ensign continued to rant. He glared at the man, while stabbing at him with his index finger at the same time. "I've had enough. I'm no longer taking it."

The other man looked at him with glowing bright eyes. "I haven't done anything to you, Ensign," Jassat ak Namur said calmly.

Na Bukh snatched Jassat's glass from the counter, raising it like a missile. "Oh, really? So we're *not* here because of you? You and your kind are *not* endangering all of us?"

"The only one in danger here is you, Ensign." Jenna Kirk sat on a stool to the left of Jassat. So far, she had been watching her subordinate's temper tantrum in silence, but now she got up and stood next to Jassat. "In danger of inspecting Jefferies tubes for the rest of the mission. You will shut your stupid cakehole right now, or I will transfer you to the tightest tubes the ship has to offer—and believe me, I know quite a few of those."

Na Bukh lowered the glass, but not his anger level. "Commander, he's a Renao!"

"And a friend of mine among other things." Kirk stood with her fists on her hips. "Do you have a problem with that?"

"You should have one!" Na Bukh was sweating because he was so agitated. "These people are our enemies, not our friends."

"Everyone who serves on my ship is my friend," the chief engineer said. "Everyone who has the same convictions as me, is on my side. And I consider all others to be on my side also, Ensign, unless they prove me wrong. Call me naïve, but I believe in the good in all of us. If I didn't, I wouldn't have any reason to get up in the morning and drag myself out of my cabin."

Jassat's gaze wandered from her to Na Bukh. He seemed visibly embarrassed by the whole situation. "You should go to sickbay, Ricat," he gently said to the Triexian. "You're not yourself. This is the cluster talking. It's not your fault."

"Reason is talking here!" Na Bukh screamed. He turned his bald head as if he wanted the whole bar to get involved. "Are you too blind to see that? These red-skinned devils are just playing with us! They think we're stupid and …"

"*Ensign!*" Adams shouted, standing up. All eyes turned to him. His thunderous bass silenced even the technician. Adams allowed the shocked silence to settle before continuing, in an only slightly lower tone. "You heard the lieutenant. Go and report to sickbay. Now."

Na Bukh blinked, obviously out of his depth. He hadn't expected the captain. "Sir …" Adams cut him off. "That wasn't a request, Mr. Na Bukh."

"Come on, Ricat." Jassat got up, taking the ensign's middle arm to steer him gently towards the exit. "I'll take you there."

"The hell you will." Na Bukh angrily yanked his arm free. He glowered at the Renao. "I can make my own way there, thanks." The ensign turned on his three heels and left Starboard 8.

Much to Adams's dismay, three of the twenty remaining customers—Ensign Simanek from security, and Kowalksi and Gliv from engineering—also rose from their tables and left without a word, but with accusatory looks in Jassat's direction.

"What was that all about?" Kirk stared after them, puzzled.

"A statement." Adams sighed as he and Roaas had joined the chief engineer and Jassat.

Roaas quietly shook his head and crossed his arms in front of his chest. "And proof yet again that Ensign Na Bukh isn't the only one aboard who has problems with your presence, Lieutenant."

"I'm not the enemy," Jassat said quietly. "And neither are my people."

"Of course not," Adams said. "But some of us are either too stupid or too short-sighted to realize that. Terrible, how quickly some people lose their manners." He looked at Kirk. "You take care of the radiation protection, Commander, and the shields. I'm afraid we will soon need them more than ever."

"Aye, sir." Nodding, Kirk emptied her glass and touched the combadge to make an appointment with Mendon.

"Superficial knowledge," Roaas murmured when Adams and he went back to their table by the window. "You were right, sir. Stupidity *is* the biggest threat of them all."

Adams nodded gravely. "And this could get much worse before it'll get better, if we're not careful."

"So let's be careful."

"My sentiments exactly, Commander."

For a while, neither of them said a word. Moba scurried past them, taking fresh drinks to the adjacent table, where three male nurses were spending the end of their working day. Even the Bolian seemed embarrassed by the latest racist outburst.

Finally, Roaas looked up. "I will inform Kromm of our suspicions regarding the *Valiant*, correct?"

"Absolutely." Adams sighed again. "Being open is imperative. We can only advance together." He was absolutely convinced of that, but some days made it difficult for him to maintain that conviction.

23
NOVEMBER 24, 2385

Bharatrum

The blood on Klarn's knuckles was still fresh. It reflected the bright flashes from the cloudy night sky of this forsaken world. It reminded Klarn of the reason why he was here, and he grinned. "Koddoth, can you hear me?" he whispered into his communicator, while he wiped his bloody hands on his armor. It wasn't his blood, and he didn't need to be reminded of his deeds.

The answer of the deputy team leader came promptly. *"Loud and clear, Lieutenant."*

"Are you ready?"

"Have been for weeks." Koddoth's triumphant grin was almost palpable in his voice.

Klarn had a like grin of his own. They'd all been waiting for a moment like this since the mission had commenced. There had been moments when they had wondered whether this moment would ever come because the powers that be—especially the ones on Earth and on the bridge of the *Prometheus*, but also the old fools in the High Council—had been far too naïve to recognize the signs of the time, and to act accordingly.

But since Xhehenem, a lot had changed for the better. Klarn had never had noteworthy problems with Captain Kromm—since Xhehenem, he more or less admired him.

Kromm had at last transformed into the leader that the *Bortas* and this mission so urgently needed: a man who didn't care about others when dealing with wrong or right. Someone who did what had to be done.

Just like me, Klarn thought. He clenched his fist again, but the two Renao who had felt it only moments earlier were long gone. They still lay in their small temple on the outskirts of the desert settlement of Bosoon.

The small town consisted of three arcologies, none of them higher than twenty levels, towered in the middle of nowhere. The glass of their façades was almost opaque, having suffered from wind and the many sandstorms in this region. Flashes and rainless clouds dominated here. Crumbling bridges connected one Renao building to the next. These also had been eroded by time and the elements.

Klarn and his three companions hadn't encountered anyone when they had first moved into town. They didn't see any movement anywhere, except for the wind. This hadn't come as a surprise, as the place looked uninhabitable to Klarn when he had flown over it with his small *Kivra*-class shuttle not long ago. But his on-board sensors had said otherwise, which had aroused both his curiosity and his bloodthirst.

After issuing orders not to be fooled by the derelict looks and the unfortunate geographic location of this settlement, he had landed the shuttle on the edge of the town, armed his team, and then set off to take a closer look at the assumed emptiness.

After a few minutes, he had found two inhabitants in a small temple on the edge of Bosoon. The building was no more than a ruin with the symbol of the Purifying Flame painted on its walls next to some of these bizarre sphere drawings that Klarn didn't comprehend. Candlelight was visible through some cracks in the door, which Klarn had kicked down, taking the two Renao by surprise.

If it bled, it wasn't dangerous. On the contrary, if it bled, it was well advised to be scared of Klarn because if it bled, it could be killed.

One shot from his disruptor and a few punches later, the second Renao had been convinced to open his mouth, instead of sharing his dead partner's fate.

"Where is he?" Klarn had hissed at the survivor, who was a whining, pitiful picture of misery. "Every cult has a leader. Where is yours?"

The Renao had gazed at the wall with the drawings of his Home Spheres. He had looked at them, pleaded with them, as if they would come to his rescue.

Klarn had shaken him. "Your circles won't help you. You can only help yourself by talking. Where is he?"

After another two punches, the young weakling had finally talked, and shortly thereafter, he had died. Klarn didn't need any witnesses to reveal his presence. And promises given to enemies of the Empire weren't binding at all.

All that had happened less than twenty minutes ago. Now, Klarn stood at the eastern entrance to one of the arcologies with three armed warriors of the *Bortas* behind him. Koddoth—his second-in-command during this mission—stood with three more men in front of the western entrance of the circular building. They had split up in order to cover all entryways to the building.

Klarn looked over his shoulder. "Status?"

M'puq, a female *bekk* with great skills in operating sensors, lowered her scanner, grunting impatiently. "Difficult to say, sir. The storms and the atmospheric interference make using our technology difficult. I'm still reading the same exotic radiation that we noticed during our approach on Bharatrum, but that's it. No life readings, no indication of weapons or even a trap."

"The radiation comes from this town of ruins?" Klarn didn't believe what he was hearing. Was it really that easy?

"No, sir," M'puq answered. "It's ... everywhere. It overlays almost everything else on this world. So I can *assume* that one person is inside this building, just like the witness said earlier, but I can't guarantee it." She raised her hand-scanner. "At least not using this."

Klarn nodded. "Fine. We do it the old-fashioned way then. That's more honorable, anyway." He looked at his other two companions and noticed with satisfaction that they were also nodding. He brought his communicator to his lips. "Koddoth?"

"Sir?"

"We're going in. Don't forget—I need the leader alive."

"What about the others, sir?"

"We don't know if there are indeed others," Klarn said. "But if there are, I don't care about them."

There were no others. Klarn saw the disappointment in his warriors' faces when they searched the small wind-worn flats without finding an opponent. The inside of the arcology had been abandoned ages ago. They saw cracks in the walls that allowed wind and sand to blow in, and the structure was crumbling. Doors stood half open, furniture was coated in thick layers of desert sand and dust, and the floor was also covered in everything that wind gusts had blown through the cracks and other openings.

"Fifth floor, sir." Koddoth's voice came from the comm

device just as Klarn's team of four was searching yet another empty Renao dwelling. *"We have him."*

Klarn looked at M'puq and the others. Their faces showed determination. "Understood, Koddoth. Don't make a move until I arrive."

"Aye, sir. Koddoth out."

They rushed to the fifth floor. Koddoth waited for them at the staircase. "Sir," he greeted them with a triumphant grin on his face. "We have him."

"So you said. How?"

"The dust, sir. We saw footprints on the western side. They were fresh, and we followed them here."

Grateful for the cracks that had let so much dust into the structure, Klarn followed his deputy through the narrow corridor. Koddoth's three subordinates stood in front of a closed door on the western side, where the ground was considerably less dusty than the rest of the corridor.

Who needs sensors when they have eyes? Klarn thought, grinning. "You all know the plan. You know what's important."

Koddoth, M'puq, and the other five warriors checked the settings of their disruptors. When they had finished, they looked at Klarn, expectantly.

He didn't let them wait for too long. "Go!" The lodging was similar to all the others in the building—small and far from luxurious. Two and a half rooms, blind windows, high ceilings. But it was considerably cleaner than the other flats and the walls weren't as perforated. Elaborate paintings adorned the walls; they were almost as beautiful as those in the temple. Klarn recognized the sphere circles, the many planets of the cluster, and in their midst the legendary world Iad from Renao mythology.

He was not here for the art, though. As soon as he and

Koddoth reached the back room of the flat, they were faced with an armed Renao.

The man was naked and stood next to a bunk where he must have been sleeping before he had been disturbed. His skin was old and wrinkled, his body thin and undernourished. He held a Romulan disruptor gun in his trembling hands, aiming at the door and the Klingons. Madness flickered in his eyes.

M'puq reached the room and started, "Sir, we—" She couldn't finish her sentence, as the Renao fired, and M'puq disintegrated into glowing energy.

Klarn reacted instantly. With a guttural growl, he lunged forward. Klarn smacked the disruptor from the Renao's gnarled hands and dragged him down to the floor. The fight was short and imbalanced; the Renao didn't stand a chance. Klarn grabbed the red-skinned man's arms, yanking him to his feet and pushing him back at arm's length, before pointing his disruptor at him.

While Koddoth and the others began to tear his small abode to pieces, opening chests and toppling bookshelves, Klarn asked a simple question: "Where is the headquarters of the Purifying Flame?" Klarn was sure that this old fool was a part of the group. And he wouldn't be hiding in the middle of nowhere if he didn't have any secrets. Klarn pressed the disruptor barrel under his prisoner's chin. "Talk!"

The Renao didn't say a word, but his eyes spoke quite eloquently of his hatred and his defiance.

Klarn hit his disruptor's stock against the Renao's temple. The man instantly fell to his knees, blood trickling from where he'd been hit. Klarn grabbed his hair, pulling his head back. "I swear I'm only just getting started! You can remain silent all you want. I've got a lot of time … and I have the means to make it very uncomfortable for you."

"Sir!" Koddoth's voice echoed through the flat's narrow corridor. Klarn looked up. The warrior hurried into the room, carrying a small box in his hands. It was covered in the now-very-familiar symbol of a flame surrounded by a sphere. "We found this in a stash in the back room. It looks like what Rooth and the human woman found on Xhehenem."

Klarn nodded. "It does indeed. What's in there?"

The naked Renao, still kneeling on the floor with Klarn's fingers clutching his hair, moaned quietly.

"Yes?" Klarn prompted the old man. "Do you want to tell us yourself, or should we take a closer look?"

The man pressed his lips together. His glowing yellow eyes sparkled with hatred but he remained resolutely silent.

Klarn looked at Koddoth. "Will that thing explode when we open it?"

Koddoth grinned. "We already opened it. Look." With his free hand, Koddoth opened the small box. Inside were some isolinear rods, carefully arranged in brackets. These data storage devices were used by many cultures, and they were similar to those that Rooth had discovered on Xhehenem—only these appeared undamaged.

"Let's see whether these are in better shape than the others." Klarn left the Renao in the hands of another warrior. He took one of the isolinear rods, went to the Renao's computer console and started looking for a place to insert it.

The Renao finally spoke: "You can't stop it. Nobody can. You're too late, Klingon."

"Too late for what?" Koddoth asked, kicking the man in the back so hard that he doubled over onto the floor. "What are you planning here? Where are your people, you pathetic *Ha'DIbaH*, and what are your next goals?"

"Your demise, you wretched aliens! We are awakened. We will destroy you. Iad will destroy you!"

Iad. Klarn realized that this might be one of the preachers who had been traveling across the cluster worlds, carrying unrest to the people, motivating others to join his wretched cause. On Xhehenem Klarn had learned about these people, and he despised them from the bottom of his heart.

"Tell me about Iad," the Klingon said. "What about it?"

The naked man laughed derisively. "Iad is everything. The Son of the Ancient Red has awoken, and now Iad will show you the error of your ways. Iad will awaken every last one of us. Home … is calling! And we can hear it, Klingon. Oh, how we can hear it."

That was enough. Klarn looked into the man's jeering face, saw his complacency, heard his arrogance—and suddenly he lost his temper. With a loud battle cry, Klarn struck the Renao's temple with the barrel of his disruptor, again and again. He only noticed that he had gone too far when the preacher slumped dead to the floor.

Panting, Klarn backed away. He looked at Koddoth and the others. None of them had even moved a muscle while he had been raging.

Now, Koddoth nodded. "He deserved that."

"They all do," said Klarn—and for the first time in a long while he felt really good.

24
NOVEMBER 25, 2385

U.S.S. Prometheus, in orbit above Bharatrum

He saw her again in his dream. Richard Adams hadn't been sleeping much or very well since this mission started, but on those rare occasions when he did sleep, there was no present, no consequences, and no temporal burdens. In his dreams, there was no Lembatta Cluster, no Typhon Pact, and no High Council. In his dreams, his wife was still alive, and the Borg invasion of 2381 had never happened.

"I'm here," Rhea said in the dream, and she smiled at him, just like she used to do when they had met at Starfleet Academy. Both were teachers there at the time. "You see, Dick? I'm here. I was never gone."

Summer wind played with her hair. Her eyes sparkled brighter than the sun in Southern France. The memory of that summer was so vivid, as if had been only ten minutes ago rather than ten years. Behind his wife, Adams saw the ocean and the horizon … a seemingly endless vastness full of endless possibilities.

"I thought I had lost you," he heard himself say in his dream. Relief washed over him. The burden of many lonely years suddenly lifted and was replaced by pure joy. "I thought the Borg had come, and had taken you …"

Rhea shook her head, like she always did, when he was foolish and refused to see reason. "No one can do us any harm. After all, we belong together."

"Yes," he said, as if this one word said it all. As if it was protection against the insanity and the brutality of the universe.

A familiar signal sounded across the French coast, and the ocean disappeared.

Adams frowned. Panic welled up inside of him. What was happening here?

The sound was repeated, and this time it took away the sky. Bewildered, Adams looked at Rhea.

She smiled. Until the noise sounded a third time and took her away, as well.

"Bridge to Captain Adams."

Squinting, he opened his eyes. Instead of looking at his wife on a coast in summer, he was faced with his darkened cabin on the *Prometheus* in the middle of the night. The sweat-drenched blanket proved that his dream must have tormented him. Again.

"Adams here," he said, clearing his throat in an attempt to become master of his broken voice again. He looked at his chrono. It was well past midnight. Gamma shift was on the bridge. "What's up?"

"I regret having to wake you, sir," said Roaas, who also should have been in bed at this hour, *"but there's something happening that requires your attention on the bridge."*

Adams swung his legs over the edge of his bed, rubbing the sleep from his eyes. "I'm on my way. What's this about?" He thought about Kromm and ak Behruun and envisioned all sorts of terrible possibilities.

But Roaas surprised him. *"It's about Ensign Winter, sir. Our whiz kid has struck again."*

A few minutes later, Adams rode the turbolift to the bridge. Lieutenant Shantherin th'Talias, the watch commander for gamma shift, stood in the center of the room next to the command chair. Clasping his hands behind his back, the Andorian regarded Bharatrum on the main screen while the rest of gamma shift performed their duties.

Adams nodded at th'Talias to greet him, then went to the communications station to join the two members of alpha shift who were still on the bridge during the night shift: Roaas and Winter.

"Weren't you able to sleep, gentlemen?" Adams asked them.

His first officer's face was as inscrutable as always. Winter swiveled around in his chair in front of Roaas and was positively beaming.

"I had the good sense not to give it a try, sir," Roaas said. "Not before Mr. Winter's experiment was finished."

Adams frowned. "What experiment?"

"Ensign?" Roaas prompted the young man.

Winters straightened his shoulders. "Captain, I believe I have found a trace of the *Valiant*."

"Really?" Adams felt excited. "Show me, Ensign."

Winter leaned forward, touching a few controls on his console. Many of the data columns, which Adams couldn't comprehend anyway, vanished from his displays, replaced by new ones that were just as incomprehensible. "Here, sir," Winter said , as if that was all the explanation needed. "This data is admittedly pretty vague. However, I'm almost entirely certain that *that*," and he pointed at one particular area of the data columns, "is an echo of the *Valiant*."

Adams squinted. "Help me, Ensign. What am I looking at?"

The German with the Sudanese roots blinked confusedly before wincing slightly. "Oh, of course. I'm sorry." Again he touched several controls. "Sometimes I forget that not everyone is able to read raw data."

Another display changed. The columns with technical parameters disappeared, and Adams saw an animated, analytic graphic display of typical Starfleet design: undulating graphs in discreet light blue, arranged in three horizontal lines.

"This," Winter began, pointing at the top graph, "is the general and omnipresent background noise out here in orbit. The normal conditions generated by atmospheric interferences, nebulae, radiation, and so forth. Any sensor that's taking readings has to make do with these limitations. I can quite easily compensate for them as far as our communications go because I've programmed a subroutine into our comm system that generates new frequencies every two hours …"

The captain raised his hand. "You make up for them. That's all I need to know. Carry on."

He thought he saw the corner of Roaas's mouth twitch.

"This is the standard beacon from one of Starfleet's log buoys, which were in use approximately one hundred and twenty years ago," said Winter, pointing at the middle graph. "These buoys were used during exploration missions into uncharted territories for the transmission of data packets when the distance to the recipient, such as the next subspace relay or space station, had become too great, or when the environment was too rich in interference for a transmission."

Adams nodded. He knew the principle all too well, and he began to anticipate what Winter was getting at. The third and last graphic curve was very similar to the second one.

"And that one down there …?" he prompted.

"Exactly, sir." Winter was beaming again. "That's a beacon of the same type."

"A log buoy from the *Valiant*?"

"It would appear so. The signal is extremely weak, and it originates somewhere beyond Bharatrum. The *Prometheus* is unable to pick it up, and even if she could, it would have been drowned out by the background noise in this region."

"Can't pick it up?" Adams shook his head, dumbfounded. "What are you talking about? Didn't you just say that you *did* pick it up?"

"But not with the ship's technology," Roaas said, quietly proud. The Caitian pressed one of Winter's controls, and another monitor sprang to life. Adams saw complex data columns—some kind of raw version of computer software.

"Sir, this is TRAFA," Winter said a little sheepishly. "It's something I've been working on since the Academy."

"TRAFA?" Adams asked.

"A trans-spectral frequency amplifier." The dark-skinned comm expert nodded. "At first, it was just some crazy idea. Something I could keep myself busy with between boring seminars. But in time … well … I never stopped working on TRAFA, and it became a hobby bordering on an obsession."

"You have … developed a new communication software?" Adams didn't know what baffled him more—Winter's seemingly endless energy, or the feeling that he was surrounded by experts whose statements always needed to be translated into a language that he could understand.

"Well, until today it was more hypothetical," Winter said almost apologetically. "One that had never been put to the test. I didn't think it was finished, and I believed it to be flawed."

"But?"

He sighed. "Sir, I really didn't think it would work. After all, we don't really know where exactly the *Valiant* disappeared out here. But … I simply hooked TRAFA up to the *Prometheus* sensors and told it to look for twenty-third-century probe signatures."

"You did absolutely the right thing," Adams said. "Don't worry, Ensign—nobody has ever been reprimanded for being successful on this bridge."

Roaas nodded.

Adams looked at the TRAFA graphs. "Can we track the log buoy?"

"Theoretically speaking, yes," the Caitian answered in Winter's stead. "The local interference prevents a reliable answer. We're also unable to ascertain with any certainty whether Mr. Winter did indeed find a remnant of the *Valiant* that has been stranded in space for more than one hundred years. We're just assuming that he has."

Deep in thought, Adams stroked his chin. What else could it be? Except for the *Valiant*, there had never been any Federation technology left behind in the Lembatta Cluster—not even during the brief years of the association agreement. What's more, Winter's signal indicated an old buoy, and not a new one. If Starfleet Intelligence had "forgotten" any secret spy probes after the closure of the borders by the Renao in 2380, they would have been much younger.

"Let's give it a try," Adams finally decided, looking at Winter. "Do your best to find the source of this signal. Until we find evidence to the contrary, we will assume that this is a previously unknown data packet from the *Valiant*. I will inform the *Bortas*. Oh, and Ensign?"

"Sir?"

"Well done. I hope you will remember us mortals once this TRAFA has made you a galaxy-wide celebrity." Winking at Roaas, he left the comm station.

* * *

"*Iad.*"

The word lingered in the conference room like a cloud of manifested absurdity. Looking up, Jassat ak Namur stared at the Klingon visible on the wall monitor with a mixture of disbelief and amusement.

Captain Adams also didn't seem too keen on Kromm's suggestion. He sat at the top end of the long table, a cup of steaming hot, freshly replicated coffee in front of him. Just like everyone else present he was staring at the monitor. "Come on, Captain. Iad is a myth, nothing more. You might as well look for the coordinates of *Sto-Vo-Kor* or the sunken continent of Atlantis on Earth. Those are just tales. Councilor ak Mousal himself confirmed that back on Onferin. There is no Iad."

Leaning back in his command chair, Kromm placed his gloved hands on his armrests and was seemingly unimpressed. "*And yet your old ship might have crashed somewhere around here?*"

"On a world of old fairy tales?" Jassat blurted out before he could stop himself. Horrified, he put his hand over his mouth, but Adams invitingly nodded at him, so he continued. "Captain, believe me—there are more than enough feasible possibilities for the *Valiant*'s doom. We don't have to focus on imaginary ones."

"*Your fellow countrymen were not wrong about you, Lieutenant, do you know that?*" Kromm addressed Jassat directly. He sounded scornful. "*You're definitely not a true Renao.*"

Jassat swallowed hard—and at the same time, he swallowed the anger that this obvious insult aroused in him. A Starfleet officer didn't bite that easily.

"What exactly are you trying to say, sir?" he asked as calmly as he could.

"*Down there, Adams,*" said Kromm, as if Jassat was no

longer present, *"Iad is far more than just a fairy tale. They hardly speak about anything else."*

The captain frowned. "You mean on Bharatrum? That's impossible, Kromm. Our away teams report nothing of the sort, and the talks with Custodian ak Behruun …"

The Klingon snorted derisively. *"That's because you're looking in the wrong places. Again!"*

As well as Jassat, who had been asked to join this impromptu conference with Kromm for his knowledge about the cluster, Commander Roaas and Ambassador Alexander Rozhenko were also present. Adams exchanged a frustrated glance with them.

The ambassador shook his head. "What's your point, Kromm? Have you gone off on your own without telling us again? You do know that that violates the agreement we have with the Renao!"

Kromm stroked his thin black beard. He seemed like a complacent ruler blowing his own trumpet while not realizing the state his empire was actually in. *"You're searching ports and assembly halls, the administration and legislative centers of a world. Official places. But our opponent is moving in the shadows. They won't greet you at the spaceport when you visit their world. If you want to find them, you need to look for them* everywhere.*"*

"What do you think we've been doing for weeks?" Adams snapped.

"I can tell you what I'm *doing. I am discovering facts, and they point toward Iad."*

Jassat hesitated. Kromm's words might be absurd, but the Klingon commander sounded absolutely convinced.

"Let me tell you a story, Captain, about a man who went into the desert in order to hate." He nodded at someone off-camera.

His visage was then replaced by an aerial image from an abandoned settlement in the middle of the wastelands of Bharatrum. Kromm's voice still commented. *"What you can see here is the enemy."*

A beep sounded and a tinny voice came from Jassat's combadge. *"Trik to ak Namur."* Jassat briefly glanced at Roaas, who sat next to him. The commander had noticed the interruption, and nodded affirmatively. Jassat got up, walked to the back of the conference room and tapped his combadge.

"Ak Namur here," he said quietly.

"Lieutenant, I hate to disturb you, but …" The Emergency Medical Hologram sighed. *"If you could spare a minute, we urgently need your help down here."*

"Is this about ak Partam and ak Yldrou?" Jassat asked, recalling the radiation, Jenna's brusque behavior, and Mendon's hopes regarding the shield modulators.

"That's correct, Lieutenant. We—" A bloodcurdling groan interrupted the holographic doctor. *"Well, you can hear it for yourself."*

And he wasn't the only one. Adams, Roaas, and Rozhenko also looked over to Jassat now. Kromm realized that no one was listening to him and glowered.

"Go," Adams said, nodding.

Gratefully, Jassat nodded back, before turning and leaving the conference room. "I'm on my way, Trik. Ak Namur out."

Since his return to the Lembatta Cluster, a stinging pain had been tormenting Jassat ak Namur that he'd never experienced before. It was born from sadness and nostalgia, and he was frightened both for and of his people. He was back home, but he hardly recognized the place. With everything that his people did to themselves and others, it hurt him immensely.

Now, as he stood speechless in the doorway to sickbay, Jassat felt this pain more than ever. *This is us*, went through his head repeatedly, while his gaze was fixed on Kumaah and Alai. *This is all of us.*

Kumaah had managed to tear one of the padded straps that was keeping his arms restrained. Now, he flailed uncontrollably, but he mostly struck himself. The veins on his neck stood out. Alai also seemed to cramp up in every single muscle. Her usually beautiful face was distorted; her eyes had virtually lost all their glow. Doctor Barai, Trik, and Nurse Chu scurried back and forth between the two Renao. The three medics tried in vain to calm their patients. Jassat wasn't a physician but even he only needed one look to realize that medication wouldn't work anymore to rid Alai and Kumaah of their madness and send them back to a merciful sleep.

"I'm glad you're here, Lieutenant," Barai said with a glance over his shoulder. Although he tried to stay calm, Jassat could hear stress in his voice. "I'm afraid we need your expertise here."

Jassat entered the room and the door closed behind him. Ensign Flores from security remained outside the door. "My medical knowledge is limited." Quizzically he looked from Alai to Kumaah and back. He wanted to help—so much so, as if their pain had become his own through and through— but he didn't know how.

"We don't mean them," Chu said. The Korean woman deftly evaded Kumaah's strong arm, and seized her chance to apply some medication to the Renao's neck with a hissing noise from the hypo. Kumaah relaxed instantly. His arm fell back onto the bed, his eyes closed, and the readings on the monitor above him approached more tolerable values.

"Finally," Chu sighed, looking at Trik, who stood behind Barai at Alai's bed. "The new dosage is working, Doctor."

"About time too." Relieved, the holographic doctor also grabbed a hypo and adjusted the settings, before applying treatment to his female patient.

Although Alai immediately calmed down, she didn't fall asleep again. Unlike Kumaah, her eyes remained open even after Trik's treatment. Her mouth was twitching, and her sweaty head slowly turned to the right, to the left, and back.

"Alright." Taking a deep breath, Barai wiped his brow with his hand and stepped back from Kumaah's bed. He looked over both Renao's monitors. "We managed to buy some more time for them."

"We won't be doing that for much longer," Chu said.

Barai nodded silently.

Trik turned to Jassat. "And that's where you come in, Lieutenant. At least, we hope you will."

Helplessly, the young Renao shrugged. "But what can I do? If the medication won't be enough to ease their pain ..."

"... we will have to find another way," Barai said, "to treat the reason for their suffering, instead of the symptoms." He approached Jassat, putting a hand on his shoulders and nodding towards the quietly mumbling Alai. "Lieutenant, she's speaking. That's how their latest tantrum started, and that's why you're here. Alai ak Yldrou doesn't just utter meaningless noises anymore, she's speaking in complete sentences. She's telling us something, Jassat. And she's calling somebody. My colleagues and I were hoping that you could help us to understand her. We need answers ... and trust an experienced doctor on this—the best source for those is usually the patient herself."

She was talking? Jassat approached Alai, looking at her. She didn't acknowledge him, just like she didn't notice the rest of her environment. She was trapped in her own reality, and a faint whisper came from the slightly parted lips of her twitching mouth. Jassat leaned down to her.

"*The Reds.*" Alai whispered that, her breath warm on his cheek. She groaned quietly and her eyes closed for a moment.

"What is she talking about?" Barai asked.

Jassat shook his head, clueless. Again, he brought his ear to the poor woman's mouth, focusing on her whispers. "What's wrong, Alai?" he asked quietly, almost pleading, although she probably didn't understand him. "Tell me. Help me to help you."

And he winced when Alai suddenly opened her eyes. "The son!" she blurted out. She gazed into space, and her body writhed in the straps. "The Son of the Ancient Red! He's close!"

"Not that again." Sighing, Trik looked at Jassat. The hologram stood with his hands on his hips, grimacing. "The same mumbo-jumbo as before. Does that mean anything to you, Lieutenant?"

Jassat nodded slowly. Memories of Onferin came flooding back ... about old friends and new mysteries. "*Where* is he, Alai?" He saw Evvyk in her. The thought was nauseating and weighed on him heavily. "Where is the son?"

Alai turned her head toward him. Her fingers touched his wrist. And from her mouth escaped just one word—one that sent cold chills down Jassat ak Namur's spine: "Iad!"

25
NOVEMBER 25, 2385

Starfleet Shuttle *Lawrence Glendenin*, 0.1 light years off Bharatrum

Mendon saw red. And nothing else.

The Lembatta Cluster's nebulae were so dense in this area that they completely blotted out the blackness of space. Navigation by stars was impossible. The Benzite scientist felt as if he was moving through the depths of a crimson ocean that might be concealing dreadful horrors.

"And you're absolutely sure that this is the correct course?" he asked.

Ensign Robert Vogel, sitting at the helm of the *Glendenin*, chuckled quietly. His seatmate, the third and final member of this away mission, answered Mendon.

"No, Lieutenant," said Winter, who was at the shuttle's tactical station, "I'm not. Just like I haven't been sure the last five times you've asked that question. TRAFA is an experiment, not a guarantee."

The shuttle quivered, and the lighting flickered, when they were caught by a solar wind from the system's immensely inflated central star. It glowed far too close to the port side, lurking like a portal into hell. Vogel's hands danced across the console, and he stabilized their trajectory.

"Our return home also doesn't seem to be a given, if you ask me," Mendon muttered, wiping over his bald blue head. He sucked in the white, salty steam from his respirator as if the mixture of chlorine and enriched moisture did not only ease his breathing, but could also calm his nerves. Mendon was one of the last members of his species to be dependent on such a device, but due to his individual genetic disposition he would need to use it for his entire life.

"Every new day poses a new risk." Winter kept his tone lighthearted. As far as he had understood Mendon, the shuttle sensors, the comm functions, and TRAFA had formed a mission-specific symbiosis. "You knew that when you joined Starfleet, Lieutenant."

"Much earlier," Mendon said dryly. "You didn't know my mother's cooking."

Vogel laughed again. The ensign's hands danced across the control panel. Somehow he managed to steer the *Glendenin* safely through the nebula, while maintaining the course that Winter's program and the ominous beacon determined.

"And you don't know TRAFA yet," Winter said. "Have some faith, Mendon. I know I do."

He touched a display on the tactical console, and a graphic simulation of their shuttle flight path appeared. The *Glendenin* was heading for an object they assumed to be the *Valiant*'s log buoy. But so far, the computer had been unable to calculate the exact location. The interference within the cluster prevented a precise approach.

Despite these issues, Captain Adams had given the team permission to head for the object. It would have been even more difficult to salvage it with the *Prometheus* employing transporter or tractor beams. TRAFA's data was too vague for such an attempt. Their only chance might be at close range with a shuttle, provided they were able to get precise lock-on data. Assuming this buoy did exist, in any case. Mendon hoped it did—he loved his profession but he didn't like to risk his health in vain—but the uncertainty troubled him. The ensign might ask him to have faith, but given the quivering shuttle, the quiet warning noises ringing through the cabin, and the red horror outside the cockpit window, he found it difficult to comply with that request.

"By the way, have you ever noticed that Doctor Barai and Lieutenant Commander zh'Thiin have a sexual relationship?" he suddenly asked, and surprised himself with the nervous outburst, born of an urge to distract himself. Mendon wasn't one for gossiping, and usually he refrained from blurting out the observations he had made regarding the crew. He chided himself inwardly. But then again, he hadn't been this insecure and unsettled for a long time.

"The commander and the doc?" Vogel's expression was skeptical. "Impossible, Lieutenant. I saw both of them just last night in the gym on deck seven. There wasn't any love lost between them, believe me."

"Maybe they're trying to keep it secret." Winter had a mischievous grin on his face.

"If you ask me, they don't want anything to do with each other," Vogel said. Mendon remembered now that the two humans sitting in front of him in the shuttle were friends. "The way they glared at each other … man, if looks could kill … Especially from the security chief. Barai looked like a tribble in crosshairs: helpless and harmless."

"Tribbles are anything but harmless," Winter said. He touched a few keys on his console, and TRAFA corrected the simulated flight path on the graphic display. "My uncle on Regulus III once wanted to breed them. Huge mistake! They reproduced faster than he could blink."

Vogel frowned. "Regulus? Didn't your uncle live on Starbase 133?"

"Among other places," Winter said. "He's been *all over* the galaxy."

Mendon leaned back in his seat, grateful for the change of subject. It was completely inappropriate to discuss the private life of two esteemed colleagues, and he was annoyed at himself for bringing it up in the first place. Besides, Vogel and Winter might have been correct in their dissenting view of the relationship, although Mendon generally had a good instinct for these things.

Minutes went by with discussions about distant relatives, vacations at the famous cliffs on Sumiko V, and about the hytritium deposits on Sigma Erandi. Mendon didn't participate in the casual conversation, but he listened intently as a means of distraction. He wasn't much interested in the subjects they were discussing, but he was fascinated by the way they effortlessly changed from one to the next.

Finally, Vogel looked up from his displays. "Target coordinates ahead, Lieutenant."

Mendon didn't need a second invitation. He had brought up Winter's TRAFA readings on his own sensor display already. Now, he opened a second program, and began a whole new sensor scan. "Search activated."

Silence fell over the cockpit of the *Glendenin*. Only the quiet humming of the engines and frequent signal noises from the shuttle's systems were audible, while the short-range sensors did their important work. Finally, they would determine whether Ensign Winter was on a wild goose chase, or whether there was indeed a remnant of the *U.S.S. Valiant* that had survived all this time out here in the bright red nothingness.

Mendon checked the initial scanner results and realized that it was possible. He realigned the scanners, launching another search. "Initiating scan phase beta."

From the corner of his eye he saw Ensign Winter. The young human stared intently out of the cockpit window, as if he could will the log buoy into existence.

A loud sound suddenly came from the sensor station. Mendon stared at the display.

"Am I hearing what I think I'm hearing, Lieutenant?" Winter asked, excited.

Mendon nodded. "I … I believe so, Ensign. The sensors have found an object. Distance: 3,720 kilometers. Transmitting exact coordinates to helm." Datastreams scrolled across his monitor, and he studied them with growing excitement. "Shape and structural composition seem to indicate that this is indeed an old Starfleet buoy."

"Setting course," Vogel said.

Mendon got up and stood behind the two men at the cockpit controls as Vogel steered the shuttle to the coordinates.

"Here we are," Winter said. "Where are you, little log buoy?"

For several seconds, all of them stared out into the red space that surrounded them, though they saw no sign of their prey yet.

"Five hundred kilometers," Vogel said. "Throttling thrusters."

Mendon narrowed his eyes, surveying their surroundings through the cockpit's front window.

"Approaching coordinates."

Winter was almost bouncing in his seat from excitement. "The signal that TRAFA picked up is definitely getting stronger. I think you can hear it now." He touched a sensor button, and suddenly a quiet, rhythmic beep mixed with static noises came from over the shuttle's speakers. "That's it! An emergency log buoy from Starfleet, configuration 2260. No doubt about it."

"There!" Vogel pointed through the window. "I think I can see it."

Mendon focused on the point in the whirling red space that the pilot had indicated.

"Can we lock onto it with our transporter?" Vogel asked.

"I hope so," Mendon said, moving to the transporter controls in the back of the shuttle. He made some adjustments and checked the transporter lock. This procedure was so much more difficult here, being close to the system's sun. He wished that he had brought Chief Wilorn. But he had to make do. A flicker on the console confirmed that a target had been locked onto. He glanced at his colleagues. "Ready?"

Winter grinned. "Have been for hours."

Mendon took a deep breath from his respirator. "Energizing."

A familiar hum filled the cabin, and a familiar column of shimmering light appeared on the platform, which coalesced into an approximately hip-high, rectangular object with a smooth surface, rounded corners, and a metal-gray casing. Several dents that were likely the result of collisions with other objects made it difficult to make out the lettering, but a closer inspection revealed the following:

U.S.S. VALIANT NCC-1709.

"Bingo," Winter said.

Mendon actually forgot the nebula and its dangers for a brief moment.

All they could see on the bridge's main screen was staticky chaos. Sighing, Captain Adams rose from his command chair, looking from the distorted mess of colors and streaks to Ensign Winter at the comm console. Two hours had passed since the *Glendenin*'s return from its successful hunt. His tension grew with every passing minute. "Still no luck, Ensign?"

Winter stood at his station. The young man was extremely focused, and his fingers moved over the console keys that no one else could handle as well as he did. "Give me another moment, sir. The buoy obviously took more damage out there than it could handle. I'm trying to compensate, but it's more difficult than I had hoped."

Adams nodded confidently, although he didn't feel like that at all. "We're relying on you, Mr. Winter."

He went over to Roaas, who stood next to Jassat ak Namur at conn. The Caitian had also turned his back on the recording on the main screen that refused to start.

"I guess we've run out of luck," Adams said quietly.

Roaas shook his head almost imperceptibly. "Keep the faith, Captain. Winter does."

"So far." Adams chided himself for his pessimism. Roaas was right. Finding the buoy was a breakthrough, no matter what information was stored in it, or whether they succeeded in accessing it. After one hundred and twenty-one years this was finally a trace of the *Valiant*. That in itself had been worth all the effort—and if Winter was unable to access the buoy's data, the Federation had plenty of specialists who would be able to take a crack at it after their return home. Even if Winter failed, the heritage of the *Valiant* needn't be lost.

But we need that information now, dammit! The Valiant's *fate could be of vital significance to our mission. It won't do us much good if we don't find out until later.*

"Careful, Captain," Roaas whispered. "Are you coming

under the influence of the radiation?"

Adams winced. His eyes widened, and he stared at his second-in-command, both questioning and angry.

"Your face," Roaas answered the unspoken question. "I can see how much the situation frustrates you. And the Richard Adams I know wouldn't be provoked by something like that. So that must be the strange influence that's all over the cluster, and not you."

Adams was mortified. Could that be true? Of course it could. No one was immune to this mysterious radiation, not even he. But he could not afford to let it impair him. The mission needed a leader with a clear head.

"Thank you, Commander." Adams took a deep breath, chasing the fury away. He succeeded, albeit with more effort than usually required. "If it happens again …"

"I'll be here," the Caitian said with reassuring confidence.

Adams sincerely hoped so.

"Sir," Winter said, "I believe I've got it. I can play at least one of the stored log entries. If I read this correctly, it should be the last one they entered."

Which could be the most interesting, Adams thought, and the tension returned. "Good work, Mr. Winter." Out of the corner of his eye he saw the door to the turbolift open. Ambassador Rozhenko and Doctor Barai entered the bridge. Their timing, he thought, was impeccable.

He turned toward the main viewer. "On screen."

"Playing recording … now," said Winter.

And the gates to insanity opened before their eyes.

"Help us!" a blonde woman shrieked into the camera. Panic flickered in her eyes. Her hair was disheveled, her

face blood-smeared, and her blue uniform was in shreds. *"They're all going mad! They're killing each other!"*

Behind her, some sort of guttural scream could be heard, as if someone had released a horde of wild animals. Suddenly, a report from an old projectile weapon shook the room, and the blonde woman ducked out of sight. Apparently, she was on the bridge. But what was going on had nothing to do with the normal business of a command center on a Starfleet spaceship. Wall monitors had been smashed, steam rose from consoles, and red blood was splashed all over the turbolift door in the back of the bridge. Most of the light panels had been damaged, so it was hard to make out details, though that was something of a blessing given the carnage.

Several figures were wrestling as if they wanted to kill each other. A blond man wearing a yellow uniform stood on the captain's chair, his legs spread, and wielded something that looked surprisingly like an archaic shotgun.

"You won't get my ship, you bastards!" he shouted at two security officers who were clearly attempting to reach him.

"Calm down, Edwards," one of the men yelled back. *"We don't want to hurt you."*

"I do," the man next to him—a dark-skinned giant with curly hair—announced. *"He slept with my sister. I'm going to wring his neck. I should have done that ages ago."* He reached out with his enormous hands, but Edwards fired his shotgun. The security officer was thrown backward in a shower of blood and entrails.

The blonde woman reappeared. The recording was obviously made by one of the few remaining functional bridge cameras. Hectically, she glanced around. *"None of us will make it out of here,"* she whispered, leaning forward.

Tears welled up in her eyes. *"We're all going to die. Damn the captain for bringing us here. And damn the slit-eyed bitch Nozawa for talking him into that landing party to the ruins."*

A man jumped into the image from the left. His uniform top was half charred, as if he'd been lying on a burning console. His face showed blatant lust. *"Come here, Green! We're not done yet."*

The blonde woman screamed. *"Schwartz! You were dead!"*

"You're wrong, sweetheart." He laughed, grabbing her small shoulders. For a moment, they wrestled in front of the camera. Suddenly, the air shimmered. The man called Schwartz cramped, his body glowed red, and then he disintegrated.

Green raised her left hand, staring at the phaser she held. Disgusted, she threw it away. Finally, she turned back to the camera. Behind her, Edwards had just killed his second opponent. Now he jumped with one leap from the command chair to conn.

"I'm going to eject the log buoy," Green said hastily. *"As a warning to all ships out there. Don't ever come here, or you're dead. You're dead!"*

Suddenly, a howling that sounded like overloading engines started. The bridge was shaking and shuddering. On the bridge's monitor that was visible on the right edge of the screen, the planet's surface seemed to grow.

"Yeeeessss!" Edwards shouted feverishly. *"You won't get my ship! None of you. Over my dead body!"*

Green put a hand over her mouth and started crying. *"I'm so sorry, mummy. I should have listened to you. I love you."*

Behind her, Edwards screamed triumphantly. Green's hand came forward, pressing a button.

The screen went dark.

26
NOVEMBER 25, 2385

U.S.S. Prometheus

The silence in the conference room was almost palpable after the log buoy's last entry had been played. Ensign Melissa Green's last words had made a devastating impression. Lenissa zh'Thiin sat on the right side of the long conference table, glancing through the room. She saw only horrified faces. Mendon blinked frantically, Kirk had involuntarily clenched her fists, resting them on the table, Counselor Courmont was pale, and Geron and Ambassador Rozhenko stared at the floor.

Spock and Roaas, who sat next to each other across from zh'Thiin, were the only inscrutable ones. Though, to be fair, the same could be said for the Klingons. The four officers from the *Bortas* didn't give off any sense of empathy, as far as zh'Thiin was concerned. Nuk, the stout chief engineer, seemed to have slept through the recording. Next to him, Rooth calmly stroked his beard. L'emka was obviously seething and tried in vain to establish eye contact with Spock. As for Kromm, he was shaking his head contemptuously. "Pathetic *nuch*. And that was the elite from Starfleet's past days of glory? Drooling men and whining women? I'm astounded that you ever won a battle against Klingon ships."

Adams stared at his counterpart incredulously. "Surely, Captain, you can see that the crew was no longer in control of themselves! We shouldn't pass judgment on them, we should regard their fate as a warning."

Kromm spat. His eyes sparkled belligerently when he looked at Adams. "Surely, *Captain*, you do not believe that Klingon warriors would be so susceptible to this mythical power of yours."

Adams snorted scornfully. "Don't overestimate yourself, Kromm. Not you, of all people."

The Klingon jutted his chin forward, glowering. "And what is *that* supposed to mean?"

Adams smiled viciously. "Oh, believe me, Kromm, there is a great deal I could say about you, especially after everything you've done during the past few days."

"That's enough!" Commander Roaas got up. Leaning forward, he rested his hands on the table. His gaze went from one person to the next. "Verbal jabs won't get us anywhere. They would only be the first step toward suffering the same fate as the *Valiant*."

Captain Adams nodded gratefully. Apparently, it took quite an effort to push his anger aside, because he seemed extremely focused for a moment. Finally, he started speaking again, much more calmly than before. "Doctor, Counselor, what do you think of what we've just witnessed?"

Courmont sighed quietly. "Well, sir, it's obvious that some form of madness had befallen the entire crew of the *Valiant*. Extreme violence, definite signs of paranoia, aggressively enhanced libido … It seems to me that this is some kind of mass psychosis that enhances predominantly destructive emotions. Males seem to be more receptive than females. The extreme degree of the psychosis is extraordinary. The *Valiant*'s crew were apparently stricken so suddenly that they weren't able to send a regular report to Starfleet.

Yeoman Green's message can definitely not be classed as a regular log entry."

Adams folded his hands in his lap. "I was under the same impression. And am I the only one wondering where in the world that shotgun came from?"

"No sir," zh'Thiin said, shaking her head. "No, you're not. But more importantly, we're here now, not a hundred years ago, and we're *much* less affected by this exotic radiation, if it's the same thing that struck the *Valiant*. Right? Even the Renao are nowhere near *that* irrational. How does that make any sense?"

"The effects of the radiation are individually different," Geron said. "At least that's one working theory, which is supported by the initial results of my investigations conducted on the captured Renao and affected crew members. Also, there are one hundred years between the *Valiant*'s crash and us. Maybe the radiation has changed since then. And lastly, we don't have any guarantees that we won't suffer from a similar madness soon."

The captain turned to the chief engineer. "I was hoping *you* might be able to guarantee that, Commander Kirk."

Jenna sighed. A small pile of padds was in front of her on the table, and there were dark bags under her eyes. "We're working on it, sir. This radiation is extremely difficult to isolate. It's still just guesswork more than it is definite readings. Our experiments with the shield modulators are accordingly difficult."

"So it's impossible to use the shields against the radiation?"

"I didn't say that, sir," Kirk replied snappishly. Like Adams, she was struggling to keep her anger at bay. And like him, she seemed to understand that it was based solely on the radiation, for all the good that did. "We're working on it."

The captain nodded. "Work faster, Commander. We need that defense more than ever."

"Aye, sir."

"Captain," Geron said, "I just had a thought. Maybe I can help Jenna and Mendon."

"You, Doctor?" Adams sounded skeptical.

"If Commander Kirk lacks definite readings, maybe a telepath is required to evaluate those feelings."

"Not a bad idea," Kirk said. "We can modulate the ship's deflector until you tell us that you sense less psychological influence."

"That's my hope." Adams nodded. "Very well. Go ahead." He turned to the Benzite science officer. "Mr. Mendon, how is the rest of the data storage retrieval coming along?"

The science officer straightened his shoulders. "Sir, worse than we had hoped. As Ensign Winter already indicated, the buoy has sustained considerable damage during its long years in the cluster, and that might be irreparable. We're doing our best to retrieve as much information as possible, but I regret having to inform you that we can't make any predictions regarding the extent of the lost data yet."

Ambassador Spock spoke for the first time since the meeting commenced. "Does the data contain information pertaining to the location where the *Valiant* might have crashed? Yeoman Green's rather dramatic log entry indicates *how* the *Valiant* was destroyed, but not *where*. That knowledge would take us directly to the root of all the fury in this region."

Mendon tilted his head respectfully. "I wish I had something for you, Ambassador, but I must disappoint you. We just know one thing: Haden and his crew were exploring a star system with six planets. And ... erm ..." He hesitated.

"Lieutenant?" Adams prompted.

"That must be an error. According to our information and that of the Astronomical Institute on Onferin, there are only two systems with six planets in the Lembatta Cluster. One of them is Onferin, the other one LC-23, but the *Valiant* did not map either system."

"Meaning?" Rooth asked. The gray-haired Klingon raised a bushy eyebrow. His tone was skeptical. "Are your people too stupid to even count?"

Mendon took a quick breath from his respirator. "Unlikely. My working hypothesis right now is that one of the seven cluster systems with five planets used to have an additional world back then."

"That sounds rather questionable," said L'emka. "For decades, we have had sensor arrays surveying the cluster, just as your Federation has. We might not have been looking for your precious *Valiant*, but we've been observant, nonetheless. Even if the radiation prevents exact observations, an event such as the destruction of a planet would not have gone unnoticed." She looked at Spock.

"That is indeed not very likely," the ambassador said. "Especially since such a destruction would have left distinct remains as well as gravitational shifts within the cluster."

"Unless ..." L'emka swiveled around in her chair, staring out of the window pensively.

"Commander?" Spock said when she didn't finish her sentence. "Please share your thoughts with us."

The Klingon woman turned back to Adams. "Sir, is the Renao of yours aboard this ship?"

"Lieutenant ak Namur? Of course."

"Summon him."

Adams seemed a little surprised that she so casually seemed to issue an order, but he nonetheless didn't hesitate. "Adams to ak Namur."

"Ak Namur here, sir."

"Lieutenant, we need you in the conference room."

"Understood, Captain. I'm on my way."

"What are you getting at, Commander?" Kromm asked his second-in-command.

Zh'Thiin looked at them and could practically feel the tension between them. There was obviously a lot of bad blood between captain and first officer.

"Iad," L'emka said.

Spock raised an eyebrow. "Fascinating. You believe that the *Valiant* crashed on the very world that even the Renao have been searching for in vain since they first embarked on space travel? The world that the modern Renao deem to be a myth?"

L'emka nodded. "Precisely. But is it really just a myth? The captain said recently that Iad is frequently mentioned whenever we encounter the fanatics. There seems to be a connection between the madness and Iad."

"Still, the planet is nowhere to be seen," Rooth said. "And we don't have any clues about its destruction. If it really did exist, it simply ... vanished."

Spock pointedly looked at the *Bortas'* security chief.

Rooth shook his head and laughed. "By Kahless, are you seriously trying to tell me that Iad has become invisible? Ambassador, I always thought that Vulcans didn't make jokes."

"We do not, Commander, as a general rule. But just because an explanation sounds peculiar, it should not automatically be dismissed. I have been traveling through space for more than one hundred and thirty years, and I can assure you, I have

seen much stranger phenomena than a disappearing planet."
He faced Adams. "We know about an exotic radiation and
assume its source to be somewhere beyond Bharatrum. We
have the information from the log buoy, according to which
the *Valiant* crashed on one of the cluster worlds. We have also
seen the paranoid, aggressive madness that is very similar
to the mental state of the Purifying Flame. And Iad plays an
important role with the Flame."

"That's an awful lot of puzzle pieces," zh'Thiin said.

Spock nodded. "Absolutely, Commander. And I believe
they are beginning to form a picture."

The door hissed open, and Jassat appeared in the
doorway. The Renao wore his uniform, and the gold jewelry
typical of his species. He looked concerned. "Reporting as
ordered, Captain."

"Sit down, Lieutenant," Adams said. "We would like to
talk to you. About …"

"About Iad, sir?" Jassat interrupted him.

Surprised, Adams looked at him before nodding.

"You're not the only ones," the Renao said, settling into
a chair.

"What do you mean?" L'emka asked.

"Down in sickbay." Jassat looked at Geron Barai, who
nodded knowingly. "Alai ak Yldrou has been talking about
nothing else for hours. She's delirious, that much is obvious,
but she keeps constantly referring to the innermost sphere,
and to the Son of the Ancient Reds and his blazing fire. My
former friends also mentioned the Son back on Onferin."

"Because she's a member of the Purifying Flame," said
Kromm. "That phrasing is typical of them."

"Maybe," Jassat said. "But perhaps they refer to more
than that."

"I have the same suspicion," L'emka said. She ignored the angry look coming from Kromm. "I have spent quite some time with Evvyk ak Busal and Moadas ak Lavoor in the past few days."

Jassat gaped. "They're … alive?"

Zh'Thiin winced. No one had informed the young Renao that his childhood friends weren't dead. It had obviously slipped everyone's mind in the heat of the moment. It pained her to see the anguish on his face, and she felt ashamed.

"They are in moderate health, given the circumstances," L'emka said, facing Jassat. "They react to the cluster in much the same manner as Doctor Barai's patients."

Jassat swallowed. "Are they receiving medical treatment?"

"Yes," Spock said. "Do not be concerned, Lieutenant. They are now being well looked after."

Zh'Thiin couldn't help but admire the old ambassador. Anyone else would have given Kromm a reproachful side-glance, or would have mentioned Kromm's role in the imprisonment of the Renao aboard the *Bortas*. Spock, apparently, didn't care much for such recriminations, be they justified or not.

Adams nodded. "I give you my word of honor, Jassat." He briefly glanced at Kromm.

"And I mine," L'emka added.

"I want to see them." Jassat looked at the captain. "May I see them?"

"Later," Adams said. "Right now, we have more urgent matters to discuss. Commander?"

L'emka continued her report. "Evvyk babbled considerably in her delirium, and much of it was about Iad."

"It is the same with Alai," Jassat said quietly.

The Klingon woman nodded. "What do you know

about Iad, Lieutenant ak Namur? You come from here. Your knowledge should surely surpass ours."

"Not much, I'm afraid. Iad has always been a fairy tale for me, nothing more. A fantasy."

"Tell us," Adams said. "And Commander L'emka, you should feel free to contribute anything from Evvyk ak Busal that might help—no matter how surreal or bizarre it might sound."

Leaning forward, Jassat rested his slender forearms on the table and began to narrate.

The stellar cartography lab was located deep in the *Prometheus*'s belly. It was one of the most modern technological facilities on the ship. Visitors entered a circular "island," hovering approximately one meter above the floor inside a spherical room. Owing to embedded holotechnology in the walls, this room could transform into any star system that was stored in the ship's computer. Currently, three people stood on this island; only one of them looked at the holographic three-dimensional Lembatta cluster.

"Fascinating." Looking up from the computer console where he stood, Spock faced Mendon. "Wouldn't you agree?"

The Benzite stood at a second console next to Spock. "Absolutely. A very impressive legend."

"One that becomes increasingly believable with every new puzzle piece that this mission brings to light," said Ambassador Rozhenko, the third person in the room. Pensively, he regarded the holographic display of the region's three-dimensional map. "Lieutenant ak Namur's childhood fairy tale may just be the key to the mystery surrounding the Lembatta Cluster."

"It would explain the *Valiant*'s fate," Mendon said. "At least to some extent."

After the mission briefing with the two captains, Spock, Rozhenko, and Mendon had withdrawn to this lab in order to find out more about Iad. Using the details that Jassat, Commander L'emka, and the four Renao in medical care had provided, and accessing several files with information about the local lore that Shamar ak Mousal—the president of the Renao Home Spheres—had made available from Onferin, they had successfully developed something like a chronology of Iad. The longer Spock studied it, the more it fascinated him. Of course, a large portion of it was speculative. It was based on the statements of mentally and physically deranged people, on legends, and countless theories. That didn't change the fact that it all seemed to add up to something. It was simply a matter of determining what.

"Let's assume," Rozhenko started, facing his two colleagues, "that all Renao come from Iad, as Councilor ak Mousal indicated when we visited Onferin."

"He did initially indicate it but he then promptly reversed his comment," said Spock. "His exact words when I asked him to elaborate were that Iad was an idea."

Rozhenko nodded. "But he also acknowledged that his people have been living on Onferin for a maximum of ten millennia. There are no archaeological finds older than that, and there is no way that the Renao originated on Onferin or on any of the other worlds where they now live. Our away teams on Lhoeel, Xhehenem, and Bharatrum have verified that."

"Indeed." Spock pensively folded his hands in front of his face. "Ten thousand years ago—according to ak Mousal and the legends that Lieutenant ak Namur remembers—the so-called *transfer* occurred, when they were relocated to Onferin."

"That poses the question, how that came about," said Mendon.

Rozhenko moved closer to the rectangular computer console. Spock stepped aside, and the Klingon's hands flew over the keys. The holographic environment changed. So far, the "island" had hovered above Bharatrum; now the display zoomed out.

Suddenly, Spock saw all the systems of the Lembatta Cluster in front of his eyes. Next to the respective celestial bodies, their names given to them both by the Federation and the Renao were displayed. Spock noticed that some suns had different names from the planets where the Renao lived; for example, Onferin, which orbited the star Aoul or LC-4. In the center, however, were at least two systems where the suns had the same names as the planets that the Renao had later colonized: Bharatrum and Acina. The reason for that was unknown.

Rozhenko programmed a green circle into the Lembatta Cluster's center—a shapeless variable—floating somewhere between LC-13, LC-19, LC-20, and LC-21.

"Iad," he said. "We don't know where this world once used to be, nor whether it even existed, but let's assume it is real for now. If so, the Renao come from Iad. They all used to live there until about ten thousand years ago when ... they had visitors."

A red dot appeared next to the green pseudo-planet, much smaller than the planet, but its meaning was clear.

"The Son of the Ancient Reds." Spock nodded. "An alien being or civilization appeared, interfering actively with the development of the early Renao, resettling them."

"One might interpret the fever fantasies of the Renao in sickbay that way, yes." Stepping back, Rozhenko stared skeptically at the holographic display, resting his hands on his hips. "And as Mr. ak Namur's childhood stories tell us, a stranger once came down from the red suns to herd the Renao people into darkness. This legendary figure and the mysterious Son of the Ancient Reds might be one and the same entity."

Again, the half-Vulcan nodded. "A plausible theory. But why? What was this Son attempting to achieve? What were his intentions?"

Mendon said, "I would say not good ones. A thousand years of darkness are not really the best of hospitality gifts. Isn't that how the legend continued?"

The corners of Rozhenko's mouth twitched. "Let's not forget the second figure from ak Namur's tales: the White Guardian." Again, he touched the console. Next to the red dot, a white dot of similar size appeared.

"A classic figure from many mythologies: the shining light to oppose the bringer of darkness."

"The Guardian also came to Iad, challenging the Red Son," Mendon said. "A terrible, violent battle ensued."

"But the Guardian failed to defeat the Son." Rozhenko pointed at the red dot in between the stars. "Instead, he locked him up in a vault beyond time—in a place where he would never be able to bring misfortune to the people of the Renao ever again." He gave a voice command, and the computer melted the red dot with the green circle, and only the white dot remained in the vastness.

Spock raised an eyebrow. "Of course. The Son's prison is Iad."

"The intruder couldn't be driven away," Mendon said. "So instead, the Guardian drove away his victims: the Renao. In order to protect them from the stranger, he took them to other worlds within the system. And they remained there until today."

"And to ensure that they would give Iad a wide berth in future," Rozhenko continued, "the Guardian made the planet simply disappear."

"Oh well," Mendon said. "Now we have a wonderful legend to support my theory that there had been six planets instead of five in one of the systems. But the question remains: Where is Iad? Where did the *Valiant* crash? Where is the source of the radiation that drives everyone mad? And if this Son is the cause of the radiation, why do we feel its effects when this Son has been locked up in a vault? Shouldn't that have solved at least this problem?"

"Those are all excellent questions, Commander Mendon," said Spock. Deep in thought, he stared at nothing. "It is to be hoped that we may answer them with dispatch."

The *Prometheus* had two different engine rooms. The larger one was capable of splitting into two smaller sections along with the hull section. Jenna Kirk and Rooth both stood in this engine room, brooding.

"Are these schematics for the *Scorpions*?" the Klingon security chief asked. He pointed at one of the monitors. Kirk had begun to analyze the data rods that Klarn had found in the ruins of Bosoon. Unlike those of Xhehenem, which had been written off completely by now, the new ones turned out to be quite useful.

Kirk's hands moved over the interface. "Looks like it."

They had found ship schematics, analyses of hull structures, information about the solar-jump technology ... very little of what she found here was new to her. Kirk knew the structure of the rebuilt *Scorpion* attack fighters, not least because of the wreckage they had found at Starbase 91. As far as the solar-jump engines were concerned, Onferin's industrial minister had provided them with all information they required—voluntarily.

"They've got a fleet," Rooth said as he scrutinized the information. "Or they're building one. One way or another, Commander, I can't help but feel that everything that has happened so far is only the beginning."

Kirk looked at the Klingon security chief. If he was right, the powers of the quadrant were facing an attack that would easily dwarf the incidents on Starbase 91, Tika IV, Cestus III, and Korinar.

The engineer swallowed hard, before tapping her combadge. "Kirk to Adams."

"Go ahead, Jenna."

"Sir, I believe we have a problem. Lieutenant Rooth and I surmise that the Purifying Flame has or is working on an entire fleet of attack ships. These would probably be similar to those ships that were used at Starbase 91: small, fast, and lethal."

There was a pause. Kirk almost sensed the horror that had gripped Adams upon hearing these words.

"Are you able to locate this fleet, Commander? Do you know where the Flame is working on it?"

Iad, thought Kirk, but that was nonsense. Or was it? Iad didn't exist.

She looked up at Rooth, but he shook his head.

"I'm afraid not, sir," Kirk said. "Your guess is as good as ours."

Suddenly, a white icon appeared on the edge of the monitor.

"Maybe I can help you out, Commander—at least, I hope I

can," said Adams. *"We just forwarded a starchart to you that Ensign Winter calculated by analyzing the flight data from the Valiant buoy."*

Kirk frowned, opening the file by tapping the icon. A map appeared immediately on her display. A red line was drawn from the place where they had discovered the buoy near Bharatrum further into the center of the cluster. It ended in system LC-13.

"That's the distance the *Valiant* buoy covered before ending up here?" the engineer asked.

"Mr. Winter is hopeful that it's much more than that," her captain said. *"Commander, you might be looking at the route to Iad!"*

27
NOVEMBER 25, 2385

I.K.S. Bortas

"Don't you have anything better to do, Lieutenant?" Sighing, Rooth rubbed his face with his calloused hand. Sometimes, he felt as if he was talking in circles. "Do you really have to waste everyone's time with *this?*"

"Sir?" Lieutenant Klarn straightened his shoulders, looking at Rooth inquisitively. His gaze wandered to the other two people whom the security chief had summoned to his office: Commander L'emka and Ambassador Spock. Their presence seemed to disconcert him. "How exactly am I wasting your time?"

Rooth folded his hands in front of his belly, leaning back in his chair. Silently, he examined the lieutenant. "We're almost at war, Klarn. We are on the cusp of either a historic reconnaissance mission or of a bloody conquering expedition. Yet you continue to expend energy and thought on this pathetic Rantal?"

It seemed like half an eternity to Rooth, since he and Nuk had found the ill-treated *bekk* in the engine-room maintenance tubes. But it had just been four very eventful days. Only now, during the calm before the gathering storm, did Rooth at last find the time to take care of this unfinished business.

"Raspin?" Klarn slumped his shoulders, shaking his head scornfully. "Sir, I can assure you—this white worm is the last thing I'm concerned with right now."

"Oh, really?" L'emka snapped at him. She stood behind Rooth's chair next to Spock. But unlike the Federation diplomat who followed proceedings with an inscrutable face, the first officer didn't hide her contempt for Klarn. "And how do you explain his injuries? The state his quarters are in? That *jeghpu'wI'* hasn't left medical bay for days because of his great fright. You have traumatized our best ops officer beyond his ability to perform his duty!"

The lieutenant was visibly perplexed. "What are you talking about? What injuries?"

"We all know how little you think of Raspin," Rooth said. "You've stood here in front of me often enough to complain about him."

"Because he's a disgrace to our ship. And a danger!"

L'emka snorted. "You're the only danger here. Just ask the two Renao next to Raspin in the medical bay."

"Above all else, the *bekk* is a member of this crew," Rooth said. "And as such we need him, especially now."

This time, Klarn snorted. Fury stood in his eyes. "It's a sad state of affairs when the *Bortas* 'needs' an inferior being … sir."

Rooth was no longer the short-tempered warrior he had been in his youth. Since he had met the great Kahless fifteen years ago, he had realized that true strength and wisdom derived from sobriety. The young man who had always been hell-bent on getting his own way had turned into a calm strategist who reached his goals by other means—better means, as far as he was concerned.

But at this moment, the young hothead returned, and he hammered his fist on the desk, almost toppling his computer monitor. "You know exactly what I mean, Klarn! Raspin may be *jeghpu'wI'*, but as L'emka said, he's an excellent ops officer. And if we wish to honor the Empire and finish the task at hand successfully, we need him. More fundamentally, we must stand together, be strong together." He rose, resting his big hands on his hips. His reproachful gaze was fixed on Klarn. "You, Lieutenant, attacked a *bekk* and vandalized his quarters during a critical phase of this mission. You not only dishonor your rank and position, but also your ship. It's not Raspin who's the saboteur of this journey, as you have claimed so fervently for weeks, it's you, Klarn. And therefore …"

Suddenly, Ambassador Spock came forward and stood next to the security chief. Rooth was so surprised that he fell silent in the middle of his sentence. Spock wore a gray jacket and matching pants. His silver-and-black hair shimmered in the light that shone down from the ceiling, and the deep wrinkles in his face bore witness to the experience he had gained while traveling among the stars for more than a century.

"I believe you are wrong, Lieutenant Rooth," he said gently, raising an eyebrow. "I believe Lieutenant Klarn is not responsible for *Bekk* Raspin's condition."

"How sad that a Vulcan knows me better than my crewmates." Klarn crossed his arms belligerently in front of his chest.

Rooth hesitated. "Ambassador?" Far be it from him to chide a living legend, but Spock obviously didn't know what he was saying.

"Before you pass judgment on Klarn," Spock said, "I wish to speak Raspin."

Incredulously, Rooth's eyes widened. Klarn also looked at the Vulcan as if he had lost his mind.

However, the ambassador's equanimity had served to remind Rooth of his own calmness. The tantrum he had indulged in now seemed disgraceful to him. "Very well, Ambassador, you shall get your wish." Rooth glowered at Klarn. "You stay at the ready, understood? As soon as I need you, I'll see you again right here!"

"Absolutely, Lieutenant Rooth," Klarn said mockingly, a belligerent glint in his eye. "We need to stand together, after all, don't we?" With these words, he turned on his heel and left Rooth's office.

L'emka led the way to the medical bay. The ward was small, windowless, and near the main cargo holds. They didn't have far to go, but what should have been a simple conversation with Klarn had turned into something much more complicated and time-consuming. He wondered if his inquiry to Klarn about having anything better to do should have been directed at himself.

But Rooth hated loose ends, and he had postponed dealing with the Rantal's abuse for too long already. Of course, he was only dealing with it now because Ambassador Spock insisted, expressing a peculiar interest in Raspin's fate. Since Spock was an honored guest, as well as a great figure of Klingon history, Rooth had no choice but to accede to his wishes.

Upon reaching the medical bay, they learned that Raspin had returned to his quarters at his own request. The medical staff, who seemed relieved no longer to have Raspin in their care, believed that the Rantal had been scared of the two Renao.

"A constructive coincidence," Spock said, "as I wish to inspect his quarters. I assume they have not been cleaned since the attack?"

"I shouldn't think so," Rooth said, leading the way to Raspin's small abode. "No one will clean up after *jeghpu'wI'*."

The state of the cabin where the *bekk* with the snow-white skin lived had indeed not changed at all since Rooth had been here last: dried blood on the walls, traces of feces, smashed furniture. Raspin sat in the back corner of the room, his knees drawn up to his chest, watching the three newcomers with big black eyes.

"Did anyone scan this room?" Spock inquired. He stood next to the Rantal, pointing at the walls.

Rooth swallowed. "I'm afraid not, Ambassador," he admitted, exchanging a rueful look with L'emka, who also hadn't thought of that. "The events of the past few days have kept us too busy to spend much time on a—"

Spock finished Rooth's sentence with a slight tinge of disdain. "A *jeghpu'wI'*, a conquered person." He pulled a Starfleet tricorder from his clothing, pointing it at the smudgy walls. "I thought as much. This is not blood from a Rantal. And the feces come from a Klingon, not from him."

"Klarn!" Rooth clenched his fists. "That dishonorable runt has lied to me for the last time!"

Spock raised one hand. "A moment, Lieutenant." He turned to the cowering *bekk*. "Do not be afraid, Raspin. We are here as friends." He showed the tricorder display to the Rantal. "Do you understand that? I certainly can do so. And I believe I know why you did it."

Rooth hesitated. "He did what?" He crouched next to Spock, who was kneeling before the Rantal. "What are you talking about, Ambassador?"

"About hatred," Spock said quietly, and for a brief moment, Rooth believed he heard deep regret in his voice. "We have, it seems, spoken of little else for weeks."

Spock asked L'emka to sit with the *bekk*. He rose and pulled Rooth to the other side of the tiny room, where he showed him his tricorder display. "These are medical scans that your sickbay made of Raspin when you had him admitted. I asked your medical staff to make them available for our investigation. If you look at the broken bones, and at the scratches here ..."

Helpless, Rooth shook his head. "I'm afraid my knowledge of Rantal biology is extremely limited."

"An unfortunate deficiency," Spock said. "Otherwise, you might have noticed what surprised me while looking at these files ... and horrified me. Lieutenant Klarn may have devastated your ops officer's quarters. *Bekk* Raspin's injuries, however, are self-inflicted."

Rooth stared at the ambassador incredulously.

L'emka's eyes also widened. "What? With all due respect, Ambassador, that is nonsense. Why would he do such a thing?"

"Self-loathing, Commander," Spock said. He went back to the Rantal and gazed into the eyes of the hairless creature. "That is what happened, is it not? You have been on board the *Bortas* for several months, and have been made to feel unwelcome for all that time?"

Raspin silently stared at Spock, and didn't move a muscle. His chest rose and fell with each breath.

"Right from the beginning, I'm almost certain of it," Spock said. "It might surprise you to know, *Bekk*, that I am intimately familiar with the feeling, and have been since I was a child. I know the looks that being the only person who is different from everyone around him will provoke. I know the skepticism, the fear, and the anger. Many sentient beings fear what they do not know, Raspin, as regrettable as that may be. And some even allow this fear to dictate their actions." He pointed at the smashed furniture, the dirt on the walls—and finally at Raspin himself. "Some are even worn down by it."

Rooth watched this moment, equally fascinated and irritated. Some kind of nonverbal exchange between the ambassador and the *jeghpu'wI'* seemed to take place.

Spock continued: "You have been called unworthy so many times that you eventually looked upon yourself as unworthy. This ship has taught you to despise yourself the way the Klingons on board despise you."

L'emka exchanged a glance with Rooth, before looking at Spock. "He did it himself? All these injuries … out of self-loathing?"

"He did what everyone else did," the ambassador explained with a grave, low voice. "He hates the *jeghpu'wI'*. And hatred—as we have witnessed many times during this mission—breeds violence. Sometimes external, sometimes internal."

This theory was absurd and plausible in equal measure, but one look into the Rantal's black eyes made Rooth realize that it was true. "Very well, *Bekk*," he asked the ops officer. "What do you want?"

The Rantal swallowed and then spoke in a whisper. "Take my post."

It was the first time that Rooth heard Raspin's voice. As far as he knew, it was the first time that the Rantal had spoken at all since he had been aboard the *Bortas*. And although he had only said a few words, they opened Rooth's eyes. All this *jeghpu'wI'*, who was despised by everyone and who had been openly accused of sabotage by Klarn, wanted to do was his duty, just like every warrior on this ship. He wanted to be a part of the crew, and his talent at ops had proven that he had the required expertise.

"Integration, Lieutenant," said Spock, looking up to Rooth. "That is the solution. Infinite Diversity in Infinite

Combinations. The strength that derives from acceptance, respect, and candor." He got up and went to the door, before turning back to the two Klingons. "Far be it from me to meddle in your ship's internal affairs. But should you wish to take my advice, I would urgently recommend having *Bekk* Raspin report to his station immediately. I guarantee that it will be to everyone's benefit."

U.S.S. Prometheus, en route to LC-13

Moba stood unhappily behind his counter in the Starboard 8. The bartender had a reputation for being unwaveringly cheerful, so this unhappiness was uncharacteristic to say the least. His eccentric drink creations and his hilarious *bon mots* from his homeworld of Bolarus were as integral a part of the *Prometheus* crew's everyday life as multi-vector missions or the EMH wandering through the corridors.

But Moba had been struggling for days to remain his cheerful self.

This mission in the Lembatta Cluster was troubling him. Part of it was the cluster itself. The deeper they advanced, the more eerie the view outside the windows on the other side of the counter became. The cluster's heart seemed to be one giant mass of red stellar matter. Space itself, the vast blackness dotted with stars, had made way for the foreboding crimson mist. At warp speed, the red turned into psychedelic streaks, reminiscent of human blood streaming past the windows—not an uplifting view by any stretch of the imagination.

Moba loved space. Looking at the stars always evoked a sense of vastness and transcendence. Now all he felt was trepidation and the irrational anxiety of a swimmer in the open sea who had just remembered that beneath him were thousands of meters of abyss, and that he could neither see nor hear the dangers unless they suddenly surfaced in order to devour him. He had, of course, spoken to Ensign Gupta, the xenobiologist of the *Prometheus*. It was completely unlikely that there were monsters lurking in these red nebulae. But what his head knew and what his gut tried to make him believe were two different things.

Your stomach knows better what it can digest than your head, was an old Bolian idiom with which Moba wholeheartedly agreed.

Even worse than the depressing view from the window was the increasingly irritable atmosphere on board. Laughter had become a rare commodity in the Starboard 8. At best, the patrons were sitting at their tables with grim expressions. There had been several altercations, and that was something that Moba hadn't seen before. It didn't matter to him whether the reason was stupid xenophobia directed at Jassat ak Namur, or this exotic radiation everyone was talking about. His club was meant to be a place of joyfulness, and this gloomy atmosphere depressed him.

Today was worse than ever. Since they had left Bharatrum almost ten hours ago, the Starboard 8 had been deserted. Some enlisted and lower officer ranks had shown up for dinner just after alpha shift had finished. Once they had wolfed down their meals, they had left. Moba hadn't seen any of the higher-ranking officers.

Now the ship's clock showed 1900, and the club was deserted once again. The last two guests, Lieutenant Meyer and Crewman Peshtal-Ynri, had taken their leave ten minutes ago, after finishing their dinner. Moba halfheartedly sorted some glasses behind his counter, watching the door in the hope of new customers. But no one turned up.

Maybe I should close early, he thought. *We're so close to the end of our journey—who needs recreation?*

These phases of increased vigilance occurred occasionally. The *Prometheus* was a battleship after all. Still, the situation was different this time. The danger they were heading toward was vague. Nobody knew what they would be facing—and whether they would be able to fight it.

Moba ran his hand over his bald pate. He felt his blood pulsate beneath his cartilaginous ridge. Inside of him, he felt an unrest that made him feel sick. And then he uttered an order he had never given before: "Computer, close windows."

"Closing windows," the unnervingly calm voice of the *Prometheus* central computer confirmed. The metal plates that were part of the ship's ablative armor slid over the window panes with a quiet grating noise. At the same time, the intensity of the ceiling lamps increased.

Moba lowered his hands, breathing deeply. Without the direct view of the nebula, he could convince himself that it didn't exist. Outside the window covers was the endless space, a black velvet night where a myriad beautiful stars sparkled. "Everything will be alright," Moba said aloud. "It always is. The *Prometheus* has fought plenty of battles and won. Even against the Borg! What kind of danger could be out there that's worse than the Borg?"

He reached under his counter, pulling out a triangular bottle that contained a shimmering, orange liquid: *yobbcha* from his homeworld. Along with Andorian ale, Earth whiskey, and Saurian brandy, Moba considered *yobbcha* to be a cornerstone of any cultivated drinks cabinet. He poured half a glass, raised it, and gulped it down all at once. Moba grimaced, making an unarticulated noise when the alcohol burned its way down his throat. Heedless of Starfleet regulations that expressly forbade the consumption of alcohol by personnel on duty, he permitted himself a second glass. *Yobbcha* was infernal stuff. Another two glasses, and Moba would feel ready to take on the terrorists of the Purifying Flame singlehandedly.

"We're a battleship!" he shouted into the empty club. "Nothing can take on the *Prometheus!* Do you hear me, Lembatta Cluster?"

A yellow panel started blinking at the door, and an acoustic warning signal sounded at the same time.

Yellow alert! Fear struck Moba like a hungry predator. Quickly, he poured another *yobbcha.*

Richard Adams sat in his command chair on the bridge, staring at the main screen. Although beta shift was supposed to be on duty, every member of his senior staff was at their respective post. This part of the mission was more important than any recreational time.

Several minutes ago, they had come out of warp as they were approaching the coordinates that Ensign Winter and the other specialists had extracted from the *Valiant* log buoy. Space around them looked like the antecourt of hell from Dante's *Inferno*. Thick fog prevented them from seeing the stars. The only identifiable celestial body was the vague red-orange disk of a sun straight in front of them. Starfleet records designated the star to be LC-13, while the Renao called it Souhla. On the left side of the screen, strange lightning flickered in the distance. Additionally, a slight image noise was visible all across the screen. That still irritated Adams but *Prometheus* technicians had been unable to filter out all of the cluster's interference.

According to the buoy, six planets orbited the sun. The outer three planets were gas giants. One of them was so big that it showed initial signs of a deuterium-fusion in its core, which would classify it as a brown dwarf. Adams suspected that Mendon would love to investigate a brown dwarf in the gravitational field of a red giant. But right now, only one planet in this system mattered: LC-13-II a.k.a. Iad.

"Captain, this is strange," Sarita Carson said from ops.

Adams looked away from the main screen. "Report, Commander Carson."

"Sir, the sensors pick up an enormous radiation zone near the sun. Diameter is approximately one hundred million kilometers. It's impossible to penetrate it."

Adams rose from his chair, stepping forward. Excitement washed over him. "Is that the source of the exotic radiation we're looking for?"

"Negative, sir. I mean, I don't think so. We haven't picked up that kind of radiation yet anywhere in the cluster."

"What kind of radiation is it?"

"That's the weird thing, Captain, I can't tell you. The computer is incapable of classifying it reliably. I receive permanently fluctuating readings. One minute, it looked like tachyon radiation, and now I see fields of polaron and tetryon radiation. I've never seen anything like it."

The captain turned to the back of the bridge. "Mr. Mendon, can you explain that?"

"I'm sorry, Captain, not at the moment," Mendon said. "I need more data before I can say whether that phenomenon is a radiation zone with multiple sources, or a single source. If it is a single source, it's in a state of hyperphysical fluctuation, where characteristics of various high-level radiation patterns manifest spontaneously, before they vanish again. That would contradict everything that established theories postulate as possible. Highly interesting."

"Are you trying to say that the conditions in the core of the Souhla system are in contrast to the physics of our universe?"

Mendon hesitated. "I hesitate to put it quite like that, sir. Each phenomenon that we discover must inevitably adhere to our universe's laws of physics; anything else would be plain impossible. A phenomenon like this one, which purports pure chaos, does, however, push us to the limits of our currently existing explanatory models."

"Fair enough," Adams said quickly, having neither the time nor the interest to get into such minutiae. "Let's leave the debates about the nature of this radiation zone to the scientists. I just want to know three things: Where is Iad? Where did the *Valiant* crash? And where is the source of the madness?"

"I can't answer these questions yet."

"That's not good enough, Mr. Mendon! It required a lot of effort to get this far, so I want some answers, dammit!"

Adams realized that he had raised his voice more than he had intended to. Squinting, he wiped his face with his hand. *Stay calm, that's the radiation talking.* So far, he had only perceived a subliminal influence, but suddenly he felt an unfamiliar surge of agitation. *Another indication that we must be close to our destination.*

He was just about to touch the intercom key on his armrest to summon Doctor Barai and ask him for a mild sedative, when the physician's voice boomed across the bridge. *"Sickbay to bridge."*

That's what I call telepathy, Adams thought wryly. "Go ahead, Doctor."

"*Captain, I can sense a significant increase of aggression levels everywhere on board. The radiation is having an increasing impact on us as well. I ... I wasn't sure about it before, even doubted it. But now ...*"

"Understood, Doctor." Adams looked up. He understood Barai's doubts very well. It was time to put Kirk's, Mendon's, and Barai's work on the shields to the test. "Red alert. Raise shields. Maybe we can block the radiation that influences us."

"Aye, sir." Roaas at tactical executed the order.

"Doctor Barai, do you sense any changes?"

"*I'm not entirely sure, sir,*" the Betazoid telepath answered. "*The increase of angry emotions occurred slowly, as you can verify yourself. It might take a while for them to subside again.*"

"Understood. Let's hope for the best."

Adams closed the channel before opening shipwide communication. "Attention all decks. This is the captain. We are approaching our destination, which we hope is the source of the Renao's delusional state."

The bridge crew all turned toward him, listening intently: ak Namur, Carson, zh'Thiin, Roaas, Winter, Chell, and Mendon.

"You might have noticed," Adams continued, "that we're also affected the closer we come to the source of this madness. I therefore call upon all of you to keep calm, and to remember that every angry thought that comes into your mind does not come from within you, but from an external influence. Remember your training and your duties as Starfleet officers— and that your fellow crew members wear this uniform because they are exceptional people. These are unusual circumstances, but I know that I can rely on you. Adams out."

He glanced at his bridge crew, establishing eye contact with every one of them in turn. They all knew what was at stake. Failure was not an option. Everyone seemed keen on doing their part to prevent that from happening.

Adams nodded, satisfied. "As you were. Let's find Iad, so we can unravel this damn mystery."

"Sir, that might be more difficult than anticipated," Mendon said.

"What do you mean?"

"I have checked the system and compared the data with that of the *Valiant*. The good news is that we're in the right system. The charted planets match, insofar as we're able to ascertain from the log buoy's data fragments. The bad news is that LC-13-II is missing. That should be Iad. And the way things look that planet is in the radiation zone ahead of us."

"The vanished planet," Carson muttered.

"That's right," said Mendon. "Which explains, by the way, why only five planets are charted in the LC-13 system of the Renao starmaps. The antiquated sensors aboard their explorer ships were unable to process the radiation zone."

Adams raised his eyebrows. "You're telling me that our sensors aren't any better, either?"

The Benzite scientist straightened his back. "No, Captain, not at all."

"Glad to hear it. Work with Commander Carson and Commander Kirk, and find a way to locate the planet."

"Right away, sir."

Settling back into his command chair, Adams said, "Mr. ak Namur, one-quarter impulse. Let's approach this radiation with all due caution."

"Aye, sir." The young Renao tapped on his console.

Winter turned around at his communication station on the port side. "Captain, the *Bortas* is hailing us. It's Captain Kromm. He sounds … agitated."

In spite of himself, Adams clenched his hands to fists. This Klingon jackass was really getting on his nerves. The Klingons were only guests in this part of space. The Federation was calling the shots ... Adams was calling the shots. And if Kromm decided to throw yet another temper tantrum, Adams would for damn sure put him in his place.

No! That's not me. We are being influenced. I need to stay in control. He wished that Spock was still aboard. If anyone knew how to keep his mind clear and focused, it was him.

The captain straightened. "On screen, Mr. Winter."

"Captain!" Kromm bellowed as soon as his face was on the screen. *"Are your people completely incompetent?"*

"What do you want, Kromm?" Adams replied with a stony face. In the background, he noticed L'emka and Spock. The Klingon first officer seemed irritated by Kromm's outburst, and the Vulcan's face was calm, as always.

"Your communications officer claims he's found the way to Iad. And now we're here, and there's nothing but gas giants and dead pieces of rock. Not a hint of a world with life-supporting conditions."

Adams turned to Spock, who was standing just behind Kromm. "Ambassador, no doubt the radiation zone in the center of the system hasn't escaped your attention."

"Indeed, Captain," replied Spock, stepping forward. He folded his hands in front of his stomach. *"And I have already explained to Captain Kromm that Iad is probably located inside of that zone."*

Kromm snarled. *"How does that help us? Have you forgotten that the red-skins are building an attack fleet? And that zone of which you speak is huge. How are we to find Iad in time?"*

"Captain!" Mendon cried from the back of the bridge. "I believe I have found a solution for our problem."

"Let's hear it," Adams said.

"We will run a program analyzing the incoming data of the passive sensors, and then we apply an automated deflector filter. The deflector dish will serve as an adaptive polarizer. That way, we should be able to come up with a slightly better image of what's inside the radiation zone."

Spock raised an eyebrow. *"Fascinating. But did you consider that there are several layers within that zone, leading to multiple changes of the radiation characteristics?"*

"Could you elaborate on that, Ambassador?" Adams hadn't understood half of the conversation of the two scientists.

"Of course, Captain. The radiation in the zone ahead of us is changing frequencies too quickly for the Prometheus*'s deflector to compensate, even if you use the majority of your computer's capacity to do so."*

"The *Prometheus* has a high-performance computer at its disposal, Ambassador."

"I am aware of that. The problem lies in the processing speed of the deflector dish itself."

Carson spoke up. "What if we used four deflectors instead?"

Adams nodded. "You're suggesting we separate the *Prometheus*?"

"Precisely. That way, we can use the deflectors of the primary hull and those of the upper secondary hull as well. If we then add the *Bortas*, and link all four systems, we should have enough processing capacity to penetrate the chaos."

"Mr. Mendon? Ambassador Spock? Opinions?"

"That should work, Captain," the science officer replied.

"It is definitely worth a try," said Spock.

"Were you planning at any point, Adams, to actually ask my permission to use my vessel's deflector?"

Adams glared at Kromm, rising from his chair. "I don't

like your tone, Captain. And don't forget who's in charge of this operation."

"How could I? You keep reminding me every chance you get." Kromm pointed an accusatory finger at Adams. *"But perhaps we should change that. Empire and Federation citizens alike are murdered, and here we are flying in circles around the Lembatta Cluster, searching for a mythical power that's allegedly behind it all. It would be much more efficient to put the Renao in their place."*

"Last time I checked, we had exhausted that subject above Xhehenem. Do you really want to engage in a pissing contest when we've almost reached our goal? Do I really have to force you to be reasonable?"

"You can't force me to do anything, human!"

Adams took a step toward the main screen. "And you …"

A furry hand grabbed him by the shoulder. "Captain." Roaas had come from the tactical station to stand beside him, regarding him with extreme caution and compassion. "Calm down, please. Remember where we are."

Initially furious about the intervention, Adams whirled at his first officer, intending to give him a piece of his mind, before coming to his senses and realizing that the Caitian was right. *Dammit, this force is insidious.* He slumped his shoulders, exhaling deeply.

"Captain Kromm, please accept my deepest apologies. The influence that has been driving the Renao crazy is tightening its grip on all of us as well. As you know, my officers have been working on a modulation of our shields, hoping to neutralize the psychic energies that Iad is probably emanating. Unfortunately, the results still leave a lot to be desired. But we're hoping for a breakthrough soon. If our efforts are successful, we will send you our results so you can modify the *Bortas* shields as well. Until then, we all should try to remain as calm as possible."

Kromm glared at Adams, and for a moment it seemed as if he was about to respond with another harsh verbal attack, but he seemed taken aback by Adams's humble words. Instead, he nodded tersely, grumbling something unintelligible.

"If you have no objections, I will contact Commander Kirk," Spock said. *"Now that we are all exposed, I might be able to provide some helpful insight as to its nature."*

The captain nodded. "I'd like that very much, Ambassador." Adams trusted the abilities of his crew, but a talented telepath and seasoned scientist like Spock might be helpful in obtaining an even more favorable result. He turned back to Kromm. "We will prepare the program for the adaptive radiation filter and be in touch. It shouldn't take longer than an hour."

"Understood. In the meantime, the Bortas *will circle the radiation zone once. Perhaps we can find something interesting. Kromm out."*

The Klingon's image disappeared and was replaced by the billowing orange fog. In the distance, the flickering of discharging energy increased. It felt as if they were headed toward an enormous storm front. Adams hoped that the *Prometheus* could withstand it.

28
TIME UNKNOWN

Location unknown

Flickering, followed by static noise. Finally, an image: endless rows of black shimmering one-person ships.

Dim light reflects from their hulls and the transparent aluminum of their windows … and from the barrels of their massive disruptor cannons.

Between the ships, which look very similar to Romulan *Scorpion*-class attack fighters, stands a Renao man. He's wearing loose clothing, but his face is clearly visible.

"Is this sufficient for you?" he asks with a harsh voice full of hatred. "Is this sight enough to convince you that we are serious? We're coming. We're coming to make you feel the same pain that you're inflicting on the galaxy. We're coming to put an end to your sacrilege. We're coming so you can feel in your own spheres what it means to sin against harmony. You have brought pain and suffering to space. Countless civilizations are being harmed because you're too blind to see the error of your ways."

He approaches one of the streamlined, dark ships. He seems proud, as he strokes the hull and one of the support struts with his right hand. "You know we're coming, and you know what we're capable of, and willing to do." He stares straight ahead, creating the illusion that he's talking directly to the recipients of his message. There's no distance anymore, no space, no time, just infinite hatred. "We don't fear death, because we know we're dying for a just cause. Our end means the end of the sacrilege."

The Renao lowers his hand. He leans back against the black fighter ship's hull, crossing his arms in front of his chest. "*We* don't fear death. Do you?"

NOVEMBER 25, 2385

San Francisco, Earth

Lwaxana Troi stood by the large conference hall's window, staring down onto the lush sunlit gardens of Starfleet Headquarters, and beyond them at the Golden Gate Bridge. She didn't really notice them, though, because she still saw the images of the Purifying Flame's latest message in her powerful mind. Those images were more compelling than all the beauty in the world.

"A fleet!" she heard Admiral Akaar rant behind her. "An entire fleet of reconstructed *Scorpion* attack fighters, and still no response from Romulus?"

Troi shook her head. What was the Romulan Senate supposed to say? That they condemned the threats and the deeds of the terrorist Renao group? Of course they did … not least because they were also a target, just like the Federation. That they were horrified about the way their—unlawfully acquired—weapons were being used? Of course they were. But did that make any difference whatsoever? Weapons were weapons. They had been built to kill, so they would kill. Neither the weapon nor its origin was the problem. The problem was that civilizations still relied on weapons and deemed them necessary. A weapon was life's great enemy; it was as simple as that. Troi had come to that realization long before the Jem'Hadar and the Cardassians had invaded her homeworld; those atrocities had merely confirmed what she had already known.

No, Romulus didn't have to respond to the terrorists' latest manifesto. Not if the response consisted of trite phrases and horrified looks. In order to stop the Flame and to prevent further deaths, they needed to act—and they needed to go down roads that politics rarely used: at the frontline.

"Any word from the *Prometheus?*" Troi asked, turning her back to the window.

Akaar sat at the head of the big, circular table. A pile of padds was in front of him, his aide Sendak and two more of his assistants stood behind him, and he could see all of the almost two dozen analysts, strategists, and ranking officers occupying the rest of the chairs at the table. Most of them were immersed in their work—they kept in touch with other governments and worked on statistics regarding combat strength, or the inner security of the main member worlds. Troi knew that world leaders, security people, and normal citizens everywhere in the Federation were all eyes and ears, trying to find traces of these *Scorpion* attack fighters. The Federation was more vigilant than ever.

Additionally, members of the crisis management group that Akaar had formed here in San Francisco were frantically analyzing the communiqué that the Federation had received less than half an hour earlier in order to find clues as to where it might have been recorded.

Akaar looked up to the Betazoid woman and sighed. "Captain Adams believes that they may have finally traced the source of the radiation that is radicalizing the Renao. His and Captain Kromm's teams are checking it out as we speak."

"He *believes* that?" Troi said.

The admiral shrugged helplessly. This gesture that was quintessentially human, and Troi was inappropriately amused at this sign of how long the Capellan had been living on Earth. "That belief is all we have right now, Ambassador. If Adams is right, that might take the proverbial wind out of the xenophobes' sails."

Again, Troi remembered the two men in the café in Paris with their demagogic slogans and alarmingly unreflecting opinions. What might happen if the Jeromes of this world had their way? What would the present look like if there were Renao among the population of this planet, if they were part of this cultural community rather than living just within their region? Would they really be building detention camps as Jerome had proposed only a few days ago? It seemed to be in direct contrast to humanity's evolution, behavior that they should have left in the dustbin of history. Would an entire species have to face collective punishment in this modern day and age, just out of pure fear?

She didn't know. Until several weeks ago she had assumed that the modern civilization within the Federation's borders was beyond disgusting traits such as intolerance and xenophobia. But the experiences of the past few days had clearly proven that even on Earth an imminent terrorist threat and fear were able to open the floodgates to unreason and stupidity. Of course, only marginal groups and minorities were the ones speaking out against the Renao and the allegedly "lax ways" of the political leaders. But every fire was ignited by a little spark. Before coming to Earth, Troi had been convinced that the spark called "radicalism" wouldn't find any fuel within the Federation, and now she was ashamed to realize that she might have been wrong.

Aloud, she said, "So Adams agrees that the *Valiant*'s disappearance might have been the result of external factors."

"He shares that sentiment, yes," Akaar said. "And the longer I think about it, the more plausible I believe it is. The recordings of the *Valiant* log buoy are fairly conclusive."

That prompted another memory that made Troi shiver. The *Prometheus* had forwarded the *Valiant*'s last log entry to its most recent communication.

"We need more information." Akaar had risen and walked over to Troi at the window, leaving the table with its piles of padds and hard-working people behind. "And Adams and Kromm have the means to acquire it. We just have to hope that they're successful, and soon. For our part, we need to find a way to track down this fleet of rebuilt *Scorpion* attack fighters—preferably before it sets off."

Troi nodded. The terrible images from Cestus III, Korinar, Tika IV, and the wreckage of Starbase 91 were still vivid in her mind, as was the Purifying Flame's arrogant claim of responsibility. These fanatics directed their wrath against virtually every Alpha Quadrant power. That their anger might have been triggered by external sources made it no less lethal.

We need to be faster than the violence, faster than the destruction. That's the only way to prevent another disaster from happening.

Silently, she gazed around the room. Once again she resisted the impulse to read her companions' emotional states. It wouldn't be polite. And it wouldn't change anything. No, she only had to take one look at the focused expressions on everyone's faces to know how seriously they took the current situation. The latest news—from Akaar, the Flame, and even the long-dead Yeoman Green—had made a determined crisis-management team even more determined. This news had led to the opposite of what terrorist tactics were meant to achieve: rather than distance themselves from one other, the worlds of the Federation had closed ranks against the fear.

That thought helped everyone cope with the horror, thought Troi. Even a glimmer of hope still existed … not just for an end to this threat, but for the character strength of the Federation members as a whole. Civilization standing together in the face of adversity, and—if necessary—mourning together. Maybe they could even wipe out the memory of the handful of xenophobic idiots among their ranks for whom the disgusting deeds of the Flame confirmed their twisted worldview.

Maybe, there's hope after all, Troi thought, and a feeling of confidence washed over her. "Let's give it a try."

Akaar looked at her. Tension and concern were mirrored on his face but she saw the belief in a better tomorrow in his eyes. And the wish to take the fear away from her and everyone else in the Federation. "There are always possibilities, Ambassador Troi," the admiral said as encouragingly as he possibly could. "A wise man once said that, and I have learned to rely on him. The one thing we currently need is wisdom."

She frowned, skeptically. "Without a doubt, but your wise man is probably far away and long dead."

"Far away, yes, but quite alive," Akaar said gently. He took Troi's arm, escorting her to the conference table—away from her ruminations and back to the present. "Ambassador Spock is currently right in the thick of things. As is typical."

With the help of Ru, who had as always waited silently in the background, and who put her chair in place for her now, the Betazoid woman sat down on the leather chair next to Akaar. "Who am I to doubt such a distinguished expert?" she asked with a smile.

"I think," Akaar replied wryly, "you would be—as they say here— 'only human.'"

Troi glared at him. "If you're trying to insult me, Admiral…"

Then, filled with new courage, they turned their attention to the matter at hand. And they did what no radiation, no terrorists and no right-wing movements could take away from them: they harbored hope.

29
NOVEMBER 25, 2385

I.K.S. K'mpec, at the border to Federation space

General Akbas marched up and down on the *K'mpec*'s bridge with a grim face, holding a cup of hot *raktajino* in his right hand. Akbas of the House of Tor'ash was a tall, strong man and a seasoned veteran of many battles. His fame had not only earned him his own ship—a heavy cruiser starship of the *Qang* class, the cream of the Defense Force crop—but also the command of the Ninth Fleet, a group of fifteen battleships. The *K'mpec* was their flagship.

The general had always believed that fame was gained only through actions. Being condemned to wait for the expiration of the one-hundred-hour ultimatum that the High Council had given the Federation was agonizing for him.

"How long?" he barked at the gunner behind his command chair.

"Fifty-two hours, General," the man replied glumly. It was obvious that he also wanted to fight, just like the rest of Akbas's crew.

The general took a sip from his *raktajino*. He would never have admitted it but he was addicted to that stuff. Without the hot brew he would have challenged one of his subordinates to a duel for the most trivial of reasons ages ago. Waiting made him sick.

"Fleet status?"

"All ships ready," his first officer, Commander Lursk, reported. "We are controlling the border to the Lembatta Cluster across a distance of two light years in both directions."

Akbas just growled. Under normal circumstances that would have been enough to stop Renao fanatics from invading the Klingon Empire. But with the revelation of the Purifying Flame's solar-jump technology, everything had changed, and their efforts seemed laughably inadequate. Reports were that the Renao ships could cover a distance of up to thirty light years in seconds. The only thing they required was a sun as their target destination, so they could recharge their engines.

He had consulted the star charts. In all, they could reach twenty systems—four of them inhabited—with one jump from the Lembatta Cluster. He needed more ships to cover such an enormous region of space. And he would get them, but it would take at least another two days before General Klag arrived with his Fifth Fleet to support Akbas's forces. *At least they'll be here in time for the finale,* he thought cynically.

Akbas respected Klag more than most of the other generals. The Hero of Marcan V had earned his generalship, fighting battle after battle. He had even repudiated his own brother, the former shipmaster of the *K'mpec,* when his dishonorable deeds necessitated it. Akbas owed his command to these events, but that had nothing to do with his attitude toward Klag. And while the general wasn't too keen on sharing glory, not even with Klag, he had to admit that there would be plenty of glory to spread around once they had conquered the Lembatta Cluster and put the insolent Renao in their place.

He took another sip from his *raktajino.* "Any news from the *Bortas?"*

Lursk shook his head. "None, Captain. Last we heard, they had left Bharatrum and were heading toward the core of the Lembatta Cluster. The crew of the *Prometheus* allegedly found the source of the radiation that is influencing the Renao. They said that they analyzed the data of some ancient buoy, and that they're now following up on a trace."

"Starfleet and their methods ..." Akbas snorted. He knew that the Klingon Empire and the Federation were allies on paper, but the hesitant methods of the humans and the Vulcans and the rest of their motley collection of aliens left a nasty taste in the general's mouth. If you wanted to achieve something, you didn't analyze data—you grabbed the enemy and pressed a disruptor against his chest. Fanatics like those of the Purifying Flame didn't understand any other language.

"If Captain Adams doesn't come up with results within the next fifty hours, we will take over this fight."

"Fifty-two," his first officer said.

Akbas glowered at him.

"General!" The *K'mpec*'s communications officer turned around from his station at the back of the bridge. "We're receiving a message. The fanatics have issued yet another threat."

"On screen," barked Akbas.

A Renao appeared on the main screen, surrounded by a fleet of small, agile fighter ships. *"Is this sufficient for you?"* the red-skinned fanatic asked with a harsh voice full of hatred. His eyes glowed belligerently. *"Is this sight enough to convince you that we are serious? We're coming. We're coming to make you feel the same pain that you're inflicting on the galaxy. We're coming to put an end to your sacrilege. We're coming so you can feel in your own spheres what it means to sin against harmony. You have brought pain and suffering to space. Countless civilizations are being harmed because you're too blind to see the error of your ways."*

The general listened silently to the hateful words, his face contorting into one of fury. When the Renao was finished, he cried out, "If I get my hands on you, I will crush you like ripe *naran!*" But his anger betrayed his helplessness. *They will come. And we can't stop them. I need more ships …*

"Commander Lursk," he said, "deploy the fleet. I want to have two ships in every system within a distance of two light years. Only the *Drovana*, the *Chong'pogh*, and the *Nukmay* remain here with us."

"Right away, General," Lursk said with a nod.

Abruptly, Akbas turned on his heel and crossed the bridge. "I'll be in my office."

"General?" Lursk sounded confused.

Akbas bared his filed teeth. "I must contact the High Council, and urge them to withdraw this pathetic ultimatum. We mustn't wait until the Renao invade our space again. We need to attack!"

U.S.S. Prometheus, within the Souhla system

Geron Barai pressed his hands against his temples. A pained groan escaped from his lips. Everywhere, he felt this hunger, this all-encompassing hunger for any type of violence.

If this incompetent imbecile Meyer botches up the gel packs one more time, I'm going to kill him!

How could you snatch Moore away from under my nose, Ciarese? I hate you!

The lieutenant is watching me. He doesn't trust me.

Damned blue-skin.

These Renao killed my brother. They don't deserve to live. We should kill them all, ak Namur first of all.

"Are you alright, Doctor?" Kirk asked with a concerned look from her console.

"No, Commander." Barai took a deep breath, trying to reinforce his mental walls. "This isn't easy for me. The influence of this strange radiation continues to grow, the closer we get to Iad. Don't you feel it?"

"The fury?"

I'm going to kick his teeth in if he grins at me like that one more time!

Who does this arrogant, pointed-eared knucklehead think he is?

Geez, she's a real pain in the neck.

He nodded.

The chief engineer pressed her lips together briefly. "Yes, I suppose I do. I'm furious at the engineers of the fleet dock Beta Antares for constructing one of the most modern ships and providing it with shields that can't keep this radiation out. I'm furious at the technicians on Deep Space 9 for servicing the ship without fixing that deficiency. I'm furious at myself for never even considering such a radiation, and not being able to keep it out of my ship. I mean, how often have we met beings with the power to influence our minds? My great-great-uncle's log entries are full of them! We should've developed mechanisms against that by now, and …"

Closing her eyes, she paused, letting out a frustrated noise and hitting the edge of the console. When she opened her eyes again, some of her building fury had abated. "Okay, I guess that was blatant enough. I'm sorry."

I'm going to wring her neck, and soon!

My brother needs to be avenged!

I swear you're going to get it, T'Shanik!

"Don't be." Barai swallowed. It took a lot of effort to block out the voices in his head. The other crew members' fury wasn't his own. He mustn't forget that. "Everyone on board is fighting their emotions like you are. And unfortunately, I'm one of the few who can perceive that. Sure, I could put up a mental block against it but if I did, how would we ever find the shield modulation to protect us from Iad's influence?"

"If that modulation even exists. I'm beginning to doubt that. Our efforts so far have not been particularly successful. It's so frustrating. I feel as incompetent as a first-year cadet." Sighing, Jenna Kirk shook her head.

With a weak smile, Barai put his hand on her shoulder. "Let's keep trying, Commander. After all, it's not just our peace of mind that's depending on it."

New determination showed on her face. "You're right, Doctor. No one bearing the name Kirk has ever been brought down by some space phenomenon. I'll be damned if I'm going to be the first in the family to allow that to happen."

Adams felt as if a heavy burden had been removed from his shoulders, a burden he hadn't even noticed before. A few seconds later, he heard Kirk's voice.

"Kirk to bridge."

"Adams here."

"Captain, we did it! Doctor Barai claims that the aggression levels everywhere on board are finally decreasing."

"Yes, Commander, we can also sense that. Good work. Transmit the shield parameters to the *Bortas*."

"Right away, sir. Oh ... and Captain?"

"Yes, Commander?"

"Lieutenant Tabor has studied the program data for the adaptive radiation filters that Mr. Mendon sent us. He believes that we can not only enhance our sensors with them, we might even be able to stabilize our shields should we enter the chaos zone."

"This is Mendon," the Benzite said from his station. "It's encouraging to hear that you're able to modify the program accordingly. I have been thinking about that because my calculations indicated that the permanently changing radiation characteristics might have put an enormous strain on the shields. Our stay within the chaos zone would have been limited to a maximum of one hour."

"I can't promise that the reinforced shields will withstand the region completely," Kirk said, *"but the adjustments should buy us more time than your hour. There's one catch, though."*

"What's that?" Adams inquired.

"We'll need the entire capacity of all three deflector systems, as we did with the sensors, if we want to get a maximum result from the program. That means keeping the separated Prometheus *inside an expanded shield bubble."*

"That would require an extremely precise formation flight under difficult conditions," Roaas said from the tactical station. The first officer's gaze wandered to the main screen where the radiation zone had taken the shape of a menacing, multicolored cloud formation with heavy energy discharges. "Captain, I recommend controlling both of the *Prometheus*'s hull sections with the ship's computer. Our pilots are not quite used to working as a team yet." He glanced briefly at Jassat ak Namur.

Adams nodded. He didn't want to insinuate with his order that a member of his crew might not be capable of fulfilling his duty with maximum efficiency, but ak Namur had only just graduated from the Academy. So far, he had not participated in a formation flight maneuver with the *Prometheus*. The risk was too high that something would go wrong in the radiation zone for that to be his first shot at it.

"Lieutenant ak Namur, link the flight controls of all three ship sections so that the computer keeps all hull sections in sync while you control the bridge section. Maintain a flight distance of fifty meters." He looked up. "Is that sufficient for a shared shield bubble, Commander Kirk?"

"Yes, sir. That'll work."

"Prepare everything. Ensign Winter, ask the *Bortas* about their status."

Lenissa zh'Thiin spoke up. "Captain, how are we going to protect the *Bortas* from the radiation? She can't separate. And her shields are nowhere near as strong as ours."

"That *is* a problem." Adams gave his first officer a wry look. "I don't suppose we could convince Captain Kromm to stay out of the radiation zone?"

"So we can claim all the fame once we find Iad?" Roaas' whiskers twitched in amusement. "Not a chance, sir."

"Commander Kirk, is it possible to extend the shield bubble to the *Bortas* without forfeiting too much efficiency?"

"I think we can, Captain. As long as we keep the cruiser in the center, between all three of our segments, it should work. I just hope the Klingons have a competent pilot, because we're going to snuggle up quite close."

Adams exchanged a knowing look with Roaas. Now they would find out how well the cooperation between the two crews actually worked in an emergency.

"Filter program loaded."

"Flight controls connected."

"Battle bridges staffed."

"The *Bortas* reports ready."

Satisfied, Adams received the all-clear reports of his bridge officers as he settled into his command chair.

"Alright. Here we go. Computer, initiate separation sequence."

"Initializing separation sequence. Automatic separation in ten seconds."

With a dull rumble the primary hull including the bridge section separated from the upper secondary hull. Adams watched on the main screen how the radiation zone shifted when the secondary hulls separated and swerved.

"Mr. ak Namur, take position above the *Bortas*," Adams said. There was no need to give any instructions to the other two sections of the ship. Everyone knew what to do, and not just because Roaas and Carson commanded the respective battle bridges.

Space glided to one side, and the *Vor'cha*-class cruiser came into view. Adams couldn't help but grin. L'emka was at the helm of the *Bortas*. Before she had become first officer, she had served as a pilot for years, and she had much more experience than the helmsman on duty. Adams was grateful, not least because L'emka had proven to be the most rational and reasonable person under Kromm's command.

The three sections of the *Prometheus* placed the *Bortas* in their center by positioning the two secondary hulls below the cruiser's left and right warp nacelles respectively. It looked as if the three sections formed a ring around the Klingon ship.

Adams addressed the chief engineer at the port-side engineering station. "Commander Kirk, activate shields, and connect them with the other sections."

"Aye, sir."

"Mr. Mendon, start filter program. Ensign Vogel, link the deflector data of all four ships."

His crew acknowledged and carried out his orders. For a moment, tense silence fell over the bridge, only interrupted by the electronic whispers of the bridge's controls and the slightly different humming of the recently activated secondary engine room, located one deck below the bridge.

"Shields up and connected," Kirk said. "The shield bubble is stable, sir. Passing shield controls to main computer."

"Filter program is running, sir," Mendon said. The Benzite breathed faster with excitement.

"Receiving confirmation from the three other ships that all their systems are active," Winter said from communications.

The static on the main screen decreased, and the image became clearer.

"It's working, sir!" Vogel at ops exclaimed. "I'm receiving data from within the radiation zone." The stocky man faced Adams, his face beaming. "Sir, I'm locating a planet right in the center of the zone. It appears to be Class M."

"Iad," Adams whispered. "We really found it. So the Renao legend is true."

Kirk glanced at him. "Now we need to find out if the Son of the Ancient Red really was incarcerated there. And if he was, whether he still exists, and is responsible for this whole mess."

Adams rose from his command chair, straightening himself. "Let's find out, Commander. Mr. ak Namur, one quarter impulse. We're advancing into the radiation zone."

30
NOVEMBER 25, 2385

I.K.S. Bortas

Spock sat on the floor in his tiny cabin aboard the *Bortas*, meditating. Klingon ships didn't have windows, but he had set the monitor on the small desk to show the radiation zone and its chaotic energy discharges. The only other light source in the room was a small meditation candle burning in a bronze holder in front of Spock. Though they were approaching Iad and even Kromm would not have been able to keep Spock from being on the bridge for this historic occasion, Spock had felt an odd sense of familiarity since entering this system. In order to examine this sensation, he had withdrawn to the silence of his cabin.

Spock withdrew deep within himself, studying this strange perception. The *Prometheus*'s modulated shields, which surrounded the *Bortas* like a cocoon, dampened the feeling, but it was still strong enough for an experienced telepath like Spock to perceive.

So far, they had not been sure whether the phenomenon that influenced the Renao had an artificial or a natural source. Spock's theory was that it was the former. There seemed to be an intelligence behind what had been happening, something actively controlling the events in the Lembatta Cluster—and beyond. There was a connotation of hunger to the actions of the Purifying Flame—as if a forceful presence was out there, yearning for hatred and fanaticism, like someone who was drowning yearned for fresh air.

Spock had sensed this hunger once before. But he could not easily determine when. It was definitely long ago, when he served under Jim Kirk on the *Enterprise*, before his death during the battle against the insane superhuman Khan and his subsequent resurrection on the Genesis planet.

His time serving on the NCC-1701 had been so full of wonders that even some extraordinary events remained concealed under the veil of forgetfulness. He tried to pierce that veil, to recall which being they had encountered that might be related to these events: V'Ger, the intelligent machine entity. Flint, the immortal. The omnipotent child Trelane. The god Apollo. The evil angel Gorgon. They had frequently encountered such powerful entities, and many of them had attempted to force their will upon them. However, none of them had caused such an orgy of violence.

But there was something else, another encounter with a strange life form ... Spock focused and recalled events that were almost one hundred and twenty years in the past when they responded to a distress signal at Beta XII-A ...

Spock sat up straight. Suddenly, the memory had returned, and it horrified him deeply. Extinguishing the candle, he rose to his feet. Without taking off his meditation robe, he left his quarters. He needed to go to the bridge and warn both captains.

Disgusted, Kromm stared at the russet world that they were just about to orbit. "That planet is one of the ugliest dustballs I have ever seen. No wonder the Renao ran away from there as soon as they were able."

"According to the legend," Lemka said from the conn, "they didn't leave voluntarily. They were translocated by the White Guardian."

The captain snorted. "If so, he did them a favor."

The door to the bridge opened, and Spock walked in. Irritably, Kromm looked at the ambassador. He didn't even wear his gray clothing anymore, but instead, a flowing long robe. It seemed the old Vulcan had mistaken the *Bortas* for a monastery.

"Captain, please open a channel to the *Prometheus*," said Spock. "I must confer with you and Captain Adams."

"We don't have time for conferences," Kromm snapped. "We're a bit busy right now."

Spock was unintimidated and undaunted. "What you are busy with is precisely what I must speak to you both about, Captain. The matter is extremely urgent."

Scowling, Kromm motioned to Klarn. *"Ruch!"*

It took a minute before the image of the red and gray planet was replaced by the *Prometheus*'s main bridge.

"Captain, what can we do for you?" Adams asked, sitting on the far side of the navigation pit in his command chair.

"Ask the ambassador." Kromm pointed at Spock.

The old half-Vulcan diplomat walked forward. "Captains, I have made an important discovery regarding our mission."

Leaning forward, Kromm stared at Spock from beneath his bushy brows. "In your quarters?"

Spock tilted his head. "Indeed. When we approached Iad, I was overcome by a curious sense of familiarity, but one I could not localize within my memory. I withdrew in order to meditate, and my meditations bore fruit. During my time as first officer of the *U.S.S. Enterprise*, we responded to a distress call from the colony on Beta XII-A. However, there hadn't been an attack—indeed, there was never any colony on that world. At the same time, a Klingon ship—the *Voh'tahk*, commanded by Kang—was also summoned to Beta XII-A, where it was heavily damaged and hundreds of Klingons died. Kang believed us to be responsible, and took our landing hostage. His goal was to take over the *Enterprise*. A vicious fight for control over the ship ensued, fueled by an unusually strong hatred. Our phasers were replaced by swords and knives— archaic weapons created to inflict pain and prolong suffering. All wounds healed without treatment, even fatal ones. Everything was aimed at prolonging the battle that we were fighting into all eternity, while the *Enterprise* was hurtling out of control towards the edge of the galaxy."

L'emka chimed in. "That sounds extremely similar to the *Valiant* log entry. As I recall, the sand-haired human who stood on the command chair fired a projectile weapon of some manner. And Green mentioned belief in having killed an attacker who later came to life, did she not?"

"Your recollection is accurate," Spock said.

"Captain," Rooth said, "I have made a study of the life of *Dahar Master* Kang, and I recall that particular battle of his. It was some manner of energy being that was behind his conflict with Kirk and his crew, and it fed off hatred and pain."

"That is also correct." Spock nodded. "An eminently dangerous being, as it could manipulate not only emotions and memories, but also matter."

"How did you defeat it?" Adams asked.

"The captain overcame it in a very … human way: He laughed at it, along with Kang and his people. The positive energies drove the creature away. We did not encounter it again."

Adams seemed skeptical. *"And you think it's down on Iad's surface now?"*

The Vulcan shook his head. "Unlikely, as the Son of the Ancient Reds is said to have arrived here some ten thousand years ago. However, I believe that the creature that we referred to as the Beta XII-A entity is related to, possibly the same species as, the creature that the Renao refer to as the Son of the Ancient Reds. It is also far more powerful than the entity that we encountered a century ago, with effects that are more far-reaching by several orders of magnitude."

Silence fell over both bridges for a moment. Adams stroked his chin pensively, nodding slowly.

"And how do we win against this thing?" Kromm asked sardonically. "With laughter and cheerfulness? Should I have a barrel of bloodwine brought to the bridge?"

Spock regarded the Klingon skeptically. "I do not know, Captain."

On board the *Prometheus*, Adams saw Ambassador Rozhenko enter the bridge, and after giving him a brief nod, looked up. "Computer, I need all information about the creature known as the Beta XII-A entity."

"Beta XII-A entity," the computer voice said, *"according to Captain Jean-Luc Picard also called (*)."* They heard a noise that didn't bear any resemblance to any name that Adams had ever heard. He assumed that it was some kind of electronic approach based on Picard's statements.

"First contact at stardate 3372.7 on the planet Beta XII-A with Captain James T. Kirk of the U.S.S. Enterprise, NCC-1701."

The computer repeated matter-of-factly what Spock had already told them. But it wasn't done yet.

"Next confirmed contact at stardate 51604.2. Captain Jean-Luc Picard of the U.S.S. Enterprise, NCC-1701-E was abducted by the entity Q during an exploration mission and taken to the galactic barrier where he encountered the Beta XII-A entity. A detailed final report is available. Security clearance for access is Sigma 9."

"Q?" Zh'Thiin's antennae bent back until they were flat on her white hair. Obviously, she wasn't too keen on the omnipotent jester who had been frequently haunting Starfleet members for the past twenty years—notably Picard and the *Enterprise* crew.

Adams raised his voice. "Computer, identify Captain Richard Adams, WA-711-282. Play final report."

The computer whistled affirmatively. *"Identifying Captain Richard Adams. Security clearance Sigma 9 confirmed. Playing final report."*

"Limit playback to facts concerning the Beta XII-A entity," Adams said.

"Beta XII-A entity brought into our galaxy by an entity by the name of 0 and Q with the help of a guardian of time. It is several billion years old and originates from another universe. As per report from Captain Jean-Luc Picard, the Beta XII-A entity is believed responsible for the destruction of the Tkon Empire as well as the planet Cheron."

"The Tkon Empire?" Vogel sounded horrified.

"Do you have anything to add, Mr. Vogel?" Adams asked.

"Sir, the Tkon were an immensely advanced civilization. They were capable of things that we can only dream of today. History says that a supernova destroyed their homeworld, which is what led to the empire falling. If this Beta XII-A entity was in truth to blame for that …" The ensign at ops trailed off, swallowing hard.

Adams nodded, uneasy. "I see what you mean." Now he understood why the report had been classified. He looked up.

"Computer. Continue report."

"The Q-Continuum became aware of the deeds of 0 and his companions, and intervened. The Beta XII-A entity was driven away, and it was stripped of the majority of its power."

"Well, one thing is clear," Kirk said. "If one of these beings really exists down there on Iad, the Continuum doesn't seem to be interested in *this* creature. They had the best part of ten thousand years to get involved and drive it away from here."

Mendon spoke up. "Sir, I believe I have found the location with the highest radiation intensity on the planet's surface. I'm also locating ruins of unknown structures at that location. Apparently, there used to be a city or a very large building at that location. And ..." The scientist trailed off, taking a few deep breaths from his respirator.

Curiously, Adams faced the Benzite. "Mr. Mendon?"

"Captain, I've found something else. I'll put it on the main screen."

The image of the *Bortas*'s bridge slid to one side. On the left side of the screen, an aerial view of the planet's surface from a great height appeared. Adams saw a coastline where a gray ocean lapped against red-brown rocks. Several kilometers further inland appeared to be a forest where the remains of stone structures seemed to cover a large area.

Mendon shifted the view slightly, and Adams frowned. An enormous crater gaped in the landscape near the antique city. Its diameter was probably several kilometers wide.

"What are we looking at?" the captain asked.

Slowly, Mendon said, "The crash site of the *U.S.S. Valiant*, sir."

Adams's heart skipped a beat. He got up, stepping toward the screen as if he could identify any pieces of wreckage of the lost *Constitution*-class spaceship. Of course that wasn't possible just from the visual view Mendon was providing. "Are you sure?"

"Yes, sir," Mendon answered with a choked voice. "I'm detecting remains of hull alloys."

Suddenly, many of the loose ends tied up. The strange Renao legend that didn't seem to match the events in the cluster. The mysterious disappearance of the *Valiant*. The seemingly impossible radiation zone, and the inexplicable fanaticism of the Purifying Flame. Suddenly, Adams felt a terrible weight upon his shoulders as if someone had doubled gravity aboard the ship. "My dear God ..." he whispered. "It's our fault."

Rozhenko next to him tilted his head quizzically. "Captain?"

Adams faced the young man. "It's our fault, Ambassador. Whatever happened down there some hundred years ago, the *Valiant*'s crash must have destroyed the Son of the Ancient Red's prison—the vault, where the White Guardian had imprisoned him. Ten thousand years he had been sleeping in there, and we woke him. We freed him!"

"*You don't know that, Adams!*" That was Kromm, still following everything from the *Bortas*.

"We don't?" Adams pointed at the panorama on the left side of his screen. "Look at the evidence. Examine the crash site with your sensors. I'm sure that it's true. Cruel, but true."

A murmur was heard across the bridge when the crew realized the magnitude of that realization. The captain remembered Zefram Cochrane's famous words: *This engine will let us go boldly where no one has gone before.* The *Valiant* had ventured too far—and the Renao were paying the price for that. Oh, the irony … the Federation was being branded by the fanatics of the Purifying Flame as the root of all evil—and now it turned out that they might indeed be responsible for everything that had gone wrong within the Lembatta Cluster.

Adams straightened himself, determination showing on his face. "Let's put this right. No matter what the cost. I swear upon my life: The *Prometheus* will not allow this entity to plunge this galaxy into another war."

"*And the* Bortas *will not be brought to her knees by some ghostly power*," Kromm added. "*We're Klingons. We fight to win!*"

We fight to win! These words echoed through Adams's mind. An overwhelming apprehension washed over him. He fervently hoped that they were not doing what their enemy had wanted them to do the entire time.

EPILOGUE

The universe knew how to die.

It had witnessed the demise of many civilizations, as well as the doom of single beings—mighty or insignificant. It had seen so much—the end of the Iconians, and that of the Shedai ... the extinction of both the Australopithecine and the inhabitants of Kataan; so many, innumerable deaths ... And it had remained silent and it had prevailed.

"And it will prevail again," the foreman said. "The Klingons and Romulans, the Ferengi and Cardassians, the humans and Vulcans ..."

Satisfied, he walked along the rows of matt-black ships under construction, inspecting the progress of the work that had been executed here inside this asteroid. And he envisioned how these ships, the fruit of their efforts, would appear above the worlds of the great powers. For the good and the blessing of the Home Spheres, they would finish what their creators had begun. They would secure the future.

"The blasphemers must die," the foreman said quietly, and the words warmed him inside. They filled him with the certainty of being part of a huge and enormously important endeavor. "Only then can the universe survive."

The sphere was everything. Home—each and every home—had to remain intact and pure. Every being and everything had their predetermined place. Whoever disregarded that sinned against their own and against all spheres of the universe. They brought chaos to perfection, suffering to innocent people.

The sphere was everything. Its protection was far more important than the life of alien beings. *In order to save the harmony*, the foreman thought, *the harmony's opponents must die.*

It was as simple as that. Happiness washed over the foreman when he realized once again that their fight—his and that of the Purifying Flame—was only another perfect stone in the glorious, immense mosaic of destiny. It was part of a whole, another step on the way to harmony.

"We are the instruments of the universe," he said enthusiastically. "What we do is as natural as a sunrise. It's part of the plan, like wind and rain and night. It's the way it should be! We're not constructing death, brothers, we are constructing life!"

"Life!" Hundreds of workers shouted simultaneously, and their cheers rose to the ceiling of the vast construction caves like a battle cry. "Life!"

The foreman closed his eyes, enjoying the chorus around him, and the strength that kept him warm inside. *Life*, he thought. Death was the same as life—one arose from the other. Once the powers of the quadrant had fallen, peace would return, the harmony of spheres.

And they would most assuredly fall. Soon. They would die pitiful deaths, just like their deeds had brought dismal deaths to others. The Flame would make sure of it.

Because the universe knew how to die.

APPENDIX

1. U.S.S. *Prometheus* Personnel

1.1. Alpha Shift

Commanding Officer Captain Richard Adams
First Officer/Tactical Commander Roaas
ConnPilot/Lieutenant Jassat ak Namur
Second Officer/Ops Lt. Commander Sarita Carson
Communications Ensign Paul Winter
Security Chief/Environmental Lt. Commander Lenissa
zh'Thiin
Chief Engineer Lt. Commander Jenna Winona Kirk
Science Officer Lt. Commander Mendon
Chief Medical Officer Doctor Geron Barai

1.2. Additional Crew members

Commanding Officer Beta Shift Lt. Commander Senok
Commanding Officer Gamma Shift Lieutenant
Shantherin th'Talias
Deputy Chief of Security Lieutenant John Paxon
Deputy Chief Engineer Lieutenant Tabor Resk
Deputy Chief Medical Officer Lt. Commander Maddy
Calloway
Transporter Officer Chief Wilorin

Counselor-Isabelle Courmont
Barkeeper-Moba
MHN-II (MHN-XI) Doctor Tric

2. *I.K.S Bortas* Personnel

Commanding Officer Captain Kromm
First Officer Commander L'emka
Second Officer/Tactics Commander Chumarr
ConnPilot/Lieutenant Toras
Ops Bekk Raspin
Communications Lieutenant Klarn
Security Chief Lt. Commander Rooth
Chief Engineer Commander Nuk
Science Officer Lieutenant K'mpah
Chief Medical Officer Doctor Drax
Transporter Operator Bekk Brukk

ABOUT THE AUTHORS

Christian Humberg is a freelance author who has written for series including *Star Trek* and *Doctor Who*. His works have so far been translated into five languages and won German-language prizes. He lives in Mainz, Germany.

Bernd Perplies is a German writer, translator, and geek journalist. After graduating in Movie Sciences and German Literature he started working at the Film Museum in Frankfurt. In 2008 he made his debut with the well-received "Tarean" trilogy. Since then he has written numerous novels, most of which have been nominated for prestigious German genre awards. He lives near Stuttgart.

For more fantastic fiction, author events, exclusive
excerpts, competitions, limited editions and more

Visit our website
titanbooks.com

Like us on Facebook
facebook.com/titanbooks

Follow us on Twitter
@TitanBooks

Email us
readerfeedback@titanemail.com